D0766978

SOLD AS SEEN

Please return/renew this item by the last date shown on this label, or on your self-service receipt.

To renew this item, visit **www.librarieswest.org.uk** or contact your library

Your borrower number and PIN are required.

LibrariesWest

4 4 0175112 9

CINDERELLA AND THE VICOMTE

JESSICA GILMORE

THE SINGLE DAD'S ITALIAN INVITATION

SUSAN MEIER

MILLS & BOON

First Published in Great Britain 2022
by Mills & Boon, an imprint of HarperCollins*Publishers* Ltd,
1 London Bridge Street, London, SE1 9GF

www.harpercollins.co.uk

HarperCollins*Publishers*
1st Floor, Watermarque Building,
Ringsend Road, Dublin 4, Ireland

Cinderella and the Vicomte © 2022 Jessica Gilmore

The Single Dad's Italian Invitation © 2022 Linda Susan Meier

ISBN: 978-0-263-30215-8

04/22

MIX
Paper from
responsible sources
FSC C007454

This book is produced from independently certified FSC™ paper
to ensure responsible forest management.
For more information visit www.harpercollins.co.uk/green.

Printed and Bound in Spain using 100% Renewable Electricity
at CPI Black Print, Barcelona

CINDERELLA AND THE VICOMTE

JESSICA GILMORE

MILLS & BOON

CHAPTER ONE

'"FOR NEVER WAS a story of more woe, than this of Juliet and her Romeo."'

For one breathless moment the silence seemed overwhelming and then, like one of the waves crashing onto the shore behind her, loud applause rang out. Clemence Beaumont lay perfectly still for one last second as the still-real emotion swirled through her and then, as reality started to return, she raised her head and allowed Ed, her co-star, to pull her to her feet, letting the dagger fall to the floor. Taking his hand, she walked to the front of the curved stage, the rest of the cast falling in behind them, and bowed. Straightening with a grin, she took in the audience for the first time since she'd stepped onto the stage in answer to the nurse's call.

Semicircular seating rose up away from the stage, the outdoor theatre more amphitheatre than traditional auditorium, respectably full for an amateur fundraising performance. Clem bowed again as the whoops and cheers rang out, the welcome and much-missed post-performance adrenaline flooding her veins. Blinking, she started to make out individuals in the crowd: her best friend, Sally, who must have found a babysitter after all; Mrs Atkins, her favourite primary school teacher, beaming away; Mr Reynolds, her English teacher, nodding at her in approval, he adored Shakespeare and tried to make sure all his pupils did too; her neighbour Trinny, dressed to the nines as always; her sister...

Hang on. Her gaze skittered back. Her *sister*? Arrosa was *here*, in Cornwall? How had she managed to get away—not just get away but also seemingly alone? Clem couldn't see her bodyguard anywhere although she knew Henri couldn't be far behind. Arrosa hadn't gone out in public without the special-service-trained protection officer in the last decade.

Her seatmates didn't seem to have recognised her although her face regularly adorned front pages and gossip sites, probably thanks to the hat pulled low over her sleek, dark curls and the thick-rimmed glasses shading her face, but Clem would have recognised her in twice the disguise. After all, a similar face looked out at her from the mirror every morning. The sisters shared the same cheekbones and nose, the same dimples and long-lashed hazel eyes. But whereas Arrosa was a princess, legitimate daughter of King Zorien of Asturia, Clem was the unplanned result of a gap-year romance, her existence hidden away from half her family and the country her father ruled. A country she had never even visited.

She continued to bow and smile mechanically, but her mind was no longer on the performance and applause. What on *earth* was her sister doing here? Clem had sent her an invite of course, but she hadn't actually expected her to come. She never had before. It was hard for Arrosa to get away.

Finally, the applause came to an end and the cast

filed backstage, chattering loudly as the post-production euphoria spread through all the crew and actors.

'Everyone back to ours,' Ed proclaimed, his arm around Tybalt, normally known as Tom and Ed's other half. 'Clem? Ready to party?'

'It's not that I don't want to…' she started, and his face softened.

'You were sensational tonight, Clem, and you should celebrate. I know it's not the same, but she'd want you to.'

Not the same without her mother, he meant. Simone Beaumont had produced and directed many of the village plays, been at the forefront of the restoration campaign that had transformed the neglected open-air theatre. If she were still alive she would be spearheading the Save Our Theatre battle against a local developer who wanted to change the beloved community asset into yet another commercial venture catering to tourists. Her mother had loved a cause. Clem had lost count of all her campaigns and passions long ago. It had used to infuriate her, feeling that her own feelings and needs came second to whatever—or whoever—her mother was championing at the time, but now she would give anything to walk into the kitchen and see her mother furiously making a placard—*Save the Seals*, *Save the Birds*, *Clean up the Sewage*, *Save our Post Office*. Simone Beaumont. Champion of the underdog.

'We'll give you a lift,' Tom added, but Clem shook her head.

'I'll try and make it, but I think I saw my cousin in the audience.'

'Bring them along.'

'I'll see what she says. We don't see each other often

so she may want to catch up at home. Enjoy the party. You were both brilliant tonight, thank you.' She kissed both men on the cheek and headed off to change. She'd been looking forward to the post-show celebration but knew her promise to try and make it wouldn't be fulfilled. It had been a long time since Arrosa had dared to be seen publicly with her, or even attend a party without prior clearance; her half-sister might have the title, a luxurious lifestyle, more money than Clem could imagine, and a real relationship with their father, but Clem knew she had a freedom Arrosa could never have.

She changed quickly and removed her stage make-up and within fifteen minutes she made her way out of the theatre to walk the short distance home. She'd been born and brought up in the pretty coastal village her mother had moved to after she'd found out that her lover wasn't just a fellow student at the Sorbonne, but a prince with an arranged marriage due to take place imminently. Three months after moving to Cornwall Simone gave birth alone in a strange town—and six months later the birth of a new princess was celebrated in Asturia. Clem couldn't imagine how alone her mother must have felt, an orphan, single mother and betrayed lover. But she knew that Simone had loved the curve of the harbour, the pretty fishermen's cottages that clustered up the cliff, the wide sweep of beach, and Clem did too; she wouldn't swap her home for any palace. Which was a good thing because here she was, recalled home by her mother's long, lingering illness.

In the six months since her mother had died Clem had toyed with the idea of returning to London, to keep trying to make it as a professional actress, but making any decision seemed too hard, her grief still paralyzingly raw. In a world where she had no one, leaving the familiarity of home was more than she could manage.

She turned in at the small path that led to the cottage Zorien had bought them all those years ago. Clem hadn't been able to bring herself to change a thing. Her mother's clothes still hung in her wardrobe; her wax jacket swung from her peg in the hallway.

Arrosa had her own key and when Clem walked into the sitting room, her sister was curled up on the sofa. She'd discarded the hat and glasses, her long dark curls tumbling free, her expression thoughtful and more than a little wistful as she stared into the unlit fireplace. She looked up as Clem opened the door, jumping to her feet and rushing over to give Clem a warm hug.

'It's not that I'm not happy to see you, Rosy, but what on earth are you doing here?' Clem asked as she accepted a glass of the excellent wine Arrosa had brought with her and inspected the delicious array of goodies spread out on the coffee table, more crammed inside the Fortnum & Mason's hamper by her feet. She selected a piece of cheese and sat back.

'Apart from watching my sister play Juliet? Clem, you were brilliant.' Arrosa's English was perfect thanks to a British nanny and five years in an English boarding school, with no trace of an accent unless she was emotional or excited. Which was a shame. Clem loved her sister's accent, a reminder of the country she had never known. The small and much contested independent kingdom was positioned between France and Spain and the dialect was close to French, but the accent owed more to their Spanish neighbour.

'You've never come to see me act before.'

Arrosa curled back up on the sofa. 'I wish I had.

Clem, I'm so sorry I didn't come to Simone's funeral. I loved her so much, but...'

'That's okay, she would have understood. And you sent such beautiful flowers.'

'But you're my sister, I should have been there for you.'

'It's hard for you to get away. I know that.' But Clem had looked for her that long, sad day and her absence had hurt. Clem wasn't lying, she *did* understand the restrictions on their relationship, but there were times she was tired of being the skeleton in the family cupboard. Of shouldering life's burdens alone.

'It was easier when we were children. Especially when I was at school and could spend my exeat weekends here as well as some of the holidays.'

Some people might have found it strange that Simone had agreed to Zorien's request that Arrosa spend time with them anonymously, posing as Clem's cousin so that she could get to know her sister, but Simone, with her trick of embracing lost causes, had taken one look at Arrosa and enfolded her into the family. 'A palace is no place to raise a child,' she would say. 'She needs some fun, to be allowed to run wild.' And run wild they had, long halcyon beach days drenched in sun and sea.

Halcyon days that had ended as they'd left their teens and Arrosa had had to take on state duties. Now they barely got the chance to meet, their long weekly phone calls their sole communication.

And Arrosa hadn't mentioned anything about a visit the last time they spoke just a few days ago.

'Fess up, why are you here apart from coming to see me as Juliet? Don't think I'm not pleased to see you, but I know you and impulsive isn't in your schedule. Is everything okay?'

Arrosa took a swig of wine, a shadow passing over her face. 'I'm not sure. I think I just asked someone to marry me.'

'You think or you did? Are congratulations in order?' Clem tried to keep the surprise off her face. She was sure there was no one special in Arrosa's life. No one *not* special either. Asturia was a small patriarchal society with old-fashioned values and their Crown Princess was supposed to embody those values. 'Who is the lucky man?'

'Akil. He's the Vicomte d'Ortiz, a rising star of the opposition. His father, the Duc d'Ortiz, was one of Papa's most vocal critics. Our families have been enemies for generations, you know how Asturians can be, but Akil and I are friends of a sort. We have a lot in common. Family honour and expectations and that kind of thing.'

'Friends? You're not even dating? Is this a friends-to-lovers thing? Rosy, marriage is a big first step. Why not start off with dinner and a film? Besides…' Clem topped up their wine glasses before turning to face her sister '…what do you mean you *think* you asked him to marry you?'

Arrosa reddened. 'Akil has been instrumental into getting the opposition parties to agree to the change in law that will allow me to inherit the throne. You know, it's really important that there's consensus, it's such a change. Asturia is so traditional that any hint of controversy, even a politician voting against the change, could make it harder for the people to accept me.'

Arrosa had told Clem more than once how relieved

she was that the Asturian primogeniture laws meant
she would never have to become Queen, but when it
had become clear that no son would succeed him, her
father—their father—had thrown himself into changing the law. Now, eight years later they were just weeks
away from the law being ratified and Arrosa becoming
the official heir to the throne. Whatever Arrosa's personal feelings about her new destiny, she had shouldered
the change with her usual, intelligent grace.

'Oh, now I get it, in return for his help he gets half
the kingdom and the Princess's hand in marriage. That
still is the going rate?'

But Arrosa didn't answer her teasing smile, taking
another sip of her wine as she stared pensively into the
empty fireplace. 'Clem, everyone—my parents, my ad-
visers, the newspapers—has been pushing me to marry.
To start thinking about an heir of my own. And the
country will see me as more settled, more mature, if I
am married. I don't like being rushed, but I see the sense
in it. The problem is, not only am I single, but I don't
see that changing. On the rare occasion I meet someone
I like the whole princess thing scares them off. Queen-
to-be is going to make that a hundred times worse. I
like Akil, and he understands the court and my world,
and we have similar ambitions for Asturia… We were
talking about what I wanted to achieve as the heir and
realised how aligned our goals were, and I suddenly
thought, well, he's the right age, single, understands
my world. I could do a lot worse.'

'So you asked him if he'd do you the honour?' She
knew the situation wasn't funny, but humour was all
that Clem had right now. Pity wouldn't help anyone,
least of all her sister.

'Not exactly. I just said maybe he'd achieve more as Prince Consort and then fled the scene in mortification. What if he says yes?'

'Do you *want* him to say yes?'

'It's not what I dreamed of as a little girl. But it *would* make things easier.'

'The last of the true romantics. What's he like? Is he good-looking?' Other words hovered unsaid—is he kind, will he respect you, can you fall in love with him?

'I think so. He's pleasant enough to look at.'

Arrosa handed over her phone to Clem, who sucked in a breath. *Pleasant enough to look at?* Understatement of the century. With cheekbones sharp enough to slice through ice, a determined chin, sensuous mouth and a knowing glint in dark eyes, the Vicomte was film-star handsome. And if Arrosa couldn't see that then she really shouldn't marry him.

'Yes, pleasant enough,' she said wryly.

'He's a good man.' Was Arrosa trying to convince Clem—or herself?

'But?'

Arrosa rubbed her eyes. 'Queens make sacrifices for the common good. I know that. But I'm giving up any last hope of privacy, of choosing my own path. Is marrying someone I don't love one sacrifice too many? Being the monarch is lonely enough. It would be easier with a real partner by my side. Someone who wants to marry me because of me, not my title. But I'm not sure that person is out there. Akil is a sensible choice. Maybe that should be enough.'

'Rosy, I think this is something you need to take some time and think about. Really think about.' In fact, she shouldn't be making any decisions while she was clearly overwhelmed. Clem had never seen her sister so pale, never seen such huge shadows under her eyes or her usually laughter-filled face so solemn. 'You need a break.'

Arrosa sighed. 'I know. It's been intense. But don't worry, I'm slowing down for the summer, I've cleared my diary for the next few weeks leading up to the ratification as things will get really busy once I'm confirmed. Papa wants me to take on some decision-making duties straight away. There's a lot to learn. He's still young, but of course he inherited the throne long before he thought he would. He wants me to be ready.'

'A break? So you'll go on holiday?'

Her smile was wan. 'I wouldn't go that far. There's a lot to do, to organise, but at least I've got no engagements or formal meetings.'

'Then organise it from here.' Clem turned to her sister eagerly. 'Stay here for a few weeks, Rosy. You know the Cornish air does you good.' And then they could spend some real time together. Maybe for the last time.

'I'd love to,' Arrosa said wistfully. 'But I'm heading back tonight.'

'Tonight? Oh, Rosy.' Disappointment hit Clem hard. She hadn't realised how lonely she was until she had seen her sister sitting high up in the amphitheatre. She had friends, lots of them, but nobody who was hers alone.

How she wished she and Arrosa could actually *be* sisters properly. Have more than a weekly phone call and a few snatched hours here and there.

'I know, but I'll be missed if I'm gone too long.'

'You said yourself that you have no meetings.'

'I don't, but the speculation if I'm not seen even from

the distance could be damaging this close to the ratification. I didn't go anywhere for a couple of weeks when I had flu last year and according to the tabloids I was having a facelift, had joined a cult and eloped with a soldier. I know it's silly and I shouldn't care but it's not just that I don't want any rumours circulating at home—eventually the press would find me and then they'd start wondering who *you* are and that's the last thing you need. It's safest for you if we're not seen together, Clem.'

'*If* they find you. After all, why would they look for you here?' But Clem knew all too well that Arrosa was always tracked down eventually. Once Arrosa had turned eighteen the press had turned their lenses on her and she had become a front-page staple. There weren't many beautiful, young single princesses around and what she wore and ate, who she spoke to and where she went were all put under intense scrutiny.

But no one in Cornwall had ever realised that the child and teenager who spent so many holidays with the Beaumonts was the Asturian Princess. In fact, some of Clem's friends and neighbours still asked after her cousin. People saw what they expected to see, and nobody expected to see a European princess eating ice cream on a Cornish beach. And look at her! Worryingly pale and thin. She obviously needed a proper holiday. One here in the Cornish air. Time away from politics and diplomacy and Court. Time to decide if marrying someone because he had done her a good turn and understood her world was really what she wanted.

Maybe there was a way to make it happen.

'I could go back to Asturia in your place,' Clem said slowly, trying the words on for size.

Arrosa started to laugh but the sound died away as her eyes grew big with shock. 'You're serious? Clem, no one would ever think you were me.'

'Up close, no, but in the back of a car, hair all neat like you, in your clothes, with those big sunglasses you wear… Why wouldn't they? People see what they expect to see.' She repeated the words she'd just thought, the truth of them becoming clearer with every second. 'We're the same build and height, the same colouring. And I'm an actress, I can walk like you, hold myself like you. You could have the summer here and I'll spend it in Asturia making sure the press get enough glimpses to think you're busy preparing for the ratification, leaving you free to get some serious relaxation. I talk about my cousin all the time. No one here will think anything of it if we say I've got a job and you're cat-sitting. The only unbelievable part will be that I've been cast in anything. I'll have to claim I ended up on the cutting-room floor.'

'That's the craziest thing I've ever heard. We'd never get away with it.'

A tendril of hope in Arrosa's voice made Clem push away her own doubts.

'If you lived in the main castle or had dozens of servants then I agree, it would be impossible…'

'But I have my own cottage in the grounds of the Palais d'Artega,' Arrosa said slowly. 'I make my own meals when I'm there, people do come in to clean but not when I'm around. Only Marie is there regularly, but of course she and Henri would need to know if there was any chance of this succeeding… But it would be lonely, Clem. You'd have to be careful that no maids, no gardeners, no staff at all saw you. Some are new but some have been at the palais since I was a baby. What would you do with yourself?'

Lonely. That was a state Clem had got all too used to over the last year and a half. 'I'll make sure the press see Henri drive me around, dressed as you, of course, but in between I'll wear my own clothes, let my hair go back to natural wildness and explore Asturia incognito. I've always wanted to go but somehow I never have.' She'd always hoped that Zorien would find a way to invite her over, but of course he had always said it was too risky. 'It would be a chance for me to see our father too. It'd be easier for him to spend time with me if I'm living at yours. No one would question him visiting you.' She tried to keep the bitterness from her voice. She knew Zorien was a distant father to Arrosa in many ways too, but at least they had a real relationship, not just an awkward meeting every few years. She was grateful for the cottage and for the money he'd settled on her but would gladly swap both for a real father.

'But what's the point of me being here if you aren't?'

'Well, Gus needs feeding, for a start.' Clem pointed at the slim black cat occupying the window seat. 'The sea needs swimming in, scones need eating, beaches need walking on and you need time to be you, not the Crown Princess and future Queen. This gives you that time. And I need a change of scene too. I've been putting off making plans for my future, just existing for too long. Maybe some time away will give me some much-needed perspective. You'd be doing me a favour.'

'Sure, *I'd* be doing *you* the favour.' Arrosa shook her head affectionately at Clem.

'We'll do each other a favour. We both need some time away from our lives, so why not swap for a while?

Your mother's not at home, is she?' She knew that Iara Artega rarely spent much time in the Artega country estate, preferring to spend her time socialising in the small capital or journeying abroad.

'No, she's spending the summer on Ischia on a re-treat.'

'Then we're safe.' Arrosa's mother knew about Clem, but the two had never met and Clem sensed the Queen would prefer to keep it that way. 'We could do this. Your call, Rosy. What will it be? Six weeks of avoid-ing Akil, ducking away from the press and worrying yourself into a shadow or all the cream teas you can eat and a summer lazing on the beach?'

'We must be mad to even consider this would work.' But there was a hint of the old fire in Arrosa's eyes and Clem knew she was close to agreeing.

'It's easy enough to swap back if we need to,' she pointed out and Arrosa nodded then laughed.

'You're right. Let's give it a week and see where we are. Thank you, Clem. Cornwall is just what I need, and I think maybe Asturia is where you need to be as well. To a change of scenery.' She held up her glass and Clem clinked it with hers.

'To the princess swap.'

CHAPTER TWO

AKIL STRODE ACROSS the ornate hallway and into the formal receiving room. His own taste ran to simple but the decor in his ancestral home had clearly not got the memo. Gilt and marble prevailed, every piece of furniture was priceless, old and incredibly uncomfortable and portraits of bewigged disapproving ancestors glared down from every wall.

Every one of them no doubt had an opinion on the dilemma he'd not been able to stop turning over and over since his last conversation with Arrosa had taken an unexpected turn.

It was an enticing prospect, an effortless climb to the very top of Asturia but, then again, he was doing pretty fine as he was. More than fine: Shadow Minister of the Interior at thirty with the possibility of making it to party leader before forty, a decade before his father had achieved the title. And as leader of the opposition, maybe even First Minister one day if the swing away from the traditionalists continued, Akil would wield a lot of power, the kind of power he had been born and bred to wield. But in Asturia the throne still held a lot of influence and nothing happened without the court's approval.

And that was the heart of his dilemma. Because he couldn't deny that if he were right next to the throne, married to a woman he knew shared many of his ideals, then together they could enact real change. The change so desperately needed if Asturia was ever to move forward, to be more than a curious little country sandwiched between France and Spain, a pub quiz answer and a quirky holiday destination. More, it would ensure that Ortiz blood would run in the veins of future kings and queens. He knew what his father would say. He would tell him to stop hesitating and act. Propose formally and marry her before she had a chance to change her mind.

But it wasn't that simple. He liked Arrosa, admired her grace and intelligence, appreciated her beauty, but he didn't *know* her, not in the way he should know a woman he was considering marrying. Akil knew that he needed to marry carefully, strategically; after all, as his mother knew to her cost, being married to a politician meant sacrifices. But he did want compatibility. Companionship. Not the chilly battleground he'd grown up in.

Blinking, his eyes readjusted as the door swung shut behind him. The heavy velvet drapes were pulled against the midday sun, the large, dark room dimly lit by lamps. His mother lay on a chaise, barely mustering a smile as Akil walked over and bowed over her outstretched hand.

'You look more like your father every day.' It wasn't a compliment.

'Mama.' He suppressed a grimace and sat down on the low stool beside her. 'You look well.'

'That's very kind of you, *cheri*.' Her tone made it

clear that she didn't find him kind at all. His mother made a study of ill health and excelled, but Akil found it hard to indulge her when, thanks to his volunteering work, he saw real ill people in the overstretched public hospitals. 'But my head has been bad recently. I thought you knew, but of course you are so busy, how could you remember such an insignificant detail?' Her sigh was perfectly calculated to sit midway between heartbroken and plaintive.

It should be perfectly calculated. She'd worked on it long enough.

Nerea Ortiz was still nearer fifty than sixty, her dark hair owing more to nature than her hairdresser's art, her figure still slim and toned, her face unlined. But she reclined as if she were a Victorian great-aunt, a small, fat lapdog snoring at her feet, a shawl around her shoulders and a selection of herbal remedies cluttering up a small table that also held a china cup half filled with weak tea and a matching plate holding two wafer-thin biscuits. A water bottle sat on another table—that was if it was water. Early as it was, it could easily be gin.

Not for the first time, Akil thought that his mother lived in entirely the wrong era.

'I'm sorry to hear that,' he said with the patience born of long practice. 'But I'm here now and I can assure you that you have my full attention.'

Akil managed a dutiful hour by his mother's side before pleading work duties and taking his leave. As he left the room his eye was caught by a photo. His mother at twenty, beautiful and glowing, full of life. It was easy to forget that when Akil had been young, very young, she had been that vibrant young woman. But years of his father's disapproval and dislike had worn away all her *joie de vivre* until ill health became her only defence against her husband's scathing tongue. His weapons were anger and contempt, sarcasm and noise, hers tears and shrinking, martyrdom and illness.

And drink. Never spoken about, never acknowledged, all too often present.

No wonder Akil had spent as much of his childhood and now adulthood elsewhere, only coming back to the Ortiz ancestral home when duty commanded. Now he was the head of the family he had to visit more often but had resisted moving back to the place where he had been so unhappy, his father's disappointment still reverberating in every room. Although, since recovering from the heart attack that had felled him eight years ago, his father now spent most of his time in the family's Swiss villa.

Apparently not alone.

Akil sighed. Thoughts of his father were always complicated: guilt, dislike and yet, still, that frustrating, inexplicable and yet ever-present need to make him proud—and to beat him. To show that Akil had everything it took to be the Duc, the head of the family, to bear the Ortiz name. His father had always urged Akil to marry tactically. 'Don't let your head get turned by some pretty lightweight like I did,' he'd told Akil more than once. 'Marry a woman who brings influence and power. Who can further the family cause.' Who better than the Crown Princess?

The beep of his phone recalled him to his surroundings and Akil paused on the top of the wide stone steps that led from the grand double-height entrance way down to the curved driveway. He pulled his phone out of his pocket and glared at the screen, the tension leaving his body when he saw the name on it.

Elixane.

'Hey, what's up?' He walked slowly down the steps, an invisible load lifting more with every inch he moved away from the house. His car was right in front of him but he carried on, turning onto a gravelled path that ran across the front of the house and into the walled garden, which had been Akil's favourite hiding place as a small boy.

'I meant to return your call before now but things have been crazy,' his sister said. 'Everything okay?'

Akil hesitated. He'd called Elixane right after Arrosa had—possibly, maybe—suggested he consider becoming her Prince Consort, desperate to talk the conversation over with someone, but the more time passed, the less he felt able to articulate what had been said. 'Everything's fine.' He paused. 'I've just visited Mama.'

'How is she?'

'Much the same.'

She sighed. 'That's not good. I did try and suggest she drank less last time I saw her, but she pretended she didn't know what I was talking about. It isn't even the quantity I worry about, it's the drinking alone. How about Papa?'

'Last I heard he was much the same too.'

'You mean he's also drinking too much and eating too much and probably spending too much time with the mistresses we're not supposed to know the old hypocrite has, while you fulfil his dreams for him?'

She had a point. 'He nearly died.'

'Of bad temper. Eight years ago.'

'Early retirement was the best option.'

'For who? Not for you, that's for sure. I still can't believe he guilted you into dropping your studies to take over from him.'

'Elixane,' Akil said warningly. 'I made my own decisions then and I make my own decisions now.'

'Which is why I'm the one doing a surgical residency in New York?'

'And I couldn't be happier for you.' He stepped through the small, hidden archway that led into the garden and the last of the tension left him as he entered. Old, twisted fruit trees covered with fresh green leaves, blossom petals carpeting the grass, little winding paths darting between them, wildflowers populating the grass.

'Now what can I say to that?' Elixane complained. 'Maybe you are better off as a politician. You always know what to say.'

'Not always. I had an interesting conversation with the Princess the other day and I had no idea how to respond,' he said, his eyes fixed on a bee busily divesting a flower of nectar. 'She's being pressured to marry.'

'Poor Arrosa, I can just imagine.' Elixane was the same age as the Princess and despite the family rivalry the girls had been friends of a sort growing up. 'You're in the Senate, you know what that bunch of dinosaurs are like. They still think a woman needs a man's steadying hand. I don't envy her. She's got an uphill battle with that lot.'

'She recognises that. She's not afraid, but I think she feels it would be easier if she wasn't facing them alone. She…' He coughed, the words feeling as ridiculous as he knew they would sound. 'She asked how I felt about being the Prince Consort.'

'She *what*? She *proposed*?' Elixane's voice rose to shrill frequency and Akil winced. 'To *you*? I didn't know you two were that close.'

'We're not, and no.' Akil wasn't sure exactly what had happened in that conversation, but he was sure about that. 'She didn't propose exactly. It was more of a sounding me out, I think.'

'And you said how flattering but no thank you.'

'I didn't say anything.' He hadn't had a chance to formulate any kind of response before Arrosa had blushed furiously, made an excuse and left.

'My brother a prince. That would bring Papa hotfooting it home from Switzerland. But it's ridiculous, of course. Please let me be there when you tell him you had the chance to marry into the royal family and turned it down.'

Akil didn't answer and Elixane's voice tightened. 'You are turning it down, aren't you?'

'I don't know. Not yet. I'd be a fool not to at least consider it, Elixane.'

'But, Akil, you don't love her. You barely know her!'

'I've spent some time with her recently and I like her. Respect her. Besides, love isn't necessary for a happy marriage.'

'Love doesn't guarantee a happy marriage but it sure as hell helps. You can't base your decisions on the disaster that's our parents' marriage. They didn't love each other. They were infatuated and that's a whole different ball game.'

'Love or infatuation, it's undeniable that everything they wanted and needed in a marriage was incompatible and I will never make that mistake.' Never raise children amongst the hostility and unhappiness of a toxic marriage. 'If I marry, then I need a politician's wife, someone diplomatic, intelligent, with shared goals. Why not Arrosa? Being part of the court rather than parliament would be a different kind of politics but together we could achieve great things.'

'At what cost?'

'There's always a cost to power, Elixane. You just need to decide what you're willing to pay.'

'I haven't seen Arrosa for years,' his sister said after a long pause. 'We were friendly but not close. She's not close to anyone as far as I know, but I liked her. Like her. She's nice.'

'Yes,' Akil agreed. 'She's nice.'

'And that's enough?'

Akil leaned against a tree. 'It's a hell of a lot better than not nice,' he pointed out. 'Look, we both want this country to move beyond ancient feuds, we want a modern democracy.'

'And marriage is the only way to achieve that?' Akil could hear the scepticism in his sister's voice. 'It's the twenty-first century.'

Akil couldn't help his wry smile. 'In the rest of Europe maybe, but you know as well as I do that for over half this country it might as well be the seventeenth century.'

'You know what I think you should do?'

'Do I want to know what you think?'

'I think you're insane and you shouldn't give this any more thought, but if this is something you are really considering then you should get to really know her. Don't make any decisions either way until you've spent some time with the woman, not the Princess. Make sure this marriage is something that you both can live with.'

Another fat bee buzzed past Akil's ear before landing on a climbing rose. Akil watched it move from flower to flower as he considered his sister's words. He didn't know what he felt about Arrosa's surprising proposition or if she had even meant it. Spending some time with her when they weren't working on bills and treatises might be the way to find out if they were compatible. 'You may be right.'

'I *know* I'm right. You might think that you don't have to fall in love with her, but you have to admit that you need to know that you can live with her.'

Elixane's words hung in the air until a beep reminded Akil that he had a meeting to get to. 'Look, I've got to go. Thank you.'

'Call me if you need me. Any time.'

And with that she was gone. Akil pocketed his phone, frowning. His little sister was annoyingly right. If Arrosa had meant those softly spoken words—and if he was truly considering agreeing—then they needed to see if they could live in harmony. His parents' marriage was an example of everything he didn't want: thwarted passion, disappointment, anger and resentment. He wanted civilised, compatible and mutual respect. Maybe it was time to stop thinking and talk to Arrosa, discover if she had been serious and then decide what, if anything, that meant for him.

Before Akil left the Palais d'Ortiz he cancelled his morning meetings, and instead of heading back to the city drove further out into the countryside towards the huge Artega estate. He'd hesitated over whether he should ask his assistant to forewarn Arrosa that he was on his way; after all, even a rising politician working closely with the Princess shouldn't just rock up uninvited at a royal residence. But if he and Arrosa were to discuss something as important as marriage then surely they should be able to discuss it without formality and pomp—and a possible fiancé shouldn't need to make an appointment to see his intended.

Akil had visited Arrosa at home enough times to be waved through by the guards at the gate and he drove up the long, tree-lined drive, past the imposing chateau with its fairy-tale turrets and intricate stonework and headed towards the villa half a kilometre away where Arrosa resided. As he pulled up in front of the pretty white one-storey building he felt a momentary pang of unaccustomed doubt. Whatever they discussed here would set the tone for the rest of his life and he still didn't know what the outcome would be—or what he wanted it to be.

The nineteenth-century villa had an idyllic setting with its lakeside location and flower-filled gardens, a small orchard to one side. But despite the peaceful pastoral feeling, Akil knew that at least one secret service agent would be concealed somewhere close by, and that CCTV cameras meant that his every move would be fed back to the soldiers at the gate. It was a sobering thought; he was used to living with a certain degree of high security, thanks to his father's position and now his own, and he had spent time himself in the special forces during his national service, but he had never been watched twenty-four-seven.

Unexpected pity for the Princess flooded through him; never alone, never private and now asking a man she surely didn't love to be her husband.

Akil strode down the paved garden path to the front door and knocked on it. The last couple of times he been here either Arrosa herself had opened it or her maid, Marie, would usher him in. Arrosa had no live-in staff at the villa. In fact she lived a surprisingly self-sufficient life; apart from the staff who ran her office from the court in the capital city her only permanent staff were Marie and her bodyguard.

He waited but nobody answered the door, although he could see several open windows and hear the sound of music from within the house. He rapped on the door once again and when there was still no answer headed around to the back of the villa. The long, terraced garden led down to the lake, where he could see a small boathouse and changing hut positioned by a short wooden jetty. Arrosa sat on the jetty, her back to him, her hair cascading down, wilder than he'd ever seen it before.

She didn't turn as he made his way down the garden towards her and Akil hesitated before he called out, not wanting to startle her.

'Arrosa,' he said softly and saw her whole body stiffen. 'I did knock but nobody answered. I'm sorry to show up without notice.' Every sense told him that something wasn't quite right; he felt wrong-footed with no idea why. 'But what I have to say is too important to wait, and under the circumstances I felt some informality was warranted. I hope it goes without saying that I very much enjoy working with you, and I hope whatever happens that we will continue to work together over the years ahead. I have also come to value your companionship, friendship almost.'

Arrosa didn't speak, nor did she turn to face him. He couldn't read her body language at all. She was still rigid, like a deer scenting a predator, unsure whether to run or try to fade into the background.

'But marriage is a big commitment and not something either of us should enter into lightly,' he continued. 'If you didn't mean what you said the other day, if I misread your intention, or if you changed your mind, then I'll leave right now with no hard feelings and a promise never to mention it again. But if you did mean it then I think we need to spend some time together without titles between us, without work as a commonality, to see how compatible we are when all that is stripped away.'

Something about her stillness made it hard for him to let the silence fall but he made himself stop, wait for her to respond as the silence lengthened, the tension thickening with every long second until finally she spoke.

'Thank you.'

Akil frowned, that sense of wrongness intensifying. Just two words but they sounded off, her voice lower, her accent subtly different.

'But now isn't a good time...' she continued slowly. 'Could we do this later?' She hesitated. It was as if she was measuring every word. 'I know this is important.'

Was she ill? Upset? Hurt? Akil couldn't just walk away without knowing Arrosa was all right. Princess or no princess, possible fiancée or not, she was a human being without many people to confide in. Whatever the future held, he could at least be her friend. Akil stepped onto the narrow wooden jetty and in a few decisive strides reached the still seated figure.

'Arrosa? What's wrong?' He squatted next to her and touched her shoulder, turning her gently towards him. But her face was at once familiar and yet strange. There was the same dark waving hair, the same hazel eyes, although these were subtly lighter, more gold than brown, the same olive skin, even that same tilt to the nose adding personality to a face that otherwise could have been blandly beautiful, and the same full mouth.

But this was not the Princess. This was not Arrosa.

His hand dropped and he straightened, taking an instinctive step back. 'Where's the Princess—and who on earth are you?'

CHAPTER THREE

CLEM STAYED COMPLETELY still for another long moment, unsure how to play this. She had no script, no director's notes. It was a good thing she had done so many improvisations but unfortunately this time she had no idea what her part should be.

After all, less than twenty-four hours ago she had been readying herself to play Juliet with no plans beyond the play and the party. But in the end she'd barely had time to remind Arrosa to water the plants and feed the cat, before finding herself hustled into the car that had brought Arrosa to Cornwall and whisked off to the private jet her sister had commandeered. It had been long past midnight when she'd arrived at the Palais d'Artega and Henri had shown her to the pretty lakeside villa Arrosa had moved into on her twenty-first birthday where, despite all her excitement and trepidation, she had fallen asleep straight away. No opportunity to have second thoughts or wonder how this madcap scheme might work in practice.

No opportunity until now. Unfortunately she had still been trying to get her thoughts in order when Akil Ortiz had inconsiderately shown up and complicated an already difficult situation. Who just showed up without calling first? Especially when calling on a princess?

However, she did know one thing. She wasn't having this conversation sitting down. Slowly she clambered to her feet and brushed the dust off her skirt before tilting her chin and turning to face Akil, meeting his suspicious gaze squarely, only to falter as she took him in.

If her first thought was, *Wow, that photo really didn't do him justice*, then her second was *Lucky, lucky Arrosa*.

Clem had been to one of the UK's most prestigious drama schools and as a result some of her classmates were now global heart-throbs. But not one of the attractive charismatic men she'd studied with, acted with, and sometimes dated had anything near the sheer magnetism of the Asturian Vicomte.

He was tall and broad, with his almost black hair ruthlessly swept back, but Clem could see hints of a rebellious wave in the strands that fell over his brow, strong brows framing keen dark brown eyes, a straight Roman nose turning his good looks characterful. His powerful body was showcased by a navy suit that had clearly been made to fit him, his olive skin set off by the crisp white of his linen open-collared shirt.

To her horror Clem felt a jolt of attraction pulsing low in her stomach, tingling through her whole body.

No, down, bad girl, she told herself fiercely as she summoned up her most regal smile, the one she'd used when playing Olivia in *Twelfth Night* during their third-year showcase.

'You must be the Vicomte d'Ortiz. I'm sorry, but Arrosa isn't here right now.'

'I see.' Suspicion lurked in his dark eyes as he surveyed her. 'When will she be back?'

'Not for a while. I'm house-sitting for her.' Did princesses who lived on their family estate surrounded by servants need house-sitters? Judging by the way Akil's eyes narrowed, he didn't think so. 'I needed a place for a while,' she added hurriedly. 'Really she's the one doing me the favour.'

'And you are?'

'Clem, Clemence Beaumont.' Surely knowing her name wouldn't do any harm? She wasn't linked anywhere with her father and sister. If he searched for her online all Akil would find would be some reviews of plays, her profile on her agent's website and her mother's obituary where Clem was buried beneath all the causes Simone had supported. 'I can let Arrosa know you dropped by, or you could tell her yourself, of course.'

'She didn't tell me she was going away.'

'It was all very sudden. And she doesn't want it to be common knowledge so please don't tell anyone.' She took a step forward but he didn't move. The only way past meant either brushing past him or going into the water and neither appealed. 'I'm sorry you had a wasted journey, but it was really nice to meet you,' she said pointedly. 'I'd offer you a coffee, but I really have to get on.'

If only that were true. Now she was here, Clem had no idea what to do next. Arrosa had promised to contact their father straight away to let him know what they were doing and she was anxiously hoping to hear from him. In the meantime her plans to explore had been thwarted by the realisation that Arrosa didn't have her own car and that she was driven everywhere by Henri. That was fine for the times she planned to dress as the Princess and be driven somewhere in order to make it seem as if Arrosa were here in Asturia, but the bullet-proof limousine was far too conspicuous for her to use to be a tourist. Lovely as the villa was and inviting as the lake was, she didn't want to spend six weeks alone with nothing to do. She could do that back in Cornwall.

'You didn't say how you know Arrosa.' He clearly wasn't shifting. Maybe it was a good sign, this protectiveness. Although Arrosa already had a bodyguard watching her every move.

'No,' she said lightly. 'I didn't. Now if you'll excuse me.' He moved then, slowly and clearly reluctantly, and she slipped past him. 'I'm sure you can see your own way out. After all, you found your own way in.' She didn't look back as she headed up the path but she could feel his gaze boring into her as if he were trying to strip her secrets from her.

The garden was split onto three terraces. Lawn abutted the lake, then steps led up to a colourful flower-filled area, alive with bees and butterflies. The third terrace was paved with pots of plants providing shade and colour, an outdoor sofa and chairs on one side and a dining table and chairs on the other. It seemed to take an age to get to the French doors that led into the house and safety, and it wasn't until her hand was finally on the handle when he spoke.

'Wait.'

Reluctantly Clem turned. Akil had followed her onto the top terrace and he stood by the table, hands clenched.

'Just tell me, is Arrosa all right?'

Clem paused, trying to read him. Did he care about her sister as a person, or was he thinking about the power and influence she could give him?

But Arrosa had said that he was a good man and she was a shrewd judge of character. She'd had to be. And Clem had overheard words never meant for her ears after all. Words which, although she still wanted a lot more for her sister than a diplomatic convenient marriage, had gone a long way towards reassuring her that Akil wouldn't take advantage of her sister.

'She's fine.'

'Is there anything I can do to help? I got the impression the other day that she needed a friend. I hope she knows she can come to me if she's in trouble.'

It clearly cost him to ask the question, to look that vulnerable in front of a stranger, a stranger who he had already inadvertently spilled secrets to. The situation needed rebalancing. He deserved some truth from her. And this was a good chance for her to evaluate the man her sister definitely didn't love but thought of highly enough to consider entrusting her future happiness to.

'Maybe I do have time for a coffee after all,' she said. 'Do you?'

Clem still didn't know her way around her sister's well-appointed kitchen and it took some time to locate everything she needed and to load it onto a tray and carry it to the outside table where Akil awaited her. Despite her invitation, Akil hadn't sat; instead he stood at the edge of the terrace gazing out towards the lake. As Clem exited the house, he turned and quickly strode towards her, relieving her of the tray despite her protestations and setting it onto the wooden table. Clem followed him and took a seat, reaching for the cafetière gratefully. She was definitely in need of caffeine.

There was something peculiarly intimate about sitting opposite someone, asking them how they took their coffee, pouring it and adding the milk. Intimate and yet distancing, the lack of knowledge a sign that they were strangers. Although here at least she had the advantage. She knew who Akil was; he had no idea she even existed.

He accepted the coffee but made no move to drink it, instead setting the cup onto the table and looking at her with a frown. 'I spoke to Arrosa just two days ago and she made no mention of going away. The ratification is in just a couple of months' time. This is no time for her to disappear. What's going on?'

Clem sat back and regarded him steadily. 'Once the law has been ratified and Arrosa is officially the Crown Princess, how much time will she have to go away? How much privacy? She's already constrained in so many ways, guarded at all times, and it's only going to get worse. This is a perfect time for her to have some space. Maybe the last chance she has.'

He inclined his head briefly as if acknowledging her point. 'But that doesn't explain what you're doing here or who you are, Clemence Beaumont. I don't believe I've heard Arrosa mention you before.'

'Does Arrosa know all your friends?' Clem asked sweetly and only the slightest narrowing of his eyes showed his displeasure with her answer.

'Your resemblance to her is quite startling, too startling for it to be a coincidence although Beaumont is not an Asturian name. You must be related, but I know all her relatives around your age and you're not one of them.'

'You've done quite the study on her genealogy.'

To her surprise Akil laughed, transforming his face from an austere, remote handsomeness to something warmer—and dangerously attractive. 'Asturia is a small country and everybody knows everybody. And *I* know that I've never seen you before and I've not heard your name and so I'm wondering why someone who looks so like the Crown Princess is living in her house when the Crown Princess has unexpectedly disappeared.'

'You have a vivid imagination. You should write crime books.' Clem took a sip of coffee and smiled. 'But there's no mystery here. Text Arrosa, she will tell you that she is fine.'

'It just seems a strange coincidence that just a couple of days after our conversation she disappears.' He stopped then, his mouth tightening as if he'd realised that he'd said too much. But it was a little bit too late to pretend ignorance about the possible match between her sister and this disturbing man when she'd heard his opening speech.

'Look,' she said, setting her cup onto the table. 'I can't pretend I didn't hear what you said earlier, and I can't pretend that I don't know what you're talking about. I also can't comment on where Arrosa is or why she's there. That's her personal business and if you need to know more than that you should ask her. She has her phone. I spoke to her this morning. As for me, I'm here partly because, like Arrosa, I could do with some time away from my life, but mainly to give her this time. You know how hard it is for her to have any peace. As you said, we look alike, and from a distance, with the right hair and make-up, through the windows of her car most people would mistake me for her. If I make sure I'm seen dressed as her two or three times a week from a distance, then nobody will think to go looking for her. I'm giving her the space she needs. Nothing more sinister than that.'

Without taking his eyes off her Akil pulled out his phone and dictated a quick message.

Arrosa, I'm at your house with Clem, let me know everything's all right.

He put his phone down. 'Okay, that's why you're here. But I still don't know who you are, or that I can trust you.'

'Arrosa trusts me, shouldn't that be enough?'

'It would be if you didn't know more about my personal business than I'm comfortable with.' He sat back and folded his arms. 'I'll tell you what I do know. Number one, you resemble Arrosa so closely you have to be a near relative, number two, she's never mentioned you but you clearly know a lot about her life, number three, you're not Asturian, you speak the language well but there's a hint of an accent. Not French, not Spanish. If I had to bet I'd say English. So why is an English girl in Asturia pretending to be the Crown Princess?'

'I'm an actress.'

'So this is a job? All above board? Signed off by the King?'

'It's more of a private arrangement.'

'Give me one good reason why I shouldn't alert the guards to your presence here.' He didn't take his eyes off her and she knew he wasn't bluffing.

'Because I'm her half-sister,' she said. 'The family secret. And no one in Asturia is supposed to know I exist. Happy now?'

What had she just said? It took more than a few seconds for Akil's brain to process the words he'd just heard.

'You're Arrosa's half-*sister*?' He knew that the King and Queen lived largely separate lives, but he'd never heard rumours of any affairs—and certainly none of any other children. But Clem's resemblance to Arrosa was startling, sisters made perfect sense. How had this scandal been hushed up for so long in this small country? Who else knew?

Clem nodded. 'I'm six months older than Rosy. Look, my existence is only known to a very, very few people.' She looked across at him pleadingly. 'Please don't tell anyone. If the truth got out it would hurt Rosy more than me. Any family scandal might rebound on her even though she's obviously not responsible for anything apart from treating me as much like a sister as possible. The next few months are key, you know that. Maybe I shouldn't have come to Asturia, maybe it was too risky, but Rosy lives such a quiet life outside her duties I didn't think anyone would find out if I stuck to her villa and slipped out to explore incognito. Shows how much I know. I managed less than twenty-four hours here before you found me.'

Akil sat back and sipped his coffee, his mind racing. Clem had a point—more than one. If news of her very existence got out then the ensuing scandal would overshadow the new hereditary law, and possibly disrupt the ratification. Change came slowly to Asturia and a consensus was still very much in the balance, as was public opinion, especially amongst the older generations. But Clem was also right about Arrosa's need for time away. She'd looked increasingly pale and thin over the last few months and Akil knew her offer to him came from a need for companionship and help, not from any deeper feelings. Some time away was exactly what she needed—and if he hadn't turned up unexpectedly then who was to say that the ruse wouldn't have worked the way the sisters had planned it?

'I won't say a word,' he promised. 'But how is this even possible? You're six months older than Arrosa, you say, which must mean Zorien is your father? Who's your mother?' It was unlike Akil to be so overtly curious but he was intrigued beyond politeness by this secret at the very heart of the court.

Clem flushed, her eyes fixed on her cup. 'One thing you need to know is that this isn't easy for me. I have never told anyone who I am, not even my old boyfriends, or my best friend. Anyone from home who has met Rosy thinks she's my cousin. Just saying the truth aloud feels like I've broken some law.'

'You don't have to tell me anything you don't want to,' Akil assured her and her answering smile was grateful.

'I know. But in a strange way, I do want to tell you. It's probably better that you know the whole truth rather than leaving you with just bits of it. I would hate for you to think badly of my mother, or even my father. He's not exactly been there for me, but I do understand how difficult things were for him and he has ensured that Rosy and I know each other. I will always be grateful to him for that.'

Akil did some rapid mental calculations. 'Arrosa

was born a year after Zorien and Iara married—so you would have been conceived three months before?'

Clem nodded. 'What you have to remember is that Zorien's marriage was brought forward after his father's illness meant he decided to abdicate in favour of his son. There had been an informal agreement between the families that Zorien and Iara would marry but they weren't technically engaged when Zorien dated my mother. It's a bit of a technicality because the marriage was very much in the pipeline, but my father wasn't a *total* cad. A bit of one but not a *total* cad.' Her voice rang with sincerity. It was obviously important to her that Akil believed this—that she believed it.

Akil had never really thought about the King's marriage before, or how it had come to be. But this was Asturian politics, nothing happened without planning for the long game, his own parents' disastrous marriage aside. 'Queen Iara comes from an old and wealthy aristocratic family with links to European royalty on both sides. I believe it was a popular marriage among the people and politically sound,' he remembered. 'And for the most part it seems to have worked well; apart from her propensity to take long retreats abroad, she's a good queen. Not loved, exactly, but respected.'

'From what I've gleaned they live mostly separate lives but put on a united front. Neither had any romantic fantasies about the marriage. Iara's family wanted her to be Queen and she liked the idea. Zorien knew his position as a young king would be stabilised by a good marriage. After the plans were agreed, but before they got engaged, Zorien was allowed to go to the Sorbonne for a year's MBA as reward. He enrolled anonymously and that's where he met my mother. They fell in love. At least, my mother told me it was love.' Her voice softened, became wistful. 'He told her the truth when his father's declining health meant the court decided to bring the engagement forward, followed by a wedding just six weeks later. What neither of them knew when they parted was that she was pregnant with me. By the time she found out the wedding was less than a month away and the abdication planned. A different man might have broken off the engagement and married my mother despite the court's objections and weathered the scandal, or even walked away from the throne altogether, but Zorien decided to put Asturia first, go ahead with the wedding and make sure no one knew about my mother or about me.'

'That must have been difficult for your mother.' And for the daughter, which made her presence here today rather remarkable. Made *her* rather remarkable. Strong, forgiving, compassionate.

Beautiful.

Desirable.

The realisation made him catch his breath. Yes, she resembled her sister, but she was very much her own person; there was a piquancy to her features that differentiated her, made her unique. Made her desirable in a way Arrosa wasn't. Not that Akil had any right to dwell on either her beauty or her desirability.

Clem's mouth twisted into a wry smile. 'My mother was a doer not a dweller.' Akil noted the *was* and the way she blinked sudden tears away at the word. 'She moved to England where I was born, fell in love with Cornwall and retrained as a teacher, although Zorien was very generous, money-wise at least. She never married, never really dated seriously as far as I know although she had plenty of suitors. Instead she threw herself into campaigns and causes, never happier than when she was directing the village play or organising a march or painting a placard. To be honest I'm not sure being a queen would have agreed with her. She liked to say exactly what was on her mind, to take action. Diplomacy wasn't really her thing.'

'How did you and Arrosa get to know each other?'

'Apparently Zorien told Iara about my mother and the pregnancy before they married. When it started to seem likely that Arrosa was going to be their only child she agreed that we should be allowed to meet. In the end Rosy used to come to us, incognito of course, for most holidays and nearly all of the summer. She loved the chance to do normal things. To go surfing or bowling, to eat chips on the beach. To get dirty and have tangled hair and old clothes. We had amazing summers. We don't get to spend time together now but we speak weekly. She's my sister, my closest friend. I love her and her happiness matters.' Her gaze was direct. 'So I am glad you and I got the chance to meet. To talk.'

Her meaning was clear. 'She told you about her proposition?'

'Yes, and that's why I urged her to stay in Cornwall. What the two of you decide is your business, but she was too tired, too run-down to make any life-altering decisions right now. I hope you will respect that she needs time and space. Her parents married for an alliance, because it made political sense, and nothing she has ever told me has persuaded me that it was a good match. I want more for her than that.'

'Understood.' He did—and he admired the way Clem had her sister's interests at heart. He'd thought Arrosa alone but how could she be with her sister on her side? He pushed his chair back. 'It was nice meeting you, Clem. Thank you for entrusting me with your secret. I promise it's safe with me. What are your plans for the next six weeks?'

She winced. 'That's a good question. I'd hoped to get to know Asturia. I've never been here before and I have always wanted to explore it. But we're miles from anywhere, Rosy doesn't own a car and the limousine isn't exactly inconspicuous. I'm not really sure how to get out and about. I can't just call a taxi when as far as anyone knows the person living here is Arrosa and never goes anywhere unaccompanied and without clearance. I'll figure out a way, but it's more complicated than I realised.'

He sympathised with her, but her predicament was none of his business. His life was complicated enough without embroiling himself in the affairs of the King's illegitimate daughter. But there was something about the wistful look in Clem's eyes and the way she tried to cover it with her cheery matter-of-fact tone that spoke to him. It *was* a shame that she couldn't get to know the country her father ruled over and her sister would one day inherit.

'I cleared my diary for the rest of the day so I could take you out this afternoon if you wanted,' he said, surprising himself with the offer. 'If you put your hair up and sunglasses on, the guards at the gate will assume you're Arrosa—I've driven her to the city before and I trained with the secret service during my national service, which means clearance has never been an issue before. The guards will assume we're working. And once we're away from here you should be fine. You don't look so like your sister that anyone would mistake you for her close up, especially if you don't dress formally.'

Hope sparked in the hazel eyes but almost immediately dimmed. 'That's very kind but I can't ask you to give up your afternoon for me.'

'You didn't ask, I offered. Your choice, Clem. A chance to explore or an afternoon staring at the lake. What will it be?' Akil didn't want to analyse why he really wanted her to say yes.

She laughed at that, the sound unexpectedly rich and melodic. 'It's not really a choice when you put it that way. Thank you, I really appreciate it and I would love to accept. Let's explore. Just give me five minutes to get ready.'

'Take as long as you need.' Akil ignored the sense of anticipation creeping through him at the prospect of an afternoon spent with the English girl, the pleasure that she had accepted his offer. He was doing a favour for his friend's sister. Nothing more, nothing less.

CHAPTER FOUR

ANTICIPATION FIZZED THROUGH Clem as she pulled on a pair of Arrosa's oversized sunglasses and added one of her sister's bright scarves and a large, low-brimmed hat. The perfect disguise as all three could be discarded as soon as she had safely left the estate grounds. She tipped her own sunglasses, phone and purse into one of Arrosa's bags and practically ran back outside.

'Ready!'

Akil was frowning at his phone but as he looked up a slow, approving smile curved his mouth and a jolt of attraction hit her low in her stomach, the heat spreading through her. 'You really were just five minutes.'

'I'm an actress, remember? Quick changes are my trade.'

'When my sister says five minutes I usually know I need to settle in for half an hour at least.'

'You have a sister?'

He nodded. 'Elixane. She's in New York at the moment, doing a surgical residency.' A shadow, so fleeting she wasn't sure if she'd imagined it, crossed his face. 'She plans to be Surgeon General here one day.'

'A woman with ambition. I approve.'

Clem quickly sent a message to Marie and Henri to

let them know her plans and then followed Akil round to the front of the villa. She let out a low whistle as she took in his car. A sporty two-seater, so far so playboy but the classy silvery blue colour he'd chosen suggested a car bought to drive and enjoy as opposed to a mere status symbol. 'What a beauty! Can we have the top down?'

'If you want.'

'I do, although maybe when we're away from here and I can shed the hat. It would be a bit inconvenient if it got blown off by the wind just as we got waved through!'

Akil unlocked the car and Clem slid in, luxuriating in the comfortable leather seats. The car might seem a cliché in a less skilled driver's hands, but he handled her beautifully, the car purring under his guidance. Clem sneaked a look at Akil as he accelerated down the drive, sunglasses shading his eyes, his face intent on the road ahead, muscles taut on his bare arms, and her pulse accelerated. He really was a ridiculously attractive man.

His arrival at the villa could so easily have been a disaster but it was looking as if it was a blessing in disguise. Not only was she finally getting an opportunity to explore Asturia, but this was an unexpected opportunity to find out who Akil really was behind the hot body and the political career, her chance to make sure he was worthy of her sister, to find out what he really thought of Arrosa's proposition.

She tensed up as they reached the gate and Akil gave her another of those slow smiles, her stomach flipping in response. 'Relax,' he said. 'You're doing fine.' Sure enough, the soldiers saluted as they opened the gates and within seconds they were accelerating away, Clem discarding the hat and sunglasses, replacing Arrosa's designer dark sunglasses with her own quirkier vintage ones and wriggling back in her seat.

'Where are we going?'

'I can tell you,' Akil said. 'Or it could be a surprise. Your call.'

Everywhere was new to her and she wanted to see it all. 'I trust you. Surprise me. I'm sure anywhere you choose will be fine.'

Akil nodded as he pressed the button to lower the roof and the whistle of the wind combined with the purr of the engine. Clem stared around at the countryside, taking it all in with avid eyes. She'd seen so many pictures, read so many books, watched any programme or film set here and now she was actually here, breathing Asturian air.

Asturia was as beautiful as she had hoped, green and unspoilt with verges filled with wild flowers. Her very soul felt repleted as she inhaled the tartly fresh air as if something in her had always craved it. As if she were home. Asturia might be backward in many ways but that meant its countryside was relatively undeveloped and the country was now getting a reputation for biodiversity and attracting eco-conscious tourists. Rolling hills and fields gave way to mountains at the further end of the horizon, the sun beating down from a cloudless sky. She sighed in appreciation. 'It's so beautiful.'

'It really is,' Akil agreed. 'There's nowhere else like it.'

'And so quiet. As if there's no one else here.'

'Hmm.' He glanced in the mirror. 'Apart from the car that's been tailing us since we left the castle. Is Henri not with Arrosa? I thought he never left her side?'

She looked round at the sleek black car hanging a discreet distance behind. 'Poor Henri. He was torn between returning with me and staying with Rosy. As people are meant to think I'm her he knew he needed to be here for business as usual, but he takes protecting her very seriously. It took some persuading for him to agree that she'd look too conspicuous if he stayed. No one expects my cousin to have a bodyguard! Although I expect Zorien has dispatched someone to keep an eye on her.'

'Your father knows you've swapped?'

'Rosy messaged him last night. I was hoping to hear from him today but of course he's very busy. This would be such a good opportunity for us to spend some time together.' She could hear the self-pity in her voice and winced, relieved when Akil didn't pursue the subject.

They crested a hill and as they reached the top and the sea came into view Clem gasped. There it was, laid out before them, turquoise and silver and so dazzling she was glad of her sunglasses. She took in a wondering breath as Akil began to navigate his way down the curving road.

'It's like something out of a fairy tale,' she said softly, transfixed as the flower-covered cliffs came into view, the sea tumbling against them. Asturia wasn't the most famous of tourist resorts, but there was no coastline to rival it, not even her beloved Cornwall. 'Just like I imagined,' she almost whispered.

They carried on heading along the coast road until Akil turned off down a narrow lane, heading towards the sea and a tiny cluster of houses dotted around a wooden, slightly tatty harbour. Clem knew that there were plenty of glamorous beaches along the coast, home to exclusive beach clubs and harbours filled with fancy boats, but this seemed like the kind of place she loved, small and known only to a few locals.

Akil pulled into a car park and killed the engine. Clem looked around eagerly. Fishing boats bobbed by the wooden pier, bigger boats moored further out, a mix of working and leisure craft. In front of them a small hut overlooked the sea flanked by a few plastic tables and chairs.

'Okay, then,' he said. 'Here we are. I hope you're hungry.'

It was as if Akil had seen inside her soul and knew exactly what she craved. She followed him to the hut and took a seat on a battered but clean and comfortable plastic chair perched on the edge of a tiny stone harbour, fine white sand inviting her on the beach to their right.

'What do you fancy?' Akil asked. 'I can recommend the fried clams.'

'Clams and fries? Perfect.'

'The local beer is good, or they make their own lemonade.'

'A beer sounds good. In a way I am on holiday, I suppose.' Not that she'd been gainfully employed for longer than she cared to remember. Money wasn't an issue, thanks to the money Zorien had set aside for her, but she needed an occupation. She needed a purpose, a reason to exist. She pushed the thought away for another day and tilted her chin. 'Besides, this is my first outing in Asturia. I should celebrate.'

Akil held her gaze for one charged second, the corner of his mouth turned up in amusement—and approval. Clem's pulse thudded under his studied gaze and she turned to exclaim at the view, breaking the spell with a stream of meaningless words.

The food was as wonderful as promised, the clams fat and salty, tasting like the sea, the fries crispy on the outside, meltingly soft inside, tart with vinegar. The salad wasn't the token collection of browned limp leaves Clem was expecting, but sweet crunchy leaves, tiny, delicious tomatoes and tart red peppers, another reminder that she was in the Mediterranean, not on the English coast.

Even better was the view. On one side the sea, calm and bright and endlessly beautiful, and on the other Akil. Six feet of broad-shouldered, olive-skinned, dark-eyed deliciousness. And she *really* needed to stop thinking about Akil that way. She wasn't here on a date. She didn't know him, nor he her. He was just being kind to a lonely girl. And no doubt it suited him to do it. He must know that Clem would tell Arrosa all about the afternoon.

But she couldn't deny that this really was her idea of a dream date. And that spelt trouble in all kinds of ways she wasn't going to allow herself to think about.

Instead, she was going to keep busy and push the words *dream* and *date* right out of her mind.

'That was amazing,' she said, jumping to her feet and collecting up the plates and beer bottles and returning them to the hut with a smile. 'Thank you for bringing me here.' She didn't return to her seat, leaning over the railing and looking out to sea, her pulse hammering with nerves. *Keep talking, Clem.* She glanced back at Akil. 'So this is a favourite place of yours?'

'Since I was a boy,' he confirmed, lounging back in his chair. 'My aunt has a holiday home near here, me, my sister and our cousins spent our summers sailing on these waters and spending all our money on snacks here at this very shack. Not that it spoiled our appetites.' His grin was reminiscently boyish and her stomach tumbled. She could cope with him being handsome. She wasn't sure she could manage charming as well.

'I was brought up by the sea. I love sailing. Surfing, paddle-boarding, kayaking, I did it all. I just love being out on the water.'

'It can be arranged, just say the word. My boat is moored here.'

He had a boat? Could he tick any more boxes? Regretfully she shook her head. 'I can't let poor Henri follow us in a dinghy.' She grimaced. 'I'd never realised how limiting it is being followed all the time. I know that Henri is kind, careful not to impose, but he's always there. I don't know how Rosy manages it.'

'What she has now is freedom compared to how her life will be once she's the heir to the throne.'

It was a sobering thought. No wonder her sister wanted companionship. Two sisters equally lonely but for very different reasons. Maybe Rosy should marry Akil. He was kind, intelligent and understood her world.

But then again she didn't love him and, of all people, didn't her sister deserve love?

'Maybe I should stick around and be her body double for good and then she could escape whenever she needed,' she half joked and Akil grinned.

'Maybe you should. Although poor Henri would definitely want to clone himself if you two made a habit of this.' He nodded towards the beach. 'Fancy walking some of that off?'

'Absolutely. I'm dying to explore.'

The beach was a long straight strip of white sand, the sea lapping at the edges. In the distance Clem could see a gentle curve and a high tumble of rocks against the high cliff that marked the end of the bay. They started to walk, first slowly and then faster as they took the measure of each other's stride, and Clem enjoyed the pace, the stretch in her muscles as she matched Akil step for step. She could hear the occasional hum of a car, the screech of gulls out at sea, but otherwise it was as if it were just the two of them—and Henri, several hundred yards behind.

Neither spoke, their strides perfectly matched. Clem was totally aware of Akil's every movement, the swing of his arms, the flex of his hands. She swallowed, trying to ignore the all-encompassing awareness of him that seemed to grow with every passing minute. *Behave*, she scolded herself, aware that she needed to stop staring at his wrists, stop finding herself transfixed by the pulse at his throat, stop dwelling on the lines of his mouth, stop allowing herself to trace the outlines of his strong, broad body.

It was just attraction, but it was inconvenient and misjudged.

'Are you seriously considering it?' she asked abruptly. 'Rosy's idea?'

Akil's brows drew together in surprise, a haughty expression crossing his face, and she winced at her gaucheness, scrambling to explain. 'I meant what I said earlier, it's your decision and not really my business. But in some ways it *is*. I've spent just a few hours in my sister's shoes and I can see why she feels she needs someone permanent on her side, in her team. It's pretty lonely being a princess. But I still think rushing into an engagement, into a marriage, is just a temporary fix. Because if you're not right for each other she'll end up lonelier than before. I love her,' she said awkwardly. 'And I hate that I can't support her the way a sister should. So maybe I'm interfering but I can't just pretend that this situation isn't worrying me.'

Akil's face softened as she spoke. 'My parents are the perfect example of a hasty ill-thought-out marriage so please be assured I would never rush into any kind of decision. My father was an ambitious man, my mother a country girl. Theirs was a summer romance which should have stayed a lovely memory but instead became an unhappy marriage.'

'That sounds tough. They're still together?'

'Legally, but in reality they see very little of each other. My mother resides at the family home, my father retired after a heart attack eight years ago and now lives mainly in Switzerland.' A heart attack Akil had been responsible for. He could never forget that.

'What happened?'

He didn't answer for a while, instead he paused and turned, his gaze far away on the horizon. 'My mother understood little of politics and hated my father's absences,' he said at last. 'She didn't want a husband who spent most of his time away from home, whereas he wanted a hostess to work the room, someone to charm allies and rivals and know all the gossip, not a shy, paranoid wife who drank too much to work up the courage to have a conversation. They were very different, too different. They made each other unhappy, everyone around them unhappy. With different partners, in another life, they might have been better people, happier people, but we'll never know. If I marry, then I know to look for shared goals, compatibility, not momentary attraction.'

'And love? Do you want love?'

'Love can complicate things. It's not essential for me. Liking and respect mean more to me than love.'

She nodded. 'Thank you for your honesty.'

'And?'

'And what?'

'Did I pass?'

It was her turn to pause and think, to search for the right words. 'I like your honesty and self-awareness and I like the fact that you understand my sister's world and aren't intimidated by it. But I still think she should wait for someone who loves her, not her job, someone who would marry her if she ran the shack on the beach or cleaned her office. And we both know that's not you. But,' she added hurriedly, aware she was interfering in a way she had promised herself not to, 'this isn't about what I think. You two have to decide what's best for you. But can I ask you something?'

'Anything. It doesn't mean I'll answer but you can ask.'

'What's in it for you? You don't strike me as the kind of man who likes to play second fiddle, and I know what a macho culture Asturia has. Do you really see your-self as a consort?'

Akil was floored by Clem's directness, by her honesty. Floored—and intrigued and more than a little im-pressed. It was so far from the kind of language used in the Senate and at Court, no dancing around, no double-speak. Instead she aimed straight for the heart of the matter and hit it.

'Power,' he said simply. 'If I marry your sister, if I became Prince Consort, then I will always be at the very heart of policy, of government, a decision maker, and influencer.'

Her brow furrowed. 'And that matters to you?'

He laughed shortly. 'I'm a politician. Power is all that matters, Clem.'

'Power for power's sake?'

He hated the uncertainty in her voice. 'No, but without power nothing can be achieved. My family has been at the heart of government for generations, carrying on their work is my destiny whether I like it or not. I haven't always agreed, but when my father had his heart attack and had to take early retirement I promised him that I would fulfil his dreams. That promise means a lot to me. But, as I said, I know the pitfalls of marrying rashly and wrongly. I could achieve great things in my current role too. I just need to weigh it all up.'

'You're close to your father?' He could hear the wistfulness in her voice as she asked the question and winced.

'I wouldn't say close,' he said wryly. 'I don't think anyone is. My father is…very single-minded. He sees no views but his own, brooks no opinion but his own. He's not an easy man.'

'But he must be proud of you,' she argued. 'Rosy said that you are the youngest, most influential politician in Asturia. And look at your sister, a surgeon in New York. Surely that success means a lot to him?'

'The only thing that would make my father proud is if my sister marries someone he approves of and if I keep climbing the political ladder. Would he approve of me marrying your sister? Without a doubt. Does that influence me? It shouldn't, but…' he shrugged '… I can't deny that his approval is something I seek. Maybe it's a weakness.' He strode on, appalled at how much he'd said, how much he'd revealed, how much he'd exposed. It wasn't like him to speak about his family, about his own insecurities and complicated feelings around his father's push for Akil to do more, to be more. What was it about this woman that made him speak without fear or thought?

He sensed Clem catch up beside him and they walked along in silence for a little longer. 'I understand better than you know,' she said at last, her voice quiet. 'I've only met my father a handful of times, he's never seen me act, never said well done after an exam result, he wasn't there the day I buried my mother. I should hate him, sometimes I do, but more than anything I want him to notice me, want him to be proud of me. I want him to acknowledge I exist.'

Akil didn't know what to say, so instead of words he reached out and took her hand. It was warm in his, fitted him as if made for him to hold. 'I'm sure he knows. He's like my father, not a man to show his emotions.' Akil reluctantly dropped her hand, his own instantly cold.

'True, but knowing it's not personal doesn't make it any easier. I hate that I care. I'm twenty-seven, a grown woman. I shouldn't let the way I feel about him affect my life. But it does. Sometimes I think the only reason I became an actress was to be seen. For the moment the applause rings out for me and I relish the validation that gives me. Pathetic, isn't it?' She shook her head, her mouth compressed tight.

'Not at all,' he said softly. 'We all need validation.

What about your mother? Did you have a good relationship with her?'

Clem stared down at the sand, digging into it with her trainer toes. 'I did, we were very close, and I miss her every day. But my mother, she was a force of nature. Not many women would take in their ex-lover's daughter every summer, but my mother loved every waif and stray. Every cat we owned was a runaway she ended up feeding. She was a woman who embraced causes, was at the heart of every campaign, her life was big and filled and sometimes it felt like there was little room for me. Everything was open to anyone who needed it, from Christmases to time together. She just had this endless capacity to scoop people up and look after them, but it meant I always had to share her.' She gave a little laugh. 'I know that I sound so selfish, so spoiled. But sometimes I just wanted to be first with one of my parents just once. If I ever marry, if I ever have kids, it will be different. Maybe it's boring, but I want the house and garden and the kids playing on the trampoline and a husband who loves me. Who sees me. And I want that for Rosy too, because she needs it just as much, more in some ways.'

Akil turned to face her. 'Are you warning me off?'

'No.' She shook her head. 'Not at all. And I'll tell Rosy all about this conversation. I just want you to know that there's more to her than the practical Princess and I bet there's more to you than the ambitious politician and you both need to take that into consideration.'

'I will,' he vowed, and he meant it. 'Come on, I'd better get you back.'

'Have I frightened you off?'

He laughed at that. 'No. In fact you've intrigued

me. I'm glad I met you today, Clem. I can't help thinking that in another time, another place, we might have been friends.'

That was only partly true, because in another time and another place he would have liked to have known her a lot better, to have explored the attraction he could feel building between them.

'Friends?' she echoed. 'Yes, I would have liked that. Thank you for today, Akil. Not just for the trip and the food, but for listening.'

'Any time.' And he meant it. It was just a shame their paths were unlikely to cross again.

CHAPTER FIVE

HEART POUNDING, LEGS ACHING, Akil reached his apartment door, opened it and staggered in to collapse on the sofa, his water bottle within reach. Ten miles in the heat of the early afternoon at that pace had been foolish but he'd needed the exercise.

Needed to get Clem out of his mind.

It had been *one* meeting. One afternoon. Just a few hours spent together. But somehow in those hours he'd been more honest with her than he had been with any other human being for years—including himself. He couldn't hide from the question she'd asked him. Instead it swirled throughout his mind relentlessly.

What was in it for him if he married Arrosa?

The answers came quickly and glibly. The same answers he'd given her: power, the ability to get things done, a place at the heart of all decision-making, marriage to someone compatible without any of the emotions or passions that could so easily turn dark and disrupt the equilibrium he craved. And most importantly of all, a chance to show his father that he was not only a true Ortiz, but he was better than him, had achieved more, to not just keep his promise, but to surpass it. Surpass him.

To show himself that giving up his own dreams had been worth it. Arrosa would never have made the suggestion if he'd become a doctor, no matter how skilled or successful he might have been.

Akil sank onto the sofa. They were all compelling reasons, but no matter how often he repeated them he couldn't make them ring true. He liked Arrosa, respected her, but he couldn't imagine spending a lifetime with her. Couldn't imagine treading someone else's path, not again. He'd already compromised his life's purpose once and had vowed never again.

And there were other reasons to refuse, as compelling as those in favour. The Ortizes were an old family but not known outside Asturia. Whoever married Arrosa would be instantly targeted by the world's press. Look what that meant for the royal family, even the unacknowledged daughter: Clem never having the opportunity to build a real relationship with her father, Arrosa resorting to subterfuge to get time alone, bodyguards always around. It wouldn't take much digging to uncover the truth about his family, about his mother's drinking and his father's affairs. There was no way Akil wanted their dirty laundry spread all over the Internet.

At that moment his phone rang and Akil reached for it, only mildly surprised when he saw the Princess's name flash up. She'd messaged him yesterday in reply to his question checking in on her, but of course she'd have had the opportunity to speak to Clem since then. The question was, what had Clem said about their time together? Would the Princess want to pursue her idea or was this call to let him down?

Either way his mind was made up.

'Your Highness, you're alive,' he said as he answered

it. 'I have to say it comes as some relief. I've been hoping that I wasn't taken in by a very clever con artist.'

Arrosa laughed, sounding far more relaxed than he'd ever heard her sound before. 'Clem is definitely good enough an actress to be a con artist, but she's far too straight talking.'

Akil smiled wryly. 'I noticed that myself.'

'Yes, I bet you did. She gave me a very interesting account of your conversation. I'm not going to apologise, it's nice to know that someone is looking out for me, but I hope it wasn't too bruising.'

'Bracing maybe, but not bruising. She certainly made me think.'

A trace of caution entered Arrosa's voice. 'She's good at that. That's why she insisted that I take some time away, to give *me* time to look at what I really want for my future. And I have. I know I've only been gone a couple of days but being away from Asturia, away from the court, away from all the pressure and hysteria around the ratification, has been exactly what I needed.'

She paused and he heard her inhale. 'Look, Akil, I think I owe you an apology...'

And there it was, his get-out-of-becoming-royalty card. The relief that filled him was surprisingly overwhelming. 'You don't need to say anything,' he said. 'Let's just pretend that the end of that last conversation never happened.'

'I shouldn't have said anything. I was tired and honestly a little scared of what's happening this year...'

'Listen, I'm flattered, but Clem's right. You deserve more.'

'She said that?'

'And the rest. Arrosa, I hope it goes without saying

that I will continue to do all I can to support you, and I hope we can work together for many years. More than that, I hope that we can become friends, real friends.'

'I'd like that. Friends sounds good.'

'In that case, Arrosa, as your friend, can I ask if you're okay?'

She paused again and when she spoke her voice broke a little. 'Yes, in some ways I'm more okay than I have been for a long time. And with Clem covering for me I'm perfectly safe. Life in Asturia can be very suffocating. I am appreciating having the chance to breathe.'

'That's good.'

'It really is. Although I feel guilty that Clem must now be feeling hemmed in, especially as she can't really go out and meet people. So thank you for taking her out, for giving her a chance to see something of the country. I really appreciate it.'

It seemed wrong to be thanked for one of the most enjoyable afternoons he'd had in a long time. 'You don't need to thank me. Your sister's an interesting woman. I enjoyed her company very much—and it strikes me that she knows exactly what she signed up for and is determined to see it through.'

'I offered to swap back, but she won't hear of it.' The relief in Arrosa's voice was palpable; no wonder Clem had insisted on maintaining the charade a little bit longer. Admiration for the Englishwoman filled him. He knew it wasn't easy for her trapped alone in the villa, no matter how beautiful the outlook and luxurious the furnishings.

'I think she's made up her mind to make sure you get a good long break. It's an honourable thing she's doing. She has integrity.'

'She's the best sister I could have. I just wish I could tell the whole world who she is, that she could be part of my life openly. I hope she's not too bored. I know she won't tell me if she is. Life at the estate can be confining, even though I insisted on moving out of the palais into the lake house, and of course she doesn't have work to keep her occupied. She says she's fine and it's a change of scene, but six weeks is a long time to be stuck in one place and alone.'

'I could pop in and check on her, if you want.' Akil's tone was nonchalant but he could feel his pulse speed up at the thought.

'That would be really kind. I would really appreciate it.' Was that amusement in Arrosa's voice?

'I'll see if I can spare the time.'

'Thank you, Akil. For everything.'

'Enjoy your break.' As Akil ended the call he couldn't shake the feeling that he'd been set up in some way.

Maybe checking on Clem wasn't such a good idea. He couldn't deny that he was attracted to her, was intrigued by her, but she was only here for a short while and he had too much going on to invite the kind of complications she posed further into his life. Better to leave her as a memorable momentary encounter.

It was definitely safer and wiser that way.

But he couldn't help wishing that she had been someone else.

For the next few days Akil kept himself too busy to dwell on might-have-beens and if-onlys. It was the parliamentary summer recess and, although there were always briefing notes to read and events to react to, it gave him more time to do the things he truly loved. His dream of being a doctor might have died the day his father had collapsed with a heart attack, but his desire to help, be part of and reform the creaky, unequal health system in Asturia hadn't and he had undertaken mountain rescue training and now volunteered whenever he could. It wasn't what he'd once hoped for, but it was better than nothing and the insight the volunteering gave him helped him push for the reforms the country needed. Even his father approved—a politician who got involved with mountain rescue played well in the polls. Now it was early summer there were plenty of inexperienced hikers walking Asturia's famous mountain trails spraining ankles and getting lost and Akil could easily spend twelve hours a day either coordinating searches or out himself. By the time he got in most evenings he was no good for anything but feeding his cat, grabbing a beer and a sandwich and collapsing on the sofa.

One night he had ended up being called out late to help locate a missing couple who had gone out to look at the stars and not returned and it was the early hours before he got back in. Too wired to sleep, he didn't get to bed until it was almost dawn, sleeping in until noon, almost unheard of with his busy schedule. Looking around, he realised the toll the last few days had taken: he had little food in and his usually neat apartment felt both untidy and unlived in, his cat grumpy and aloof as if indignant at being left alone for so long.

After toasting the end of the loaf and whisking up his last two eggs, he sank onto the sofa and switched on the TV to catch the news. His counterpart had made an announcement about a new security law, and although Akil had read some of the online reactions he was interested to see what the state TV news would say. It was the lead item, and once it was finished he fumbled for the remote to switch over to the sports channel when the sight of a familiar profile made him pause.

To any casual onlooker the profile through the tinted window looked enough like Arrosa for there to be no doubt that this was the Princess being driven back to her home from the capital city. Huge sunglasses shielded most of her face, but the features were familiar, her hair was up in the kind of complicated knot Arrosa favoured and her posture and half-smile were so like Arrosa's own he'd have been fooled himself if he hadn't known better. Warmth filled him as he watched the brief clip of Clem doing what she'd come here to do: fool the press into thinking Arrosa was safe in Asturia.

Warmth that soon faded as he remembered his unfulfilled promise. What had she been doing for the last four days? Had her father come to see her? He doubted it. She was probably all alone.

But she shouldn't be because he'd promised Arrosa he'd look in on her and, unlike many other politicians, he prided himself on keeping his promises. It was wrong of him to stay away just because he was attracted to her—after all, he'd been attracted to lots of women in his life and been perfectly capable of spending time with them.

Before he could think better of it, he quickly texted Arrosa and asked for Clem's number. The reply came back lightning quick, as if Arrosa had been waiting for the question. Akil saved the number and sent a quick exploratory message. There, it was up to her now. He didn't mind either way.

So why was he checking his phone to see the message had been read?

'I'm a fool, Tiger,' he said to his cat, who as usual ignored him. But just as he put his phone out of reach, determined to concentrate on the game, his phone pinged.

His pulse sped as he reached for the phone and checked the name of the sender. Clem. She'd replied. His finger hovered over her name; it shouldn't matter if she gave him a polite brush off or an acceptance, but Akil couldn't deny the thrill of anticipation as he contemplated the message.

Nor could he deny how much he hoped her answer was a yes.

Clem was doing her best to put a Pollyanna spin on her experience. Number one: the weather was beautiful and her tan was coming along nicely. Number two: Arrosa's villa was luxuriously and comfortably furnished with everything she could need and more besides, including some seriously luxurious toiletries, which turned every day into a spa day. Number three: she had the lake at her disposal. The small rowing boat in the boathouse was perfect for spending a couple of hours sculling up and down the lake in, and the water, although cold, was clean and clear enough for some serious swimming. She had got into the habit of taking both a morning dip and sunset swim and on a hot day could be found spending most of the afternoon in the water as well. She just hoped this behaviour wasn't so out of character that it was raising eyebrows amongst bodyguards and staff who saw her from afar. Number four: there was a castle kitchen at her disposal. All she had to do was order her food and it turned up, like magic in her kitchen although she'd never seen anyone bring it over or put it out for her. Even when she didn't order anything the kitchen was mysteriously stocked in her absence, freshly made bread, cream butter, sharp cheese, olives and delicious little cakes replenishing themselves or so it seemed. Her sister might live independently, but she definitely had all the perks of living at home. Her laundry disappeared too, only to return clean and pressed.

And, last but not least, she had the time she needed to think about her future. Time away from Cornwall and the memories of her mother. Time to ready herself to move on to whatever the next stage of her life entailed.

But even Clem at her most determined couldn't be Pollyanna all the time, and when she stopped the reality of her situation came crashing down on her. She had been here nearly a week and her father still hadn't found time to come and see her. She wasn't so naive as to expect him to drop everything and rush over straight away, although that would have been nice, but she had hoped that now she was just a half-hour drive away he might have been able to carve out a little bit of time to see her. *Idiot*, she scolded herself. She should have known better than to expect anything from him. He'd made sure she was materially provided for and that was all she realistically could and should expect.

Plus, although she'd told herself that what she needed was time away, it turned out you really could have too much of a good thing. Her days seemed endless and her mind was whirling with possibilities and fears. It seemed impossible that less than two years ago she had been sharing a flat with friends in Battersea, filling her days with classes and auditions and sometimes even work, her evenings with bars and restaurants and plays. She'd never doubted that she would make it, that her talent and drive weren't enough. It was just a matter of when her break would be, not if.

But then she'd received the call from her mother and all that fell away, her life became a worried regime of hospital appointments and waiting rooms, too brief moments of hope and long days of bitter grief, watching her home turn slowly into a hospice for those last long, painful months.

For the three months after the packed-out funeral she had been numb with grief, wandering along the beach, curling up in her mother's bed, until the opportunity to play Juliet and the possibility of the theatre's privatisation had galvanised her back into some kind of action and routine. She'd joined the Save Our Theatre campaign, aware of just how proud her mother would have been, attending planning meetings and organising petitions, turning the cottage into a campaign headquarters just as it had been throughout her life. But although both had filled her thoughts and hours, neither were a solution to the question of what came next. In the end she'd followed her sister's advice and written a list of possibilities along with pros and cons and scores out of ten for how each one inspired her. It was time to revisit it.

Almost reluctantly she brought up the file on her tablet and set it before her on the outside table. She had a fresh coffee and a bowl of mixed fruit so she couldn't distract herself with a trip to the kitchen. Taking a deep breath, Clem read through the short list.

First and most obvious: acting. Not only had she trained for it, but she still had an agent somehow, despite her long break. Plus, she'd loved playing Juliet and was enjoying impersonating her sister and getting into character as the Crown Princess, even if it was for just an hour sitting in a car. But she knew that at some point in the last eighteen months she'd lost the resilience she needed to face the constant rejection that awaited every aspiring actor. Did she really want the high point of her month to be a recall for a toothpaste ad? Did she want to spend another three months as an understudy, sitting in the dressing room every night trying not to wish a broken ankle on the star? At twenty-five that had just been part and parcel of the process, but at twenty-seven she needed more than constant knock-backs and waiting around for her break.

Secondly, and maybe even more obviously, she could follow so many of her drama school friends into teaching. Clem sighed. It was a worthy career and her mother, with her zeal and passion for change, had been a wonderful teacher. But she didn't feel a vocation and surely that was important?

Or she could carry on putting off making a decision and go travelling, hoping she would find her vocation as she did so. After all, her mother had backpacked around the world more than once before enrolling at the Sorbonne. She had been full of stories of the time she had worked in a school in Ecuador or had crewed on a Greenpeace ship. Simone Beaumont, trying to save the world even as a backpacker. She'd always encouraged Clem to follow her example and why not? It wasn't as if she didn't have the money and the time. But she didn't want to do it alone.

She didn't want to do any of it alone, not any more. She wanted people of her own to live and laugh and love with. That was what mattered to her. That was what she needed.

But that wasn't something she could just make happen.

Clem sat back and rubbed her eyes. 'Get over yourself, Beaumont,' she muttered. 'You are luckier than so many other people. You have a home and you don't need to worry about money, you have qualifications and prospects even if you're not sure what they are yet. Stop feeling sorry for yourself. What would Maman say?'

Simone Beaumont had had no time for self-pity.

Her phone pinged and, glad of the distraction, she picked up her phone to look at the notification—an unknown number.

'Ooh, what kind of spam will it be? An uncollected parcel or a tax rebate? Or maybe it's not spam but a producer hearing about how devastating I was as Juliet and wanting me in the West End.'

She missed her mother's cat. Talking out loud didn't feel as foolish when she was addressing Gus, who always seemed on the verge of saying something wise.

She clicked it open, unprepared for the thrill of anticipation that ran through her when she saw who it was from.

Akil.

It had been five days since their lunch. After their parting she'd not expected to hear from him again, although a tiny part of her had hoped to be proved wrong, especially once Arrosa had told her that they had decided to remain just friends and colleagues after all. But after a couple of days had passed with no word from him, she'd done her best to put him out of her mind. Now here he was. What did he want?

The message was short and to the point.

If you're still finding it hard to play tourist, I have a spare afternoon tomorrow. Shall I pick you up? Let me know. Akil

Clem sat back, unable to stop a small smile playing on her mouth. The part of her that had stopped knowing how to enjoy life over the last eighteen months, the part of her that knew that sometimes the worst did happen, advised caution. But the part of her that had propelled her here, that acknowledged how very attractive she found Akil—and was all too aware that Akil was now unattached—urged her towards acceptance. Without stopping to think she pressed reply and quickly typed.

That sounds great. I'm due another trip out as Arrosa, so why don't I get Henri to take me somewhere where I can do a quick change afterwards and then meet you at your apartment? Send me your address and let me know what time. Thanks so much. Clem

She read it over quickly, and then before she lost her nerve she pressed send. Excitement and nerves warred but she pushed both back. It was an afternoon out, nothing more, nothing less. She deserved some fun.

Clem did her best to return her attention to the list, but right now the future seemed far away. Tomorrow she was going sightseeing with an attractive man. That was good enough for now.

CHAPTER SIX

AKIL STRODE ACROSS his apartment to pick out a different shirt and realised that he was whistling. Again.

Actually, he'd been whistling all morning. He'd even sung in the shower and it was a long time since he'd done that. Not since he'd accepted his role as a politician in fact. Yet here he was. Whistling and deliberating over his outfit. As if he were fifteen again and arranging to meet a girl on a beach.

At least his hands weren't clammy, and he'd learned not to gel his hair in the last fifteen years. But maybe he should channel that boy and lose the suit. It was a little over the top for an afternoon sightseeing. He checked his watch. Clem would be here soon so if he was going to change he'd better do it now. He didn't want to greet her half naked.

He'd just finished changing when his buzzer sounded and he strolled across to the videocam and pressed the button but, instead of Clem, Henri, suited and stern, filled the small screen.

'Subject ready. All clear?' Henri barked and Akil resisted the urge to salute.

'Everything's fine, send her up,' he said easily and pressed the button, opening the front door.

Akil waited by the open door, trying to ignore his heart hammering with anticipation. Light footsteps tripped up the stairs and there she was at his door, dressed like the tourist she was rather than the Crown Princess she'd pretended to be earlier that day, in a pretty vintage-style green sundress teamed with a denim jacket and trainers, and white sunglasses, her hair cascading loose and wild.

She looked utterly beautiful.

'Hi,' he said, mouth dry.

'Hi.' She hovered on the other side of the door, and he stood back.

'You found it okay? No problem getting here without anyone thinking you were your sister?'

'All good thanks to Henri,' she said. 'I did a quick change in a secret underground car park he knows and then he brought me here in a different car. I feel like a glamorous spy!'

'Where is he?'

'Lurking outside in case anyone followed us. Obviously a high level of paranoia is part of all bodyguard training.'

'A prerequisite,' he agreed. 'Ah, do you want to come in?'

'I thought you'd never ask.' Her hazel eyes gleamed, more green than brown today, thanks to the vibrancy of her dress. She stepped inside and glanced around. 'So this is where Asturia's most promising young politician lives?'

'It's where *I* live.' Akil tried to see his home through her eyes. His apartment was in a medieval building, all thick stone walls and tall arched windows. The floor gleamed honey brown, the old wood polished to a shine and covered by antique faded rugs. The walls were exposed stone, bookcases lining one wall, filled with books picked up over the years. Faded brown leather sofas grouped around the fireplace, one occupied by a fat ginger cat. Arrosa gave a little cry of delight and went straight over to rub its head.

'You have a *cat*?' She couldn't have sounded more incredulous if he'd had a panther in his apartment.

'You're not allergic?'

'No, I love cats. What's his name?'

'How do you know it's a he?'

'Ginger cats usually are.' She smiled as the cat rolled over to expose a fluffy white tummy. 'Oh, aren't you handsome? Name?'

'Tiger.' Akil tried not to grimace as she unsuccessfully tried to hide a smile.

'Oh, very original.'

'I didn't name him.'

'Really.' She gave him a disbelieving look. 'Who did?'

'A neighbour's kid. Tiger belongs to them really but they had to move abroad and couldn't take him so I said I would look after him.'

'So a cat man not a dog man. Interesting!'

'I wouldn't say that. But I live in an apartment, I work a lot. It wouldn't be fair on a dog. You?'

'I like both.'

'Very diplomatic.'

'And true. We always had cats growing up. Maman said we were too busy for a dog, it wouldn't be fair. But one day I will have one—and several cats too.' She scratched the top of Tiger's head again and the feline tilted his head up, eyes half closed, purring under the caresses. Akil felt a stab of something that felt remarkably and absurdly like jealousy.

'Come on, I'll show you the rest.'

It didn't take long to show her the open-plan kitchen and dining room and the small second bedroom he used as an office. They didn't go into his bedroom; it felt too intimate. Instead he swung the door open to show her the neat room, and he just indicated the bathroom. Clem noted every detail, asking about the photographs and paintings he'd chosen, lingering over his books and greeting them like old friends.

'I like your apartment,' she said, leafing through a poetry anthology. 'But it's not what I expected.'

'What did you expect?'

'Something to match your car, all modern and sleek and styled. This...' She waved a hand. 'This feels like a home.'

'Thank you.' He tried for light, but he was surprisingly touched by her words. 'I think so too.'

'So what's the plan?'

'We're going to be tourists in the city. I hope you're wearing sturdy shoes. We have a lot of ground to cover.'

She didn't answer for a long moment, anxiety creasing her forehead, and he looked enquiringly at her.

'The city?' she said at last. 'That's pretty busy. Is it safe?'

'Asturia's one of the safest countries in the world.'

'I mean for me, for you, for us to be seen together? Won't people wonder who you're with? You're not exactly unknown and in my experience young, single, prominent men attract attention, especially when accompanied by women.'

'The Asturian press is a lot more respectful of pri-

vate lives than most of the European press and most
people aren't interested in what politicians do in their
own time as long as they're not obviously corrupt. If I
took you to an official event or we were seen together
at the races or a regatta or some other society occasion,
then we would expect to be photographed and questions
asked, but not if we're just walking around the city.
And although you look a lot like your sister, you're not
so alike that anyone would seriously mistake you for
her, especially when you dress so casually. We're safe.'

She exhaled and he saw her visibly relax. 'Okay,
that's reassuring. In that case what are we waiting for?'

'You to stop reading poetry.'

She closed the book and carefully reshelved it.
'Done! Come on, then, let's go.'

'After you.' He held the door open for her to precede
him out and closed it behind him, realising how much
he was looking forward to the afternoon. To spending
time with Clem, to showing her the city he loved. This
might only be their second meeting but he was already
comfortable with her in a way that was unusual for Akil.
His family, his position, his own natural reserve created
barriers between him and most people, but somehow
Clem had effortlessly battered them aside without him
even noticing. This afternoon was supposed to be a favour for Arrosa, a day out for Clem, but it was turning
into an unexpected treat for him too.

Clem broke into a skip as she walked through the busy
streets at Akil's side, relieved to be out and about, surrounded by people like a normal person once again.
Akil was right, nobody gave them a second look, even

though Akil still cut an imposing figure dressed down in jeans and a T-shirt.

Although maybe he was *especially* imposing dressed down in jeans and a T-shirt. The grey T-shirt was faded, clearly well worn, but it looked as if it had been expensive, well cut and fitted, clinging to toned arms and showing off the breadth of his chest and shoulders, the flatness of his stomach. His jeans were perfectly cut, riding low on narrow hips and showcasing what she couldn't help but notice was a very nice butt—she was only human after all—and clinging to muscled thighs.

The sun shone, a perfect Mediterranean mid June day, and she was glad of her sunglasses as it bounced and sparkled off the paved streets, marble pavements and shop windows as she eagerly looked around, drinking in every sight, sound and smell.

The Asturian capital city, Asturia Valle, was a medieval city set in a large valley and ringed by the mountains that made up the bulk of the small country. Beautiful as the coastline was, it was the mountains that lured the tourists in, skiers in winter, walkers in summer, the blue lakes that dotted the valleys and mountain shelfs a magnet for skaters, swimmers and water sports enthusiasts.

Clem wanted to explore every inch of her country. And this was the perfect start. Akil knew exactly where he was going, steering her to one of the tourist booths dotted around the city, where he left her for a couple of minutes, reappearing with a map and a couple of tickets.

'I've got us these,' he said, handing her one of the tickets.

Clem squinted at it as she made out the small printed words. 'A one-day city pass?'

'This gets us in everywhere.'

'Everywhere?'

'The castle, the city museum, the zoo, the cable car, the funicular railway, the steam railway, the cathedral, the walking tours, all five of them, discounts at the theatre and the opera house and several restaurants and cafes. Pretty much everywhere.' His smile was smug, but she had to allow he deserved it. This was a great idea.

'That *does* seem to cover pretty much everywhere. What time is it?'

'Just after one.'

'And they are one-day passes?'

'Yep.'

'Then we have no time to waste.' She whirled around to look at a nearby sign with a city map displayed on it. 'Okay. We need to approach this strategically. What is the nearest attraction?'

Akil stared at her, clearly bemused. 'You want to do it *all*?'

'Well,' she conceded. 'Maybe not *both* the theatre and the opera house, and obviously trying all the restaurants and all five of the walking tours would be a stretch, but let's try and do as much as we can before midnight when the tickets run out.'

'Is this a challenge?'

'Are you up to it?' She removed her sunglasses and met that cool amused gaze, her mouth responding automatically to the smile in his eyes.

'I'm an Ortiz. I never turn down a challenge.'

'Good to know. Okay, where shall we start? Where's nearest?'

'The castle.' He paused. 'Are you comfortable with

that? Your father doesn't make a habit of crossing over into the public areas, but you never know. This might be the day he makes an exception. It could be awkward if you bumped into him in public.'

Clem bit her lip as she considered it. The castle was a much rebuilt and redesigned fortress perched on the edge of the valley overlooking the mountain pass that had once been the only way into the city. Most of it was now open to the public, who could tour the old state-rooms, the rooms occupied by long-dead royalty, the courtyards and gardens, as well as the dungeons and defensive walls showcasing the country's often violent history.

But well away from the public areas were the royal apartments and the offices of the court, with a private entrance to parliament, whose equally impressive medieval building was right next door.

The royal apartments comprised living quarters for the King and his family as well as rooms for courtiers and staff and reception rooms for ambassadors and other dignitaries, plus rooms of varying sizes for official events.

As it was the parliamentary recess most parliamentarians and the aristocrats who made up the upper chamber were at home in their country estates or their seaside retreats. But the King, as Clem knew too well, rarely returned to the Palais d'Artega, staying at Court year-round. Which meant he might well be in the castle right now and she would be in the same building as him for the first time in almost a decade. But as a tourist she'd be as removed from him as she was when she was at home in Cornwall.

'He knows I'm here,' she said, trying to keep the bitterness from her voice. 'But to be honest he hasn't seen me for so long he'd be more likely to recognise you than me. Let's do it. I've always wanted to visit.'

She shook the lingering sadness off and consulted the map in front of them, tracing the routes with her finger. 'Okay, I propose we spend an hour in the castle, half an hour each in the cathedral and the city museum, get the cable car up the mountain and the funicular down and then take the railway to the zoo for the hour before closing time. If we leave promptly we should make the evening walking tour, which possibly gives us time for tonight's concert at the opera house. We'll need refreshments so a snack after we've gone up the cable car and dinner after the concert. What do you think?'

Akil pretended to sag against the post, holding the map. 'I'm exhausted just listening to all that.'

'Too much for you?' She turned to face him, hands on her hips, allowing a flirtatious challenge to enter her voice, even as she acknowledged to herself that she was skating on very thin ice. This wasn't a date. But that didn't mean she couldn't enjoy it.

He held her gaze, suddenly serious, and Clem felt the air suck out of her lungs.

'Too much for me? Not at all. But I'm worried about you, my lady. Can you handle it?'

'It's my suggestion, remember. Come on, we're wasting precious time.' Clem rammed her sunglasses back onto her face, glad to break the disturbingly intense connection, and marched away, knowing he was right behind her, laughing as she strode as fast as she could as he effortlessly matched her stride. It was companionable. Nice.

She just needed to dial the flirting down to zero.

The castle was as fascinating and informative as Clem had hoped, and far more macabre than she'd expected, especially the dank underground rooms full of terrifying-looking devices.

'Nice types, my ancestors,' she muttered as she took in the rusted manacles stained with what she fervently hoped wasn't blood.

Akil nodded. 'Mine too. Before they dominated parliament they were generals and military leaders. I bet they condemned a lot of people to these rooms.'

'What does that do?' She wandered over to a tall, beamed contraption hung with ropes to read the horribly visual interpretation board and shuddered. 'I could have quite happily lived without ever knowing that.'

'What kind of mind even invents something like that?' Akil was standing right behind her. At least two inches separated them, but she was acutely aware of every part of him, the proximity between them lighting up every nerve.

'No wonder they put this bit before the Crown jewels. We'll need all the glitter and pomp to wipe this out of our minds. If I never come down here again it's too soon.'

The tour led them through a bewildering array of corridors and courtyards and Akil kept her entertained with what Clem was pretty sure were completely made-up facts about every part. She couldn't remember the last time she'd laughed, really laughed, the last time it had been this easy to be with someone.

The last time it had been this easy to just be.

Finally they reached a dark, heavily guarded building where they followed the path around display cases filled with fur-trimmed cloaks and padded surcoats, jewelled scabbards and wicked-looking swords until they reached a big display case set into a thick wall. Sightseers were kept well back by a rope, and, more effectively, guards at either end holding serious-looking rifles, in case anyone decided to try and steal the valuable items.

Clem stared at the state jewels in a mixture of awe and a painful melancholy, a sense of loss she couldn't quite explain. This was her family history but she had to see it as a paying tourist, always on the outside, held back by ropes and shatterproof glass and guards. She tried to hide her feelings, her voice unnaturally bright. 'The crown is huge! It must be really heavy. Like wearing a concrete hat.'

'It's very bling,' he said, blinking. 'I've seen it plenty of times but I'd never really noticed how many jewels it has before. And just how *gold* it is.'

'Maybe because the chain of office is equally bling.' Clem stared at the heavy gold chain studded with rubies. 'The sceptre is pretty big too. The whole lot together is very dazzling. I wouldn't say it's particularly tasteful though. All that velvet and gold and those huge rubies. It's a bit try hard.'

'The King makes it look so effortless,' Akil said. 'He makes the crown look like it weighs nothing. Whether you agree with him or not politically, he is good at what he does. He works well with the Assembly and controls the Senate. It needs a strong person to wear that crown.'

'Rosy is strong, one of the strongest people I know,' Clem said, still transfixed by the crown. 'But no one should have to bear that weight alone. If only I could be by her side, support her the way a sister should, make sure she wasn't alone. Seeing this makes it all much more understandable.'

'It all?'

'What she asked you. I almost wish…' She paused and he looked down at her, his expression inscrutable.

'What do you almost wish?'

'That things were different and you could have said yes…been what, who she needed.'

His expression didn't change, his eyes dark pools she was losing herself in. 'I could never have been who or what she needed. I knew it straight away, I think. I just had to work through it. And I am glad I realised in time.'

'In time?'

Clem couldn't breathe, couldn't move, all she could do was look up at him, so close she could see his dilated pupils, the rise and fall of his chest. It would be so easy to close the small distance between them and press herself against him but she was paralysed by the blood surging through her, the roaring in her ears.

'It's one thing to marry out of respect and friendship and support. They can be good bedrocks of a successful union, I believe that. But it would be unfair to marry one woman while attracted to her sister. Don't you think?'

Thinking was beyond her. She was caught in his mesmerising gaze, dark and hot, stirring desire throughout her. 'I…' She stared at him a moment longer, trying to find something to say—*I think you're attractive too. What does this mean? Kiss me*—when the sound of a family approaching, children arguing noisily, broke the spell and Akil stepped back, a rueful smile on his lips.

'Come on,' he said. 'We've got a long itinerary and I think we're at least five minutes behind.'

Yet as they walked away she couldn't help but look

back at the case and the glittering crown that represented her sister's future. Akil might find her attractive—and she might reciprocate his feelings—but she had no place, no future here. She couldn't let herself forget it.

CHAPTER SEVEN

AKIL COULDN'T REMEMBER the last time he'd enjoyed an afternoon so much nor the last time he'd had the leisure—or inclination—to dedicate a day to nothing but fun. It had been a genius plan to explore his city with fresh eyes, joining the tourists on the well-trodden trails around the sights. They'd done a mad dash around the cathedral and the city museum and made up the lost time as they did so because—as Clem said a little guiltily—there were only so many religious paintings a person could admire before they all merged into one.

'Do you think they'd ever actually seen a baby before?' she asked as they checked out their twentieth old master rendition of a Madonna and Child, this one with a baby Jesus almost the same size as his mother. The one before the baby had been the approximate size of an orange. 'They remind me of my attempts of art at school and I always got a *Could do better.* Who knew I was actually painting in the style of the fourteenth century? My teachers should have given me more credit.'

After the museum they enjoyed the breathtaking views from the cable car that ascended up to the mountain shelf overlooking the city, a popular day-trip destination, where they stopped for a snack before taking the funicular back down and catching the small steam train to the zoo.

'I have very conflicted feelings about zoos,' Clem said as they wandered around the world-renowned attraction, known for its ground-breaking breeding programmes and successful conservation work. 'I know that if this tiger wasn't here it wouldn't be roaming free in the jungle, it wouldn't exist at all. And I know that if it wasn't for places like this there might be no tigers at all in a few years' time, but it seems wrong to see such beautiful creatures caged up, for us to be able to stand and stare while they have nowhere to hide.'

Her face softened as she watched the tiger prowl, its tail swishing irritably. 'I wish I could set you free.'

'Now that would make an interesting headline. *Fake Princess Sets Tiger on Horrified Population.*' He gave her a keen glance. 'Do you think you might be over identifying?'

'Hmm?'

'Beautiful creature locked away?'

She laughed a little nervously. 'I'm not…'

'Beautiful? I hope you know that's not true.'

Their glances caught and held and Akil could feel his blood thundering around his body as her cheeks pinked, her pupils dilated. He'd felt in his very bones that this attraction was not one-sided, but her reaction gave him all the proof he needed. Primal jubilation filled him as he ran one finger slowly down her cheek. She stood acquiescent, quivering under his touch, her gaze still fixed on his.

'Akil…' Her voice was husky, half protest half entreaty, and he dropped his hand, fighting the urge to pull her close, to taste those full lips. 'I…' She cleared her throat, adorably flustered, still flushed a rosy pink. 'I was going to say locked away. I can get out, you know, it's just not easy. Besides, it's only temporary. Come on, we need to get on or we'll miss the walking tour.'

'Yes, ma'am.' He saluted. 'Begging your pardon for forgetting the itinerary, ma'am.'

She threw him a mock stern look. 'I'll let you off this once.'

Despite Clem's protestation that they would be late, Akil insisted on stopping at the food cart at the zoo exit to buy them tart chilled lemonade and toasted cheese sandwiches, hot and oozing with melted cheese.

'We've walked miles already and your schedule doesn't allow for dinner until after the opera,' he said as he handed her the sandwich. 'A man's got to eat. Especially this man.'

'That's good to know about you. Hangry unless fed, noted. Mmm, that's delicious.' She took another, bigger bite, laughing as she tried not to spill any cheese on her dress, and Akil couldn't help but join in as he watched her inelegantly scoop up a glop of cheese with her tongue.

It had been a long time since he'd laughed this much, talked this much, about nothing and everything. Clem was easy company—apart from the way his body reacted to her every move, the way he wanted to pull her close and kiss her until they were both breathless.

But she was here for such a short while and her life was complicated enough. It wasn't for him to complicate it further than he already had and it would be too easy to do so, considering how thrown she'd been when he'd told her how attractive he found her.

'You are very good at saluting,' Clem said as they

walked along the pretty pedestrianised street that led back to the centre, flowers in planters on either side and leafy trees protecting them from the worst of the sun.

'You can thank national service for that.'

'Of course. It seems so strange to me that you have to give up two years of your life! Even Rosy had to enlist before she went to university.'

'Every Asturian does, even royalty. Your sister and mine worked in the medical corps together. But it wasn't two years for me, it was four. Two in the infantry, like all good Ortiz men, then two in the secret service. I came out at twenty-two to go to university.'

'What did you study?'

'Economics and politics of course.'

'Of course. Was that what you wanted to do?'

And that was the million-dollar question. Usually Akil went along with the fiction that studying politics in readiness for taking the Ortiz seat in the upper house was his own ambition. It was easier that way.

But he didn't want to dissimulate with Clem. It was nice having someone he could be himself with. 'Truthfully no. I had a place at medical school.'

'Really? Like your sister?'

'Only I'm older and got my place first, so really she was copying me.' He couldn't help grinning as he said it. 'The sibling rivalry between us is real. Elixane hates that she's both four years younger than me and a girl in a country which still favours male heirs.'

'You should be flattered that she wanted to follow in your footsteps. It's nice that you inspire her.'

'I don't think she'd put it that way, but I'll be sure to mention it to her.' His grin widened as he imagined his sister's indignant response if he referred to himself as her inspiration. 'Honestly, I'm not sure why we both chose that path. There are no medics in the family.'

'So what happened? Why didn't you take up your place?'

Akil carried on walking, deliberating how much to say. He rarely allowed himself to think about that time. 'I don't know if you know this, but the seats in the Senate, our upper chamber, are hereditary—and the line of inheritance is on the male side. Even when things change next month those seats which belong to the old aristocratic titles, like mine, will only go to males—it's the same in the UK.'

'I am beginning to sympathise with your sister,' Clem murmured.

'We're making some headway in reforming this, but we have a long way to go.'

'Of course,' she said consideringly. 'Inheritance really should go through the matriarchal line. Before DNA testing, it was obvious who the mother was but the father was taken on trust.'

'You would get on far too well with my sister, she often makes the same point, although, as I tell her, I am still older and that makes me the head of the family and future Duc no matter if the law changed.'

'I'll bet she loves that.'

'She really does, although occasionally she will admit that she is much happier as a younger sibling—there's a lot more freedom for her than for me. But what you need to understand is that the Duc d'Ortiz has always been an important person in Asturia, for centuries we were in charge of the military. Sometimes the Duc was the Crown's right hand, even Regent on two occasions, sometimes its most implacable opposition. Since the Second World War, as Asturia's military need has waned, my family have turned to politics to build power and influence, with the Duc using his hereditary seat to make sure they are right at the centre. My father made it clear that I was shirking the responsibility inherent in my future title by not pursuing politics.'

Clem frowned. 'But your father is still alive, right? So why couldn't you do both? Be a doctor now and then a politician later?'

Exactly what he had pointed out eight years ago. 'My father is not a man to do things by half, not work, not food, not drink.' Not women. 'Nor is he a man to take his doctor's advice. He has little time for the medical profession. He sees it as a job for the bourgeoisie, not his heir. His health was not good eight years ago so when we disagreed and it got far too heated he collapsed. He nearly died of a heart attack.'

A heart attack Akil had known was a risk, and yet he still hadn't walked away when the argument had started to get out of hand, had still allowed all his anger at his father, at his selfishness and implacability, to pour out. Had enjoyed reducing his father to incoherent rage, out-arguing him. What kind of man did that make him? No better than his father for all his self-righteousness.

Clem stopped, her hand flying to her mouth as she turned to him. 'Oh, Akil, I am so sorry. It must have been terrifying.'

'It was. Worse was the knowledge that I was responsible.'

Her forehead creased. 'How? You said yourself that he didn't take his doctor's advice. Surely that's on him.'

'True,' he acknowledged. 'But I was young and implacable as only the young can be, convinced I alone knew the right path. I wanted to be a doctor and yet I allowed a man I knew to be at risk to get agitated to lose control. Worse, I goaded him. Pushed him beyond what was safe. What kind of son, what kind of aspiring doctor, does that?'

'Families make everything complicated. We're not always our best selves with them,' she said, laying a comforting hand on his arm. 'So you gave up your dream? As what? Atonement?'

In part. 'I promised him that if he just held on I would do my duty as the Vicomte d'Ortiz. So when he recovered he stepped down on grounds of ill health and the Senate voted to allow me to take the Ortiz seat early. My father now spends most of his time in Switzerland still not looking after his health and I am as you see me. Fulfilling my promise.'

'Do you ever regret it?'

'I don't allow myself to regret it.' Suddenly he regretted saying so much. 'Come, there's still a lot to fit in.' Without looking back, he marched on. Because that was what he did, eyes fixed on the future, no dwelling on the past. It was easier that way. It was safer. It was what he knew.

Clem stole a glance at Akil as they walked towards the medieval square where the walking tour was due to meet. He'd been silent over the last few minutes, seemingly lost in thought.

Not that it was surprising. It must be hard, living one life when you had once had a vocation for something else. But then again wasn't that the future she was facing? It would be some consolation if she was as successful in her second-choice career as Akil was in his.

But she still ached with sympathy for him. Maybe it was better having a father as hands off as hers rather than one who raged and manipulated and used a promise extracted on a possible deathbed to push his son down a path he didn't want. And it wasn't as if Akil wanted to give it all up to become a pop star or something equally ridiculous! He wanted to be a doctor— every parent she knew would throw a party if their child expressed such a wish.

Her mother would have. She'd supported Clem, it hadn't been in her nature not to, but she'd have preferred Clem to have chosen something more worthy than acting.

She peeked at Akil again; his expression was still far away. 'What's the tour?' she asked, wanting to break the silence.

He blinked as if he had forgotten where they were going. 'Hmm? Oh, the twilight tour. Apparently it's ghosts, ghouls and gore. Ready?'

She pulled a face. 'I'm not sure I can face ghouls and gore after the dungeons earlier. I'm already dreading the nightmares.'

'This is our heritage. We should embrace it.'

'Not too enthusiastically, I hope.'

'We don't have to go on the tour,' he reminded her. 'We could always skip it and do something else.'

'Skip it? And lose the challenge? Absolutely not.'

'Of course.' She was relieved to hear laughter in his voice. 'The schedule. How could I forget?'

'So this finishes at seven, conveniently right by the opera house, which gives us time to get our tickets. I hope they're not sold out. What is it?'

Akil pulled out his phone and checked. 'There are

tickets and it's *Tosca*—oh, good, there's a warning. Contains depictions of torture, murder and suicide. There's a definite theme to the day so far.'

'In that case I want to eat at the cheesiest, most kitsch restaurant as possible afterwards,' Clem warned him. 'I'll need it after all the horror and death.'

'I'll see what I can do,' he promised.

They lapsed into another silence, but this one was more companionable, their stride perfectly in time, arms swinging together, so close their fingers almost touched. Almost.

As they entered the square she saw a small group of people waiting by the meeting point. A couple of families, several older couples and a young couple who smiled as Akil and Clem approached. They probably saw a mirror of themselves, a couple enjoying a romantic break in the picturesque ancient city, and Clem allowed herself to bask in the fantasy that she and Akil were here properly together. Before she thought better of it she reached out and took his hand, slipping her fingers through his. She felt him momentarily freeze before his fingers clasped hers, warm and strong, his thumb circling the back of her hand, a minute gesture that shuddered through her.

'Okay, gather round.' A tour guide dressed in the colourful Asturian national costume called out in English and then again in French. 'Does everyone have their tickets ready? Great. Okay, let's begin right here, with the great siege of 1412.'

Despite the theme the tour was a lot of fun, the guide engaging as well as knowledgeable, and Clem found herself laughing uncontrollably as he took them on a whistle-stop tour of the least palatable parts of Asturian history, pitching his spiel perfectly between scaring the children just enough and amusing the adults. Throughout the tour she was aware of Akil's hand in hers, the breadth of him, height of him, the sheer handsomeness of him taking her breath away, the wonder that he wanted to be here with her—the wonder that he wanted her—dizzying her. Possibility hung thick between them, the possibility that this adventure wouldn't end when the tickets expired at midnight, but this Cinderella might keep her bewitched existence a little longer.

Just a few hours ago she had been reminding herself that she had no future here, warning herself to be careful, but now those sensible thoughts belonged to someone else. What did the future matter when there was now?

The group clustered around a cannon that pointed out towards the mountain pass and was, they were informed, haunted by a young soldier who had refused to abandon his post when the city was under attack and stayed there still to protect Asturia. The guide's voice had dropped to a carrying whisper as he told the tale and the children on the tour pressed forward, eyes wide in the deepening dusk, only to jump back in exaggerated fright when he boomed out the end. As they jumped, one tripped and before anyone could catch her fell into the road—and straight into the path of a car. Time seemed to slow as the small body was scooped up onto the low bonnet as the car screeched to a desperate but too late halt.

Everyone was paralysed with shock and fear—everyone but Akil. He dropped Clem's hand and sprang into the road even as the car finally braked, shouting instructions to call an ambulance. He bent over the girl, his finger on her neck, and then ran his hands carefully over her.

'Stay back, she needs space,' he called out. 'Where are her parents?' An American couple were at his side in seconds, one holding a smaller girl, faces pale and shocked. 'She's breathing,' he reassured them. 'That's a good thing. Her leg is certainly broken, and I can't rule out internal bleeding or concussion, but the hospital isn't far.'

'Are you a doctor?' the woman asked, and Clem was proud to see he didn't wince as he shook his head.

'No, but I volunteer with the mountain rescue and I am paramedic trained. She'll be in good hands, I promise.'

It took the ambulance less than ten minutes to arrive and Clem stayed back as Akil assisted the paramedics as they moved the still unconscious girl onto the trolley and checked her over. The rest of the group were still huddled together, silent, and as she was loaded into the ambulance Akil came over.

'I am going to accompany her to the hospital,' he told Clem quietly. 'Her parents don't speak Asturian or French and it will be helpful for them to have a translator.'

'Of course,' she said hurriedly. 'I told Henri I'd call him as soon as we were done, so he can collect me and I can transform back on the way back to the palais. It's dark now so I only need to get through the gates and the guards never check Henri anyway.'

'I'm sorry we didn't make the opera.'

'Another time.' But even as she said it she could feel the possibility slipping away. In the cold light of day would this live-for-the-moment promise she had made to herself last? Or would she remember all the reasons getting close to Akil—to anyone in Asturia—was such a bad idea?

Akil drew her close, his arm an anchor. 'Of course. We'll rearrange and we can pick up our schedule. Carry on as we planned.'

'That would be lovely.' She could hear the lack of conviction in her words and she knew he heard it too. Before she could back away he bent his head and brushed her mouth with his. It was the briefest of caresses, almost chaste, but the touch lit her up, flames swooshing through her from the tips of her fingers to the ends of her toes. All she could do was look up dazed as Akil smiled ruefully and stepped away. 'I'll see you soon.'

Clem stared after him, drinking in his tall figure, allowing herself one last look at the way his jeans encased him so perfectly, the fit of his T-shirt, the strength and grace in the fully muscled body. She swallowed, fighting the need to run after him, to call his name, to kiss him once again. Instead she watched him step into the ambulance and exchange a few words with the paramedic before the doors shut and he was driven away.

'Goodbye,' she said at last. But whether she meant for tonight or for keeps, she didn't know.

CHAPTER EIGHT

IT WAS LATE by the time Clem returned to the villa but despite her exhaustion she found it hard to sleep, replaying the events of the day over and over, lingering on the brief kiss until she had no idea what was memory and what was fantasy. When she finally got up the next day she was convinced she hadn't slept at all, and her activity watch confirmed her suspicions. With a groan she took her coffee and a book onto the comfortable terrace sofa and curled up, promising herself a lazy day.

She'd messaged Akil last night to check on the injured girl and he'd promised to send her an update. To her relief when she checked her phone, she found a message from Akil sent some time early that morning letting her know that although the girl's leg was broken and she'd severely bruised her ribs, there was no internal bleeding and she'd somehow managed to avoid concussion. The hospital were going to keep her in for several days for observation but she'd been very lucky.

Clem pressed the reply arrow and then sat there for some time staring at the blank screen before typing a simple thank-you. After another couple of minutes' thought she added:

You were brilliant yesterday.

Before she could think better of it she sent the message and then lay back on the sofa and stared up at the cloudless sky, mind an exhausted whirl.

What would have happened if there had been no accident? Would they have gone to the opera? For dinner? Would possibility have hung in the air throughout? Would she have gone back to Akil's apartment? And if so, then what?

She'd never know...

At that moment her phone vibrated and when she picked it up her sister's name filled the screen. Clem took a deep breath and then answered it, injecting as much vibrancy into her voice as she possibly could.

'Hi, you, what are you up to?'

'Just checking in,' her sister said, and Clem felt some of the tension leave her as she took in just how relaxed Arrosa sounded. 'Is everything okay with you? Have you heard from our father yet?'

'Not yet.' Clem tried to sound breezy, as if the continued silence didn't bother her at all, but of course her sister knew better and she didn't try and hide her sigh of exasperation.

'Honestly, what's he playing at? Do you want me to say something?'

'No, no, it's fine.' Clem *did* want to see him, but more, she wanted *him* to want to see *her*, not for him to pay her a duty visit because his other, legitimate daughter had scolded him into doing it. 'There's plenty of time yet. I'm sure we'll catch up sooner rather than later.'

'You're sure? And you're fine to stay? It's been a week now and I feel a lot better so if you're bored of being driven around like a ceremonial doll, just say.'

'I'm fine. It's very relaxing sitting in the back of a limousine in designer clothing, so let me enjoy it a little longer. What have you been up to anyway? Did you and Sally have that cinema trip? And did the theatre action group find somewhere else to meet?'

Clem sat back and sipped her coffee as Arrosa filled her in on all the local news and told her all about meeting Sally for a couple of drinks at the local pub. Not exactly the most rock and roll evening for a single twenty-six-year-old, but probably the most freedom her sister had had in years.

'Clem?' A diffident note had entered her sister's voice and Clem put her coffee down, all senses on alert. 'What do you know about Jack Treloar?'

'Jack Treloar? As in our "local bad boy done good, trying to take over the town theatre and commercialise it" Jack Treloar?'

'That's the one.'

Clem's first instinct was to demand an explanation why Arrosa was interested in *Jack Treloar* of all people but, knowing what it must have cost Rosy to ask the question and provoke the inevitable reaction, she made herself hold back.

'Not much,' she said, sifting through her scant knowledge and trying to exclude gossip and hearsay. 'He's about four years older than me so we were never in the same school year and didn't hang around with the same group, although from what I remember he was always quite solitary. His dad was absent a lot, drifted in and out of his life, his mother did her best but he had a real reputation. If there was ever any trouble it was attributed to him. Then he took up with the local big-wig's daughter, next thing she was pregnant and they got married. I don't think they were more than eighteen, it was quite the scandal. They disappeared off to London where somehow he made money hand over fist. I think she died tragically a couple of years back, then six months ago he returned with his daughters and bought the most expensive house in the village. No one knows why he came back. Goodness knows he can't have many happy memories of living in Cornwall. He left the town under the shadow of a scandal and has returned the same, especially now he's trying to strong-arm the council into selling or leasing the theatre to him.'

She paused before giving in and asking the burning question. 'Why? How have you come across him? He usually doesn't descend from his clifftop mansion to mix with us mere mortals.'

'He was at your play, so sometimes he does. Anyway, I've found myself babysitting for his daughters,' Arrosa said, an evasive tone in her voice, and Clem nearly choked on her coffee.

'You are *what*? How on earth did that come about?'

'It's a long story. I'll fill you in some other time.'

'I've got time now,' Clem offered, but her sister was clearly not going to be drawn.

'Honestly, it's not very interesting. But what *is* interesting is what's going on with you. Has the gorgeous Akil contacted you yet?'

'I didn't think that you thought he was that good-looking,' Clem countered, and her sister laughed.

'Objectively I can see that he is, but more importantly I know that you think so. Come on, spill the beans, what's going on? He asked for your number a couple of days ago. Has he been in contact?'

'We met up yesterday but nothing is going on, he's just being kind.' It was Clem's turn to prevaricate as her sister let out a disbelieving—and most un-princess-like—snort.

'If you say so. I've known Akil a long time and he has a real sense of honour and justice, but I wouldn't have called him kind, not in the "give up a second afternoon to entertain a stranger" way.'

'I don't know, it seems completely in character to me. Did you know that he works for the mountain rescue?'

'I've seen it mentioned in interviews, but he's usually pretty quiet about it. Not really one for sharing at all. So he's mentioned it to you, has he?'

'I saw him in action. There was an accident and I just froze, it was horrid, but he knew exactly what to do. It was impressive.'

'Handsome and heroic. He's quite the catch.'

'Rosy. Tell me honestly, are you having second thoughts?'

Clem held her breath while she waited for her sister's answer. Arrosa and Akil belonged in the same world, the same social circles, the higher echelons of the same country, had shared goals. It would make perfect sense for her sister to have reconsidered, and if she did then it would be Clem's duty to step aside and hide her own feelings. She might not be a princess, but she was a princess's sister and she knew what that entailed. She'd seen the weight of that crown yesterday.

'Not a second or a third or a fourth thought,' Arrosa said emphatically. 'And I can tell you something, nor is he.'

'How do you know?' Clem hoped her sister couldn't hear how desperately she wanted that to be true.

'Because he's attracted to *you*, Clem. It was so obvious when I spoke to him. And it's obvious that you like him so what kind of sister would I be if I came between you, even if that's what I wanted? Which for the record I don't.'

'He kissed me,' Clem confessed and winced as her sister let out a whoop.

'I knew it!'

'It was only a brief kiss goodbye as he was heading for the ambulance.'

'But you wanted more?'

Clem closed her eyes and relived the feeling of his mouth brushing hers again. 'Yes,' she confessed.

'This is *marvellous*. I'm so excited for you. What's the next step? When are you going to see him again?'

'I don't know, Rosy.' Clem tried to gather her racing thoughts. 'Akil lives such a different life from me. For a start he lives in a different country. And he knows what he wants while I'm floundering. He has his life all planned out. Plus, he wants a well-connected wife who knows his world and understands politics and diplomacy. I'm a walking national scandal. That's the last thing he needs.'

'I hate that you see yourself that way,' Arrosa said softly.

'It's not how I see myself, it's how others see me. It's how our father sees me, how the very few people in the court who know I even exist see me. The truth is that although Akil can squire me around he couldn't be seen with me anywhere that matters. We both know that's true. So what future could we possibly have?'

There was a startled pause. 'You feel that strongly about him? Are you falling in love with him, Clem?'

'Am I *what*?' Clem winced as she realised just how ridiculous she was being. 'I've only met him twice, of course I'm not. In lust, yes, and I like him a lot. But it's way too early to even think about love.'

'In that case,' Arrosa said, 'what's the harm in spending some time with him? What's the worst that could happen, Clem?'

He might reject me because of who I am. He might realise I'm not good enough.

But of course she couldn't say that aloud, not even to the sister she loved.

'You're right,' she said instead. 'I'm being a drama queen. It comes with the job, you know that. But if I see Akil again will you promise me something? Be careful with Jack Treloar.'

'Only if you promise *not* to be careful.' And, laughing, her sister hung up, leaving Clem staring at her phone. She hadn't lied to Rosy; it *was* far too early to think about love. But she was in far deeper than two meetings should warrant and that left heartbreak as an inevitable outcome.

She would allow herself to see what, if anything, happened next, but she would guard her heart and her soul. It was the only way to keep herself safe.

It had been another long night. By the time Lucy, the injured American girl, had been settled in and checked, and all her family's questions answered and concerns addressed, it had been after three a.m. Akil had stumbled back to his apartment, luckily less than half a mile away, and collapsed on the sofa, where he'd fallen into a deep sleep only to awaken three hours later when Tiger had jumped on him and insistently demanded some breakfast. Akil had drunk some water and eaten the very last of the bread before sending the promised text to Clem to fill her in on Lucy's progress, and falling back asleep. He'd woken a couple of hours later, neck stiff but feeling refreshed. Coffee, a quick shower and change of clothes and he was ready for the day ahead.

But for once, for the first time in longer than he could remember, he had no plans. There was of course work, recess or no recess his inbox was overflowing, but his assistants were filtering it for him and there was nothing urgent to address. He wasn't rostered in to be on call with the mountain rescue and wouldn't be again until next week after all the shifts he'd recently pulled.

He strode around the apartment restlessly, his gaze falling on the poetry book Clem had looked at just the day before, and smiled wryly. Maybe he'd unconsciously kept the time free in case he and Clem wanted to spend another day together. After all, if things had gone the way they'd been heading last night, she might have been here with him now. They might have been planning another day of exploring and getting to know each other. Or they might still have been in bed.

It was an intoxicating thought. He wasn't sure why the Englishwoman had got under his skin like this. She was beautiful, yes, but he knew plenty of beautiful women. It went beyond a physical attraction. She was both funny and straight talking, a combination he appreciated, and there was a hidden vulnerability that made him want to take care of her, to make her smile, to make her feel appreciated.

Goodness knew, someone should. It might be none of his business but one day Akil would tell Zorien exactly what he thought of his parenting style.

He picked up his phone and reread the message she'd sent in reply to his update.

Are you free? If so come over. Let's go out.

He should reply, but he just wasn't sure what to say. Or was it actually better that last night had been cut short? Was it safer for them both not to take this attraction between them further? There was no future after all.

But did he always need to plan for the long term? Couldn't he occasionally just enjoy life as it was. It was summer; she was here for a finite time. Why was he overcomplicating this?

One thing he did know: he wasn't going to make any sensible decisions on an empty stomach.

Akil headed out of the apartment, popping into one of the many local cafes for a quick savoury pastry and a small cup of the potent espresso Asturians loved. It took him less than a minute to finish his breakfast and he decided to go back to the hospital and check in on Lucy and her family before making any further plans. Clem would want to know how they were, after all.

Lucy had been placed in a small private room, and Akil made his way there, stopping to chat with a couple of the nurses and a doctor he knew and catching up with one of his fellow volunteers who had just finished a shift. It was nearly lunch time by the time he reached the children's ward to be buzzed in by a nurse who recognised him. Lucy's door was ajar and to his surprise he could hear a familiar voice within. What was Clem doing here?

He stood there for a moment, pleasure and apprehension warring inside him. Whatever happened next between them would be decided soon whether he was ready or not. As he waited, he began to make sense of the words within and he realised that Clem was reading to the small girl. He stepped a little closer and leaned against the door frame listening.

She was good, very good, her rich voice bringing the text to life, giving each character a distinct voice. Lucy was still pale, her leg extended before her, lines of pain on her small face, but she was smiling, looking eagerly at Clem as Clem continued to read, clearly transported to the magical world Clem was bringing vividly to life. Akil waited until the end of the chapter before pushing the door further open and entering the room, not wanting to break the spell Clem cast.

'How's the patient?' he asked in English and Lucy smiled at him.

'Clem came to read to me. She's really good.'

Clem met his eye although her expression was adorably flustered and she'd reddened. 'I wanted to see how Lucy was doing so got Henri to drop me near here. I didn't expect to be allowed in but I saw her mother outside getting some air. Her family seemed exhausted so I insisted that they went back to the hotel to get some food and a change of clothes and promised I'd keep an eye on her.'

Akil eyed the small girl keenly. 'She seems to be

doing pretty well, but she looks like she needs a bit of a rest. Do you want to try to get some sleep, Lucy? We will wait just outside until your parents get back so if you need anything or you get lonely just press that button.'

'I am a little sleepy,' the little girl admitted. 'But can we read another chapter later, Clem?'

'Of course.' Clem brushed her fringe back and smiled down at the wan face. 'I'd love to. Are you comfy? Those pillows okay?' Akil watched as she expertly settled the child with soothing hands. Of course, she'd helped care for her mother and recently too. Being here must bring back some difficult memories. His admiration for her deepened.

Once Lucy was settled, Akil steered Clem out to the comfortable chairs in the adjacent waiting room. 'You want a coffee or anything?'

'No, I'm fine. How about you? What time did you get to bed?'

Akil grimaced. 'Not so much bed, more the sofa, but I've had some sleep. It was kind of you to come and check on Lucy. Even kinder to offer to watch her.'

Clem brushed the compliment aside. 'Not at all. I've spent a lot of time waiting in hospitals, I know how time takes a different element here. And her parents have another child who was definitely at the exhausted and fractious stage. I wasn't sure how they'd feel about leaving Lucy with me, but I managed to persuade them that they would be much more use to her if they were rested, fed and changed. I don't think her mother will be gone long, but a shower and time away from here will do her good.'

'It was a clever idea to read to her. You definitely put her at her ease.'

'It was no big deal. I actually really enjoyed doing it.' She sounded surprised and he quirked an eyebrow at her.

'You're an actress, don't you grab at any opportunity to perform?'

'After my mum died, I didn't think I'd ever want to set foot in a hospital again. But now I'm here, I'm remembering all the things that helped. All the volunteers as well as the nurses who made such unbearable times surprisingly bearable. The value of having people who would sit with Maman just to listen, to be there, allowing her to say all the things she couldn't say to me. The same for me, people who would listen when I was angry or selfish or frustrated. That was invaluable, priceless. Reading to one small girl is a very, very small way of giving back.'

She looked so small, almost defenceless, and yet there was an indomitable spirit about her that he was drawn to. In two steps he was next to her, drawing her up into his arms. Akil looked down into the heart-shaped face, at the gold-flecked eyes shadowed with exhaustion, and knew that for once he didn't care what the future held, he wanted her, he needed her, and by some miracle she wanted him too.

'It wasn't small to Lucy or her family. It was everything.'

'Being here is helping me too. It might be a different hospital in a different country but the smell, the look, is pretty much universal. It's making me realise how my life pretty much just stopped eighteen months ago. No wonder I don't know what to do next, I've forgotten how to move forward. But I'm ready, Akil. I'm ready to live, not just exist at last.'

She cupped his face with her hands. They were warm against his skin, the gentle touch setting him on fire, and he closed his eyes briefly to allow the sensation to soak in.

'Help me live again, Akil,' she whispered, and he was helpless against her soft entreaty, against her touch.

Slowly, deliberately, not wanting to rush a single moment, he dipped his head and captured her full inviting mouth with his for a second time. But this was no mere brush, no promise, but an intent and she responded in kind, opening up to him, her hands moving to the nape of his neck as he moulded her body to his. He pulled back slightly to look down at her, eyes glazed, mouth parted.

'Anything,' he promised her. 'Whatever you want, whatever you need, anything.' And he kissed her again, the sounds of the hospital fading away, the feel of her, the taste of her all he wanted, all he knew.

CHAPTER NINE

CLEM TURNED IN to the pretty medieval square where Akil lived, aware of Henri standing watching her, making sure she was okay. It was funny how used to his discreet presence she'd got, no longer troubled by the knowledge that even when she couldn't see him he was only a few seconds away. The only time he wasn't close by was when she was with Akil. His secret service training meant that Henri usually didn't accompany them, although he was always on call and, she suspected, never that far away.

They'd fallen into a routine over the last couple of weeks. Every morning Henri drove her out, ostensibly to the court but in reality facilitating the discreet change that allowed her to explore the country with Akil or head to the hospital, often both, then reversing the process late each evening. Her life couldn't be more different from that first lonely week. Now her days were packed. She spent a lot of time at the hospital; Lucy had been discharged over a week ago to fly home, but news of Clem's reading had spread throughout the children's ward and she now did a group session for those in the big general ward. She enjoyed it far more than she had expected to. It wasn't acting exactly, but she was transporting them into other worlds, creating magic, and that, for Clem, was as fulfilling as a big production, although if she had more time she would have liked to look into doing something bigger, maybe trying to stage some kind of small production. The volunteering was certainly opening up some possibilities and, although she was deliberately not worrying about the future just yet, ideas were percolating away.

And when she wasn't at the hospital she was with Akil. He still volunteered two days a week, and spent most mornings buried in his inbox, but the afternoons and evenings were hers. They had finally made it to the opera and to the theatre—this time a comedy, much to her relief—and to several friendly neighbourhood restaurants, the kind where a prominent politician wouldn't expect to be photographed. Any high-profile venues were out, any events where society people mingled too dangerous, but Akil was sure that if they stuck to the tourist trail no one would give them a second glance. So far that had been true, and it was getting easier and easier to forget that she was here under false pretences and not a tourist at all.

They'd hiked some of the mountain trails, pausing for cold beers and well-stuffed sandwiches at the cafes at the summit, and explored some of the picture-perfect villages and towns dotted throughout valleys and mountain shelves, cliff tops and riversides. One day they kayaked along a river, racing each other, another day they abseiled down a mountainside. She felt fitter and more resilient than she had for a long, long time.

And then there was Akil himself, his slow smile and intent gaze, his sure touch and sweet, sweet kisses. They were still at the courting phase, and although their

kisses and caresses were getting increasingly heated—
and increasingly intimate—neither had been in any rush
to move to the next stage. It was as if they had all the
time in the world.

Only of course they didn't.

Checking her watch, Clem realised she was a little
early so rather than head straight to Akil's apartment
she decided to have a little explore around the neighbourhood. He lived in a charming part of the old quar-
ter, filled with cafes and local artisan shops. Just the
kind of place she liked.

Fixing her sunglasses firmly on her nose, Clem
headed along the nearest alley, emerging into a narrow cobbled street. Cafes and shops nestled next to each
other, the old buildings four storeys high, their upper
levels lurching drunkenly over the street. This part of
the city was centuries old, the country's history in every
cobble, every plastered and timbered front, the butch-
ers and tanners giving way to tourist-friendly jewellers
and art galleries. Clem moved slowly along, enjoying
examining all the enticing wares laid out in the shop
windows, the sun warming her arms, the sounds of the
city a lively soundtrack.

She paused in front of a jeweller and examined the
tree-inspired bracelets in silver and gold. Her mother
would have loved them. Everything she'd worn had had
some kind of link to nature whether it was the floral
prints she'd preferred or the delicate swallow earring
she'd always worn. Maybe she should buy one. Not that
she needed jewellery to remember her mother, but she
couldn't resist the impulse and headed in, emerging a
few moments later clutching a bag, having bought a
bracelet for herself and one for her sister, and a pair of

cufflinks for Akil. They weren't really at the present stage, but she wanted him to have something to remember her by when this was all over.

Finally she stopped to look at some delicious pastries, her mouth watering at the sight of the nut and honey confections; she'd developed a taste for the local delicacies over the last couple of weeks. She couldn't resist popping in to buy some and they were still warm when she returned to the square and rang the buzzer to Akil's apartment. She took the now familiar stairs up to his first-floor apartment two at a time and as she reached Akil's front door he opened it.

'Hi,' she said a little stupidly as he leaned against the door frame, his dark eyes glowing in admiration as he looked her up and down. Clem resisted the urge to smooth her shirt down, glad she'd picked the floaty sunshine-yellow silk skirt and teamed it with a short delicate lace white blouse. It wasn't the most practical of outfits, but she liked how feminine she felt, liked the way the skirt swirled around her calves, the flattering fit of the shirt, deceptively demure with its high neck, yet cut to flatter her every curve—and Akil's not too subtle once-over proved it did.

'Hi. You're looking beautiful today.' His voice was a low rumble and she felt it vibrate through her.

'Thank you. You're not looking too bad yourself.' Now that was an understatement. He was delectably handsome in a white linen shirt and jeans, off duty and perfectly masculine. 'I've bought pastries.' She handed him the bag and he unleashed one of his devastating smiles.

'Now you're doubly welcome.' He bent his head to drop a lingering kiss on her mouth and her body responded enthusiastically. This kind of passion was so different from anything she'd experienced she'd never actually gone weak at the knees before.

Clem entered the apartment and headed straight over to Tiger, who uttered a miaow as she reached him, stretching out so that she could reach his cream and ginger tummy.

'Hello, gorgeous,' she crooned, and Tiger stretched even further demanding worship. 'How are you?'

'Is it wrong I'm jealous of my cat?' Akil asked and she threw him a mischievous grin.

'Cats need to be paid their dues first, you know that.'

She continued to croon at Tiger while Akil put the pastries onto a plate and poured fresh coffee, bringing them over to her and sitting next to her on the big leather sofa. She loved the domesticity of it, cuddling up to him, ignoring the world outside.

'How was the hospital this morning?'

'Good. There's a couple of new kids in, but they came to the reading. I still can't believe that this is something I do! I keep waiting for someone to ask who I am and why I'm there. To throw me out.'

'They're always looking for ways to make it an easier experience for the children. And don't worry, I vouched for you.'

'And it's that easy? No background check, no references?'

'You're not alone with the children at any time, are you?'

'No, of course not. But I didn't mean for it to get to be a regular thing. What happens when I leave in three weeks' time?'

'I'm on the hospital board…'

She turned to face him. 'You never said.'

He shrugged. 'It didn't come up.' No wonder no one had challenged her presence. 'But you've shown that we have a need for this kind of entertainment, maybe in more than the children's ward. It's being looked at.'

'Look at me influencing hospital policy.'

'You have good instincts and a good heart. It would never have occurred to me if you hadn't shown me the way.'

An unexpected pride washed over her. She might not be the Crown Princess, but she might have achieved some good in the time she was in her sister's country.

'So what's the plan for today?' she asked as she finished the pastry.

Akil flashed a grin at her. 'I was thinking that it's time I introduced you to the most important woman in my life.'

Clem stiffened. His *what*? Surely he didn't mean his mother? She had never got the impression that they were that close and it was way too early—and too temporary—for that, and wasn't his sister abroad? He must have seen her alarm because he hastily added, 'My boat.'

That was more like it. 'I love boats. Did you know I grew up by the sea?'

'You may have mentioned it a hundred times or more, which is why I hoped you would like this idea. Then it's a date?'

'Absolutely!'

'Let's pick up some provisions, then…'

'Look at you with the nautical terms.'

'I'll have no insubordination on my ship, thank you. Tell Henri I'll drive you back. It may be late.'

She saluted, her smile cheeky. 'Yes, Captain. Anything you say, Captain.' With a roar he pinned her to the sofa, strong body moulding round hers, kissing her until she was breathless, tickling her until she begged for mercy and promised that she would be properly respectful once on the boat.

Just the two of them, out on the sea. Anticipation quivered through every nerve. She was loving this slow sensual discovery but maybe it was time to take things to the next level. She pulled Akil down to her again, luxuriating in the weight of him, the strength of him, the sureness of his kiss. Today was going to be a very good day.

Akil knew that this thing with Clem couldn't last, and he was also all too aware that the closer they got, the harder their inevitable parting would be, but paradoxically he didn't care because every day they spent together he fell for her more and more.

He liked her frank, no-nonsense sense of humour. Enjoyed the conversation that flowed so easily between them. And he had never been so physically aware of a woman in his life.

Neither of them had discussed taking it slow, but somehow it felt right, learning each other bit by bit. It was tantalising in all the right ways. Especially as they were building up to something more; they both knew it. Awareness simmered between them as they got ready for their trip, every touch searing, every glance full of promise.

Before heading to the coast they stocked up on enough provisions to last them a week at sea. Shopping together should have been a mundane task, but it was a glimpse at a future that seemed infinitely desirable, if impossible, standing in a shop debating which cheese to select and what bread would go best with their choices, deciding if they wanted cakes or biscuits or both and how many raspberries were too many. They ended up laden with bags and baskets as they loaded up the car and set off to the harbour where he kept his boat.

'Oh, I like it here,' Clem exclaimed as Akil drove into the small car park at the harbour and parked up. 'This is where you brought me that first time—only this time we're Henri free.'

Akil slid out of the car and walked round to open the door. 'It must be a relief to have some time away from him. Lucky for you that I have secret service training.'

'Don't forget my black belt in karate.' Clem jumped out of the car and joined him at the back of the vehicle as he opened the catch and let the boot spring up. 'I have skills too.'

'That you do.' He swung the first of the picnic hampers out of the car, then more cautiously lifted out the second basket containing the drinks, setting it gently on the ground.

'I'll get these.' Clem reached in and pulled out the paper bags containing the fruit they'd chosen and the box of cakes. He kept crockery, cutlery, towels and cushions on board so all they'd needed to get was the food.

'You sure?'

'Well, fun as it would be for me to skip ahead while you stumble laden behind me, I can carry my share. You're meant to be advocating dismantling the patriarchy, remember?'

'It's chivalry, not patriarchy,' he protested, and she laughed.

'Tell you what. I'll let you help me aboard.'

'It's my boat. I need to formally invite you anyway.'

'Like a vampire? Will I burst into flame if I put a foot aboard without a formal invitation? That must be an Asturian thing. I'm pretty sure we're not so formal in Cornwall.'

She gathered up the food and set off towards the harbour, Akil falling in beside her.

'I don't think poor Henri knows what to do with himself,' she said as they navigated the narrow path. 'He doesn't really do free time. I did point out to him that I look a lot more suspicious being shadowed by a six-foot-five rock of a man, but actually he does have this amazing ability to blend into the scenery. But he would literally give his life for Rosy so I guess that's a good thing. One less thing to worry about.'

'You worry about her?'

'She's going to be a queen one day. That's a tough gig. Of course I worry. I'm glad she has you as a friend though.'

They reached the small curve of the harbour and Akil exhaled as they stepped onto the jetty. It was a perfect sailing day. The sky was cloudless, the sea calm, the scent of salt and lemon permeating the air. He loved this moment of anticipation, the gorse-covered cliffs green behind him, the mountains rising majestically beyond, while turquoise seas stretched endlessly ahead. Here he wasn't the Vicomte d'Ortiz, carrier of his family's hopes and his father's thwarted ambitions. Here he wasn't a politician, a man who had put his own dreams aside. Here he was simply Akil. It was a rare pleasure.

Even rarer were the times he got to share this with someone. *Wanted* to share this with someone. And he had never brought a woman out to his boat before. Never wanted to share this most personal of pleasures. Never until now.

'Which is it?' Clem asked as they neared the end of the jetty. Most boats were moored further out, their dinghies bobbing off the jetty and harbour wall ready to ferry owners out. Akil reached his own dinghy and put the hampers at one end, before pointing out his boat.

'She's there.' He tried to keep the pride out of his voice but knew he'd failed as Clem laughed.

'You sound like a proud father. Or husband.'

'She is the love of my life,' he admitted. He was only half joking. There were so few times when Akil felt really comfortable being himself, even when he was with his sister or with his fellow volunteers at the mountain rescue. He was always conscious of the image he projected, the weight of responsibility and expectation he carried. It was only out on the water where he could drop all his barriers. It was just a shame he rarely got to enjoy it.

'I can see why you're so proud, she is a beauty. Small but perfectly formed.'

'I didn't want the kind of superyacht I needed a crew for. Something small enough for me to manage myself, but big enough to take out to sea, to spend a week exploring the coast if I wanted.'

'Sounds idyllic.' The yearning in her voice was palpable. 'I've always wanted my own boat—but I could never justify the cost for the use I'd get from one. Not that I ever had the money even if I could justify it. Jobbing actress is not a lucrative profession and although I do have a trust fund it doesn't run to luxuries like keeping a boat. Do you get away often?'

'Not nearly enough. To be honest, I *can't* justify her really. She deserves more than the few days every now and then I can give her.'

'But you're here today.'

'We're here today. So let's make the most of it. Hop in.'

Clem stepped gracefully into the small inflatable tender and sat herself at the bow as Akil untied the rope and started the engine, steering the dinghy out towards where his boat was moored. She knew what she was doing, taking the rudder as he pulled alongside and secured the dinghy to the dock at the back and climbed aboard, extending a hand to help her up the ladder. She then helped him winch the dinghy up and secure it before turning around to survey his prized possession.

'Nice,' she said. 'Very nice.'

Akil wasn't being modest, the boat was compact with just one cabin although it had a comfortable double bed and plenty of storage. But the boat was perfect for him, combining swift, comfortable handling, with plenty of space on deck including seating, a built-in grill and bar and swimming platform while its size meant he could moor up in any port or cove he wished. With the sea literally within a second's access he had no need for the hot tubs or fancy fittings many of his peers enjoyed on their larger, more ostentatious vessels.

It didn't take long to give Clem the tour, and she was suitably appreciative, helping him stow away the provisions as she admired all the gadgets and clever use of space.

'Some of my friends' families have boats, small fishing boats or glorified dinghies, but nothing like this. She's in a class of her own. But I do know my way around a rope so set me to work.'

'In that case…' Akil motioned her towards the tiller. 'Do you want to take her out?'

'Really?' Her smile was all the reward he needed.

'Absolutely. Here, you turn this to get her started and the gears are here. Let me know if you need any help. I'll get the anchor.'

Akil's faith in Clem was justified as she expertly steered them towards the open sea. He leaned against the side and watched her as she confidently found a path through the buoys marking the way out. Her hair blew in the slight breeze, her eyes crinkling as she concentrated on the horizon, her poise strong and true.

She looked utterly beautiful, a sea naiad in her natural world. Akil's mouth dried. He'd never dared dream of being fully in sync with someone. Had never imagined it could be so easy spending time with another human, being himself. The irony of knowing it was temporary was not lost on him. But he pushed the thought aside. Akil knew how to make the best of things. How to snatch at moments of happiness while steadfastly doing his duty. This time wasn't any different.

'Which way shall I go?' Clem roused him from his thoughts and he straightened, joining her at the tiller.

'Up to you. Left will take us to the glitzy resorts just along the coast so head that way if you want cocktails and sophistication. It's quite a sight.'

'I'll bet. And what happens if I turn right?'

'Then you'll see tiny coves that can only be accessed by boat, isolation, stunning views, some of the best swimming you'll ever experience and an idyllic picnic spot.'

'Hmm, difficult decision.' She angled the boat towards the right. 'How will I choose? The only thing…'

'Is?'

'I didn't come dressed for sailing, as you can see.' She flashed him a smile. 'Silk and lace are not really picnic attire but I can manage. But more crucially, I should have realised earlier when we were shopping, I don't have a bathing suit.'

Akil dropped a kiss onto her neck, his hand resting on the curve of her hip. 'Who said anything about costumes?'

Clem stilled. He could see her chest rise and fall as her breathing quickened, her cheeks and neck turned pink, her pupils dilated. He was so attuned to her every response, his own breathing sped up along with hers, heat rising throughout his body. When she finally spoke her voice was husky.

'I bet you say that to all the girls. Is this your routine? Invite a girl out for a sail and then suggest a dip but, oops, no costumes?'

'Not so far.' He paused, then said deliberately, 'You're the only woman I've ever invited abroad.'

She didn't respond, not at first, but he could see her work through the implications of that statement, before she turned and twined her arms around his neck, reaching up to press her mouth against his.

'What are we doing, Akil?' she half whispered, and he smoothed her hair back from her face.

'I don't know,' he said honestly. 'But we don't have to do anything, be anything. We can just sail or I can take us back. Just say the word.'

She shook her head emphatically. 'I don't want to go back,' she said, and he knew instinctively that she was talking about more than this trip.

'Then let's see where the wind takes us.'

She stared up at him, her eyes solemn and almost fearful until she seemed to shake her thoughts away, managing a smile as she turned back to the tiller. Akil leaned against her as she steered, his arm around her waist, holding her steady, wishing that she were someone less complicated, that he were someone without a predetermined path, that this could be the start of a longer voyage, the start of something real.

CHAPTER TEN

'THAT WAS A ridiculously delicious picnic.' Clem took another longing look at the leftovers before pushing her plate away with a groan. 'No. Don't let me eat any more. You might need to lose some ballast to get us back at the rate I've been consuming.'

She repressed a sigh at the thought of *back*. How she wished they could just sail on for ever. No worries about tomorrow, no family expectations—or in her case lack of family expectations—just the sea, a fair wind and each other. Because with Akil she was completely herself. Her hair was windblown, her skirt watermarked and her make-up non-existent and he didn't notice, didn't care. It was intoxicating.

'No more food. Got it. But we're now respectably heading towards evening so I could open the champagne and we can toast the view?'

It was a view worth toasting. Clem had kept hold of the tiller and taken them twenty miles up the rocky, dramatic coast where they'd moored up just inside a wide, deserted bay. They'd deliberated taking the tender in to picnic on the sandy beach but in the end elected to stay here on deck, the boat rocking gently with the tide.

'Champagne? Sounds good but should we drink and

boat? I guess we could get Henri to pick us up at the other end.'

Akil leaned back in his seat and stretched and she did her best not to look at the tantalising glimpse of bared, muscled stomach. 'Of course, the best thing about a boat is that you don't have to worry about sailing under the influence, you can just stay where you are.'

Her whole body tingled at the thought. 'You mean just stay here? Overnight?'

'Here or further up the coast.' His eyes gleamed. 'There are many possibilities.'

'I see, so was this trip just a ruse, a plan to spirit me away like a pirate and sail away on the seven seas?' She was a very modern woman but she couldn't help but thrill at the thought. There *was* something piratical about Akil. He was usually so well put together, but here on the boat, the top few buttons of his shirt undone showcasing a tanned, muscular vee of chest, shirt sleeves rolled up to expose strong corded wrists, hair ruffled by the breeze, she could see traces of his warrior ancestors. Ancestors who might whisk an enemy princess away on their boat.

'Tempting.' His voice was husky, and it trembled through her, setting every nerve vibrating. 'But nothing so uncivilised.'

She held his gaze. 'Pity,' she said, and her stomach tumbled at his wolfish smile.

'You see,' he said, and it was as if he were undressing her with his eyes, 'I wouldn't want any woman who didn't want me with every part of her. Who I didn't want with every atom in me. And I do want you, Clem. So, what shall we do? It's up to you, it's always been up to you. Maybe you're the pirate…the pirate princess seducing the warrior into doing her bidding.'

His voice was hypnotic, low and mesmerising and she couldn't have moved if she'd tried. And she wasn't trying. Not when Akil was so close, the scent of him wrapping around her senses, making her dizzy with that intoxicating mix of salt and sandalwood. Not when her whole body buzzed with his proximity, her nerves alight, her legs weak and her breasts full, aching for a release so tantalisingly close.

She couldn't even speak, just quivered as he drew one finger along her cheek, brushing the tender outline of her mouth. 'Your move, Clem.'

No, she wanted to cry out. It wasn't fair, he couldn't leave this decision solely up to her, not when she instinctively knew that making love with Akil would make her more vulnerable than she had ever been before. Not when she needed reassurances and promises that this was right, that she was right. That *they* were right. That they had a future, even if that reassurance could only be a lie.

For a moment she desperately thought about changing the subject, backing away, even as her body cried out for her to just get on with it already. She was so close, so close to getting in too deep. Surely making love with Akil would tip her over the edge. If she wasn't there already and, oh, how she feared she might be.

But if she didn't she knew she would regret this moment of cowardice for the rest of her life. She wanted to know him fully, for him to know her. And besides, wasn't this where they had been heading since the day of the tour? More, since that very first meeting? Wasn't this what she craved, what she wanted more than air or water? If so, then how could she not?

More importantly, how could she not when he was allowing her to set the parameters, when he was putting her first? For a woman so often left in the shadows, that power was the most seductive thing of all.

'I have decided.' She stood up and faced him. No more thought. No more fears or doubts. Suddenly it was all very clear. She wanted Akil and he wanted her and that was all that mattered. 'I do want you. Here, tonight.'

It was his turn to stand, one hand on the boat rail, his gaze locked on her, his mouth curved into a wicked smile, one that sent shivers trembling through her. 'In that case, come here.'

He was now supremely arrogant, no longer the suave suitor or the sweet-tongued seducer. He was a man who knew what he wanted—*her*—and knew his goal was within reach. But she could match him, in desire, in need and in confidence that she was desired and needed in turn. The ultimate aphrodisiac. And, chin tilted, a sway in her step, fire consuming her, she stepped forward. Just one step.

'Now you.'

He raised an eyebrow, laughter lighting the darkness of his gaze as he casually stepped forward. But she wasn't fooled; for all his amusement there was a predatory air as he moved that showed his blood was up and he was fully focused on moving in for the finish. There was still space between them and he stared at her, daring her to complete it. Instead, Clem reached for her top button and, eyes fixed on him, flicked it open. She watched him swallow and allowed herself a feline grin.

'It's a little hot, don't you think?' Another button

and then a third. 'Maybe we should cool off.' Another two and she slipped the blouse off her shoulders, her hands moving to the zip on her skirt. 'You did say this was a good swimming spot?' She stepped out of the skirt, leaving it pooled on the floor and, without looking away, undid the snap of her bra and let it fall away, feeling as much as hearing Akil's intake of breath as she did so. 'So, let's swim.' She kept her pants on, not quite ready to lose that last layer of protection as she stepped onto the swimming platform and pushed her hair back, looking back at him challengingly. 'Race you to the beach.'

It took Akil all of two seconds to react. He'd frozen in place while Clem discarded her clothes, unable to move a muscle as inch after delicious inch was bared, brown and lithe and delectable and—so it seemed—his. And then, just as he managed to wake up enough to reach for her she was gone, diving with clean precision into the sea and striking out for the beach. He allowed himself one lingering moment to take in the lines of her body forging through the water before tearing off his shirt and trousers and following her in.

The water was perfect, cool and refreshing, calm enough to make swimming a pleasure as Akil followed Clem, his blood up, closing in on his prey. Clem was a good swimmer, but he was better and he caught up with her with ease, then keeping pace alongside her until the water reached his chest at which point he stopped, reaching out to hook her and pull her close. Her hair, sleek with water, fell heavily around her shoulders, her chest rising and falling with exertion, water drying on her shoulders. She was all sea nymph, salt and water and flesh in a package he wanted to consume, like Poseidon claiming his prize. The water was deep enough to hide the rest of her body, but he knew just what was concealed, the high round breasts, a lighter shade than the rest of her olive body, the planes of her stomach and long, long legs, the triangle of silk that revealed as much as it concealed, now wet and translucent. Heat flooded him despite the chill of the water as he finally, finally, crushed her to him and took her mouth with his, not gently or sweetly but with a fierce possessiveness. A possessiveness she reciprocated. This was no coy naiad, rather a fierce and wild goddess as she wound her hands in his hair to pull him closer, her tongue entwined in his, hot and sweet, her breasts soft against his chest as he pulled her closer still.

Akil couldn't have said how long they stood, chest high in the waves, all he knew was that at some point he wanted, needed more, needed to touch as well as taste, needed to explore every inch of bared flesh. Slowly, unable to break the embrace, as if by doing so he might break the spell, he inched her back, back until the water receded, the sand soft under his feet, the early evening sun hot on his shoulders. But not as hot as the trail her hands blazed across his neck and down his back, not as hot as the flesh he skimmed as he finally, finally palmed one perfect breast, her damp skin silk under his touch. She inhaled sharply as his thumb reached her nipple, and he circled the tight bud slowly and with intent as he kissed his way down her jaw, down the proud slim column of her neck until he could replace his thumb with his mouth, cupping her other breast as he did so.

Blood surged triumphantly through his whole body, pooling at his groin, the urge to take her there and then almost overwhelming. *Steady*, he told himself. *Not yet.* He sank to his knees, pulling her with him, until she was supine on the sand beneath him, her beautiful body laid out like an offering, returning to her mouth as he straddled her.

Impatient, Clem pulled at him but Akil resisted with a low laugh, refusing to rush now that he had her here beneath him. Instead he concentrated on discovering every previously hidden inch, the places that made her gasp and buck and reach for him, holding onto his control with everything he had as his body clamoured for release.

'Now,' she whispered first softly and then impatiently but he resisted with painful restraint, pulling back to cup her face and kiss her with a melting slowness that almost undid him.

'Clem,' he murmured against her mouth. 'We need to return to the boat. I didn't get a chance to bring any protection.'

For one millisecond, Clem didn't care. For one moment she understood for the first time how desire and sensation could overwhelm common sense, but before she had time to act upon her instincts reality reasserted itself and she sat up, reluctantly, almost embarrassed by the abandon she'd displayed just moments before. 'Oh.'

'Oh, indeed. But I've seen you swim. I think we can be back on board in less than five minutes and carry on where we left off. What do you think?'

Again he was giving her the control, even though the evidence of his desire was all too visible, and that control only solidified her need. 'I think the quicker we get back, the better.' She allowed herself the luxury of run-

ning her eyes over him slowly and with intent, taking
in every plane and hollow, every piece of hard sculpted
flesh, and she could see him visibly shake with the effort of standing still as she caressed him with her gaze.

This time it was no mad dash, instead they kept
pace with each other, knowing what awaited them at
the return to the boat. Clem reached the ladder first and
climbed, Akil right behind her. As soon as she was on
the boat she turned, needing to kiss him, to hold him,
to be held in turn. The water hadn't quenched her desire, instead the wait, the anticipation, had only stoked it
and she pulled him close, entwining herself around him,
until, with a muttered curse, he swept her up, laying
her on the double sun lounger. She stayed still, drinking him in as he loomed above her.

'Don't move,' he ordered, and she obeyed, unable
to do anything but wait, every nerve quivering, every
sense greedily needy until he returned, tall and powerful and gloriously nude, a packet in his hands. He
paused despite her whimpering protest and she felt his
gaze wander over her as if he were touching her, her
flesh goosepimpling under his study. 'You are beautiful,' he breathed. 'A sea goddess.'

'No more talking,' she managed and he laughed
softly, sitting beside her.

'No? But I could write a poem to your eyes…' his
finger brushed over them '…a sonnet to your mouth…'
it moved lower still '…and a haiku about your neck.
Your breasts deserve an ode.' She sucked in a breath
as he lazily circled a nipple, replacing his finger with
a tongue. 'Your stomach an elegy. And as for the soft
skin here.' He moved his hand down to the tenderness

of her inner thigh. 'Oh, I could write an epic poem about the way you feel here.'

She was panting now, her breasts rising and falling as need built inside her higher and higher, hotter and hotter. She'd never felt so wanted before, so desirable, so tempting. But then again no man had ever looked at her as if she were the answer to all his prayers.

And she had never wanted a man so fiercely either. The play of his muscles under her eager hands, the strength in his arms and chest, the tautness of his stomach. The way he hissed as her hand moved lower as he fought fire with fire, moving lower until he was kissing her stomach, her hips, her thighs, her inner thighs, his hand moving further up, knowing and sure.

'And here,' he whispered. 'Only a ballad would do for here.' Clem cried out, she couldn't fight back now, all thought disappearing under almost unbearable sensation until at last she broke, riding the wave again and again, exultant as he joined her, as if he were made for her, as if she were made for him.

Time ceased to have any meaning until she came to, wrapped around him, limp and sated, the stars shining down on them. Clem lay there, not knowing what to say or do. It had never felt like that before, never been as intense, as overwhelming. Part of her wanted to shout out in happiness, some part of her wanted to cry and, as if he understood, Akil rolled over to pull her closer, to envelop her in his arms.

'Are you okay?'

'Better than okay,' she reassured him, then, worried, 'You?'

His laugh rumbled through her. 'Better than okay.'

'Good, that's good.'

'It is.'

They lay there breathing in time until Akil sat up. 'I promised you champagne.'

'It's fine,' she reassured him, just wanting him back next to her but he was already on his feet.

'No, you should have champagne. We have the sound of the sea, we have the stars, we shouldn't waste it.'

'Well, if you insist.'

It took him less than two minutes to return with the chilled champagne and a bowl of the raspberries they'd bought earlier and, completely unselfconsciously, they stayed on deck, sipping and nibbling on the raspberries and talking nonsense as they gazed up at the stars. At some point, most of the champagne drunk, Akil kissed her once again and desire sprang back up as if they hadn't made love earlier, Clem responding with an ardency and urgency that would have surprised her if she'd had any room to think.

Later, much later, still under the stars but under a blanket Akil had brought up from the cabin, she began to fall asleep, safe in Akil's arms.

'I love you,' she murmured, so almost asleep she wasn't sure if she was imagining saying the words or not. Nor did she know if she imagined the pause that followed or the almost breathed response.

'*Je t'aime*, Clemence Beaumont. *Je t'aime.*'

CHAPTER ELEVEN

CLEM LAY BACK on the sunbed and breathed in. It was another hot, sunny day, the kind where she was glad to have little to do but swim and sleep. And she knew she needed to make the most of it, she wouldn't be able to stay in this idyll for much longer, nor enjoy almost guaranteed sun once she was back in the uncertainty of a UK summer.

Not that there was much summer left. She couldn't believe how quickly time had flown, but here she was facing the end of her stay. In less than a week she'd be returning to Cornwall and Arrosa would come home and start preparing for the ratification. She hadn't spoken to her sister for a couple of weeks, they'd just hurriedly exchanged a few messages, and she had no idea how she felt about returning to her normal life. Clem wasn't sure how she felt about her return to normality either.

On one hand, fun as being a tourist and enjoying the benefits of living in Arrosa's house were, she didn't think she was suited for a life without purpose. Sunbathing and swimming were fun, but she got just as much enjoyment out of the sessions at the hospital, more in fact, looking forward to the moment she sat down and

transported the children away. After discussing it with
Akil she'd started to do some research into what she'd
need to do to qualify in occupational therapy and dra-
matherapy and had contacted a friend who worked in a
theatre company that specialised in working with children in hospital and other non-home settings. She still
had no concrete plans, but just having an idea of a path
was a huge step forward.

But, of course, returning to Cornwall meant leaving Akil. And if that thought had been difficult *before*
the trip out on the boat, it was almost unbearable now.
She continued to see him nearly every day, although as
summer drew to the end so his responsibilities grew,
like a warning sign their time was nearly up. The need
for discretion was as high as ever; the last thing either
of them wanted was speculation about who Clem was
or, worse, for people to start gossiping about how much
time he spent at the palais with Arrosa. So she continued leaving the estate in one outfit and changing in a
discreet location, and when they did venture out they
mingled with tourists and sightseers far away from anywhere where Akil might meet friends or colleagues.

Clem wriggled again, trying to get comfortable.
What had been fun at the beginning, an amusing subterfuge, was beginning to lose its charm. A reminder
of why their relationship had to be secret, and that an
end date was in sight. Fun as it was for them to lie in
bed building castles in the air about a life sailing around
Cornwall, she knew that leaving Asturia was not an
option for him, just as staying was not an option for
her. All she had ever wanted was someone to love her,
to see her, to put her first. Ironic really that she had

found someone who fitted the first two but couldn't fulfil the third.

At least neither of them had been foolish enough to mention love again. It didn't stop her thinking it though. Feeling it.

She closed her eyes, resolutely pushing the thoughts away although she knew that their reckoning was coming. They still had nearly a week. Maybe they would think of a solution before then. Maybe he'd ask her to stay, or she could suggest it. No one knew who she was. What did Clem Beaumont from England have to do with the royal family? Did he want more than a holiday romance? Did she? They had never discussed it.

She did her best to concentrate on the sensuous warmth of the sun across her body, the sound of the birds singing overhead and the distant drone of an aeroplane. Occasionally she heard voices from outside the villa gardens as the palais gardeners moved around, a burst of radio from one of the guards and his reply, footsteps coming down her path.

Hang on? *Footsteps.* Clem peeled her eyes open, suddenly alert. She wasn't expecting anybody. Akil was working this morning and nobody else ever came to see her. Feeling a little vulnerable in just her bikini, she sat up and grabbed her wrap, turning towards the path and the figure striding down it.

'There you are, Clemence.'

She blinked, myriad emotions whirlpooling through her, the way they always did on the rare occasions she saw her father, the less rare occasions she thought about him.

Sitting back, she peered over her sunglasses, deliberately cool and collected. 'Hello, Zorien. I wasn't expecting you. I must have missed your message.'

It was a long time since she'd called him *Daddy*; it had been made very clear to her that the word was not for her to use, not even in private, in case they were ever overheard. Safety trumped reality every time.

'You look well,' she added. 'Would you like to sit down? I'm sure I can manage some coffee.'

It had been several years since she'd last seen him, but he looked exactly the same, tall, slim and straight-backed, his hair not yet silvering. The hazel eyes so similar to hers and Arrosa's were cool and assessing, his expression inscrutable.

'Your sister stands when I first enter a room, curtseys, says *Your Majesty* and waits for me to speak.'

It was like that, was it? Clem smiled, affecting an insouciance she didn't feel. 'I missed the day my local comprehensive taught court manners. But on the other hand, we're outside so this isn't actually a room and you're not *My* Majesty. I'm not an Asturian citizen, remember?'

One of many points of contention. Zorien wasn't named on her birth certificate so she had no claim to citizenship although thanks to her mother she held French as well as British citizenship.

'But any guard or member of staff could see you not adhering to protocol. You should know better than to let your guard down, Clemence.'

'No one's looking. Besides, what will they do? Arrest me for lack of courtesy and take me to the tower?'

'You are always so argumentative, Clemence.' The first time they'd met in years and already they were at odds, the same old pattern. It was like the time he'd come to see her on her eighteenth birthday, and they had managed about fifteen minutes before she'd crashed out of the house in a rage, angry that he wouldn't be there for her last school play, one she had helped direct as well as starred in, a labour of love she had wanted to share with both her parents. Angry that he wouldn't even come for a walk with her in case they were seen. Angry that he'd refused her request to spend the summer in Asturia. She'd said bitter words, a lifetime of resentment and hurt spilling out, and in the end he had simply walked away. Soon after he'd made it clear it was no longer safe for Arrosa to spend her summers in Cornwall.

Their relationship had never really recovered; it had never had the opportunity. It wasn't as if they ever spent time together to repair it, his calls infrequent, his visits even more so.

Zorien Artega had done his duty materially. Her trust fund had been set up before she was born, more money was deposited in her account every birthday and Christmas and upon her mother's death she'd found out the house had been held in trust for her. There were times when she'd wanted to throw her trust fund back at him, to tell him that she needed nothing from him. But without it she had nothing. No family, no security net, no proof of who she was and that anyone had ever cared about her.

But he was here now, and this was what she had wanted, had hoped for. She couldn't allow her temper and age-old hurt to get in the way. 'I'm going to make coffee,' she said in as conciliatory a manner as she could manage. 'Sure you don't want some?'

He continued to survey her for another long moment, then nodded. 'Coffee would be nice.'

They didn't speak again until Clem had set the coffee pot onto the table, quickly ducking into the bedroom and throwing a dress over her bikini and pulling a comb through her hair. After a moment's hesitation she added a wrap, a dash of lipstick and some mascara. It wasn't that she wanted to impress her father, but she did want the protection of respectability. She returned to the kitchen, pouring the milk into a jug and tipping some biscuits onto a plate, carrying the lot outside. She took a seat opposite him and handed him a cup.

'It's beautiful here. I always thought the house in Cornwall the most perfect setting, and I do like to be beside the sea, but if I can't have the sea then a lake is certainly a good substitute.'

'Your sister seems happy here,' Zorien said. 'I had my doubts when she wanted to move out of her apartments in the palais, but this seemed like a good compromise. She is still protected by the palais guards, still looked after by the staff but she has some independence.'

Some was the relevant word here; Clem knew her sister's comings and goings were recorded and scrutinised but it was a compromise Arrosa had made and it wasn't for her to comment.

Zorien sipped his coffee then set his cup down. 'How are you, Clem? It can't have been easy for you the last few months.'

'I'm fine,' she said as brightly as she could. 'Aren't I always? Stay out of trouble and need nothing, that's my role.'

But he didn't rise to the bait, looking her over with

eyes that were suddenly kind, and she blinked; kindness was almost more than she could bear. 'You shouldn't have had to deal with your mother's illness alone,' he said. 'I'm more sorry about that than you can know.'

'The nurses you paid for were more than helpful.' The least she could do was give credit where credit was due. 'And Maman loved the gifts you sent. You always seemed to know what would cheer her up.' Every day something new would arrive, her mother's favourite flowers, gloriously soft cashmere socks and wraps, fresh baskets of fruit, luxury creams and lotions, delicate cakes to tempt a disappearing appetite.

'I should have been there, come to see her before the end. I think…' For a brief second, he looked vulnerable. 'I think I was in denial; your mother was so full of life it seemed impossible that life could be cut short. If anyone could beat a diagnosis like hers, I thought she would.'

There were so many things Clem could respond with. She could point out that if he had been there, if he'd seen her mother, he'd have known how ill she was, that those who cared for her day to day didn't have the luxury of dreaming that everything was going to be okay. But what was the point? 'I think we all hoped that,' she said instead.

Silence fell once again, thoughts of her mother permeating the air around them. She was the link, their common ground, the woman they both had loved. Now she was gone, was anything left in their relationship to salvage? Did her father even want to salvage it? Would it be far more convenient for him if Clem disappeared never to be seen again?

'You seem to have been very busy while you have been here,' he said at last.

Clem looked at him warily, but he seemed to be genuine. 'I've heard good reports about the impact your reading is having at the hospital. It's kind of you to give up your time. It's the sort of thing I could imagine your mother doing.'

'I kind of fell into it really, but I am enjoying it.'

'Will you continue when you go back?'

When you go back: there was clearly no doubt in her father's mind that her stay here was temporary. 'Possibly,' she conceded. 'I've been wondering what to do with my life. Taking eighteen months out has changed everything. Acting doesn't seem like the be-all and end-all any more. Doesn't seem as important as it once did. I've been thinking about maybe retraining, looking at something like occupational therapy. It's early days, I don't want to rush into anything, but it might be a rewarding thing to do.' She paused, hating how much she wanted his opinion, his approbation, but she could feel his approval warming her through as he slowly nodded.

'That sounds like a good plan. You'd be good at that.'

'Thank you.'

'I've also heard,' he continued, and something in the way he shifted told Clem that this was the purpose of the meeting. He wasn't here to catch up with her, nor to compliment her on her work at the hospital, he was here to deliver a message. She straightened and met his gaze coolly, glad of the lipstick and combed hair. 'That you've been spending a great deal of time with the Ortiz heir.'

'Akil? Yes, he's been very kind.'

'The pair of you have been very discreet and I appreciate that, but he's a young man on the rise and the press will start to take notice sooner rather than later. Will want to know who you are.'

'All they would find out is that I'm an English actress here on holiday.' She knew she sounded defensive and tried to rein it in. 'There is nothing to link me to you. That's what you're worried about, isn't it?'

'You are staying in my home, accompanied by your sister's bodyguard, there's a link. It would take one enterprising journalist to work that out. But there's more, Clem. Your behaviour is rousing suspicion. People are wondering where Arrosa is every day. She sets off for Court but no one sees her. I have put off any queries, as far as anyone knows she's with me, but people won't really believe she's shut up in my private apartments all day every day. It's stretching credulity. The gate logs from here come to me, but they also go to the Army General. They show Arrosa as coming back late or not coming back at all. Sooner or later, this will leak, people will wonder where she is, what she's doing.'

Heat flooded her cheeks; to think she'd been congratulating herself how discreet she and Akil had been. Of course her behaviour would be noticed and reported on, no matter what she, Akil and Henri did to mitigate it. And now her father was having to cover for her and Akil.

'I'll be more careful. I'm leaving soon anyway.' But she knew that wasn't the right answer. He wasn't here to ask her to be more discreet, he was telling her to stop seeing Akil.

Zorien leaned forward and although his eyes were kind, they were also implacable. 'You've done a good thing, Clem. Your sister needed time away and you made that happen. But when she returns, things are going to get more and more intense. Her life was difficult as my only child.'

Clem did her best not to wince at his words. *Only child.* That put her very firmly in her place.

'It's been very difficult as we have worked to change the law, especially as I know she has no real desire to be Queen and part of her would have been happy leaving things as they were. But nothing can really prepare her for what life will be like in just a few weeks when she officially becomes my heir. Everything she says, everything she does, will be under intense scrutiny, at home and internationally. She has to show that she is fit to rule, that she has what it takes to manage this country. Everything we do needs to support that. Do you understand what I'm saying?'

'Yes. I understand, I've never done anything but understand. Asturia comes first, I come second. That's how it's always been, isn't it, Zorien?'

He shook his head. 'Not you, Clem. *Us.* We Artegas. Asturia comes first, the family second. We are the servants of this country, and we can never forget it.'

'But it's *not* my country. That's been made very clear to me.'

'But you're here, and you love it, don't you? You've explored the mountains, the villages, and the seas. You've spent time in hospitals, eating our food, walking our streets, exploring our heritage—your heritage. Don't think that I don't know that the sacrifice you make is greater in some ways than the sacrifices your sister and I have to make.'

'But you have each other.' She hated the tears filling her eyes, the wobble in her voice. 'I have no one.' No one but Akil—and she had known she would need to say goodbye, she had just hoped for more time.

'Please don't think that I don't want to be more involved in your life, and I know Arrosa wishes she could be a proper sister to you. But this is what we do, all of us, and you have your part to play as well. The last thing we need right now is the publicity that would surround us if there was any suspicion of who you really are. I'm glad you had a chance to be here, to get to know the country, but it's time for you and Arrosa to resume your normal lives. Your life is in England, Clem. That's what your mother chose for you.'

'But what if that's not what I want?'

'What we want is secondary to what we need to do. Look at you, Clem, you're an Artega through and through. Our blood into your veins and I know I can trust you to do what's right. You've given your sister the space she needed to prepare for her future, to grow into her role. Your plans for your future sound exciting, and I will help in any way I can.'

'As long as I pursue them away from here?'

Her father nodded. 'The last year and a half have been difficult for you, and you deserved some fun, but it's time for the fun to stop. I'm sorry, Clem. I wish it could be different, but it's time you went home.'

It wasn't like Clem not to reply to his messages, but a couple of hours after letting her know he was free, Akil had still not heard from her, nor was she at the hospital. He had tried to be discreet about visiting her at the Palais d'Artega, not wanting his presence there too often to be noted, but when his third call went to voicemail his worry intensified and he headed out towards the country estate, discretion the last thing on his mind.

It wasn't just that it was unlike her to go AWOL. He needed to see her. It had been hard to settle to work that morning; every hour that passed was a reminder that summer was nearly over, and Clem would be returning to England soon. It had been easy to ignore that realisation; when they had started to get close, summer had seemed endless. Besides, they had both known the score. Theirs was just a holiday fling, some fun while Clem was in Asturia.

But what they had was stronger, deeper, than a fling. And now, as every day got dark a little earlier and the noonday sun sank a little lower, reality was setting in. He loved her.

The irony didn't escape him; he was a man who didn't really believe in love and certainly didn't believe in love at first sight, but he couldn't deny that something in him had shifted the very first time they'd met. He'd grown up to think of love as weakness, as destructive, but being with Clem just made him stronger. Talking to her, listening to her, finding out her perspective made him a better politician, a more strategic thinker—look at his plans for the hospital inspired by her. Was she the politician's wife of his dreams? No, but he was very glad he hadn't met the well-connected and diplomatic hostess he'd thought he wanted to marry. He needed someone to challenge him, someone to complement him. Love wasn't weakness, as he had feared, but strength, allowing himself vulnerability in front of another human being.

And he was sure that she needed him, too. For all her strength she needed to be loved, to be needed; she'd been alone too long. Which was why Akil was going to ask her to stay in Asturia. To stay with him. A smile curved his mouth at the thought of evenings curled up and days out exploring, of long nights loving and laughing. It was more than he'd ever thought he'd have and now it was within his grasp. How could one person change everything so completely?

He'd known since the first night on the boat that he couldn't just let her leave, but now time was running out and he still hadn't found the right time or words. He'd even considered proposing, but his natural caution urged him against making such an irrevocable move just yet. After all, his parents' marriage stemmed from a summer romance gone wrong, and he didn't want to repeat that mistake. He and Clem needed to spend every season together before making such a commitment. But he was looking forward to every one of those seasons.

He knew it wouldn't be easy. Even if she were just an English tourist here for the summer then there would still be some obstacles to overcome. Her life was overseas, she had no job here, and his work and the obligations of his title were both demanding. But she wasn't just an English tourist, she was the illegitimate daughter of the King, and from everything she'd told him he knew Zorien and those court officials who knew of her existence would not welcome her presence in Asturia full-time. But they couldn't let that stop them. If she wanted to stay, they would find a way to make it work.

By the time he reached the Palais d'Artega he'd still not heard from her, and tension gripped him as he turned in through the gates. As usual he was waved through but, this time, he was aware of some curious glances from the usually inscrutable guards and knew that he wouldn't be able to visit her here again. If his presence here was being noted, it had to stop.

As he drove along the formal driveway another car was coming the other way and Akil slowed and pulled in to allow it to pass. As it drew close, Akil saw Zorien at the wheel, his expression dark and filled with pain. His gaze met Akil's and he nodded curtly. Akil's pulse began to hammer as he noted what looked like pity in the King's eyes and the feeling of tension increased as he sped a little faster than usual past the palais and out towards the villa.

He pulled up outside and jumped out of his car, making his way around to the back of the house, instinctively knowing that Clem would be standing by the lake. He knew at times of stress she gravitated towards water and sure enough she was standing on the platform where he had first seen her, wearing a long green sundress that fell around her ankles. Her head was bent but she looked up as he approached, and he saw her eyes were red. Her father had made her cry.

He clenched his fists; he knew better than anyone that family relationships were complicated, but Clem had nobody. Surely Zorien understood that? Would it have cost him to be kind?

'Hi,' she said, her voice a little husky.

'I'm glad you're okay. I got a little worried when I didn't hear from you.'

'Sorry, my father was here. I haven't had a chance to check my phone.'

'I saw him on the way out. I'm glad he managed to visit you. How was it?'

Her smile was tremulous. 'As expected. He's given me my marching orders.'

Anger and possessiveness rose in him, almost overwhelming as he strode forward to take her hands. 'He can't do that.'

'He's the King. I'm pretty sure he can do anything he likes.'

'We're a democracy and you're of age. You can do anything you want, Clem.'

She pulled her hands away and tried another smile. 'What does it matter, Akil? We knew this day was coming, it's just a little earlier than expected. This was only a summer fling.'

He took her shoulders and looked down at her defiant face. 'Is that really true, Clem? Because it isn't for me. I love you—and I think that you love me.'

CHAPTER TWELVE

CLEM STARED UP at Akil, her eyes filling with unwanted tears. She tried to blink them back, not wanting to show any sign of weakness. 'Love is a big word, Akil.'

'It's not one I use lightly.' His voice was teasing, warm, but his face was full of concern—for her.

She twisted away, not sure she'd be able to do what had to be done if he was touching her. 'Say I was falling in love with you, what difference would it make? My life is far away from here, and there's nothing for you in Cornwall.'

'Apart from you.'

She closed her eyes, trying to regain control of her voice. 'But I wouldn't be enough. We both know that. You have your role here, your title, the promise you made to your father. You couldn't give that up for me.' Although a selfish part of her wished he could.

'No, maybe not long term, although I'd love to visit your home,' he conceded. 'But, Clem, you could stay. You could extend your role at the hospital; we could look into funding to make it a real job if that's what you wanted.'

'And what? Live with you?'

'Why not?'

'Because I don't belong here. I'm not wanted here.'

'I want you, and I bet your sister does too.'

She knew he was trying to help but how she wished he wouldn't; every word just made it worse, showing her a future she could never inhabit. 'My mother left France because it was considered too close to Asturia, too risky. At one point my father tried to persuade her that she should move to New Zealand in order to protect the secret of my existence, but she didn't want to go so far alone so they compromised on Cornwall. I don't think, judging on the conversation we've just had, that he's changed his mind.'

'This isn't about him.'

'No, it's about me. He reminded me that if word got out about who I was then life will be even more difficult for Rosy—and it's going to be hard enough for her from now on, we both know that. I love my sister, Akil, she is the one constant I have. I couldn't live knowing my existence was like some time bomb waiting to explode.'

'Have you asked her? Because I bet you anything she would tell you that she doesn't care about any possible scandal, that she would give anything to have you close by. She loves you too, Clem. She would want you to be happy.'

'But how could I be happy living so close to a father and sister who can't acknowledge me? If you and I were together then wouldn't there be times we were in the same place and at the same events? And we would have to be strangers! I can't live like that, I can't. I can't be here unacknowledged, unwanted. It would break me, Akil.' The words were torn from her, and the tears she so desperately tried to keep back made it through the barriers. 'How could I live as a stranger to my family?'

He enfolded her in his arms, and she allowed herself the luxury of leaning in against him. 'You're not unwanted, Clem. Never that. I'd be by your side throughout.'

How she wished she could believe him. 'And if we didn't work out? We barely know each other after all, it's just been a few weeks. You're the one who said that mutual goals were a better basis for a relationship than love. That love complicates things, that your parents married as a result of a summer romance and made each other miserable. What if that is us? What if we realised in a week, or a month or a year that it wasn't working? Where would I be then? Surely it's better to make a clean break before we're in too deep?' She allowed herself another second of absorbing his strength, memorising every muscle, before she stepped back, trying to keep her expression neutral, to hide how much every word hurt.

'I did say that.' His smile was rueful. 'And I meant it. But that was because I didn't know what love was. I'd never been in love before, you see. I do know now, though, thanks to you, Clem, and my feelings aren't going to change. You just need to trust me.'

'I can't. I can't, Akil. I wish I could. It's a nice idea, extending whatever this is between us, but it's not practical. Better to realise that what we have here is a summer romance, a lovely, memorable time out from reality. I'll always cherish it.'

'Or maybe it's more, maybe we have the chance of something extraordinary.'

'Maybe in another life.'

'We only get this one chance, Clem.'

'I'm sorry,' she whispered, not able to prolong the

torture for another moment. 'But you have to go. I need to pack.'

Akil stood stock-still, dark eyes blazing. 'Don't just give up on us, Clem. Don't give in without a fight.' He stared at her for a moment longer and, unable to bear the weight of his gaze, she looked away. By the time she looked back, he was gone.

Clem stood frozen to the spot for one moment and then sank to her knees, letting out a howl of such grief it shocked her, and then another one wracking her body. She crouched there, allowing the tears to flow and the sobs to pour out until she was spent with emotion, and then clambered to her feet. Her chest and throat ached, but the pain in her chest, which had tightened the whole time Akil had been here, was gone. Now she could move.

Her father had arranged for the plane to fly her back that evening, so she headed back up the garden to the villa mechanically. She'd brought very little with her, so as not to arouse suspicion, and it didn't take long to put her scant few belongings in her bag. A paper bag on the dressing table held the bracelets and cufflinks she'd bought a few weeks ago and she slipped one bangle onto her wrist, leaving the other for her sister. She held the cufflinks tight in her hand for one long moment then slipped them into her pocket—she'd ask Henri to deliver them. Her bag packed, she took it through to the hallway and then began to tidy up the coffee she'd made earlier.

She needed to keep busy. She couldn't allow herself to think, to feel, to understand that this was her last day in Asturia, that she'd never see Akil again, had no idea when she'd see her sister again.

Finally, there was nothing else to do and Clem wandered back out into the garden and down to the bathing platform staring out at the lake, at the magnificent palais in the distance. She'd never wanted to grow up here; beautiful as it was, she preferred the Cornish cottage, and was immensely grateful she'd not had to deal with all the rigmarole and ceremonial nonsense Arrosa had had to navigate. But she'd like to have been able to visit here, to share this house with her sister, for them to be sitting here by the lake together gossiping, a chilled bottle of wine awaiting them on the terrace.

If she'd said yes to Akil, if she'd been braver, stronger, would that have been a possibility? How could it have been? She and Rosy could have no public relationship; that was why she had to go home, for her sister.

Clem sat down and trailed her hand in the cold water, closing her eyes and remembering the moment Akil had kissed her in the sea, the overwhelming sensations. It had all been overwhelming. Yes, she wanted to protect her sister, but she also needed to protect herself. She was frightened of being hurt, frightened of being left behind, frightened of not being enough.

But it was too late. She had let Akil into her heart and now she was hurting, more than she'd ever imagined possible. But it wasn't Akil's fault; she was doing it to herself. He wanted her to stay; he wanted her to be with him. She was the one turning away.

She knelt down and stared at her reflection in the water, pale and big eyed. What if she did stay? What was the worst that could happen? She couldn't control what her father did or said, and she'd have to be respectful of Arrosa's wishes around any kind of public relationship, but really who would connect Clemence Beaumont with the royal family? Her similarity to her sister was striking, but wild dark curls and hazel eyes were common enough in Asturia.

Akil loved her. She rocked back as the truth of the words hit her. What must it have cost him to have said that? To have made himself so vulnerable, he who lived a life led by duty and responsibility? But he loved her and wanted her no matter the consequences. It was what she'd always wanted and yet she was willing to throw it away.

How could she when she loved him? Could she really return home and carry on living without him? Carry on as if all this had never happened? Of course she couldn't. She was no longer that grieving girl with no idea who she was and what she wanted, who had arrived here just a few weeks before. Akil had helped her find the way. And her way was with him.

She just had to find a way to tell him.

Akil didn't know where he was going to go or what he was going to do as he drove away from the Palais d'Artega, but one thing he did know for sure. This was *not* the end of the conversation. He was not going to just give up.

It would be one thing if Clem had decided to go back to Cornwall of her own volition; if she didn't care enough about him to stay. He wasn't going to pretend that it wouldn't hurt, but he'd have to accept her decision. But he was pretty sure that was not what was going on here. He had no idea exactly what Zorien had said to her but whatever it was had clearly persuaded her that she had no place in Asturia, that her very presence was a danger to her sister.

But the real danger was the secret itself. Secrets had

power, a power that only existed as long as the secret did, a power that disappeared once freed. Clem was in her twenties now, and Zorien had technically been a free man when she'd been conceived. The news of her existence would undoubtably cause some scandal, but it would be a short-lived one, especially if both the Artega and the Ortiz families rallied around her.

But what could Akil do? It wasn't his secret to spill, his call to make.

Before he could think better of it, he tapped the call button on his dashboard and commanded his phone to call Arrosa. It rang several times before she picked up.

'Akil, is everything okay?'

'Not exactly. Have you spoken to your father?'

'Funny you should ask that. He's left me a voicemail and a couple of messages, telling me it's time to come home.' He couldn't quite tell what the Princess thought of her father's command.

'He's told Clem the same thing, that her time here is up,' he said grimly.

'I guess we always knew it wasn't for ever,' Arrosa said, a shadow of unhappiness in her voice.

'You certainly couldn't keep this pretence up for ever. At some point people will want to see the Princess's face,' Akil said dryly. 'Clem needs to be able to leave the palais without disguises and subterfuge. But that doesn't mean that things should have to go back to the way they were. Don't you agree?'

There was a startled silence at the end of the phone. 'What do you mean?' she asked at last.

'We're about to begin a new era here in Asturia, spearheaded by you, Arrosa. Don't you think it's time for a new start in every way?'

'Is this about Clem?'

'I love her,' he said deliberately. 'And I think that she loves me, but she won't stay here with me, she won't put her happiness first, because your father has told her that if anyone finds out who she is the scandal would be too much for you and she loves you too much to be a burden to you.'

'But that's not it at all, Akil. I would love everyone to know who she is, I am so proud of her, but how could I do that to her? Clem has never been the target of the press. She's never been followed anywhere, she's never been commented on, she's never had her outfits dissected, her love life speculated on, her every expression misinterpreted until she had to learn to show no expression at all. She has a freedom that I can never have, and that freedom is the greatest gift I can give her. If anyone knew who she was, she'd lose that.'

'I think that should be her decision, don't you? Arrosa, don't you see, you're protecting her and she's protecting you and the only people losing out are the two of you?'

'And this is all altruistic on your part?'

'I don't deny that I would like her to stay in Asturia, that I would like to carry on seeing her, but this is beyond us, whatever we are. She is all alone, Arrosa. She is going back to Cornwall with no family, no one who really cares about her apart from you and me.'

There was another long silence before she asked, 'What do you want me to do?'

'I'm going to go see your father to tell him that I think he should come out and acknowledge her if that's what she wants. And then I am going to see if I can persuade your stubborn sister to give us a chance. I just need to know; will you back me up or not?'

'If that's what Clem wants, then yes. I will.'

'Thank you, that's all I needed.'

Akil said goodbye then hung up, and headed towards the castle, parking in his usual spot just outside parliament, and striding into the building, flashing his pass at every barrier and guard post until he'd reached the doorway that separated the royal apartments from the parliamentary building. There he was forced to halt and give his name to a footman and request a meeting with Zorien.

'He'll see me,' he said with a certainty that made the footman look taken aback. Sure enough, the man was back within minutes.

'He said to bring you straight in,' he said in obvious surprise. 'Follow me.' He led Akil through several corridors until they finally reached the heavy oak door that barred the way to Zorien's private office. The footman knocked and opened it, gesturing for Akil to go in.

The King stood at the window gazing out, turning as Akil walked towards him and made a swift bow. 'I was wondering if I'd see you today,' he said.

'Your Majesty.' He straightened. 'I think you know why I'm here.'

Zorien gestured towards a chair. 'Sit down, d'Ortiz. Brandy? No? You're sure?' He sat opposite Akil and sighed. 'It's for her own good, you know,' he said. 'For both their good.'

Akil made himself consider every word, use his politician's diplomacy, not the righteous anger that rumbled through him. 'Isn't that their decision to make now? They're not children any more, Your Majesty. They are women, strong women who have been through a great deal in different ways. They need each other, want to support each other as the sisters they are. It should be their choice where Clem lives and whether they see each other, not yours.'

'So this is an intervention on their behalf? I think both my daughters are capable of speaking for themselves.'

'So do I. But thanks to you they both think silence benefits the other. I don't know if that is deliberate manipulation or an unfortunate misunderstanding, but while they both think they are doing what's best for the other they are not going to challenge you. I, on the other hand, have no such scruples. Instead, I wanted to give you fair warning.' Akil held the King's gaze. 'I love Clem, I want to make a life with her, and I don't care whether you are happy for her to stay in Asturia or not. But *she* cares and that matters to me.'

'So you're here for my blessing.'

'I don't need anyone's blessing. But Clem does. She needs to know that you love her, that you care about her, that you want her in your life. And you should want her. She's an amazing woman, kind and intelligent—and she tells it how it is, which is a really rare quality. She could be a real asset to you, and a real asset to Arrosa. But that's not why you should acknowledge her. You should do it because it's the right thing to do. Because she has nobody else, and you are her father.'

'And you think it's as easy as that, do you?'

Akil smiled at that. 'You and I both know that in politics the easiest decision is rarely the right one. Of course it won't be easy. There will be a lot of talk and a lot of speculation, and it will be unpleasant for a while.'

'I have a wife who is innocent in all this.'

'And a daughter who is also innocent. Clem deserves to hear you stand up for her, for you to say publicly that you're proud of her. Whether you do so is up to you. It's not up to me to spill your secrets. But it's not for me to hide them either. I am going to do everything in my power to persuade Clem to make a life with me here whether you like it or not. And if I do then you will have to find a way to live with that that makes her happy— because if I see you snub her even once, if I ever see her look the way she looked after your visit today again, then this won't be such a civilised conversation.'

'You've made yourself very clear, d'Ortiz.'

'Good.'

The King sighed. 'Are you sure you don't want a drink? I think I need one.' He stood up and poured two generous measures of brandy, setting one before Akil. 'I have to say, I am half hoping she turns you down. You would be an exhausting son-in-law. But maybe it would be better to have you close. You could also be an asset as Arrosa starts to take the reins. A brother-in-law like you on her side would be a formidable weapon.'

'As would Clem, if she has a place here. You'll consider it?'

'I need to talk to Arrosa and I need to talk to my wife, but if Clem wants me to publicly recognise her, then maybe it's time. Tell her I will think about it.'

Akil stood up, his brandy untouched. 'Thank you, sir.'

'Good luck, d'Ortiz.'

Akil grinned then. 'I'll need it. Your daughter can be very stubborn, sir.'

'Don't I know it. She's very like her mother.' The

rather austere face softened. 'I did what I thought was right at the time, what I thought was right for Asturia, and I don't do regrets. Iara has been a good queen, maybe better than I deserve, and I love my daughter more than she'll ever know. But I wish I could have been a father to Clem, shown her how proud I am of her.'

'It's not too late, sir.' Akil just hoped it wasn't too late for him as well. But he came from a long line of warriors. It was time to fight.

CHAPTER THIRTEEN

CLEM TURNED AWAY from the lake and marched back up to the villa full of purpose. As she reached the terrace she saw a tall figure waiting for her. Her heart leapt, only to sink again when she realised it was Henri; his usually impassive face was full of sympathy.

'The plane is waiting for you, Your Highness.'

'Henri, you really don't have to *Your Highness* me. You never did. I'm just Clem,' she said, and a smile crinkled the usually austere face.

'No matter what, you're the King's daughter, and you deserve the title.'

'Thank you. I'm glad Rosy has you to look out for her. Just let me get my things.'

Clem collected her bag and jacket then stood in the hallway looking around for a moment, picturing her sister working at the desk in the study, stirring something on the stovetop, relaxing in front of the TV. If things went the way Clem hoped, would she be here with her sometimes?

'This isn't goodbye,' she said. 'But *au revoir*, I hope.'

She cast one look around and then followed Henri out to the car, waiting until he opened the door and ushered her inside. As he settled himself inside the driver's seat she leaned forward.

'Henri, will you do me a favour?'

'You look just like your sister when you ask that,' he said suspiciously. She smiled.

'Can we go via the beach? You remember the beach I went to with Akil that first week? I just want to walk on the beach one last time, see the sea so I can remember it.'

She crossed her fingers, hoping that Henri wouldn't point out that she lived by the beach and could see the sea any time she wanted, but simply nodded as he turned on the engine. Clem sat back and pulled her phone out of her bag, typing a brief message.

I'm on the beach. Can we talk?

It wasn't a long drive, but Clem looked out and learnt every piece of it by heart as she pondered the conversation that awaited her—if Akil showed up. She knew one thing: she couldn't allow her future to be decided by Akil. If for whatever reason he changed his mind, if he decided that he'd been right all along and that love was too messy and unpredictable, if he decided he wanted that diplomatic polite marriage after all, she couldn't blame him, nor could she use that as an excuse to run home and hide from the consequences of her decisions.

She had to decide whether Asturia was part of her future or not, not Akil. She had to set the boundaries for any future relationship with her family, not him. She'd been passive long enough. It was time she came out of the shadows. Of course she wanted Akil by her side when she did, but thanks to him she was strong enough to do it alone if she had to.

She just hoped she didn't.

It was mid-afternoon by the time they reached the beach and the car park was busier than she'd seen it, families unloading picnics and groups of teens with surfboards. Many stopped to stare curiously at the limousine.

'Don't open the door for me, Henri,' Clem asked as he pulled the handbrake. 'I don't think anybody will mistake me for my sister, but if they see you acting all chauffeurish someone might put two and two together and make six.'

Sure enough, although a few people stared at her as she opened the door and slid out, no eyes widened with recognition and no one showed any sign of being interested in taking her photo or speaking to her. How different it must be for her sister, not able to even have a simple walk on the beach without Henri's presence to keep onlookers away. If Akil was right, if her sister was prepared to risk scandal and have Clem close by, then was Clem prepared to be the scandal? To be stared at and whispered about and photographed?

With her sister and Akil by her side, she could weather anything.

Clem slipped off her shoes and walked barefoot onto the beach, heading towards the shoreline where gentle waves lapped the sand, holding up her skirt so she could wade in up to her ankles, tipping her head up to look at the sky, the same deep blue as the sea. How she loved the smell of sea air, the salt and water and air combining into something more than the sum of its parts. It smelt like home. She could live anywhere as long as she could feel sand beneath her toes and submerge herself in the sea.

She checked her phone, there was no message, no answer from Akil, but there was a brief message from her sister.

I just want to say that whatever you do decide I have your back, always. I'm proud of you and I'm proud to have you in my life and I am happy to shout it from the rooftops to anyone and everyone if that's what you want. I love you, big sis.

Clem swallowed. She'd cried more than enough today, but it was hard to read the message through blurry tears. She quickly sent a reply.

Right back atcha!

Casting a hopeful look back towards the harbour, Clem continued her slow wade through the soft surf feeling freer than she had done for longer than she could remember. Free of worries, free of insecurities, free to be herself whoever and whatever that meant.

Without allowing herself to think what she was doing, she headed back to the beach and pulled her dress over her head, wrapping her phone in it and laying them on her shoes, and then she turned to wade right back in, heading out until she was waist deep and then diving into the waves, submerging herself, letting the water wash away the last of the doubt and the insecurity. Not the grief; that would never quite go, but with time she would learn to manage it.

As Akil left the castle his phone buzzed and his heart rate sped up, only to decrease when he realised it was from Arrosa.

Whatever Clem wants, whatever Clem decides, I will always back her.

He inhaled, relief filling him. He didn't necessarily need the Princess on his side, but he did need her on Clem's. He replied quickly.

Thank you. I've just had an interesting conversation with your father, I think we've reached a similar consensus.

He sent the message and jammed the phone back into his pocket as he reached the car, unlocking it and sitting behind the wheel trying to decide where he should go, what he should do. In one way nothing had changed since he had left Clem and yet at the same time everything had changed. He understood her position a little bit better, thanks to his conversations with Arrosa and with the King, and he knew that he could promise with truth that if Clem decided to stay she wouldn't be reliant on him, but that her sister would also have space for her, that there was the possibility of a more open relationship with her father, but they were just words. How could he make her see his truth when through fear for herself and love for her sister she'd erected barriers so tall and so thick it would take more than words for Akil to battle through them?

Think, he told himself fiercely. *Think.*

Finally Akil jumped out of the car and half jogged through the streets until he reached his home, letting himself into the apartment where, after quickly feeding Tiger, he rooted around looking for his spare key. Pocketing it, he checked his watch, still not sure if Clem was meant to be heading back to the UK that night, and wended his way through the maze of alleyways behind his apartment until he reached the small jeweller's shop where he and Clem had browsed just a few days before.

The shop specialised in sea glass, and Clem had exclaimed at the beautiful turquoise and greens of the polished jewels. Akil stepped inside and selected a keyring and a matching necklace, quickly paying before jogging back to his car. He slid inside and took the key from his pocket, carefully fastening it onto the keyring, and put the keyring and necklace onto the passenger seat. Right, he had a plan, he just needed the girl.

He pulled out his phone to check it again, his heart speeding up when he saw her name. She was on the beach. That had to be a good sign. He didn't need to ask which beach, quickly starting the car and driving as quickly as he legally could out of the city and across the hilly terrain until he reached the harbour. To his relief he saw her limousine parked up at one end of the car park, Henri leaning against it, the usual inscrutable expression on his face. Akil parked next to it and got out, palming the key and necklace and putting them in his back pocket.

'Is she still here?' he asked, and Henri nodded.

'She went for a walk.'

'How strict are your instructions? Is it a case of getting her to the airfield no matter what, or is there some flexibility?'

'I think they were open to interpretation,' Henri said. 'She'll be safe with you?'

'Always.'

Henri nodded. 'Her bag is in the car.'

It was almost heartbreaking to see how little she had with her, just one small duffel bag that fitted even in Akil's tiny boot. He locked the car and nodded one more time at Henri.

'Thanks for looking after her.'

Akil set off for the beach, standing on the edge and looking out across the sands. It was busy, families gathered for picnics and groups of teens sunbathing and splashing in the waves. He scanned the scene carefully, looking for a single figure walking alone, but couldn't see Clem anywhere. He was going to have to play this one by instinct. He navigated his way through the crowds, until he reached the quieter section a little further away from the harbour. There was still no sign of her.

'Where are you, Clem?' he muttered, looking around, his attention snagged by a piece of material waving in the wind, the same green as the dress Clem had been wearing earlier. He walked over to see the dress neatly folded on a rock, her shoes underneath and, turning, he looked out at the sea. There she was, swimming strong and sure like the naiad he called her, complete in her own natural habitat.

Akil didn't stop to think, unfastening his shirt, kicking off his trainers and discarding his trousers, leaving his clothes in a heap on the sand beside her dress. He walked quickly into the surf and struck out to join her.

The sea was coolly refreshing, filling him with hope and anticipation as he recalled the last time they'd swum together and the time before that—swimming usually ended up with them in bed, salty damp limbs curled around each other. It didn't take him long to reach her; she'd stopped to tread water, her face tilted up to the sky, and he swam up to face her.

'Nice day for a swim,' he said, and she started, submerging for a second then resurfacing with a gasp. His heart pounded at the sight. She was in her underwear, a pale lemon lace, that clung to her wet curves, her hair sleeked back.

'You scared me,' she said through her splutters.

'I scared you? You're not the one who found a small pile of clothes on the beach with no sight of you to be had,' he pointed out and she smiled up at him.

'I was bored waiting for you and the water looked so refreshing. I feel more like me when I'm in the sea, like a different person, a better person.'

'I'm sure you were a mermaid in a different life.'

'I'm sorry,' she said suddenly, the smile dimmed. 'I am so sorry for what I said earlier today. It's not that I didn't love you, that I don't love you. I do, Akil.'

'I know,' he said—and he did know. Knew with every fibre in him.

'But I was scared. Scared of what my life might be like here if my father decides he doesn't want me here, scared of what my life would be like if you tired of me, if you found me too complicated. Your life is so different from mine, Akil, what you need in a partner is so different from who I am. It's not as if you're unaffected by Court decisions. If my family don't want me around then that will affect you. Affect things that are important to you. I don't want that to happen to you, but, more than that, I don't want to see the look on your face when you realise I'm hampering your career, that I'm in the way. I've seen the look before, you see, on my father's face. I couldn't bear to see it on yours.'

Akil fought to find the right words. 'Clem, you will never see that look on my face, because I will always be proud of you, always want you by my side. I don't know what the future holds for you and your family, although I hope it will be better than what you anticipate, but even if they wanted to banish you completely, never recognise you, I'd still be proud to call you mine. I'll always be proud that you're mine. And you are mine,' he said possessively fiercely, exultant as she nodded.

'I said that all I wanted was someone to love me, and put me first, then here you were offering me just that and I was too terrified to reach out and take it. I'm still scared, Akil,' she admitted. 'I like to project this image of myself as fearless, and in some ways I am, I can go on stage in front of thousands without a single nerve, but when it comes to my heart I'm the biggest coward of all.'

'I meant what I said, Clem. I love you and you will always have a home with me if you want one. I don't want some dull and respectable marriage of convenience to further my career, I want a straight-talking, big-hearted English girl who is happiest in the sea, and thinks nothing of trying to cram twenty activities into one day. I want you and I love you, and I think you and I can do great things here in Asturia; you're already *doing* great things.' He swam closer and touched her cheek, willing his truth into her. 'The work you have started in the hospital is inspiring, Clem. I meant what I said earlier. I'm sure we can find ways to expand it if that's what you want. But if your family make it too difficult for you to be here and that really hurts you, then I'm open to other possibilities. I'm not saying it would be easy, politics isn't really the kind of career that translates well to other countries, but I've had invitations to lecture before and offers of fellowships. I could make it work.'

Clem gazed at Akil wonderingly. 'You would do that for me?'

He smiled into her eyes. 'I hoped you might know by now that I would do anything for you.'

It wasn't just the words, it was the sincerity in his voice and Clem knew that he meant every word, that Akil would walk away from the promise he'd made his father, from the title, from his life here if she asked him to, not because it would be easy or he wanted to, but because her happiness mattered to him. But that kind of strength had to run both ways.

'I don't want to run away. I love it here. I love it here because of you, because of the Asturia that *you* show me, the country that *you* love. The country you dedicate yourself to with your job, with the volunteering you do, with everything you are. How could I not love it? You inspire me with everything you do. I hope that if I stay I can be the kind of asset you need. I'm not really sure how to work a room, but I can learn. It's just another form of acting after all.'

Akil laughed at that, pulling her closer, and she moved in to meet him, her hands on his shoulders, legs entwined as his lips met hers in a brief kiss that sent them both back under the surface. She held onto him as she kicked her way back up, kissing him again as soon as they hit the air.

'My naiad,' he said, smoothing her hair off her face, and she leaned into the caress. 'Could you bear to come back to shore?'

'Maybe this once,' she said, holding his hand as they made their way through the waves back to where they'd abandoned their clothes. It was still so warm that the water began to dry on her skin as soon as they left the sea, and she pulled her dress over her underwear while Akil shrugged his shirt back on, leaving it open. She reached out to run her hand down his chest, enjoying the play of muscles and his intake of breath.

'I've got something for you,' he said, looking uncharacteristically nervous as he picked up his jeans and slid his hand into the pocket. 'I don't want you to feel like you never have a home, Clem. This is yours, for always, to use every day, I hope, but if not whenever you want to.' Clem blinked as she looked at the key, attached to a beautiful turquoise oval of sea glass.

'What's this?'

'It's a key to my apartment,' Akil said, smiling down at her. 'You said the first time you visited that it felt home like. I'm glad you think so because I'd like it to be your home for a while at least. Maybe at some time we could look for a place together, somewhere by the sea, with direct access so you can swim to your heart's content.'

She turned it over, letting the sea glass catch the sun and watching the metal glinting, the symbolism almost more than she could take in. 'You've given me a key?'

'Maybe it's not the most romantic of gifts...'

'It is, it's the most romantic thing I've ever received.' She stepped over the sand and cupped his face in her hands, kissing him fiercely, putting all her love and longing into the embrace. 'It's perfect, Akil, it's absolutely perfect. Thank you, and yes, I would love to have a key to your apartment and yes, I would love to stay there with you and one day move to a house by the sea. I need to go back to Cornwall first. I need to pack up my mother's things and decide what I need and move Gus across. I hope Tiger won't mind a roommate.'

'I know parliament is due back, but I would love to come with you, to see the place you grew up and meet your friends.'

'That would be perfect. I don't believe in ghosts, but the cottage still feels like my mother. I would love her to meet you. I know that sounds silly…'

He slipped an arm around her shoulders. 'It doesn't sound silly at all. I'd be honoured.'

'Oh,' she remembered. 'I have something for you too. I was going to ask Henri to give it to you.' She felt in her pocket and brought out the paper bag. 'I bought it the day we first went on the boat, with matching bracelets for Rosy and me. My mother loved trees the way I love the sea. She always wore nature-inspired things but trees were extra special to her. The very first campaign I remember was her trying to save an old oak from demolition and she got involved with at least two bypass protests—chained herself onto branches and everything. At the time I thought it was totally embarrassing and wished she could just be normal, now I'd give anything to chain myself up next to her. Anyway, I saw these and thought of her.' She handed him the bag and said shyly, 'If you don't like them…'

'I love them.' He held up the delicate cufflinks. 'I'll wear them to the Senate and let myself be inspired by your mother.'

'Be careful, who knows what she'll make you vote for?'

'She raised you, didn't she? I trust her instincts.'

'I think she would like you, Akil Ortiz.' Clem pressed herself close and kissed him, luxuriating in the feel and taste and solidity of him. This wasn't just a fling, this was real, as real as she wanted it to be. She was no fool. She knew relationships needed work and compromise, but she also knew this man was worth it.

'I know it's too early,' he said at last. 'But I want you to know that at some point this year I am going to ask you to marry me. There's a lot to work out, where we'll live, what path we'll take, but as long as we're together we can do it.'

'And I want you to know that I will say yes,' she told him, blinking back happy tears. 'That my home is where you are. I do have one condition…'

'Anything.'

'That once a month we sail away and for at least one night.'

'I'll build it into our marriage vows,' he promised, and she laughed.

'I love you, Akil. Thank you for giving me the space to figure out who I am and what I want, thank you for believing in me. Thank you for loving me.'

'That's the easy part,' he told her and then he kissed her again until she was lost in him. She didn't need a stage or an audience to feel validated any more; she wasn't lost. Thanks to Akil she knew exactly who she was and what she wanted.

'I love you,' she whispered against his mouth and felt him smile.

'And I love you, and I am more than ready to demonstrate how much. Let's go and let your father know that, thank you, but you won't be returning to Cornwall just yet, and then I suggest a few nights at sea, while we get used to this for ever thing.'

'That sounds perfect.' She kissed him again and then, his hand clasping hers, turned towards the harbour. Akil was by her side and had vowed to stay there; she wasn't alone any more. She had a family: a sister and this man. She had a place. She looked up at the late afternoon sky, the sun still beating down, and raised her face to the warmth, sending a moment of love towards her mother, wherever she was, before allowing Akil to tug her towards the harbour. Towards their life together. Their future. She couldn't wait.

* * * * *

THE
SINGLE DAD'S
ITALIAN
INVITATION

SUSAN MEIER

MILLS & BOON

CHAPTER ONE

THE FIRST FRIDAY in June, Wyatt White's limo stopped in front of the Montgomery, one of Manhattan's premiere residences on the Upper East Side. He slid his eight-month-old daughter Darcy out of her car seat. Careful in a way only a single dad knew how to be, he hoped she'd sleep through the jostling while he moved her to the carrier on his chest. But her eyes popped open, and she began screaming again.

"You need a nanny."

Wyatt peered at his business partner, Cade Smith. With thick blond hair and piercing blue eyes, he resembled a surfer more than a businessman, but Cade was shrewd. From the look on his face, Cade had calculated the risk and knew Wyatt couldn't take his sweet baby girl to the upcoming negotiations that Wyatt had to handle.

"No kidding. But I'm wheels up for Lake Como in four hours. That's not enough time to interview and hire someone."

"Call a service."

"I'm not leaving my child with a stranger!"

"The service would vet anybody they sent over.

Candidates might be a stranger to you, but not to the service."

"That's the worst argument you've ever made about anything, anywhere, any time."

Cade snorted. "You're too damned picky and it isn't just bad for poor Darcy. It's going to cost us the biggest deal of our lives. Trace will have your head."

Wyatt winced. Trace was the third partner in what they laughingly referred to as Three Musketeers Holdings. And he *would* have Wyatt's head. If Cade was the analyzer, Trace was a fixer. He saw problems and found answers. But Wyatt was the mastermind. He saw opportunity and located the path to get what they wanted and negotiate for it.

Which was why he was the one going to Lake Como to strike the deal with Signor Bonetti to buy his shipping empire.

He had to hope the old guy liked kids. Because he was going to have to bring Darcy with him to their meetings. The only alternative was to leave his baby— his sweet, innocent child—with his stuffy socialite parents. A problem because he'd never told them they had a grandchild. He had enough on his plate adjusting to being a dad. He wasn't ready to add his grouchy parents into the mix.

The limo driver was suddenly at the door, opening it so Wyatt could slide out. Juggling Darcy, her diaper bag and his briefcase, he hoisted himself onto the sidewalk.

Even if it was true that he couldn't keep a nanny because he wanted the best for his child, this was getting old.

He leaned down to be level with the limo door and told Cade, "I'll call you when we get settled."

"I'd rather have you call me when you get a nanny."

The astute driver quickly closed the door to end the conversation and, grateful, Wyatt turned to the Montgomery. Instead of the quiet, sedate building he loved, the place was a beehive of activity. Movers carried furniture and lamps out of the lobby, hauling them to a big box truck.

He squinted at the movers, wondering why they weren't using the service elevator. Then he saw the letters *FBI* printed across the backs of black jackets.

The world stopped for a few seconds. He couldn't hear the blare of taxi horns or Darcy crying. He kept staring at those big white letters.

FBI. Someone in their building had committed a *federal* offense.

That's why they weren't using the service elevator. They were making a statement. Seizing someone's property. Probably hoping the story would be on the six o'clock news.

Darcy amped up the volume of her crying, jerking him back to reality. He rubbed his hand up and down her back. "I'm so sorry, sweetie. I don't know what I'm doing wrong, and you can't tell me. But I'd do anything to help you."

Walking into the lobby with a screaming baby, he knew he was going to have to figure this out soon. Not merely because the FBI commotion seemed to be making his daughter's crying worse, but because he had to negotiate for a shipping company.

"Pete," he called to the doorman across a stack of furniture. "What's going on?"

"You don't know?" Pete shouted to be heard above the baby who had ramped up her crying again.

Guilt that he couldn't settle Darcy raced through him. When she'd been left with him a few months ago, he'd been aces. Now, suddenly, he couldn't get her to stop crying. "I miss a lot lately."

Pete chuckled. "I shouldn't laugh. The building's been full of trouble lately. First, you get a baby you didn't know you had. Then old Mrs. Remirez gets pneumonia. Now, Sophie's been evicted."

Wyatt blinked. "Sophie?"

"Your ex."

That was the problem with living in a five-condo building. It was like a small town. Everybody knew everybody and nobody's business was sacred. "She's being evicted?"

"Not by us. By the FBI. They're seizing her condo. Her mom bought it and pays the HOA fees. Apparently, she's been arrested."

Wyatt squeezed his eyes shut. He and Sophie had met in the lobby the day she'd moved in, and it had been like being struck by lightning. She was tall, beautiful and so funny he'd been captivated. He'd taken her to dinner that night and she'd told him that her mom, owner of a small but growing investment firm, had bought the condo as an investment for a client and needed someone to live in it. Another person might think she'd offered her the condo out of guilt for leaving Sophie with her dad when Sophie was only three. But Sophie assured him her mom had no such feelings. She'd gotten pregnant in a one-night stand and "tried" to make it work with Sophie's dad. When it hadn't, she dropped them both.

If the FBI was seizing a condo supposedly owned by a client of Sophie's mom's, that meant Erica had done something really bad. Maybe even lied about who owned the condo.

He scrubbed his hand across the thick beard on his chin. "Is she gone?"

"Nope. Still up there. She didn't get prior warning, so I'm assuming she's making sure they don't take things she bought herself."

Common sense warred with common decency. It had been three years since he and Sophie had dated. After they broke it off, their schedules were such that they never even bumped into each other in the lobby. Plus, he had a private elevator to the penthouse. They didn't have a connection anymore. It wasn't his job to check up on her.

But he also knew that she'd taken advantage of not needing rent money to cut her work hours in half and enroll in university. She desperately wanted a degree, even if she was starting at twenty-one instead of eighteen, so she'd thrown herself into her studies and she didn't have a lot of friends. Most likely, her mom was in an interrogation room somewhere. Her dad had remarried, had another family, and didn't bother with Sophie much. If Sophie was still in her condo, she was up there alone.

A river of genuine pain for Sophie surged through him. She was the sweetest, nicest, funniest woman he'd ever dated.

And she was alone.

He growled in frustration. With his baby screaming on his chest, he headed for the general elevator. He was not the guy who did missions of mercy. He was the guy who cut deals, grew businesses, made money. How the hell had he become the guy with the baby, who checked up on his old girlfriend?

The elevator bell dinged, and the door opened. He stepped inside. As the doors closed, he looked down at Darcy.

"You wouldn't happen to know if your mother casts spells, creates voodoo dolls...anything like that?"

Darcy only continued to sob.

He tried rubbing her back again. "I'm just saying... I seem to have a lot of weird things happening in my life and she's the only person I know who really hates me... Well, Sophie used to."

Which could potentially turn his checking up on her into an ugly scene.

He took a breath.

It had been three years. She couldn't still be angry. And he couldn't stand the thought that she was facing this alone.

The elevator bell pinged. He stepped out into the hall and walked past the parade of agents carrying Sophie's furniture.

Darcy snuggled against his chest, a move she usually made before she fell asleep, even if it was out of pure exhaustion from sobbing. Simultaneously relieved about Darcy and hesitant about Sophie, he paused at the open door of her condo. Sophie sat on a box in the middle of her empty space, her back to him as she stared out the floor-to-ceiling window. Her long yellow hair was a mass of unruly curls. The T-shirt she wore outlined her slim back.

Attraction and memories hit him like a freight train. He'd been crazy about her. She was funny and soft. Every day with her had been filled with simple fun—

Which was why she'd deserved someone a lot better than a workaholic businessman and a head full of expectations that wouldn't come true. He'd known it. He'd handled it. He'd broken up with her when she started talking as if she expected them to be together forever. She wanted marriage, kids, a house in Connecticut—the trappings of his parents' picture-perfect, fraudulent lives.

She wanted what his parents had. Probably because she didn't know happily-ever-after was a lie.

But he did.

To him, the breakup had been logical, a way to avoid worse pain in the future. He hoped she'd realized that in the three years that had passed and was no longer angry.

He stepped into the empty open-floor-plan area. "Hey."

She turned from the window with a weak smile. When she saw him, her eyes widened before drifting to Darcy.

They hadn't spoken in three years and in that time he'd fathered a baby. The whole building knew the general story, but he'd been careful with the specifics. It was normal that she'd be curious.

"Hey."

"Everything okay?"

She sat up straight, demonstrating her fierce pride. Her mom hadn't wanted her. Her dad struggled to raise her and remarried quickly after she was self-sufficient and basically moved on without her. She had a way of pretending none of that mattered.

"Oh, sure. I mean, it's no thrill being evicted, but this condo was temporary. I knew that."

Because it was an investment for one of her mom's

clients. Still, she'd been going to school, hoping to get through enough semesters that finishing would be possible.

When they were together, she'd just begun her freshman year, but she'd lived in this condo the six months they'd dated and three years after that. The stay had lasted a lot longer than she'd thought.

"You only have another semester to get your degree, right?"

She batted her hand. "Don't worry about that."

Hope for her rattled through him. "You finished?"

She shrugged. "No, I have two left. But maybe I don't want to keep going. It was a fluke that my mom showed up with a condo that needed babysitting. With what I know now, I could easily become someone's assistant or maybe manage a coffee shop or something."

He couldn't believe his ears. Where was the formidable woman who could conquer anything? When she'd told him the story of her mom offering her a condo to live in, giving her a chance to get her degree, she'd said she was the luckiest person in the world—

She couldn't possibly want to quit.

"Of course, you should keep going!"

"Look, some people in life are meant to run businesses and make big deals." She smiled briefly. "Like you. Other people like me are meant to be worker bees."

"That's crazy talk. You have a good mind. You have a talent for making people happy and comfortable. You *will* be somebody someday."

"Stop." The optimism she'd been trying to display disappeared from her voice and her pretty face. "I don't need a cheerleader. What I need is to be realistic and I am. I always knew the day would come when I'd have to leave. I was lucky to get over three years here. Now I need to be realistic."

Seeing her brought so low made his chest ache. Even *he* hadn't hurt her this bad. Damn her mother!

He glanced down to make sure Darcy really had fallen asleep. Seeing her softly closed eyes, he strolled a little farther into the room, keeping his voice low and even, almost a whisper. "If it's a matter of money, I could have this condo back in your hands in a few days."

She rolled her eyes and mimicked his lowered voice. "I don't want your charity."

"It wouldn't be charity. I'd buy the condo, let you live here until you finish school, then sell it…probably at a profit. You know how Manhattan real estate is. The longer I keep it, the more I make."

"Did you not hear what you just said? You'd *let* me live here."

Darcy woke with a start. She glanced around the strange environment and released a wail that would have curled Wyatt's toes had they not been in shoes.

Sophie's face crumbled. "I woke her! I'm so sorry!" She bounced off the box. Tall and slim in her faded jeans and bright yellow T-shirt, with elbow-length blond hair that swirled around her when she moved, she took Wyatt's breath away.

He needed a second before he could say, "No. You didn't wake her. She's been like a bear cub with a thorn in its paw for about a week. I have no idea what's wrong."

Sophie eased over. Darcy continued to scream.

"How old is she?"

"Eight months or so."

"Does she have any teeth?"

"She's a baby. Babies don't have teeth."

Sophie gaped at him. "Babies can start getting teeth as early as three months." She raced toward the kitchen, washed her hands and dried them in a paper towel, then walked to him again. "Turn her head toward me."

Wyatt did as he was told. Sophie opened Darcy's mouth and stuck a finger inside. "There, there, sweetie. Your daddy's a newbie, but I'm not. I have two half siblings. A sister and a brother. I've been through this." She paused. "Yep. Two teeth coming in on the bottom."

"Really? And it hurts so much that she screams? Why don't I know about this?"

"Why don't you know?" She frowned. "I'd have thought you'd have researched it by now."

Because he was too damned busy with a baby, a job and two partners eager to move into the next phase of their business.

Getting exhausted just thinking about it, he ran his hand along the back of his neck as Sophie continued to run her fingers along Darcy's gums. The scent of her shampoo drifted to him. He could see the light freckling on her pale skin. It had been three years since he'd touched her, yet his palms itched with the memory of how soft she was.

Still rubbing Darcy's gums, Sophie said, "There are two things to know. First, teething is painful, but also it's a strange feeling so it scares her. Second, see how I'm massaging her gums?"

Forcing his mind off his enticing memories of her supple skin, he nodded.

"That sooths the pain. You need some things for her to chew on."

He gaped at her. "Like a chew toy for a dog?"

She sighed. "Sort of but more like a teething ring. You can even get rings you freeze so they do double duty. They give her something to work her gums, even as the ice numbs them. You can find them online or at a drugstore."

Relief rolled through him. "Thank God."

A few seconds of massaging Darcy's gums had calmed her, but Wyatt wasn't fooled. This peace wouldn't last.

Still, he wasn't done with Sophie yet. He might not want what she did out of life, but he'd always liked her. He could help her. If there was one good reason to have money, it had to be the ability to use it to help people.

"Okay. You know I need to go to the drugstore immediately. So don't argue about me buying your condo back from the Feds. Let me do this for you."

Amazed that Wyatt could be so clueless, Sophie Sanders shook her head. It would be a cold, frosty day in hell before she'd let him buy her condo back and *let her* use it. It would be a cold, frosty day before she'd let him do *anything* for her. The tall, dark-haired Adonis, with the neatly trimmed beard that made him look like a sexy stockbroker, had broken her heart into so many pieces she had doubted she'd ever get it back together. There was no way she'd depend on him.

Actually, she was done with depending on anybody. Her dad had a new family. Her mom was a thief and a liar. Even the guy trying to help her had proven himself untrustworthy. So…no. She would be standing on her own two feet from now on.

"I'm fine." *She was fine.* She was twenty-four, almost twenty-five. She had experience waitressing and almost had a degree. Her mom might have let her use the condo, but Sophie had worked for spending money. Yes, she'd be moving out of Manhattan, but there were worse fates.

"Seriously, Wyatt, you don't have to worry about me."

"You are so stubborn!"

"I'm stubborn?" She laughed. "Look, who won't even hire a nanny."

"I've hired plenty of nannies."

"You simply don't keep them." She might not have spoken to Wyatt in the past three years, but a guy didn't get a baby dumped on his doorstep without people talking. She knew one of his former girlfriends had figuratively dropped Darcy in his lap and then gone. Pete had also told her Wyatt hadn't known the ex was pregnant. But he hadn't dodged his responsibilities. Which made his not being able to keep a nanny extremely odd. The doormen even had a betting pool. No nanny ever lasted more than a week, so betters had to choose a day *and* a time the nanny would race through the lobby with all her belongings. The winner was the person who picked the day and time closest to when Wyatt fired her.

"There's always something about them that isn't quite right." He glanced down at Darcy, then back at Sophie. "She's still not screaming."

"The massage will last a bit. It would last even longer if you would go to the drugstore already and get one of those teething rings that I told you about."

His eyes narrowed. His expression shifted. She knew the look. He was calculating something in his head. "You learned all this from helping with your brother and sister?"

"I lived with them for two years after my dad got married, from sixteen to eighteen when I moved out." She shrugged. "I picked up some stuff just watching my stepmom."

"You know a lot about kids?"

She frowned. "I know a *bit* about *babies*."

"I leave this afternoon for Lake Como, Italy. I'll be there for the next two weeks or so, negotiating to buy a company. I suspect it will take ten days, but we have the extra four just in case."

Surprised by the change of subject, she peered at him. "Bragging or complaining?"

"I desperately need someone to come with me to help with Darcy. I can't take her to negotiations." He winced. "I mean, I could. I've done it off and on for months… But this deal is important."

Suddenly his calculating expression made sense. "Are you asking me to come with you to take care of your child?"

He winced again. "I know. It really sounds awful of me, but you need cash and a place to stay, and I need someone to care for Darcy." He took a breath. "I would pay you handsomely. *Pay* you. For your *help*. This wouldn't be charity."

She said nothing, even though the money she could make would be a huge plus in terms of getting a new apartment, since it might be enough for a security deposit.

He shook his head. "We leave in four hours. I'll go to the drugstore now. Give you some time to think. But two things to consider. Number one, this is a one-shot offer. When I get to Italy, I will be calling a service. I have to have a nanny. I would prefer someone I know, and someone who seems to know what Darcy needs. You fit both categories. Number two, how long do you think it's going to be before the press gets wind of this?" He motioned around her empty condo.

"The press?"

"The FBI doesn't march up and down a street in the Upper East Side without the media noticing."

"I'm not worried. I'm not the one who stole from my clients."

He snorted a laugh. "That might be the reporters' angle. Innocent daughter of embezzler loses her home. They're guessing you're upset. They're guessing you might know stuff about your mom that will make a juicy story."

"I didn't even see my mom when she offered me this place. I got the keys from the doorman. We don't have brunch or girls' night or wine Wednesday. I know nothing about her. I was an available body to live in an investment property. If her secretary had been without somewhere to live, she would have just as easily offered it to her."

"Sounds like an interesting story to me."

She squeezed her eyes shut. Her nonexistent relationship with her mother added to her mom's embezzling did make one of those melodramatic made-for-TV stories.

Damn it. She hated being thought of as pathetic.

Wyatt said, "I think you need to get out of the city. Two weeks is long enough for the story to die down and for you to prep yourself for what you're going to say if they do find you." His head tilted. "And they will."

Damn it! They *would* find her if she moved to any

one of the five boroughs...or her father's house. Sheesh, of course, they would look for her at her father's house! And that was where she had planned to stay until she found another job and a rundown apartment she could share with roommates.

"Plus, if you come to work for me, you'll be under the umbrella of my legal team and PR team. They can say no comment for you a million times. Protect you."

She froze. That sounded a lot better than dodging reporters and hiding in whatever shabby apartment she could find—that is, if she didn't get fired from her current job. Actually, it didn't matter if she got fired. Her waitressing job in a diner didn't pay enough for expenses, let alone food. As of today, she needed a new, full-time job. But if her name hit the papers, she might have trouble finding someone who would hire her. Especially as a waitress in a classy restaurant where she could earn decent tips.

"The PR department can help you control the narrative. Better yet, they can help you create one." He frowned, running his hand over his beard as he thought. "You need a story. Even if we stick solidly with the truth, it must be written in such a way that it comes out correctly. You know. The PR department creates a paragraph or two of information that doesn't leave room for questions. Something you can say to everybody who approaches you."

Her brain homed in on that. She could see herself with her head high and her shoulders back, easily reciting a prewritten line or two that got her away from reporters and explained things to prospective employers when she went for job interviews.

"Keep talking."

"Nope. That's all I have to say." He headed for the door. "I'm leaving for the drugstore. The decision is up to you. The limo will be out front at three. Have Pete bring your bags down. If you're not there, I'll call a nanny service in Italy. It doesn't matter either way to me. But I think you'd make a good caregiver for Darcy—better than a stranger—and as I said, I'll pay you."

Sophie watched him leave, then with the FBI almost done taking all the things her mother had bought, all the furniture, all the lamps, all the rugs, she walked back to her bedroom to pack her clothes.

Though the idea of a legal team and a prewritten statement by professionals tempted her, she couldn't go to Italy with an ex who had seriously broken her heart—

Could she?

No. That was—

Was what?

She had no idea. She was homeless and would be the target of God knew what until the story died down.

The reality of her situation rolled over her. The FBI seemed to realize she didn't know anything, but that could make her story more interesting to the media. She'd be the abandoned daughter. The child her mom left and didn't even call to see how her life was going. She was literally the perfect avenue for the press to make her mother's arrest juicy and titillating. Stealing from clients was bad. Not even talking to your child? That made Erica Wojack heartless.

Sophie stretched away from the suitcase she was packing. She really did need a professional to word her story.

She took a breath, thought about what she was signing up for in Italy if she became Darcy's temporary
nanny. She'd be rescuing poor Darcy from having to go
to meetings. She'd dated Wyatt White long enough to
know that his negotiation sessions lasted ten or twelve
hours a day. That poor baby would be stuck in the carrier on his chest for hours on end.

No child should have to endure that.

But those long meetings also meant that she'd barely
see him. Add that to the fact that they'd broken up three
years ago and she was over him. He'd hurt her, and she
was smarter than to make the same mistake twice.

She did need time to think all this through. Especially how she would handle it in public.

She might not be going to jail, but the internet was
forever. How she behaved would end up on YouTube
and whatever new platform was being invented. Future
employers would see her either calm and composed
or frazzled—or angry. Part of her really wanted to be
angry. When she was little more than a baby, her mom
had left her with her dad, a blue-collar worker who just
made ends meet. She'd had no chance at school until her
mom plucked her out of her dad's apartment in Queens
and gave her a shot at fixing her life.

Only to have it all snatched away—not because her
mom had sold the condo—because her mom had *em-
bezzled from clients*. If she thought about it too long,
her head wanted to explode. And she did not want that
on the six o'clock news…or the internet.

Wyatt was right. She needed a story and it had to be
solid and well-written enough that it wouldn't make her
look pathetic or like a hothead.

She also needed two weeks out of New York, a break before she had to face the repercussions of the crimes of a mother she didn't even know.

She'd be crazy not to take him up on his offer.

CHAPTER TWO

Sophie came out of the Montgomery, hiding from reporters in sunglasses and a big hat. She took a deep breath and headed toward Wyatt's limo, carrying an overnight bag and a cosmetic case, and wheeling a suitcase behind her. Pete followed her with three more cases.

Tall, slender Wyatt straightened away from the back fender of his limo. He still wore his black suit and tie, and dark-haired Darcy still slept in the baby carrier on his chest. His striking blue eyes homing in on her things, he frowned. "That's a lot of stuff for two weeks."

"That's everything I own." She looked at what was left of her life. "I have nowhere to go. Nowhere to store any of it."

Wyatt grimaced. "Sorry. I forgot. How many bags you have doesn't matter. We're taking the company's private jet. You could bring a washer and dryer and we'd have plenty of room."

She knew he was trying to cheer her up, but she didn't feel like laughing. It was one thing to totally restart her life in Queens. She would have sucked it up and found a new job and an apartment and roommates. But face the press? Answer questions about the mother with whom she had no contact? Tell the world that she was the daughter of a thief and a liar? Not be able to find a fulltime job because of all the publicity?

She needed help figuring out a response for reporters or at least some time out of town while the excitement of her mom being arrested died down.

Pete began to stow her suitcases and Wyatt pointed at Darcy, asleep in the carrier on his chest. "I'll get her settled. Join us when you're done." He walked to the passenger's section of the limo and climbed inside, closing the door behind him.

Sophie waited for Pete to finish with her luggage. When he closed the trunk lid, she offered him a tip, but he refused it. "I'm going to miss you, kid."

The sense of permanence of what was happening rattled through her. She might never see Pete again. Never have a reason to walk on this street. She'd probably never have a reason to come to this part of the city.

Her heart stuttered as she looked at the beautiful building she'd called home for three years. Still, she mustered a smile for Pete. "I'll miss you, too."

He headed into the Montgomery and Sophie slid into the backseat beside Wyatt.

"I'm glad you decided to come with us."

"Yeah, well, you always were able to see all the angles of a problem. I was so gobsmacked this morning, it didn't occur to me that the press would want to interview me, let alone turn this into a spectacle. I'm amazed they weren't waiting on the street for me."

"I paid Pete to tell them that you'd sneaked out using the service entry and were long gone."

She glanced at him, surprised he'd done that,

though she wasn't sure why. He *did* think of everything. Always.

He smiled and a bubbly feeling filled her. She was
on her way to romantic Italy with the man she'd once
been crazy about—

To care for his child.

She gave herself a shake. This was not a pleasure
trip. He'd broken her heart. It had taken her a year to
get over him. She would not forget that.

In the car seat beside him, Darcy stirred. At first,
she kind of whined, then she whimpered, then Wyatt
slid a pacifier into her mouth.

The strangest realization drifted through her. She
knew she was on a mission of mercy, saving Darcy
from hours on end at meetings, but she suddenly realized that this little girl had been deserted by her mom
the way Sophie had.

"I give her the Binky before she wakes up completely," he explained. "This might help her go back
to sleep. By the way, thank you for your advice about
teething. Spoke to the pharmacist and bought enough
chew toys and numbing agents to keep her happy for
two weeks."

Sophie tried to smile but as the limo drove into traffic, it all seemed surreal. She and her ex-boyfriend's
baby were kindred spirits of a sort. The man who'd
dumped her like a hot potato when he realized she was
getting serious, the man who'd told her he'd never marry
and forget—absolutely forget—about having kids, had
hired her to care for his child.

That stung. How does a man who breaks up with her
because he doesn't want to be a dad suddenly become
father of the year?

She settled back on the plush limo seat and took two calming breaths, telling herself not to overthink this. If she let herself imagine the possible scenarios for how he'd become so good at caring for Darcy, she'd only feel like he'd lied to her about why he'd broken up with her. And if he'd lied, what was the real reason he didn't want her around anymore?

Had she done something wrong?

Or was there just plain something wrong with *her*?

Best to keep this simple. She knew how to care for a baby. He needed someone to care for his baby. Plus, she would barely see workaholic Wyatt once they got to Italy. That was the important thing to remember. She might have to get through a ride to the airport and then a flight to Italy, but she had a book to read. She could ignore him.

She *had to* ignore him. She couldn't lose herself in those blue eyes or remember how good they were in bed together—

The air in the limo suddenly became thick and heavy. Though there was space between them, her skin tingled from his nearness. She chalked it up to the bizarreness of being beside her ex-boyfriend—being *employed* by her ex-boyfriend—and looked out the window.

But thoughts of Darcy sneaked up on her again. She knew what it was like to be abandoned by the woman who'd brought her into the world. She knew the feelings Darcy would have when she went to preschool and grammar school and even when she graduated college.

Wyatt would have his hands full.

When they arrived at the private airstrip, staff made short order of their luggage as Wyatt jogged through the light rain to the jet's small stairway, with Darcy covered up in the carrier he held. She followed behind with her cosmetic case and overnight bag, feeling like a home-less person—which, technically, she was.

Her breath stalled when she stepped inside the jet. The space looked more like a living room than a plane. Seats were white leather. A wet bar lined the back wall.

Wyatt pointed at a door beyond the bar. "There's a bedroom back there. Once we take off, I'll put Darcy into the crib."

Awestruck and seriously out of her element, she said, "Okay."

He sat and began fastening Darcy into the car seat already attached to the seat beside his. "Your things can go in that overhead bin." He pointed at the space behind the seats but before the bar. "Sit anywhere you like."

She nodded, stored her cases, then sat on one of the plush seats. As the supple leather cradled her back and butt, she almost sighed at the luxury of it.

"Once we're airborne, there's a TV. Flight's long. Seven or so hours." He finished buckling Darcy in and glanced up at her. "Once Darcy's in the crib we can have the television as loud as we want out here. Bedroom's soundproofed. It won't matter."

"No worries." She displayed her book. "I came pre-pared."

"Okay. Then you won't mind if I watch soccer."

The less contact they had the better. "No. Watch away."

The plane took off. In minutes, the jet hit the right altitude for a smooth ride, and Wyatt took the baby to the back. When he returned, he plopped down on his seat and pulled a remote from the armrest. "She's in a deep sleep. I don't think I've ever seen her this out of it."

"That's good."

"Well, we'll see if it's good when we get to Italy. Seven-hour flight. Six-hour time difference means it will be five o'clock in the morning when we arrive. She might want to stay awake and play. She'll get adjusted to the time change, but we won't." He glanced at Sophie as he flicked on the TV. "Might be best for us to catch a nap on the flight too. I'm sure Signor Bonetti will want to meet with me first thing after we land, and I promised Trace I wouldn't take Darcy to any meetings. So, you'll be the one watching her."

"That's fine. Great." Being his nanny was her purpose for going to Italy with him, but those feelings of being a kindred spirit with Darcy suffused her again.

Wyatt got comfortable in the seat to watch soccer.

Though Sophie told herself to open her book, she covertly studied him.

Memories of their breakup eased into her brain again. He'd been so emphatic about not wanting kids. He'd called marriage and kids traps. He could have changed in the three years they were apart. But could he have changed so much that he could raise a little girl who'd been abandoned? She knew firsthand how difficult it was to grow up knowing your mother hadn't wanted you.

Unless Wyatt hadn't really broken up with her because of the whole marriage and kids issue? Had it been a convenient excuse and the real reason he'd broken up with her was actually something related to *her*? Maybe telling her he didn't want kids was a breakup line? Maybe the actual reason he didn't want her would

have made things complicated? Not the easy cutting
of ties they'd had when he told her they wanted two
different things out of life, which was something she
couldn't argue.

Confusion washed over her only to be booted aside
by suspicion that he'd lied to her...

She shook her head to dislodge all those thoughts, reminding herself she was overthinking again. She'd lost
her condo that day. Her mom was going to jail. She'd
taken a job as a nanny. That was enough to stress about.
She did not need to add to her list of worries.

She read for a bit, then the motion of the plane made
her sleepy. She kept reading but her eyelids drooped.

Wyatt glanced over and saw Sophie was nodding off. He
plugged in earbuds to send the noise of the soccer game
directly to his ears. He watched to the end, then he fell
asleep too. Sophie shook him when they were about to
land, telling him the copilot had told her to wake him.

Dazed, he raced back to get Darcy who was cooing
in her crib—with a dry diaper, meaning Sophie had
been attending to her. He prepared himself and Darcy
for landing and before long, he, Darcy and Sophie were
in another limo, leaving the private airstrip and heading
to the house Signor Bonetti had rented for him near the
small town of Bellagio on Lake Como.

Even in the predawn, half-light of the twenty-minute
drive, Wyatt could see lush greenery everywhere. The
enormous lake seemed to cradle the small towns that
rimmed it in a loving hand.

As the limo navigated the circular drive to their
home for the next two weeks, Sophie gasped. "It's a
mansion!"

The limo stopped by the well-lit front door, and he glanced at the spectacular three-story pale stucco house. "It's a villa."

The driver exited the limo, as two young men ran out of the house and headed for the trunk to get the luggage.

Sophie turned to Wyatt, one eyebrow cocked. "You hired staff?"

"Signor Bonetti said the villa came with staff."

She frowned, but he laughed. "Are *you* going to cook and clean for two weeks?"

She peered out the car window at the enormous building again. "I doubt I could clean the whole thing in two weeks, let alone cook, clean and care for a baby. What a place!"

Wyatt sniffed. "It's a negotiating tactic. Signor Bonetti wants me to see he has plenty of money and doesn't need anything from Three Musketeers Holdings."

Climbing out of the limo, still ogling the gorgeous house on the enormous estate, Sophie said, "Really?"

"Yes." He shook his head. "This guy knows every trick I know. It is going to be a blast wrestling his company away from him."

Sophie faced him. "Fighting is going to be fun?"

"First, it's negotiating. Not fighting." He lifted Darcy's carrier out of the limo. "Second, if it's not fun, I don't do it."

"Yeah. Right. No kidding."

She headed up the walk, shaking her head and he followed her. He almost blamed her snarkiness on lack of sleep then he realized that since she was one of the things he'd walked away from, she probably thought she was one also of the things he considered not fun.

Which wasn't true at all. She was the most fun person he'd ever met. But their life goals weren't the same. And he didn't want to have to explain why he didn't trust marriage, or family, or commitment. He didn't want to admit that his dad cheated, and his mom tolerated it. That their marriage was a sham. A front. His dad really hadn't committed to his mom when he took his vows and ultimately his mom didn't care as long as she kept her place in high society.

Worse, he didn't want to admit that his parents had used him as a trinket, the brilliant boy they trotted out to impress friends.

As he carried Darcy up the walk, all that reasoning coupled with Sophie's odd reaction to his comment about fun, and he stopped dead in his tracks.

He'd told her he didn't want kids, yet here he was with a baby.

He held back a groan. No wonder she was behaving oddly.

He'd told her one thing and done another.

Still, they weren't dating. He'd hired her to be a nanny. He didn't have to explain anything to her. In fact, it might actually be easier to let the oddness between them take root. That way they wouldn't have to worry about their attraction finding footing in the beautiful Italian countryside.

His brow wrinkled. *He wasn't worried about that... was he?*

No. They'd been apart three years. There would be no rekindling their romance. He rolled his eyes at the stupidity of that even crossing his mind.

In the big foyer with a two-story ceiling, an ornate chandelier and marble floors, Sophie reached for Darcy's carrier. "I found bottles in the little fridge in the plane's bedroom and fed her before you woke up."

He didn't let go of the handle. "Then she should be good for a while."

"Okay, but she could probably use a change of clothes. Maybe even a sponge bath," she said, attempting to grab the carrier again. "Since it's morning here. It wouldn't hurt to start her on the schedule she'll be following for the next two weeks."

He took a step back. "I'll do it."

She took a step forward, once again trying to finagle the baby away from him. "You go call Signor Bonetti."

He tugged Darcy back out of her hands. "He'll call me."

She put her fists on her hips. "You do realize you have to leave this child with me sometime, right? Otherwise, I'm not a nanny. I'm somebody who attached herself to your trip."

An uneasy feeling wove through him. He wanted to raise Darcy totally differently than how he was raised. He did not want her left with nannies—strangers—the way he had been. Still, this was Sophie, a woman he'd dated for six months, a woman he knew, a person he liked. *A person he'd hired.*

Plus, his partners were right. He couldn't care for her while he and Bonetti conducted business. Having someone he knew as Darcy's nanny, even if it was only for two weeks, was a good way to start acclimating himself to leaving her when they returned to Manhattan.

He handed the baby carrier to Sophie.

She sized him up as she took the handle, as if she was trying to figure him out. He thought of her probable confusion over him even having a child, let alone being an overprotective father and the need to explain himself tiptoed through him again.

Luckily, his phone rang. Seeing it was Signor Bonetti, he answered it as he walked back down the hall, looking for a quiet room or an office.

"Buongiorno!"

"Buongiorno, Signor Bonetti."

"We meet this morning?"

"Sure. I slept on the plane. Name a time."

They set a meeting for nine o'clock, and after they hung up, Wyatt asked a maid for the location of the nursery. Expecting her to speak Italian, he was surprised when she spoke perfect English. After she gave him the location of the nursery, she told him about the cook and housekeepers, as well as the gardener and driver.

As the maid walked away, Wyatt shook his head. Signor Bonetti was showing him how smart he was and his level of attention to detail. This guy was going to be holy terror when it came to coming to an agreement on the sale of his shipping company.

He climbed the stairs and walked back the hall to the last door on the right. Opening it, he saw Sophie with Darcy and he froze.

"Do you like the sundress?" she was saying to Darcy. "You've been in that pajama thing all night. I figured you were probably glad to get out of it."

Darcy cooed and gooed, and Wyatt's heart swelled. He'd never really seen her behave that way with any of her nannies. Though it was farfetched to think the baby already liked girl talk, or even knew what girl talk was, she seemed to like Sophie.

"At this point, I know you're not watching your figure. So when your daddy's off the phone we'll ask him what you can eat for breakfast."

"She likes peaches."

Sophie turned away from the changing table with a smile. "I like peaches too." She faced Darcy again. "Breakfast will be yummy."

"I sometimes mix it in with cereal."

"Nice." She winked at Darcy. "Some stable carbs for a morning of playing."

The baby laughed.

Darcy had never laughed for any of the other nannies. But she hadn't liked the other nannies. So maybe there had been a good reason for Wyatt to fire them? It wasn't him who'd made the choice. It had been Darcy.

Satisfied with that reasoning, he walked farther into the simple ivory nursery with yellow, pink and blue accents in blankets, pillows and curtains that billowed in the sweet Italian breeze coming in through an open window.

"We should probably scout out the kitchen, see if there's a maid or cook or a maid who cooks."

Sophie lifted Darcy from the changing table and put her on her hip. "Lead the way."

Wyatt held out his hands. "I can take her."

"And put her in that carrier on your chest again? Let's give her a break."

"The carrier is perfectly comfortable."

"Yeah. But variety is the spice of life."

Darcy giggled up at her.

Wyatt's heart swelled again. All his qualms about leaving Darcy while he worked disappeared.

"You are the cutest little thing," Sophie cooed to his baby girl as she headed for the door. "You've got your daddy's blue eyes and black hair and I've gotta tell you, your dad's going to go nuts over all the boys who will be chasing after you when you hit sixteen."

Not sure if he should be happy or confused that his child and his ex-girlfriend had bonded so easily, he followed her out of the room. "I won't go nuts. I understand life."

Sophie sniffed a laugh. "Right."

"I know she's going to want to date."

She stopped and faced him. "Wyatt, I know I brought it up, but don't let yourself think about this now. You will make yourself crazy. Enjoy her as a baby and a little girl. Save the worry about her dating for her teen years."

He considered that, more interested in Darcy's good mood right now than her behavior sixteen years from now.

Hoping against hope Darcy's easy acquiescence wasn't a fluke, but also needing to understand it before he trusted it, he said, "She's not crying."

Darcy babbled happily.

Sophie dropped a quick kiss on her cheek. "She's a cutie pie. Aren't you, sweetie?"

The baby laughed.

Wyatt still wasn't convinced. What if she was happy now, but started sobbing when he left?

"She hasn't liked any of her nannies. Cried for every one of them. And not one of them could get her to stop."

"Were you in the room when they were getting to know each other?"

"Yes. I'd hold Darcy to make sure she was calm and happy and could see the nanny in a positive light, hear her voice, get accustomed to her. Then when I thought she was ready I'd shift her over to the nanny and she'd cry every time." He stopped to glance at Sophie. Her pretty face, soft eyes and smiling mouth. "Your smile makes me want to smile back. Maybe that has something to do with it?"

Sophie shifted away, heading down the stairs. "I think it has more to do with the fact that you weren't in the room both times I changed her and got to know her." She shrugged. "Out of sight. Out of mind. She didn't think to cry for you to take her because you weren't around."

Damned if that didn't make sense. Good sense.

Sophie said nothing, but when they got to the bottom of the steps, she paused and asked, "Which way?"

There was that smile again. Not merely an indication that Sophie was a happy soul, but a link, a feeling that a person could let their guard down with her. She was so easygoing and happy he'd always felt like he'd known her forever. Even on the day he met her. Simply because she was so welcoming.

The urge to confide in her about Darcy's birth mother rose up, but he squelched it. Talking about Shelly infuriated him. They'd literally had a two-week affair—which she'd initiated—and then she'd disappeared from his life. When he was in a cynical mood, he suspected their affair had been all about her desire to get pregnant. But that thought more than infuriated him. They'd talked about birth control. She'd assured him she handled it. Then a little over a year later she was on his doorstep with a baby, telling him she had gotten a job offer in Dubai she couldn't refuse, and he was going to have to raise Darcy.

What person wouldn't be shellshocked?

It wasn't merely a breach of trust; it was disturbing

to discover she could so easily hand over a baby. One minute, she would have kept his child from him forever. The next, she was in his living room, telling him he had to step up. He would have never known he was a father, if she hadn't decided she wanted the career boost more than to be a mom.

Anger inched through him again. He calmed himself the way he always did. With the realization that he loved Darcy and how she came into this world and his life was of no consequence. There was no point in talking about it. No point in remembering how easily Shelly had broken the bond with their beautiful daughter and left her behind. Simple acceptance of Darcy had worked to dispel the anger so he could step into the role he needed to play. He'd stick with that.

"The kitchen's just down that hall." He pointed to the end of the corridor and the oak door leading to another area. "There's a cook. Tell her what you and Darcy want to eat, and she'll make it. I've got to get a shower and make myself presentable for the meeting." He leaned forward to kiss Darcy's cheek. "I'll be home as soon as I can."

"Take your time."

"No. I'll be home when I'm done." Because he wouldn't leave his little girl any longer than he had to. Not just to keep Darcy from the lonely childhood he'd endured, but because Darcy's mother hadn't wanted her.

Though if anyone would understand that it would be Sophie. But that was actually the problem. He didn't want to create any sort of bond with Sophie. Not even friendship. She needed him. He needed her. When these two weeks were over, they would part ways.

Getting too friendly would make that difficult.

CHAPTER THREE

Sophie spent an enjoyable day caring for the baby. The weather was gorgeous with a golden sun that smiled down on them as they lounged by the sparkling pool, while the scent of flowers, rich earth and the sea somehow combined to create an intoxicating aroma that drifted around them. She'd taken Darcy for two walks, one in the morning and one in the afternoon, just looking at gardens and grottos in the incredible green space.

That evening, with Wyatt already gone for eleven hours and showing no indication of returning soon, she tucked Darcy in, thinking Wyatt had been correct. This really was the perfect place for her to clear her head and relax.

As she turned away from the crib, the nursery door opened. Wyatt walked in. Wearing the white shirt and dark suit pants he'd changed into for his meeting, with his tie loosened and the suit coat gone, he had the whole sexy businessman thing going on. Memories of their life together flashed through her head, and she understood why it had taken her so long to get over him. He was handsome, cultured and hardworking. Normal in some ways. Perfect in others. Like when he was being romantic. Nobody kissed like he did.

Her breath stuttered in and fluttered out. Those kinds of memories were why she couldn't get too comfortable on this trip. She knocked them out of her brain.

"She's asleep?"

She nodded as he walked to the crib and glanced down at his little girl.

"This is one of the reasons I didn't want to leave her with a nanny. I make it a point never to look at my watch or phone while I'm with someone, so I don't appear overeager or bored. I had no idea I'd been gone so long."

"She's fine." His devotion to his daughter made her smile, even if she didn't understand it. "And you're fine. Take a few extra minutes in the morning with her. Or, better yet, you be the one to wake up with her tonight when she cries."

He faced her and caught her gaze. "You think I won't?"

She shook her head at his serious tone. "Lighten up, Wyatt. Nothing about you surprises me."

He took a step closer. "Really?"

His nearness brought a rush of heart flutters and gooseflesh. She almost said something sassy, something flirty. But this was the precipice. The right response from her could topple them over the edge into flirting, if only because that was familiar. They'd loved to banter, to be light and silly. And his one word was as much an innocent question as it was an open door.

Did she want to flirt with him?

Did he want her to flirt with him?

In the ten seconds that time stood still, she decided to say nothing. Just in case she'd misinterpreted his encouraging tone, or made something out of nothing, she held back every possible response from silly to sexy simply by stopping her tongue, not letting it form words.

He turned to the crib for one last look at sleeping Darcy. "Since she's fine, why don't we go to the patio for a glass of wine?"

Her chest swelled with longing, but her brain told her joining him for anything was not a good idea. Though three years old, the memories of them together that popped into her brain felt fresh and real. Best not to tempt fate.

"No. I'll pass. Darcy might have settled into our new time zone nicely, but technically we were up before dawn. Despite our naps on the plane, we're still on Manhattan time. I'm exhausted. I'm going to bed."

He eased his gaze over to hers. "There are actually a few things we have to discuss."

Oh, those eyes. Blue like the ocean, but serious and curious. She could always tell his mood by his eyes.

"We haven't talked salary yet. What if you don't like what I'm offering?"

The need to be with him, to be the lovers they'd been three years ago, swept through her, but common sense fought it back. She was susceptible because she was tired. She needed a good night's sleep before she could be alone with him at night in a scented garden with stars shining overhead. She was not here as his old girlfriend, his former lover. She was here as the nanny for his *baby*.

The reminder doused her longing and might have even made her a little mad that life had been so good to him and so dreadful to her. "If I don't like your offer, I guess I'll have to take the next plane back home."

His blue eyes shone with laughter. "So, what you're

saying is I should pay you less than the price of a ticket back to the states, so you're forced to stay with me if only for a ride home?"

The urge to say something sassy returned. To walk her fingers up the buttons of his perfect white silk shirt while she gazed in his eyes and knew…absolutely *knew*…he wouldn't be able to resist her.

Every time she'd decided to seduce him, he'd gone from purring like a kitten to growling like a tiger, taking her like a man starving…for *her*. Only her.

The memory of that power was intoxicating.

This was why she'd never even let herself run into him in their building. There was something delicious and spicy between them. Sexual. Possessive. They'd been so close, so perfectly attuned, that the last thing she'd expected was that he'd let her go. Whatever they had, it had wrapped around her heart and soul and tied them up in a pretty red ribbon as a gift for him. She'd thought he felt it too. But he couldn't have.

And she couldn't invite him into her life again, only to be set free when they returned to New York. She had experience with how difficult it was to lose him. She'd be a fool to set herself up for that again.

She turned to the nursery door. "We can discuss salary in the morning." She faced him again. "And make it good. I'm going to need a security deposit on a new place. Not to mention lamps and rugs and bed linens."

She left the nursery and entered her bedroom, her heartbeat like thunder. She hadn't forgotten that odd, possessive feeling, but she hadn't remembered its power. Part of her wanted to sink into the memory of him backing her into a corner and stripping her slowly so he could take what he wanted.

The other part knew that was dangerous ground.

And the biggest reason to stay the hell away from him. No breakfast. No coffee. No drinks after dinner… Hell, no dinner together.

No matter how smart she was, he was still gorgeous and masculine. He was a serious guy who also had a sense of humor. She'd loved him enough to want to marry him and have children. He did not feel that for her. It took a whole year to get over him. It would be foolish to forget that. Even being friends didn't seem like a good idea. She should just get through these two weeks.

The next morning, she woke to sunshine pouring into her window. And no sound from the baby. She pivoted to see the clock. Realizing it was almost nine, she bounced out of bed and raced to the nursery but stopped short of the door. She could hear Wyatt talking to Darcy. Gooing. Cooing. Laughing.

She cracked open the door to see him dressed in suit pants, a white shirt and a print tie, leaning over the changing table as he slid his little girl into a sunsuit. For a few seconds she stood and watched him with the baby he wouldn't have with her, letting the insult of that take root. Tempting as he could be, she needed to be reminded that he was pain in a suit.

Then she walked in.

He glanced over with a smile. "I let you sleep in because you seemed to be tired last night."

She had been tired the night before. Otherwise, she never would have let herself open the door to all those memories. But she hadn't forgotten how overprotective he was with Darcy. It was almost as if he didn't trust her—maybe anyone—with his child.

She could understand him changing his mind about not wanting to have children, but there was something odd about the leap he'd taken from not wanting kids to being the perfect father.

Unless he simply hadn't wanted a family with *her*. That made the most sense. Except that also meant the reason he'd broken up with her had been a lie.

She walked to the baby's table slowly, wondering if she should try to figure all this out or let it go. But his gaze fell to the skimpy tank top she'd slept in with pajama pants, and their infernal attraction arced between them again.

One flick of his eyes and they were right back where they were the night before.

The sermon she'd given herself as she'd climbed into bed popped into her brain. He'd hurt her worse than anyone ever had. And he'd do it again…if she let him.

She didn't want to go through another year of the pain of getting over him. Given their attraction, she had to be a little smarter about what she said, what she did and how she dressed around him.

She broke the powerful connection of their linked gazes. "If you can keep her another minute or so, I can get dressed for the day."

He returned his attention to Darcy. "Sure. No problem."

She left the room and Wyatt blew his breath out on a sigh. He lifted Darcy off the changing table. "You know, breaking up with Sophie had seemed like such a good idea at the time but I have to admit I more than missed her." He shook his head. "But that's wrong because she deserves better. I really could have screwed up last night. I was tired and she did such a good job with you that I was feeling friendly...and I shouldn't be."

The baby cooed and he laughed. "I know she's great, right? But we want different things. And I don't make the same mistake twice. Plus, this isn't about me. It's about her. Making sure she gets the good relationship she deserves."

Darcy's head tilted as if she was confused.

"I get it. You like me so you think I'm a safe bet for everybody." He kissed the top of her head. "But there's a big difference between being your daddy and being..." He frowned again, then finally said, "Sophie's boyfriend."

The word rattled around in his head. *Boyfriend* conjured up images of football games, proms and movie dates. What he and Sophie had, had been intimate. Sensual. And close. They were as close as any two people could be.

Yet somehow, he'd kept his secrets, avoided telling her about his parents and in general let her see only the best part of his life, refusing to think about his past when they were together, let alone tell her about it.

The nursery door opened again, and he started like a kid caught with his hand in a cookie jar. Sophie walked in dressed for the day in a T-shirt that caressed perfect breasts and shorts that showed off long, tanned legs, an indication that she still studied in the park as she had when they were dating.

His chest tightened and he remembered a hundred things best left forgotten by a man who didn't want to get involved with her again. Her bubbly laugh. Her soft moans when they made love. Her soft body.

He pulled in a breath and said, "I take it you're not going into town."

She took Darcy from his arms. Easily. Naturally. And he let her, confusing himself even more.

"If we do decide to go somewhere today, we can change." She headed for the door. "Right now, I'm going to take this little girl downstairs and have Mrs. P. make her peaches and rice cereal."

His brow puckered. "Who's Mrs. P.?"

She faced him with a grin. "The cook. She makes me anything I want for breakfast, lunch and dinner. If you get a free evening where you're eating dinner here, have her make the mushroom ravioli. I had it yesterday." She closed her eyes and sighed. "It is amazing."

Her closed eyes and the sigh reminded him of a particularly good memory they'd shared in the elaborate shower of the primary bathroom of his penthouse. His breathing stuttered and when he tried to talk nothing came out.

She didn't seem to notice as she turned toward the nursery door again. "You get yourself ready for your meeting with Signor Bonetti and we'll see you when you return this evening."

His attraction to her was beginning to annoy him, particularly since she didn't seem to have the same problem. He crossed his arms on his chest. "What if my meeting isn't for hours from now?"

Once again not seeming to be suffering from the same tumble of memories that he was, she turned and motioned toward his suit pants and white shirt. "You'd be in something comfortable."

Not only was she not reliving some of the more interesting moments of their relationship, but also she really did know him a little better than he let himself believe. He should walk away, but a devil inside him wanted one—just one—hint that she hadn't totally forgotten what they had, and he wasn't letting her get away until he got it.

"I still have to eat. So, you're stuck with me through breakfast."

"No. If I remember your work habits correctly, you always go over your notes before meetings. You go to the study. I'll have Mrs. P. bring in scrambled eggs, bacon and some strong coffee."

With that she left and something hot and insistent brushed through him. No matter if she was right. He didn't like her telling him what to do.

Of course, her remembering that he always went over his notes and even what he liked for breakfast actually could be considered the confirmation that she remembered more of their relationship than she was letting on.

His body reacted with a flurry of need, but he shook his head. What the hell was he doing? Trying to revive memories that would resurrect feelings that would lead to God knew what?

Was he crazy?

No. He was under a little too much pressure. Too much was riding on this deal. He didn't merely want it. He needed it to cement his place as Manhattan's premiere negotiator. Then there'd be no question in his partners' minds that when they needed him to, he could deliver.

There'd also be no question in his father's mind that Wyatt had surpassed him. Made something more of himself than his father had.

Sophie had to fulfill her job as nanny to Darcy in

order that Wyatt could succeed and that's all there was. Their nanny arrangement might have turned out to have certain unexpected difficulties—his attraction to her—but he was a strong man who would overcome them.

All he had to do was remember that this deal pushed him past his dad. Only in his early thirties, he would be worth more than his father and better established than his father could ever hope to be.

Then maybe he could get on with the rest of his life.

But to assure that, he needed to spend a little neutral time with Sophie. First, to get accustomed to being around her so that his brain wouldn't slip into fantasy mode every time she was in the room with him. Second, to make sure she really was a good choice for nanny. She was bossy with him. And she used her knowledge of him from their past relationship as a way to control their situation.

That ended this morning.

Sophie walked downstairs, toward the kitchen, still overwhelmed by the house that had been rented for Wyatt as he negotiated with Signor Bonetti.

With plastered walls housing paintings that she recognized as originals by masters, the downstairs reeked of money…but also class. She paused on the marble floor of the foyer and spun around once, making Darcy giggle.

"Oh, you liked that?"

Darcy babbled something that Sophie was sure was agreement. She laughed and kissed her cheek, even as Cora, the housekeeper who had introduced herself the day before, came through the door, wearing a crisp gray uniform and carrying a clipboard, as if the house had a regular cleaning schedule that had to be adhered to.

"Good morning, ma'am."

So classy and dignified. "Good morning, Cora."

The forty-something woman disappeared behind a door and Sophie took a deep breath, filled with awe. Everything about this house was perfect. Elegant. Even the servants were friendly while still crisp and respectful.

For a second, she felt like a princess in a castle then Darcy babbled, and she headed to the dining room so she could get the little one her breakfast. But she stopped suddenly as reality hit her.

She wasn't a princess.

She was one of the servants.

And despite the gorgeous accommodations, and nothing to do but play with a happy baby and lie in the sun, she couldn't forget she was hired help too.

She carried Darcy into the formal dining room with a long table and twenty chairs, feeling a little foolish as she slid Darcy into a highchair that had materialized after breakfast the day before. Equal parts of wonderful and overwhelming, having her every need attended to felt like part of that fairytale she seemed to be enjoying in her mind, but she was not here to be pampered. In fact, letting herself get accustomed to this life would cause a culture shock when she returned to New York and had to find an apartment she could afford.

She slid Darcy into the highchair as the door between the dining room and butler's pantry opened. The cook entered. With her dark hair pulled back into a severe bun, she wore the same uniform as Cora, but she stretched the fabric to capacity.

"Good morning, Mrs. P."

"Good morning, Ms. Sanders."

"It's Sophie. I'm an employee just like you."

Mrs. P. chuckled. "What would you and the wee one like for breakfast?"

"Peaches and rice cereal for the baby and fruit for me, please." She straightened away from settling Darcy in the highchair and slid onto the soft velvet seat beside it. "Mr. White is in the office working this morning. I told him I'd have you make scrambled eggs, bacon, dry white toast and some very strong coffee and have it taken to him."

Mrs. P. smiled. "Yes, ma'am."

"Sophie, remember?"

"Yes, ma... Sophie."

When she was gone, Sophie faced Darcy. "This might not be my life, but you know this is your life, right?"

The baby grinned and Sophie could see the beginnings of two little white teeth on the bottom gums.

"Your dad is wealthy and brilliant." She frowned. When they were dating, he'd tried to hide it, but she'd always worried that being brilliant was something of a burden for him. People expected things from him. No. People *depended* on him. Though his partners absolutely did their fair share after a business was added to their conglomerate, when it came time to level up, that onus was squarely on Wyatt's shoulders.

She'd always believed she was his release valve. They rarely talked about work. Though she'd met his partners at fundraisers and galas, any time he wasn't working he avoided discussions of business like the plague. Because Sophie was sure he knew the value of time off, of letting his brain rest, of compartmentalizing things so he didn't burn out.

Mrs. P. returned with rice cereal for Darcy and coffee and fruit for Sophie.

"Thank you."

Mrs. P. put her hands on her ample hips. "You should eat something more than fruit."

Sophie laughed. "Oh, trust me. I will. I haven't decided yet if I want a big fancy pasta lunch or a big fancy pasta dinner. But I'll be eating some big, fancy pasta something today."

Shaking her head, Mrs. P. laughed and headed back to the kitchen.

Sophie picked up the baby spoon and scooped out a portion for Darcy. "Don't pay any attention to my eating habits," she said as she slid the spoon in Darcy's mouth and was rewarded by an "Mmm" and some lip smacking.

"Grown-up women balance their food throughout the day but for the next decade or so you need lots of calories because you are growing."

Darcy grinned.

"That's right. Enjoy it while you can."

Eating her bowl of fruit, Sophie fed Darcy, then took her upstairs so they could retrieve the umbrella stroller. "You and I are going to take a walk around the grounds."

Darcy clapped. After slathering the baby with sunscreen, she carried her and the lightweight stroller to the foyer and through a side corridor to a sunroom that led outside.

Walls of glass allowed the morning sun to envelop

the room in a golden hue, as they walked through to a door that led to a stone patio.

They'd been out the day before, but after putting Darcy into the stroller, Sophie still paused to admire the conversation groupings arranged on the various sections of the patio, the pool and the gardens among the greenery.

The joyful sense that she was in the Garden of Eden enveloped her as she pushed the stroller toward a segment of wildflowers arranged around a statue of an angel.

"Wait up!"

She turned to see Wyatt walking behind her and frowned. "Aren't you supposed to be working?"

"You're the nanny. Not my keeper."

He was right. She had to remember that and behave—and speak—accordingly. "Okay."

"Where are you going?"

"Just around the grounds." She pointed at cobblestone paths that slid subtly through the rich green grass. "I pick a trail and Darcy and I travel over to see the gardens and statues." She glanced around. "It's so beautiful. The perfect way for her to get some fresh air and sunshine before she takes her morning nap."

"Make sure she doesn't get too much sun."

She laughed. "I'm not a rookie. If I remember correctly, that's why you hired me."

He didn't laugh with her. "I hired you to be sure she's well cared for."

Any residual good humor in her gut disappeared. That was his second reference to the fact that she was an employee. Not his friend. She understood that they needed to keep things professional, but there was no reason for him to question her. "I'm taking good care of her."

"Did you put sunscreen on her?"

"When I went upstairs for the stroller." She huffed out a sigh. "I might not be a real nanny, but I know how to care for a baby. And what I don't know I'll look up. We're fine."

He said, "Uh-huh," but he didn't appear to be convinced.

She took a second to study him then wondered if all this questioning was because they'd come so close to flirting the night before. A ripple of desire wove through her at the memory, but she shoved it aside. He'd hired her because he was desperate. In those minutes, he'd trusted her. Now, suddenly, he was suspicious. That she couldn't do a good job? Or that she wasn't right for the job? Was he thinking about firing her?

After all, they'd had a fabulous relationship, yet he'd still dumped her. And he might have dumped her with a lie. He'd said he didn't want a relationship or kids. Now he had a child.

The whole situation was confusing. And tiring. Extremely tiring when she had to second-guess everything he did.

And why did she second-guess? Because he was behaving strangely.

She knew Wyatt the lover, but didn't know Wyatt the businessman, or Wyatt the obsessive dad. And she didn't exactly like that guy.

What if coming to Italy with him had been the biggest mistake of her life?

She wheeled the baby toward a group of trees at the far end of the path they were on. "Go to work, Wyatt. We're fine."

CHAPTER FOUR

Things had not gone particularly well with him trying to figure things out with Sophie that morning.

Wyatt stirred cream into his coffee, having refused a glass of wine with lunch. Too many things were jumping around in his head. He was being driven crazy by his feelings about Sophie—which were really his own confusion about his longing to sink into their attraction, when he'd ended their relationship for damned good reason. And after today's nonnegotiating session with Bonetti, he now had an odd sense that the old man really didn't want to sell his company.

No. It wasn't an odd sense. Bonetti was beyond procrastinating and foot dragging. He diverted the conversations enough that morning and the day before that he hadn't said two words about his business.

"Your mind wanders. Do you not like lunch?"

They'd eaten at a small outdoor café. Twenty feet beyond their table a fence guided tourists along a path virtually on top of Lake Como. The place was littered with colorful flowers and smelled like heaven. Scents of pasta and sauces mixed with baked goods and greenery. And the ravioli he'd chosen had melted on his tongue.

"I love it." The intense look on Bonetti's face urged

him on, but he had nothing more to say about his food. He wanted to discuss the man's company, not lunch. "I'm just thinking about—"

What? If he said he was thinking about financing, Bonetti would jump to the conclusion he was worried about money. If he asked a direct question about his business, Bonetti would deflect.

Suddenly, it all seemed pointless.

Which really confused him. Normally, he loved difficult negotiations.

He motioned for the waitress to come to their table. "You know, I'm actually leaving my child with a new nanny, and that's distracting me. I think I'll go home and make sure everything is okay."

Deflect? Change the subject? Refuse to talk?

Wyatt could do all those too. If the man didn't want to sell his company, turning the tables might flush him out.

He gave the waitress one of his credit cards and rose. "We'll pick this up tomorrow."

The look on short, bald Bonetti's face was priceless. His eyes had widened. His mouth hung open slightly.

Wyatt walked away.

On the drive back to the villa, he wasn't sure if he'd let Bonetti get away with far too much because he was worried about Darcy or concerned about his attraction to Sophie, but a day with his baby and her nanny might cure both. He might not want Sophie bossing him around, but he did want her to take good care of the baby. An afternoon with them could show her that firsthand. Plus, time with her, getting accustomed to being around her again, would probably get rid of the infernal attraction.

Then, when he was satisfied both things were handled, Bonetti had better look out. He was tired of the old man calling the shots and stringing him along.

He drove the villa's sports car onto the winding driveway to the front door, parked and jogged inside. "Sophie!"

One of the housekeepers appeared in the foyer. "She and the baby are outside, Mr. White. In the pool, actually."

He nodded once. "Thank you." Yanking off his tie, he headed upstairs. He changed out of the suit, into swimming trunks and headed to the big sunroom, then the patio, then the pool.

"Hey."

Gliding the giggling baby through the water, Sophie looked up. "Hey."

She wore a pink bikini top that showed off her ample cleavage. As longing swished through him, Wyatt told himself to get used to it. That's why he was here. Outside. *With her.* He had to get accustomed to their blasted attraction, so it would have no power over him.

Her brow wrinkled when she squinted against the sun. "Thought you were with Bonetti all day today?"

"I was supposed to be." He glanced around at the beautiful grounds, surrounded by trees. An opening caused his gaze to stop, and he peered through. "Are there tennis courts back there?"

Sophie laughed. "Yes. There's also a field with soccer goals. When Darcy gets older, you'll have to rent this place again so she can take advantage of all the stuff she's too young to appreciate now."

With one final glance around the beautiful grounds, Wyatt kicked off his flipflops and sat on the edge of the pool, dangling his feet in the warm water. He wasn't sure if it was being away from Bonetti, seeing how happy Darcy and Sophie were or the general peacefulness of the isolated grounds, but suddenly he felt foolish, ridiculous, for believing he was powerless against an attraction to a former lover and for worrying about Darcy when it was clear she was happy with Sophie.

He took a breath and blew it out slowly.

Sophie peered at him. "What's up?"

"Nothing. I just couldn't handle two more minutes with Signor Bonetti."

"Are you sure? 'Cause it sort of feels like you might be checking up on us."

He moved his feet through the water. Checking up on them might not have been his primary purpose but it had been one of three. Still, they were fine, and he had lost patience with Bonetti more than he'd worried about Darcy.

"No. I'm not checking up on you."

Her face changed. The questioning look changed to humor. "Yes, you are!"

"All right. A little." He didn't want to admit that he had odd feelings around her. The attraction was one thing. It was natural that memories of their good times would pop into his head. He believed he could end that with enough interaction that the memories would stop. His not trusting her with the baby dripped of paranoia. He could see Darcy liked Sophie. He could also see she was good with the baby.

So why did this odd feeling about her and the baby persist?

He couldn't dislike that his baby was happy with someone other than him. Not when it served his purposes.

"Truth be told, I used my needing to make sure everything was okay with you and Darcy to get away from Bonetti. He's making me nuts."

Sophie lifted Darcy to her hip then waded farther into the water where it was deeper. Darcy let out a squeal of delight. "Why?"

"Why?" He gaped at her. His nerve endings shot to high alert seeing Darcy in water that would be way over her head if Sophie dropped her, even as complete disgust with Bonetti sent his impatience into the stratosphere. "The man doesn't want to talk business. We've talked soccer. We've talked about Italy. We drink wine. We eat. His kids arrived this morning and sized me up. But we have yet to discuss his shipping company."

"It's only been a day and a half."

Annoyance rippling along his skin, Wyatt slid into the water. "I've negotiated for bigger businesses in a day and a half."

"You've also spent weeks letting a perspective buyer dangle hoping to get the price up for one of your businesses. Was it the holding company for grocery stores?"

He sighed. "Yes. But that deal made me and my two partners billionaires."

"Ah."

He frowned. "Are you saying I'm getting back what I give?"

She feigned innocence. "Me? Why I'm just a simple college girl."

He blew his breath out in disgust. "Right. You're one of the smartest people I know."

She laughed and shook her head. "Because I can keep up with you?"

"Well, yeah. Not everyone can." He frowned again,

as memories flitted through his brain. He had always enjoyed talking to her. They didn't discuss his business often, but it hadn't totally been off the table. Neither had politics, religion, art. All things he could bring up to avoid talking about himself, especially his past.

"Anyway, since I'm home I should spend time with Darcy." Walking in the waist deep water toward Sophie, he pointed at the happy baby in her arms. "We'll chill out, and I'll get my bearings back. So that if Bonetti calls to get together tomorrow, I'll be ready."

She passed Darcy to him. "Okay."

He took the baby, then watched Sophie head for the pool steps. "Where are you going?"

"Out. You said you wanted to spend time with the baby."

She climbed the first two steps of the ladder, exposing her little pink bikini bottom and long slim legs. His pulse scrambled and his breath stuttered, reminding him that he hadn't merely come home to avoid Bonetti and see Darcy. He had to get rid of this unwanted attraction. And he'd decided the only way to do that was through spending enough time together that she stopped being a novelty in his life.

"I sort of thought we'd enjoy the day together. The three of us."

She paused and faced him. "Are we back to you not trusting me?"

He winced. What else could the odd feeling he had around her be? "You've only been her nanny two days."

"Yes, but I took care of her *myself* yesterday and this morning. And when you surprised us by coming home early, you found us in the pool, laughing. She's fine. *We're* happy. Actually, we're having fun. It's very nice here."

He sighed. "I know."

She slid back into the water and leaned against the pool wall. "So what's really going on with you?"

He said nothing.

Resting against the pool, she studied him. "You want to know what I remember the most about our relationship?"

Oh, Lord. He wasn't sure if did. If she started talking about their sex life, his libido would not be able to handle it.

When he didn't answer, she said, "It was that you were intense."

He laughed with relief. That he could address. "I buy and sell billion-dollar companies. The fates of thousands of people rest in my hands. I think I'm allowed to be intense."

"Okay. I'll give you that. But I'm talking about being intense about your secrets."

His chest froze. "My secrets?"

"We dated six months. I never met your parents. You rarely talked about yourself. We went to basketball games, out to dinner, fundraisers, gallery openings. We talked about what was happening in the moment, but not really about anything personal. It was like I knew you very well but didn't know you at all. And now, here I am, nanny for your little girl and it's clear there's an issue. Since I've never done anything wrong, never given you a reason to mistrust me with her, I have to assume one of two things. First, something happened in your past to make you so suspicious of people." She caught his gaze. "Or, like you're doing with Signor

Bonetti, you're looking for yourself in other people so you can strike first before they manipulate you or cheat you or steal from you."

For a few seconds, he only breathed, so taken aback by her observations that his brain stalled. "Are you telling me I'm a bad person who expects people to do bad things because I do bad things?"

She shrugged. "I don't know. Maybe."

All his beliefs about their relationship flipped on their side. He'd thought she adored him. Only saw the good in him. Wouldn't have believed he had faults. He almost couldn't fathom that she had such negative opinion of him.

The need to defend himself could not be squelched. "That's not it at all."

"So, you're a good guy?"

He always thought he was. Wasn't he?

Sheesh. Now she had him doubting himself.

He straightened up, yanking Darcy higher on his hip. He *was* a good guy. He was fair to his employees, loved his partners like brothers, took in his daughter when her mother abandoned her.

"I *am* a good guy."

"Okay."

Her halfhearted agreement caused the need to defend himself to swell again. Especially when he began seeing their breakup though her eyes. He'd hurt her. Then he'd avoided her. Or maybe they'd avoided each other. He'd done it for her. But what if she didn't see it that way? What if she saw his silences, his unwillingness to discuss his family, as secret-keeping? And mistrust—

Of her.

Worse, she clearly saw his negotiating tactics as heavy handed.

And what if believing wrong things about him, about his motives, about how he'd felt about her had caused her even more pain?

Enough pain that she hated him?

Was that why she was so standoffish with him now? Why she hadn't jumped at the chance to get out of Manhattan but had to think about it?

Because she didn't like him?

He couldn't stand the idea that she didn't like him, that she'd gotten everything wrong because she'd judged him on the secrets he kept, not the great time they'd had together.

He had to fix that.

"Something bad did happen to cause me to be careful with people."

She peered across the shimmering blue water at him. "Had to be pretty bad if you never got beyond it."

"I got beyond it, but it was serious enough that I realize it formed a lot of my opinions and behaviors."

She studied him. "I'm going to need a little more context."

He took a breath, then another. It wasn't like his family life was a secret. Most of Manhattan knew. "My dad cheated on my mother."

Her head tilted, as if she didn't understand what that had to do with anything.

"I caught him."

Her eyes widened. "Yikes!"

The intimation that he'd caught his father in a compromising position almost made him laugh. "No. I didn't *catch* him the way you're thinking. They were at lunch." He floated Darcy through the water, avoiding Sophie's questioning gaze, as he tried to figure out how to explain this in such a way that it shed the right light on his behavior and raised her opinion of him.

"My parents had this 'perfect life' thing going on. My dad was successful. My mom was a pillar of society. I caught my dad having lunch with a woman at a pier. They were in a corner, kissing. It was an accident that I was there. A combination of skipping school and knowing a kid who had access to his dad's boat. In my fourteen-year-old enthusiasm, I confronted him. He left the woman and all but dragged me to his car. He didn't say a damned word for the two hours it took us to get home, but when we got there, he told my mom what had happened.

"They sent me to my room and had a fight, but the next day it was like nothing had happened. Eventually, my mom explained that she and my father decided to reconcile. I thought it was good news. But I caught my dad again and again and again because now he didn't have to hide who he was."

Sophie studied him. "And that makes you distrust everyone?"

"No." He shook his head. "Well, that's part of it. My parents sent me to the best school, and I was a star. But when I wasn't, there were consequences."

Her expression turned horrified. "They beat you?"

"No. They gave me sermons about who I was and what was expected of me and then they'd fly off to Europe or Japan and leave me with a nanny. I never felt like a person. I always felt like a commodity. And no one knew. Everyone saw us as this perfect family which we weren't. But, boy, my parents could pull off the lie.

Hug me in front of their friends. Brag, as if they adored me. Not tell anyone how many times I was sent to bed without supper if I got an A minus. And certainly never let on that the only time I was shown any affection was when it benefitted their image."

"That's awful."

"Yes. But in the end, I used it. I realized that life isn't always what it appears to be, and people aren't always their real selves. No one ever screws me over or cheats me. I know the tells. I know how to be careful."

She studied him. "Careful? You're obsessive."

"In a good way."

"Maybe."

"No maybe about it. I live a real life. A genuine life. And so will Darcy."

He could see she was thinking through their breakup and decided to let her draw her own conclusions. The right conclusions this time.

"Look, I don't want you to think I'm crazy. I'm just trying to make sure I get to live the life I want."

"Hmmm. Okay."

She didn't seem convinced. "You think I'm nuts?"

"No. I'm just very middle class, always have been. I've never had to worry about those kinds of things. Your upper-class upbringing was very different than mine. I'm extremely ordinary."

He laughed, thinking she was kidding. Then the expression in her pretty eyes told him she was dead serious. He looked at her with her long blond hair streaming around her and her pink bikini showing off her perfect figure and he knew she wasn't ordinary. Someday, some smart man would snap her up.

It took a second to fight through the jealousy that rat-

tled through him, but only a second. When he broke up
with her, he'd accepted that she'd find real love—with
the kind of man who deserved her. What astounded him
was that she didn't see she was as far from ordinary as
any woman could be.

"You're beautiful and smart and you are not ordinary."

She snorted. "Right."

"I *am* right." Damn it. How had she gotten him to not
only talk about things he never discussed, but to bring
his beliefs about her into the conversation? "That's why
you need to finish school. There's a place for you. A
purpose. A strong one. You're going to do something
important someday."

Sophie listened to his little tirade, knowing the big problem was that he hated people questioning him. But at
least she now understood why. His parents punished
him if he wasn't perfect.

That's a very difficult way to grow up.

The baby yawned, and Wyatt carried her to the ladder and out of the pool. Assuming he was taking her
upstairs for her afternoon nap, Sophie closed her eyes
and leaned back against the pool wall again, confused
about their conversation.

Wyatt's story explained a lot of why he acted the way
he did. But not everything. Lots of people had tough
parents and ended up perfectly fine.

There was more to the story. Something he was holding back. When they were dating, he didn't trust easily,
but she'd proven herself to him, and he'd let her into his
life, albeit with limitations. Now, when he truly needed

her, he had to trust her in a way he couldn't before and that was not coming easy for him.

No wonder he was having trouble.

Except she'd proven herself with Darcy, too.

The door to the sunroom opened and she glanced behind her to see Wyatt striding out, baby monitor in hand.

She hadn't expected him to return but watching him walk toward the pool made her heart stutter. He was gorgeous. Smart. Usually easygoing with her. Only out to enjoy himself. But on this trip, he'd been anything but easygoing.

Of course, now he had a child.

She stopped her thoughts as a realization over-whelmed her. *He had a child.* If the rumors at the Montgomery were correct, the mother of his little girl had simply shown up and handed Darcy over to him.

No wonder he was different. No wonder his mistrust of people had gone from logical to obsessive.

Unexpectedly getting a child could change a person forever.

He presented the baby monitor before he set it on a colorful round table. "We'll hear her if she cries."

She drifted a little farther down the wall so he wouldn't bump into her as he climbed down the ladder into the pool.

"I want you to know I meant what I said."

"About your parents?"

"About you. You are attractive, but there's more to you. Especially because you are so determined about everything. Once you get into the workforce, you're going to see how quick you are, and that the sky's the limit. For now, you need to finish your degree so you can get a job and start looking for your place."

She smiled. "Well, there's one thing about you that hasn't changed. You still like telling people what to do."

"I'm guiding you."

She laughed. "I can figure this out myself."

"I don't think you can. The situation with your mom is ugly. You will face controversy when you get home. But you can't let that stop you. Hell, our breakup didn't stop you."

"It might have made me more determined."

"Good. Use the negativity of your mom's arrest to push you to prove yourself."

She licked her suddenly dry lips. They'd gone from talking about him to talking about her. Though she suspected he'd done that on purpose, she didn't miss the message.

No matter that he didn't want her in his life anymore, he truly believed she was going to do something important someday.

Even as the faith he had in her added to her confusion about why he hadn't wanted her in his life permanently, it also gave her a funny feeling in her chest. She hadn't realized how much she needed someone to believe in her. Having him make a point of telling her he did gave her the sense that he was right. She might be broke and homeless, but she only had two semesters to finish to get her degree. The way to make this work might be finding the best job she could while still going to school. She didn't want to live with her dad and stepmom, but it might be possible for two semesters.

But maybe there were other answers? Other ways to get the money she needed for tuition. Other ways to fix this that she hadn't yet had enough time to come up with.

She dove into the water and swam to the edge of the pool and back again. When she returned to the wall by the ladder, he was beside her.

"So, you agree with me?"

"I'm thinking things through."

"Okay. That's part of what these weeks out of Manhattan are about. Getting time to consider all angles. And you know that if there's anything you want to talk about or anything I can do to help you, all you have to do is say the word."

This calm, reasonable guy sounded like the Wyatt she'd dated.

She looked up to find him gazing into her eyes. She guessed he was looking so intently to be sure she was listening to him, but they had always had a connection. Sexual, sure. But today there was more. He genuinely wanted to help her.

Their eyes locked. The magnetic pull she'd experienced when they were dating rose up in her. But this time it wasn't just about physical attraction. It was about his basic goodness. He had a way of wanting everyone to be successful, not just himself. He wanted everybody to be happy. And maybe that's what she'd liked the most about him. He hadn't seen her as a misfit with an absent mom and a dad who'd moved on, going to the university so long after high school she was the oldest person in all of her classes. He just saw her.

Was it any wonder she'd loved him? Deep down he was the strongest, yet kindest person she'd ever met.

And maybe remembering that was more dangerous than their chemistry. The look in his eyes said he wanted to kiss her. He might have even been drawn to kiss her simply out of familiarity. They'd been here before. Kissed a million times.

Memories of missing him, feeling lost, lonely, pummeled her. She absolutely could not go through that again.

She stepped back. "I think I'll check on the baby."

Disappointment flitted through his eyes. "I just put her—" Music suddenly erupted from his cell phone.

"Damn it."

He jumped out of the pool to get it and sighed when he saw the screen. "It's Bonetti."

"Take it." She climbed out of the water and grabbed a big fluffy towel. "I'll check on Darcy and maybe start doing some research online."

For a job. For grants and loans for her last two semesters. It didn't matter which one. She needed to plan her future. She needed something to look forward to, something to hang on to, so she'd stop noticing him, sensing his moods, understanding his new life while getting insight into his old life, feeling that horrible, wonderful attraction that made her long to touch him, to be allowed to be in love with him again.

CHAPTER FIVE

WALKING THE GROUNDS of Signor Bonetti's villa on Thursday morning, listening to the old man jabber on about family and continuity and how he'd assumed his kids would take over his business, Wyatt thought about how much he'd wanted to kiss Sophie—how close he'd come to kissing her. His lips had tingled with the need, but his muscles had quivered with the effort of holding himself back. The urge was that strong.

"This property has been in my family since the Middle Ages."

That brought Wyatt back to the conversation. "Really?"

Bonetti laughed. "You Americans. You think a two-hundred-year-old cupboard is an antique. We count time in centuries."

Not able to argue that, Wyatt nodded. "I wanted to apologize to you for leaving so abruptly at lunch yesterday."

Bonetti waved his hand. "Not a problem. I really called you over to let you know I'd be out of town for two days. I know our negotiations got off to a rocky start. So, I'll spend some time with my grandsons so we can cleanse our palates so to speak, and when I get back, we'll start over. *Si?*"

It made sense to him. As it stood now, Wyatt was losing interest in the shipping company. Which was ridiculous! He needed this purchase. It would be the jewel in the crown of their conglomerate. But when his brain should have been running at full capacity, it was focused on Sophie. Almost kissing her. Wondering why he got so antsy every time she held Darcy.

He saw Bonetti off then returned to the villa. Seeing Sophie and Darcy in the pool, he ate lunch then did some work in the office. But even with all the catching up he had to do he was done around four o'clock.

He paced a bit, knowing they couldn't stay in the house the rest of the afternoon and evening. That was too much time to have to ignore her. He wouldn't be able to do it. Even if he took Darcy outside to explore the grounds, Sophie wouldn't be out of sight, out of mind. He'd proved that when he couldn't stop thinking about kissing her, when he was supposed to be focused on buying a shipping company.

If he didn't do something, he wouldn't just lose the chance to buy Bonetti's business, he'd face the embarrassment of telling his partners he'd failed.

That was unacceptable.

What he needed to do was to go back to his original plan. Bite the bullet and spend enough time with Sophie that he'd get accustomed to being around her, so being with her didn't affect him anymore.

"Sophie?" he called walking out of his office and into the foyer.

She scrambled to the top of the stairs, holding

Darcy. "What are you doing home? I thought you were negotiating?"

"I actually came home hours ago. Bonetti wants us to start fresh when he returns from seeing his grandsons. I ate lunch and caught up on a few things."

"Oh." She started down the stairs. When she stepped into the foyer, Darcy reached for him—for the first time since Sophie came into the picture.

His heart swelled with love for the little girl. But the move also reinforced his logic about Sophie. Darcy spent more time with Sophie, so the nanny wasn't a novelty anymore. All he had to do was hang around with her the next two days and he'd be normal around her too.

"How about us doing some sightseeing in town?"

"Or why don't you take Darcy sightseeing yourself, while I get some work done. I need to look up loans and grants for school. And I should also call your PR department to discuss their crafting my statement about my mom and my lack of knowledge of her dealings."

"Right now?"

"Yeah. I need to get started on this. I should at least start investigating grants and loans and then I can call your staff—"

He couldn't believe she was arguing about this. She had to know the rest of their trip would be trouble if they didn't fix their attraction right now.

"Stop. Seriously just stop. Don't you realize how close I came to kissing you yesterday when we were swimming?"

She licked her lips, making him shake his head again. Had she been shocked by that, he would have known it was his predicament to suffer through or solve. But she was having trouble too.

"I know our problem. In the three years since we broke up, we never even ran into each other in our building lobby. Meaning, our automatic reactions to each other are still romantic because our last encounters had been romantic. We need to spend time together as nanny and boss so we can get a new mental identity for ourselves."

She laughed. "Mental identity? That's crazy."

He took a step closer to her, cutting into her personal space. "Is it?"

He'd only crowded her to prove a point, but Sophie's breath stuttered and her pulse raced. The feelings from the pool came tumbling back. Not just the physical desire to touch him but the longing to be in love with him again, to have him love her.

Damn it. He hadn't really loved her. He'd barely told her about himself. All her feelings from three years ago had been one-sided. Her side.

Still, that didn't mean he wasn't right. What if all her reactions around him were simply the result of habit? Having been hurt by him, the last thing she wanted was another romance with him. Yet she couldn't stop the yearning that rose up anytime they were together. Plus, if all her strange reactions around him were only the result of memories, learned behaviors and reactions because they'd never interacted except as lovers, then a little time spent together could get rid of them.

Or it could backfire miserably.

Sometimes life was all about taking a shot. If they didn't at least try to balance out what they were feeling they'd surely end up in bed. But facing the residual attraction head on—bringing it out in the open, not letting it boss them around—might get rid of it.

They were also in gorgeous Italy for two whole weeks. It would be fabulous to spend that time looking around, rather than staying in a house thinking about how attracted they were.

"Okay. You're right. Let me put on something pretty and we can go."

"Sophie?"

Halfway up the stairs she turned to face him. "Yeah?"

"Not something too pretty. We are trying to diminish the attraction."

The silliness of it made her giggle. Though she got his point, her heart lifted. She'd forgotten how much she loved to laugh with him. And how much it pleased her that he believed she was beautiful.

Rather than groan at the memory, she let it and feelings it inspired wash through her. If being around each other was to work to eliminate these feelings, then she had to acknowledge them and replace them with the reality that he might have always thought she was beautiful, but he'd also broken off their relationship.

The hard truth rippled through her and burst the bubbly happy feeling.

Exactly as she wanted—

No, exactly as *they* needed.

Almost an hour later, Wyatt's head tilted when she walked down the stairs to the front foyer. She'd chosen a pink sundress that complemented her blond hair and the light suntan she had from studying in the park and playing in the pool with Darcy.

When she reached the bottom step, he shifted Darcy on his hip and said, "Too pretty."

She laughed, not letting the compliment affect her as it had the first time. "For Italy? Lake Como? Famous for being the home of royalty and movie stars? Frankly, I think I'm underdressed."

He snorted. "Right." Pointing to a corridor off the stairway, he said, "This way to the garage. I found a Range Rover in there when I went looking for a car to drive to Signor Bonetti's. It's more suited for us than the sports car I've been using."

"Signor Bonetti certainly thought of everything."

Pushing open the door that led to a huge garage, Wyatt sighed. "Unfortunately."

"Why is that unfortunate?"

Carrying Darcy, he led her to the black Range Rover. "I told you. He knows all my tricks. That's why his not talking business yet is scaring me. What if there's something I don't know about negotiating that he does?"

"Then you'll use this as an opportunity to learn something new."

One of his eyebrows rose. "Really? That's your take on this?"

"Hey, there's a silver lining in everything. Sometimes it's simply the chance to learn a lesson, but some lessons are pretty damned important."

He rolled his eyes, then opened the door to the backseat and slid Darcy into the car seat that had already been installed.

"You must have gotten downstairs long before I did."

"Let's just say I dressed myself and a baby, installed the car seat and put the umbrella stroller in the trunk in the time it took you to put on that pretty pink dress."

Once again, the fact that he'd noticed pleased her.

She shoved the feeling aside and opened the passenger door. "Okay. Point taken."

He slid behind the steering wheel. "I'm not being critical. You're allowed to take time to yourself. Your only breaks are when Darcy's sleeping. There have been days, when I was the only one with her, that I had trouble finding time to go to the bathroom."

Darcy began to babble in the backseat. Wyatt glanced at her in the rearview mirror. "Do you think she's defending herself?"

She turned to look at the baby who was playing with her foot. "Not unless her toes are the jury."

He laughed and started the SUV before he pushed a button to raise the garage door.

"You're getting awfully comfortable with this place."

He backed out onto the cobblestone driveway. "I'm thinking of adding this villa to the purchase of the shipping company to make up for the pain and suffering Bonetti's putting me through."

She snickered. "Have you ever given a perk to one of the buyers of your companies for the pain and suffering *you* put *them* through?"

He gaped at her. "No."

"Okay then."

The drive to Bellagio, a village at the tip of the Y formed by the lakes, was magnificent. With the Alps in the background and greenery all around them, the views took Sophie's breath away.

To her surprise, they parked at the edge of town. "What are we doing?"

"There's not a lot of parking. The streets are narrow and filled with tourists, so it's best to walk."

"You've been here before?"

"I researched."

She laughed. "Of course, you did."

They got out of the SUV, loaded Darcy in a stroller and began the walk along Giuseppe Garibaldi, the main road. The closer they got to town proper, the more tourists milled about the streets filled with shops, restaurants, bakeries and coffee shops. Bright coral, blue and green awnings protected doorways of stucco buildings painted beige or white or yellow. Quaint cobblestone streets guided them along.

"This is amazing."

Wyatt looked around. "It's like a different world."

"It is." She inhaled the sweet air. "I'll bet we could get some really good pastries for breakfast tomorrow."

"And insult Mrs. P.?"

She wrinkled her nose. "Right. We wouldn't want to do that. The woman's a gem. I can't believe I forgot her."

He sniffed a laugh. "It's part of her job to blend in with the house."

She glanced at him. He always behaved so normally it was easy to forget he was wealthy beyond her wildest dreams. But remembering that he'd grown up in the lap of luxury, and bought companies worth more than she'd earn in a lifetime, was another good way of dissolving their attraction. When they'd dated, she'd always believed they were fated to be together, so good for each other it was obvious they belonged together, despite their different stations in life. But losing him had shown her that he didn't look at life the same way she did. And maybe remembering that would be the real way to dispatch the memories that wanted to draw her to him.

They pushed Darcy's stroller along the cobblestone

streets until they found a little coffee shop with seating outside. They wheeled her in and sat at a tiny round table. A waiter walked over.

"We've been smelling pastries for our entire walk. Any idea what we're smelling?"

"Could be anything," the waiter said with a grin. "But we have the best *miascia* in Italy. Apples, pears, macaroons and chocolate with just a bit of liquor. There is nothing quite like it."

Wyatt laughed.

The waiter sucked in a breath as if Wyatt's laugh had insulted him. "I'm not bragging."

"Okay. We'll have that and some coffee." He glanced at Sophie. "If that's good with you."

"Sounds great." It did. She hadn't had the big lunch she'd promised herself and it was getting late. Not so late that Darcy needed to be in bed, but late enough that they were officially missing dinner and her stomach was growling.

She inhaled the scent of the sea and all the wonderful pastries with which their *miascia* competed.

As the waiter walked away, Wyatt said, "It must be great to live here."

She glanced around. Even inundated with tourists, the place had a slow, happy pace. She put her elbow on the table and rested her chin on it as she studied him. "You can live anywhere you want. Why not here?"

He bent down and lifted Darcy from her stroller, settling her on his lap. "Business. I like being in Manhattan. It's where the action is."

"Yet here you are working in Italy."

"Courting a pretty tough customer."

"So you say." She frowned then glanced at him again.

"You always told me that getting someone's business from them was simply a matter of figuring out what they really wanted and then offering it to them."

"I told you that?"

She shrugged. If bringing back memories of their former relationship was supposed to diminish their attraction, then they needed to talk about their relationship. "You told me a lot of things."

He'd talked about high school and university, old girlfriends and the strong friendships he'd built with Cade and Trace, his first apartment, and the fact that he'd never actually held a job except an internship. All that was interspersed between chats about art and music, New York City, and his travels.

Funny, now that she thought about it, she realized he'd gone to Europe, Australia and Asia with friends, not his parents.

Still, there'd never been a quiet or uncomfortable minute between them. They'd talked in the back of his limo, on snowy walks in Central Park, in fancy restaurants or little burger joints, at Broadway shows during intermission or in his apartment. She could not remember a lull in conversation.

In all those talks, he'd somehow avoided telling her about his parents. Yet, he'd shared that now. When she wasn't actually in his life—except temporarily.

Because it didn't matter?

Because he was putting distance between them?

Explaining why their relationship hadn't worked?

Probably. Just as she knew they had to talk about their old relationship to get rid of it, he was opening up now.

Uncomfortable silence settled over their little table.

She'd thought he didn't like his desire to kiss her because he feared getting close again. But what if it really was just a reflex for him? No emotion attached?

Disappointment and foolishness flooded her. She kept forgetting that she'd fallen in love with him, but he hadn't fallen in love with her. He'd dumped her.

Their dessert and coffee arrived. Wyatt returned Darcy to her lightweight stroller and gave her a teether, as the waiter set the order before them.

She peeked at the waiter. "It smells heavenly."

He grinned. "I told you."

He left them and Sophie inhaled deeply, enjoying the full experience. She let Wyatt take the first bite of the *miascia*. He groaned. "Wow."

She took a bite, savoring the flavor that exploded on her tongue. "Wow is right."

"And this is just the first thing we've tried. Can you imagine trying something new every night?"

She could. Except she didn't want to go out with the Wyatt with her now. She wanted to experience it with the Wyatt she'd loved. The guy who hadn't yet broken her heart. The guy who had seemed to love her.

Going out with him in an attempt to break his bad habit of wanting to kiss her was sad and lonely. Now that she was thinking logically of how he'd viewed their relationship, it was easy to see how different he was from the guy she'd dated. Harder maybe. Or perhaps his honesty made him seem different than the guy he had once been?

"I've heard that's what vacations are for."

"True."

She studied him a second. "Have you ever taken a

real vacation? Not just gone to some great country to negotiate for someone's company?"

He laughed. "I can see how you'd get that impression. But I love to go to Cade's house in the Florida Keys. I just took Darcy there a few weeks ago."

The fondness in his voice for the child he'd said he didn't want with her saddened her even more. He was perfectly capable of loving Darcy. It was her he wanted to avoid.

She took a breath, keeping the conversation neutral, working as hard as he was now to break his romantic habits about her.

"How long did you stay?"

He shrugged and forked off another piece of dessert. "A couple days."

"Ever stay anywhere for an entire week? Just for entertainment. No work involved."

"I used to. When I was younger. I told you about those trips before I met Cade and Trace in college."

Trips without his parents. No chaperone. No supervision. Almost as if he was trying to escape them. Or they didn't want him around?

"Now, you're more of a workaholic."

"Don't make it sound godawful. I enjoy what I do."

"Except when the other guy is smarter."

He laughed. "Bonetti's not smarter. He's just got something up his sleeve and I don't know what it is. But I'm going back to my old-school philosophy about figuring out what he wants and dangling it in front of him. I'm better at this when I stick with what I know."

She smiled weakly. The young, impulsive guy he was three years ago had been charming and charismatic, but this Wyatt, the guy with substance, suddenly interested her more.

Which was pointless since they were here to get rid of their attraction. "I guess."

They ate their dessert talking about the cobblestone paths, gorgeous houses perched on the hills and the peace of the lake. The ride home was made in darkness and Darcy fell asleep, forcing her and Wyatt to be quiet.

But when they returned to the beautiful villa, emptiness surrounded her. She was beginning to like this new Wyatt. Having him open up to her made her want more. And he wanted nothing to do with her.

"Let me take Darcy to bed."

He held on tightly to the baby. "I'll take her."

Getting Darcy might have softened him in some respects, but it had also made him vigilant. Determined to love his little girl, even as he shut out everyone else.

"Or we can both take her."

He nodded. "That way we'll have her in bed twice as fast."

She smiled the way a good nanny was supposed to and ignored the tweak in her heart when Wyatt sat on the rocker in the nursery and fed Darcy a bottle before he changed her into one-piece pajamas and kissed her goodnight.

It wasn't amazing that he could be so good to his child. She'd always known that deep down he was kind. What surprised her was that becoming a father seemed to have made him even more alone.

She turned toward her bedroom which was right beside the nursery.

"Goodnight, Sophie."

She stopped and faced him. "Goodnight, Wyatt."

"We did okay tonight?"

She couldn't say. The only thing she'd accomplished was to remember old Wyatt and realize there was more to him now than a big brain and the ability to get what he wanted. Rather than that help her grow accustomed to being with him, to their chemistry, it only seemed to make her miss him more.

CHAPTER SIX

FRIDAY MORNING, when the baby monitor sent the sounds of Darcy crying into his bedroom, Wyatt bounced up in bed. His first thought was of Sophie, but instead of groaning, he congratulated himself on how well their sightseeing went. They'd had short, succinct discussions that weren't stilted. She knew him and that knowledge edged into their conversations. But nothing seemed to tip over into those romantic memories that bedeviled him.

And this was Lake Como! There were hundreds of small towns to visit, hundreds of sights to see. If that wasn't enough to keep them too busy to think about being attracted, the villa owned a boat that was moored in Bellagio. Because of Cade's island, he was very good with handling a boat. They could take Darcy out that afternoon if they wanted.

In his navy pajamas, he stepped into the nursery. "Hey, baby. What's all the crying about?"

Darcy sniffled and rolled over so she could see him. Her short black hair made spikes on the top of her head. Her blue eyes swam with tears.

"Now, now. Mornings aren't that bad." He lifted her out of the crib, his heart swelling with so much love he almost couldn't contain it. "Actually, I like to look at mornings as a new opportunity."

The nursery door opened, and Sophie ambled into the room in a T-shirt and yoga pants, but his brain didn't dart back to a memory. It didn't need to. Seeing her perfect butt cradled in the stretchy pants, he didn't need to recall feelings. New ones sparkled through him.

Well, damn.

Darcy snuggled against him and brought his attention back to where it needed to be. "That's right. Daddy will change your diaper and feed you."

Sophie walked over, her hands open to take the baby. "I'll do it. You get ready for work."

He eased away from her. "No work, remember. Bonetti's out of town, visiting his grandsons." He set the baby on the changing table and took a short breath, trying to decide if they needed more time together or less. If the feelings he had weren't connected to memories, then more time together didn't seem advisable.

Of course, they'd only tried spending time together once. That wasn't enough to know if it had worked or not. Today, he'd make double sure he interacted with Sophie enough that he grew accustomed to her.

Sophie rooted around in a drawer for clean clothes for the baby, which she set on the changing table.

She peeked around him to tickle Darcy's belly. "Good morning." The baby gooed and cooed. "I take it you slept well."

Darcy laughed and made some sounds that weren't words but showed she was grasping for them.

"I slept well too. I think it might have been the walk around town. Made me sleepy."

The baby giggled.

Wyatt didn't know why he was surprised Sophie was so good with Darcy. Not only did she have experience with babies, but she was a likeable person. He'd liked her when they were dating. Obviously, he'd told her a lot more than he typically told people about himself.

Her interactions with Darcy, though, always made him smile. "She loves you."

Sophie tickled Darcy's belly again. "I think she's pretty special too."

Something warm and fuzzy rose in his chest. He got rid of it by telling himself that it was simply love for Darcy and happiness that she liked her nanny that was getting to him.

"She had a good time in the pool yesterday."

Wyatt said, "Yeah. She did. She likes the pool at Cade's. I'm not surprised she likes the pool here."

"It's always good to put her in situations she's comfortable with. That will ease her from her regular routine into this one."

"We don't go to Cade's all the time."

"But swimming or being in the pool is something she's accustomed to."

He shrugged. "Yes. Sort of. I never thought of creating routines for her."

She peeked over his shoulder at the baby again. "Babies love routines. That's what my stepmother said. If they are comfortable, they are happy. Doing familiar things makes them comfortable, so doing familiar things makes them happy."

"That makes sense."

He snapped the last closure on her outfit, and she spit out a string of unrecognizable sounds. Again, seeming like she was trying to make sentences.

Sophie pinched her cheek. "You're so smart."

Darcy said another string of sounds.

Wyatt said, "It seems like she's trying to make sentences."

"I'd say she's mimicking us."

"Interesting."

"It's how babies learn. They watch and mimic and try to figure things out by what they see others around them doing."

Others around them? He was the only one around her most of the time. Meaning, to learn about life, she'd be watching *him*.

His usual fear rippled through him. He had a cheat for a dad and a social climber for a mom. They'd punished him when he hadn't performed. They'd alienated him. Shoved him off on nannies. He hadn't learned a damned thing about parenting from his parents—

He shook his head. He'd always told himself awareness was power. Having seen the miserable way his dad treated his friends, he'd become a better friend. Having seen his mom's love of social climbing he'd not joined the game. He knew he'd be a better parent. He would never punish Darcy for bad grades. He'd never let her feel alone or unwanted.

Still, he was a single guy, someone who used work as play—

"She's *watching* me?"

"Of course! And, right now, she's also watching me."

He said, "That's good." Then realized just how good it was. He was clueless. Sophie knew things.

Maybe instead of hanging around Sophie to get rid of his attraction, he should be paying attention to what she said and did around the baby?

Or better yet, maybe he should be taking notes. Watching what she did. Watching how she treated Darcy. How she cared for Darcy. And then writing everything down so he could refer to it.

He didn't need time to forget his attraction. He needed to learn how to care for his little girl. And he had the perfect teacher in his employ.

Sophie lifted Darcy off the changing table. "You get dressed. I'll go downstairs and tell Mrs. P. the baby's awake and ready to eat. Maybe get her a bottle of water."

He said, "Okay," then frowned at the door after she was gone.

He liked the idea of learning as much as he could while he had Sophie around, but something was happening here. Yes. He needed to learn to care for his child. But for him to open up and ask questions, they would have to become friends. He would have to trust her even more than he trusted her with the baby.

He would have to trust her with his shortcomings, the oddities about him because of being raised by parents who demanded perfection and nannies who shifted every six months or so and only did their jobs.

He'd been raised in the loneliest way possible. It made him different. He did not want Darcy to go through that.

He walked into his room, changed into shorts and a T-shirt and ambled to the dining room where Sophie sat feeding Darcy.

Weirdness tumbled through him. He'd broken off their relationship before they'd gotten too close. Now, suddenly, he was about to expose all his vulnerabilities to her.

He took a seat at the head of the table and Mrs. P.

scrambled in. He asked for eggs, toast and bacon. When she was gone, he poured himself a cup of coffee from the pot on a buffet.

"What do you think we should do today?" Coffee in hand, he walked back to his seat. "We have the whole day. We could go out on the boat."

She winced. "I really do want to have an hour or two to look up some options online."

"Did you bring a laptop?"

She nodded. "Yes. It's one of the few things I got to keep because my dad bought it for me for Christmas one year."

"Must be old. Are you sure you don't want to use mine?"

She stiffened. "I'm fine."

"I didn't mean to insult you."

"You didn't."

He surely had. But he supposed he'd be tripping over himself for the next ten days as he tried to get the help he needed and help her in return.

He took a sip of the hot coffee, knowing he had to shift this conversation. "Anyway, what if I gave you two hours, then we headed out on the boat."

"It'll be Darcy's nap time."

"Right."

"I can always do my research tomorrow."

He shook his head. "No. You're eager to get started figuring out your future. You can't do that without investigating a few things like school loans and a new apartment." He peeked over at her. "You might even want to check what's happening with your mom. Or at least see if it's making headlines in the papers or dying down."

She didn't answer for a second. "I'd rather call your PR department."

"You have to wait until afternoon for that. It's in the middle of the night in Manhattan."

"Right."

Her mouth turned down and the light in her usually bright green eyes dimmed. She set her attention on feeding Darcy who looked like she was loving whatever was in the bowl on her highchair tray.

"What's she having today?"

"Plums and rice cereal."

Darcy smacked her lips as Mrs. P. walked in with Wyatt's breakfast.

"She loves it."

"That she does," Mrs. P. said. "My kids always did."

"Good to know," Wyatt said, expecting Sophie to chime in with her own agreement, but she seemed to be off in the distance.

Mrs. P. scampered out of the dining room and Wyatt glanced at the table where a cup of coffee sat in front of Sophie but no breakfast.

"Aren't you hungry?"

She shook her head. "No. Not really."

He studied her. He hadn't expected that bringing her here would make her troubles disappear. He knew they'd dog her. He knew she'd have some things to face and decisions to make. They'd talked about it almost every day they'd been here. But now that the time had come for her to investigate possibilities for finishing university, she seemed down in the dumps.

"You're okay, though, right?"

"If you're asking if I'm good enough to care for

Darcy, the answer will always be yes. I won't let my troubles affect her."

"I'm not worried about that." He knew she'd be responsible. She always was. "Are you upset about your mom or the next few years of your life?"

"It's weird to have a plan and have it snatched away then have to scramble to figure everything out."

He laughed. "Look who you're talking to. I had a plan. A solid one. Then one day an ex, someone I hadn't even thought about in a year just bold as brass walked up to the doorman and demanded to see me. He called me, I went down to the lobby, she showed me Darcy and suggested we talk in my penthouse."

Obviously curious, Sophie perked up.

He hadn't intended to tell her this story, but it seemed appropriate given her new role as his teacher for the remainder of their two weeks in Italy.

"She told me Darcy was mine. Said I could have a DNA test done to prove it. Then said she had a job in Dubai and couldn't take the baby. Her hours would be long, and she wanted to devote herself to this stage of her career."

Sophie gaped at him. "I'm not sure if that's arrogant or heartless."

Seeing her reviving as her interest grew, Wyatt kept going. After all, most of this had been gossip at the Montgomery from the day he got Darcy.

"I couldn't tell, either. She gave me some bull about being thrilled to be pregnant and she didn't need me. She would have raised Darcy alone, but then she got this opportunity and promotions like the one she'd been given didn't come along every day and she wanted it."

"Wow."

"I know, right?" Wyatt said, catching her gaze, feeling like he had something of a kindred spirit in her. "From her story, and the way she hedged about some things, I had the sense that she might have deliberately gotten pregnant, following a whim of wanting to be a mom, and when a chance to further her career came up, she changed her mind."

"My dad said my mom was like that."

He hadn't set out to get her to talk, but he was glad she was opening up. "Selfish?"

She laughed. "No. Scattered. One minute she wanted one thing, the next day she wanted another. No one was more surprised than he was when she started the investment firm and stuck to it." She sniffed. "Now we know why. She was siphoning off money. Probably indulging her whims with other people's wealth." She took a breath, pressed her lips together then caught his gaze. "What's funny is I genuinely believe that she didn't consider anything she did wrong."

"Sophie, she was stealing money."

"Yeah, but I'll bet if I talked to her right now, she'd say she was going to give it back, only borrowing it and everything got blown out of proportion."

Wyatt opened his napkin and set it on his lap. "Unfortunately, that sounds a lot like Shelly. She's got a story for everything. I was going to break it off when she started ghosting me. I thought we were on the same page of realizing we weren't a good match. Seems I was right and wrong."

She nodded and was thoughtful for a few seconds before she said, "I can't call New York. You can't see Bonetti." She shrugged. "Maybe we should go out on the boat this morning?"

His chest filled with relief. He didn't even realize how upset he was for her until she agreed to relaxing a bit. "I think that's a great idea."

Of course, the villa Bonetti had rented for Wyatt had a boat. A simple outboard cruiser moored at a dock a few miles away. Sophie would have shaken her head in disbelief, but nothing surprised her on this trip. In some ways, Lake Como was almost magical. Not only was it breathtaking, but Wyatt had opened up to her again. He'd told her about his parents, then Darcy's mom.

After unloading the car seat from the SUV, Wyatt carried Darcy along the wood planks that took them to the boat and Sophie brought the picnic lunch made by Mrs. P.

"That's a big boat."

"Not really," Wyatt said as he boarded the cruiser. With Darcy secured on his hip he took the picnic basket from Sophie so she could climb on.

They settled Darcy in a car seat and secured her before Wyatt set out on the water. Leaning against the side of the boat, beside Wyatt who steered the craft, Sophie watched Bellagio grow smaller and smaller the farther out on the water they got. "Wow."

"I know, seeing it from the lake is amazing, isn't it?"

"You have got to buy a property here."

He chuckled and took them out to the center of the water, then stopped the boat. "Let's just get the negotiations with Bonetti done first before we start making decisions like me buying a house here."

"Okay." She'd brought up the subject of him buying property on Lake Como because she was still filled with questions about Darcy's mom. Deciding it wasn't wise to ask those, she kept the conversation on Lake Como. She pointed at the shore. "Look how pretty the houses are."

He drew in an appreciative breath. She could almost see his stress melting away. "Yeah."

Noting how he was relaxing reinforced her decision not to talk about Darcy's mom. They discussed the mountains cradling the lake, Bellagio itself, and even how everything felt different here. Then she let the conversation go. As if carried off on the gentle breeze, her thoughts disappeared, and she turned her face up to the sun.

"Darcy's asleep."

She kept her eyes closed. "It is her nap time."

"Is this good for her?"

"Sure. She's slept in that carrier before. She's comfy. She'll probably wake naturally. Just as she does in her crib."

"Okay."

Wyatt started the boat again, taking them on a leisurely trip around the first arm of the Y of the lake.

A little over an hour later, Darcy fussed and Wyatt stopped the boat, brought Darcy out of her car seat and showed her the shore.

"I hope she remembers it," Wyatt said as he sat beside Sophie on a bench seat.

Relaxing again, she didn't open her eyes. "She won't."

"She won't?"

"She's too young." She opened one eye. "I'm telling you. You're going to have to bring her back here when she's older."

He laughed. "Okay. Whatever."

They ate their lunch, then took a drive along part of the other arm of the Y that formed from the lakes, with Sophie holding Darcy, pointing out things the baby wouldn't remember.

When it was time for Darcy's afternoon nap they decided to return to the villa.

They were quiet on the boat ride back to the dock, quieter still on the drive to the house. Lake Como was the perfect place. Full of peace, it had settled Sophie's mind and she didn't want to disturb the blessed silence in her brain.

She didn't even realize Wyatt had turned off his phone until they pulled the SUV into the garage, and he turned it on again. Bells and pings filled the vehicle.

"Sounds like you've been missed."

He glanced at his phone as Sophie pulled Darcy out of the car seat and snuggled her against her chest.

"Bonetti's home."

"Already?"

"He said he wanted two days. That was yesterday and today. Tomorrow we meet again."

She refused to let disappointment rise. They'd had such a nice day. *He'd* had a nice, calming day. There was no reason to make more of that than what it had been. A break.

"It still feels like he's home early."

Reading something on his phone, Wyatt said, "Because he called today instead of tomorrow morning."

"You think it's a trick?"

He rolled his eyes. "I don't know. He could be trying to keep me off balance or he could simply be following his own timetable."

"Maybe it's better to think he's inexperienced than to think he's yanking your chain."

He snorted "Probably. Giving him too much credit is throwing me off my game."

"Exactly."

He took Darcy from Sophie's arms. "I'll put her to bed. You can call New York if you want or just use the Internet. If I'm with Bonetti all day tomorrow, you won't get a chance."

She said, "Okay," handing off the baby and heading to her room and her laptop. But she sat staring at the screen. She didn't feel sorry for Wyatt. He had everything. But after hearing him talk and sensing his isolation, she knew he also had nothing. No family who behaved like family. No connection except to two friends he considered to be brothers.

Which was cool. Better than a lot of people had. But there was a loneliness that surrounded him and Darcy.

She couldn't explain it. She thought it best not to try because she didn't want to get involved with him. And he didn't want to get involved with her.

Still, on Saturday, floating Darcy through the pool, she realized that she had only nine or so days as Darcy's nanny and maybe the best use of her time would be to help Wyatt with things he might not think to investigate.

After putting Darcy in a poolside baby swing, she got out her phone and searched *how to teach a baby to swim*.

She learned about vertical twists and assisted free floating and tried both with the baby who giggled with delight.

While Darcy napped, Sophie investigated grants and student loans again, not quite ready to talk to Wyatt's

PR department yet. She and Darcy ate dinner, then she put the baby to bed.

It was after nine when Wyatt returned.

Sophie was in the foyer to greet him. "Hey! How'd it go? Darcy and I had a great day. I googled how to teach a baby to swim and found some really neat information. Do you know babies as young as five months can be taught to hold their breath?"

"No. I didn't know."

At the weariness in his voice, she tilted her head, studying him. "He's wearing you out, isn't he?"

"Wearing me out? Wearing me down? Simply a guy who wants to have fun?" He shook his head. "Who knows. The point is, we got nothing done today."

"What did you do?"

"First, we spent the morning talking about the two days we each had off."

Sophie couldn't help it. She laughed. "Sorry."

"Oh, don't be sorry. I'd be laughing if it wasn't happening to me." He headed for the den and walked behind the bar. "After the chitchat, we played eighteen holes of golf."

"Golf?"

He got a glass from the shelves beneath the bar. "Then we had an enormous dinner with the most delicious food I've ever eaten."

"That sounds fun."

"Oh, it was fabulous. Especially since he invited his entire family. We talked about kids and grandkids, vacations, the proper private schools and even university."

"But not his shipping company."

He sighed, setting his glass on the shiny bar. "No."

She shooed him away. "Go sit. I'll pour your bourbon."

"Put some ice in it. If you don't, I'm afraid I'll just start drinking it like shots and that won't be good."

She laughed and he fell to the sofa. "The man is killing me."

She found the bourbon, poured some over ice and handed it to him as she sat beside him. "I don't get it. Can't you just work a discussion of his company in?"

"Oh, I have tried."

The expression on his face made her laugh. "Sorry. Again."

"You think this is funny?"

"I think this might be life telling you that you won't always win."

He gawked at her. "That's unacceptable."

She shrugged. "Either you have to accept his time-table about negotiations, tell him to shove off and leave Lake Como, or somehow get control."

"Yeah. No kidding."

"Come on. Talk to me. Tell me what you're missing. Sometimes saying things out loud can give you the answer."

He took a breath, thinking she was crazy, but also realizing he couldn't go on like this.

"He's so casual, it's difficult to pin him down."

"That's good. Keep talking."

"He's definitely in command at his villa."

"Which might make you feel uncomfortable about pushing him or arguing with him when you're on his turf."

He leaned back, relaxing on the sofa. "Maybe."

"No. No. No maybes. Only state facts."

He frowned at her. Not because she pushed him but

because he suddenly realized that on this trip he'd told her about his parents, told her about Darcy's mom and now she was getting him to talk about Signor Bonetti.

"I think I'd like to meet this guy."

He laughed.

"No. I'm serious. I've never seen anyone stump you. Hell, I've never seen you tired."

He laughed again.

She playfully slapped his biceps. "Come on. I think it would be fun to meet him."

He set his drink on the coffee table. "I know it would be a laugh a minute for you, but it would mess up whatever rapport I've established—or that I'm kidding myself into thinking I've established."

"I might surprise you."

He didn't doubt that for one second. Sometimes she was sunshine in a bottle. Other times she was like Attila the Hun's little sister.

The thought made him laugh again.

"You're going to have to stop laughing at me."

"I'm not laughing at you. I'm laughing with you."

Having fun, he leaned forward and placed a quick kiss on her lips. The automatic reaction stunned them both. It had been nothing but a reflex but the quick touch of his lips to hers felt like coming home. For ten seconds, they looked into each other's eyes, then she leaned forward at the same time he did, and their lips met softly.

But the softness became a frenzy of need. Their mouths opened to allow their tongues to twine, then retreat, so he could nibble her bottom lip. Visions of making love with her returned. The ease and simplicity of their connection filled his chest with longing as their mouths mated. A tsunami of desire overwhelmed him, a yearning so intense that common sense had him breaking away.

She blinked, gazing at him with sleepy green eyes that urged him to kiss her again. But his brain woke. He remembered what a nice person she was. He remembered that her life might be a mess, but that was only temporary. His life was always a mess.

And he'd told her.

He'd confided in her.

He'd put them on the slippery slope of making a genuine connection and now he had to get them off.

"I'm so sorry."

She blinked. Her dreamy expression fled. "What?"

"That was supposed to be a friendly kiss. You know. A peck between friends but there is something powerful in the attraction I feel for you and... Well, I shouldn't have risked even the friendly kiss."

Wyatt understood what he'd been trying to tell her, but even he didn't buy the explanation that had tumbled out. All his life had been about keeping secrets, except from Trace and Cade and now he was telling her things, happy when he saw her with his baby girl and kissing her?

It almost seemed that ignoring their sexual attraction had the unwanted result of real conversations and confidences. Which was weird. He could handle sex. The mindless, easy sex they'd had when they were dating had been fabulous.

But he couldn't handle getting close to her. Not for himself. *For her.* He was a horrible bet as a partner. She deserved better.

"You're saying we're friends?"

"You don't think we are?"

She studied him a second. "I guess spending so much time together we almost have to be."

Relief stuttered through him. "Yes. I think we need to be friends because of Darcy, because I want to help you and because we're in this beautiful place that we should be seeing."

"Seeing?"

"Yes. You know. Sightseeing."

Giving them something to do other than get to know each other, like each other, confide more things that would make them long to indulge their attraction.

She said, "Right," sounding extremely skeptical. He didn't blame her. But keeping them busy sounded like a good plan, and he was sticking to it.

She rose from the sofa. "Goodnight, Wyatt."

CHAPTER SEVEN

SOPHIE WALKED TO her room, shaking her head. "Friendly kiss?" She snorted. *Seriously. Was there even such a thing?*

She didn't think so and Wyatt was only kidding himself if he believed that was what had happened between them. After sliding into pajamas, she got into bed. She could still feel the tingles of excitement that raced through her the second his mouth had met hers. The roar of arousal that had followed still rode her blood.

And he thought they could be friends?

Doubtful.

Oh, *he* might be able to separate friendship and their old relationship, but her hormones were not on board.

She fell into a restless sleep and woke tired the next morning. As if he hadn't kissed her the night before, cheerful Wyatt shooed her out of the nursery and got Darcy ready for the day himself. By the time Sophie got to the breakfast table, Wyatt was eating his eggs and bacon as he fed the baby.

She tried to take the baby spoon from his hand. "Let me do that."

He pulled it away. "We're fine. Ring for Mrs. P. Get your breakfast."

He looked amazing in his white shirt and red tie with the black suit coat hanging on the back of his chair.

Amazing.

Not just good or even attractive. No. He had to look amazing.

Why did the guy she thought the most handsome in the world have to be the one guy she couldn't have?

And why had that guy kissed her?

Because she wasn't buying that friendly kiss explanation.

She grumpily walked back to her chair. "I only get a plate of fruit."

"Maybe if you'd eat a pastry, you'd be happier."

She scowled as she hit the buzzer to ring for the cook. Mrs. P. walked into the dining room all smiles and Sophie realized why her bad mood was so obvious. Everybody around her was happy.

"Are you ready for breakfast, miss?" Mrs. P. asked with so much cheer Sophie almost winced.

Instead, she forced a smiled. "Yes. Thank you."

A few seconds later, Mrs. P. returned with her fruit platter. "I added cinnamon toast."

This time she did wince. Okay. That was confirmation that her mood was obvious. But Wyatt had kissed her—

She sighed. *No. They'd kissed each other.* And that was trouble. Not only had they already been down this road, but also more than kissing was happening on this trip. They were talking. Getting close.

That was when she recognized what was bothering her. He'd told her about getting Darcy. He'd told her about his parents. They were actually discussing Signor Bonetti and his negotiating tactics.

When they'd dated, they'd talked about wine and art, music and dancing, the best places to go in New York City, their favorite plays. They'd never run out of things to talk about. He'd even told her bits and pieces of his work, but he hadn't told her the important things about himself. His fears. His past. His troubles. Now, he was. And easily. As if living together made it perfectly natural for him to confide in her.

She genuinely believed he had no idea all this talking was taking them to a level more important than sex.

And she was going to get hurt.

She had to get herself back on track, get their relationship back on track, start working toward her purposes before she ran out of time.

"How about giving me the contact number for someone in your PR department. I think I need to get that ball rolling."

"I know I suggested that yesterday, but I think it would be smarter for me to call ahead, tell them what you need and have the appropriate person call *you.*"

His plate empty, he tossed his napkin to the table, rose, kissed Darcy's forehead and said, "I'm going to phone Trace and Cade this morning. They need an update and maybe they'll have some ideas for how to get Bonetti talking."

With that he left, and Sophie slumped in her chair. Maybe some carbs were in order?

She bit into the cinnamon toast and felt marginally better. But with every bite, she got a little stronger. Or maybe her brain awoke? Like it or not, she had over a week left to deal with Wyatt. And she would do it like a professional.

Not a nitwit, who couldn't see past the fact that he was sexy and good in bed.

Wyatt walked back to the office he'd been using and plopped down on the desk chair. Before he set up the video call with his partners, he read through the financials one more time. It might be ten o'clock in Italy, but it was only four in the morning in Manhattan. He needed to be ready, so he didn't waste the time of his sleep-deprived friends.

Of course, Trace was in Tuscany. So, they were in sync. But even if Cade was on his island in the Florida Keys, he was still six hours behind.

After two hours of reading and making notes, pondering possible stumbling blocks for Bonetti's wanting to sell, he was ready to talk to Trace and Cade. He set his computer for a video call and within seconds their happy faces appeared on the screen. Cade's blond hair was a bit mussed as if he'd just crawled out of bed, but the rolled-up sleeves of Trace's shirt said he was already working. Sundays were one of his vineyard's busiest days.

"Everything okay?"

He sighed and sank back into the chair.

"You're sighing? I thought you'd be happy," Trace said with a laugh. "Lake Como is beautiful."

"It *is* beautiful. We've even taken a boat out."

Cade said, "That's great."

"Yeah, fabulous. The whole reason for my being here is to get a company, not to see the sights."

"Wouldn't hurt to see the sights," Trace pointed out, "if it would improve your sour mood."

"My mood will skyrocket when Signor Bonetti decides he wants to negotiate rather than play golf, introduce me to his family, show me his villa and in general talk about Italian food."

Cade sat up. "He's not negotiating?"

"I have no idea what he's doing. He actually left to visit his grandsons for a day and a half. Told me to see the sights."

"Maybe he doesn't like you grouchy either?"

The comment reminded him of Sophie. When Mrs. P. offered her cinnamon toast, it was clear her mood was apparent to everyone, not just him.

Because he'd kissed her?

Or because he'd brushed it off?

He used the things he'd found in the financials to take the conversation with Trace and Cade in the direction of the purpose for the call. Cade had observations, but Trace's thoughts about Bonetti struck a chord.

"He's clearly hesitant to sell his company. Maybe in the same way Marcia's dad had reservations about selling his vineyard to me."

Knowing the story of Trace's father-in-law, Wyatt said, "You think he's broke? He can't be broke. I read his financials. He's got enough money to support himself and his extended family for the next two generations."

"I'm talking more about pride," Trace said. "Marcia's dad pretended he was happy to be selling out and retiring, but being shoved out of the vineyard he'd nurtured from infancy made him feel small."

"Signor Bonetti does not feel small."

"Oh, you won't see it. He'll pretend for all the world that he's happy. That's how men like him salvage their pride. Watch for little things. Facial tics. A sudden look of sadness that he can't hide."

Wyatt rose from his seat and turned to gaze out the big window behind him. The manicured grounds soothed him, then he saw Sophie walking to the pool, holding a giggling Darcy.

Getting his mind off her bathing suit and back on the conversation with his partners, he said, "You think he doesn't want to sell?"

"I think he *does* want to sell," Trace said, "but maybe he feels odd letting go of his life's work."

"That makes sense."

Cade agreed. "I get that, too. I have a fiancée who won't desert the clientele she built up in our small town in Ohio. We should live in Manhattan...or on the island. Instead, she's caring for the people she loves. Because she's spent five years getting them to trust her and she won't breach that trust."

"See?" Trace said. "We *buy* existing companies so we don't understand the feeling that someone who builds a company from nothing would have when they sell."

"I suppose."

"Maybe be more careful with him?"

"I don't get a chance to be anything with him. He calls the shots."

Cade laughed. "I'd pay to see that."

"Very funny."

"You do have a tendency to be bossy," Trace reminded him.

He looked at Sophie, watched her slide Darcy through the water. He thought of how he'd kept their relationship in a neat little box three years ago so he could get what he wanted. "Maybe a little."

"And contrary to your beliefs, you're not always right."

Holding Darcy by the tummy, swishing her along the blue water, Sophie turned in a circle, showing him all sides of her perfect body in a little yellow swimsuit.

When he didn't laugh at Cade's snarky observation, Cade said, "What are you looking at?"

He pulled himself away from the window, sat at the desk and faced Cade and Trace again. "The nanny has the baby in the pool. I was just watching to make sure she was being safe with her."

"You hired a nanny?"

"You told me I had to."

"Well, that's good."

"Yeah, if she's careful with Darcy."

Trace shook his head. "Careful is sometimes your middle name, Wyatt, and though it's prudent to be safe, sometimes you've gotta take a risk. Get Bonetti talking about how he started the business," he said as he reached for the button to disconnect the call. "Then get back to us. I'll bet you'll have better news."

With that he ended the call.

Cade said, "I agree," then he disconnected too.

Wyatt pulled in a breath and swiveled his chair toward the window again. It was a hot day. Bonetti probably expected him to shuffle over and beg for his attention.

Well, Trace wanted him to take some risks? Maybe he would.

He called Bonetti, told him he wouldn't be over that day and headed upstairs to change into swimming trunks.

When he reached the pool, Sophie was twisting the baby, almost spinning her.

Terrified, he raced down the ladder. "What are you doing?"

"It's called a vertical spin. I saw it online. It's supposed to show her that the water doesn't have to control her. She can move in the water."

He took the baby from Sophie only to discover that Darcy was calm and happy. She babbled a few lines that sounded like an attempt to explain something to him.

Wyatt shook his head. "You liked being spun?"

Darcy grinned.

He glanced at Sophie. "Okay, maybe you have a point."

"There's tons of stuff on the internet about teaching babies to swim. Even if you aren't comfortable with it now, when she's only a few months old, at the very least getting her accustomed to the water, to moving in the water, will help her when you do think she's old enough."

"How young are the kids learning to swim in the videos you saw?"

"Six months. Eight months."

"Then she's old enough."

Sophie shrugged. "Yes. But…" She shrugged again. "Why rush things? Getting her accustomed to the water, to playing in the water, to seeing the water as fun might be as far as you need to go right now."

He totally relaxed then realized he'd tensed because he didn't want to push Darcy to do anything. His parents had pushed him his entire childhood—

He wouldn't let his mind take that unhappy trip. Not on such a beautiful day. Not when he'd finally called the shots with Signor Bonetti.

He looked around, let the greenery and blue sky calm him. "It's a perfect day."

"It is." She walked through the water to him. "Let me take her."

She reached out to take Darcy and their arms brushed. Electricity sprinted through him. He pretended he didn't feel it, though he let her take the baby.

He expected her to say something about him giving up the little girl so easily.

She didn't.

He relaxed some more. The baby giggled in Sophie's arms as she glided her through the water again, even doing the spin thing that had scared him. The sun beat down on him. The peace of the place filled him.

"I think I'll swim."

Sophie laughed. "You don't have to ask. Just swim."

He pushed off on his toes and dove across the three-foot water into the deeper area where he swam laps until he relaxed into a backstroke with a satisfied "Ahh."

"This place is more than pretty. Look around. There's so much to do. Places to walk and gather your thoughts. Tennis courts with ball returns so you can play alone. A basketball court. You could shoot hoops."

He didn't know why but hearing her say, "Shoot hoops," sounded funny.

"Do *you* shoot hoops?"

"Not really, but that's all the guys in my old neighborhood did."

He drifted closer to her and the baby.

"I'd watch them out the window."

He could see her, alone while her dad worked, not allowed outside where there was trouble. His heart did a little shimmy of sorrow for her, so he decided to steer clear of that part of the experience and took the conversation in the opposite direction.

"Didn't you learn anything from watching them?"

She laughed.

He shifted from the backstroke to treading water and reached for Darcy. "Give her to me."

She handed the baby over. Only their hands touched, but his skin prickled at her nearness. Their gazes caught. Their old connection arched between them, initiated, he was sure, by their easy conversation and the very natural way they were treating each other. Just like when they were lovers.

Baby securely in his arms, he eased into the deeper water again. He watched Sophie as she made a move to follow them, but hesitated.

He put his attention on Darcy as he casually said, "You know, if we'd let go the next few days, and just sleep together, we'd probably both be a lot happier."

He expected a horrified gasp. Instead, she ran her hand through the water.

Interesting.

Reading into her reaction, he said, "You've thought about it."

She took a breath.

"Wow. You've thought about it a lot."

Her gaze leapt to his. "So I've thought about it? But I thought about it…more as memories not planning for the future."

He laughed. "Memories *are* planning for the future."

Her face scrunched. "How do you get that?"

"You think about what was because you're really thinking about what could be."

He watched her eyes change as she understood his meaning. Then she trudged over to the pool's ladder. "Well, that just makes it official. I shouldn't have come."

That was the last thing he'd expected her to say. She was the perfect nanny. He'd been the perfect employer.

Only their attraction messed things up. And he had a solution for that.

"Come on. Come back in the pool. I think we need to talk about this."

She grabbed a towel. "You act like these two weeks are time stolen. Like we can do anything we want and just go home and pretend everything's normal. But I'm going home to trouble. I don't need to be pining for you on top of it."

Two things hit him simultaneously. First, he'd thought suggesting that they sleep together was sort of funny, a way to get it all out in the open, and yeah maybe nudge them in the direction of doing it.

She clearly had not.

Second, she *was* going home to trouble.

He slogged through the water to the ladder. "You're right."

She stopped drying herself with the big fluffy towel. "I'm right? Mr. I-know-what's-best-for-everybody is admitting he's wrong?"

"I didn't say I was wrong. I said you were right."

She only frowned at him.

"I still think we should sleep together. But I also see you've got some things to do before you can go home. Since I decided to ditch Bonetti today, we can go inside and call my PR department."

"It's Sunday."

"They're go-getters. Lots of them come in for a few hours, even on weekends. We'll set up a Zoom call to talk about the statement you'll need and also have them coach you on attitude and appearance. They'll show you how things you might do naturally can be perceived and then demonstrate how you should behave so you don't stand out in the crowd. You don't want to appear arrogant when you're doing something simple like getting your morning coffee."

The relief on her face showed just how worried she was about going home. He should have seen it or thought of it sooner, but he hadn't. While she'd been taking excellent care of Darcy, he'd sort of left her hanging out to dry.

Because he'd been afraid of their attraction.

But he wasn't anymore. And he would show her she didn't have to be either.

CHAPTER EIGHT

THE CALL WAS incredibly helpful. If Sophie had ever doubted the importance of a PR department, she had been converted to the other side. After hearing her part in the story of her mom's arrest, how she was innocent, merely house-sitting a condo, Wyatt's team made suggestions on how often to appear in public and even where to go. Coffee shops were good. Expensive restaurants were not. And no shopping trips. She didn't even want to give the appearance that she was spending money her mother had stolen.

She could have told them they need not worry about that. She had no money. She would not be shopping. But she kept her mouth shut and listened more than she spoke because that was how smart people learned.

After twenty more minutes of teaching her how to say, "No comment," without looking rude or condescending, the job of crafting her statement was assigned to a youngish-looking guy who promised he would get back to her on Monday.

She thought the conversation was over, but Wyatt went into detail about what he expected the statement to accomplish and while her eyebrows rose at his high expectations, his staff nodded and told him he'd get everything he wanted.

Of course, he would.

Not only was he the boss but his life seemed to be geared toward success. Sometimes it was almost fun watching fate turn into favor for him.

She remembered how much she'd loved that when they were dating, then memories poured into her brain like gentle rain, filling her chest with longing. She'd liked them together. They weren't exactly yin and yang, but they complemented each other. He was forceful. She was more subtle. She could pull him out of a bad mood. He could get her to come out of her shell.

He'd never thought of her as anything less than his equal. Despite her humble beginnings, they had been partners.

She'd missed that and the reminder only served to make her long for their connection.

He was feeling it too. He'd as much as said it in the pool, but his recollections seemed to be more sexual.

While hers were wistful. He was the guy of her dreams. Strong. Determined. Able to get things done. And romantic. He could be such a romantic when wooing her.

She almost sighed.

"So, everybody's got a job to do."

The people at the big conference table in his office nodded and said words of agreement.

"Okay, then. Get it done."

The simple way he commanded his staff sent that weird tingle through her and she understood what he'd been saying in the pool about their sexual tension, except she would add an "or" to his proposition. Either they had to indulge the sexual needs that wove through their conversations and daily dealings, *or* they had to stop spending so much time together.

The second choice seemed like the wiser one.

She rose from the seat across from him in the office of the villa. "You know what? I think I'm going to take the rest of the day off."

He blinked. "What?"

"You're here. You've got things under control. I just want to sightsee."

"I could—"

"You could stay with the baby."

He tossed his pen to the desk. From the expression in his eyes, she knew he was figuring things out, reasoning why she might want time on her own. "Our conversation in the pool isn't making you run away, is it?"

"Nope. Not running. Just want to see the sights."

He shook his head as if confused. "Alone?"

"There's nothing wrong with being alone." She took a breath. "Why don't you think of it as me needing a little time off after working five days with barely a break."

That struck the chord. "Oh. Geez. I'm sorry. You're working twenty-four-seven and right now I'm here to care for Darcy. You could get a break." He waved his hand. "Go. Enjoy."

"I'll be home in time to put her to bed."

"No. Don't worry about that. We're fine. Go. Have a good time. You can take one of the cars in the garage or if you don't want to drive on roads that you're unfamiliar with, Marco, the gardener is also the driver. I'm sure he'll be happy to take you to Bellagio."

"Thanks." She left to go to the kitchen to ask Mrs.

P. how to arrange for a ride into town and Mrs. P. said she would handle telling Marco.

After almost an hour to shower, fix her hair and put on a sundress, she was in a car being driven to town. That part felt weird. But otherwise, happiness buzzed through her. She was in Italy. About to tour the most beautiful small town she had ever seen. Yes, in a little over a week she'd be going home to a disaster, but right now, she was in Italy. She intended to enjoy it.

She spent the first hour ducking down cobblestone alleys with quaint shops, refusing to let her fun be stolen by thoughts of her mother and all the prep work she'd have to do with Wyatt's staff to get herself ready to deal with her mother's scandal.

But it wasn't easy. Almost a week had gone by. In another week, she'd be returning to her mother's mess made worse by the fact that she loved being Darcy's nanny and would miss her…and Wyatt.

Their relationship had ended in her heartbreak, but he had so many redeeming qualities. He was helping her. He loved Darcy. He trusted her with Darcy. He made her laugh. They could talk about things, even more than when they were together. He'd actually told her about his parents and Darcy's mother. Things he never would have done three years ago. And when they parted company, she would miss him.

The realization didn't surprise her, but as she walked through gaggles of tourists and past hand-holding lovers, she suddenly missed him *now*. They were like sunshine and blue skies. They fit. It was hell to be together but hold back saying things, *feeling* things. She saw him every morning, saw him when he returned from work, saw him when they put Darcy to bed together and she thought of him when she settled into her lonely bed—

The strangest thought hit her. No matter what happened between them, she would miss him. She wouldn't miss him any less if she spent the next week avoiding him. Or any more if they slept together.

Whatever happened, she would miss him.

Wanting to put her mind anywhere else than on Wyatt and the crystal-clear thoughts that began to haunt her, she considered buying a souvenir but decided to spend her money at the pastry shop she and Wyatt had visited. Right before she called Marco to return to collect her, she would indulge in one of those delicious desserts. That wouldn't be too much to put on her credit card, but it would make the late afternoon feel special.

Her plan made, she continued toward the town square. Tree-lined streets and statues took her attention to the point that she forgot to look where she was and simply wandered. Eventually, she found the Basilica of St. Giacomo and gaped for a minute at the gorgeous stone structure before she stepped inside.

Shimmering silence greeted her, along with a golden altar surrounded by a stone wall that formed a half circle. Ancient, but well-kept wooden furniture caught the colors that danced in through stained-glass windows. Stone walls and golden frames displayed paintings of angels and saints.

The perfection of it nearly overwhelmed her.

She glanced around. She'd never seen anything like it. She'd lived a small life until her mom bought her a condo and she and Wyatt started their affair. He'd opened up so much of the world to her and now he was doing it again. Just by giving her the opportunity to be at Lake Como for two weeks, he was showing her more of the world.

Damned if it didn't give her the feeling that she was thinking too small, letting her troubles control her.

She couldn't change the fact that her mom was in jail. She would have to answer questions. But she didn't have to cower or be afraid. She'd done nothing wrong.

And, damn it, she wasn't letting her life stop because her biological mom was a thief.

She walked out of the basilica laughing. She wasn't sure if it was letting a little time pass or if being with Wyatt had given her perspective, but she suddenly understood. She'd spent her entire life without her mother. She didn't have to either persecute her *or* help her. What she needed to do was take care of herself, take care of her own business to get her life back on track again.

Strolling to the bakery, she waited for more clarity about school, about money, about where she should live but none came. Still, she had a week before she had to make any decisions.

She took a seat at one of the outdoor tables, and a waiter hastened over to help her. She didn't speak Italian, so he shifted to broken English, which was charming but also reminded her that when they needed to smart people adjusted.

This time she chose a buttery cookie, buying six of them so she'd have some to take back to the villa. She ordered coffee, despite the late hour, and settled in to enjoy the scenery while she waited for her treat.

"Of all the—"

She glanced up to see Wyatt standing by her two-person table. He took a seat on the wrought iron chair across from hers. "I wasn't following you. I swear."

"You're supposed to be home."

He laughed. "I was. But after volunteering to watch the baby, Mrs. P. shooed me out. Said I'd have eighteen years with Darcy but how many times would I get to Lake Como."

"You told her you're rich, right?"

"Didn't seem to impress her."

She chuckled, but her heart swelled with that feeling she'd had as she wandered around Bellagio. It didn't matter if she and Wyatt spent no more time together, she would miss him when they returned home.

And even if it was wrong, she wanted to be with him—enjoy this chance she never thought she'd get.

"I actually ordered six cookies."

"Did you now?"

"I'd intended to take five of them back to the house as treats throughout the rest of the week."

"Then I won't take one."

"No, you probably should." She smiled across the table at him. "Besides, I like to share."

"I do remember that about you. You're one of the most generous people I know."

"You have your moments too."

He laughed.

And the world suddenly seemed to right itself.

"If you're really here to sightsee, I just spent an hour in Basilica of St. Giacomo. I wouldn't mind going back for a second look, if you'd like to see it."

"Really? You'd join me?"

"Well, let's see how many cookies you eat first."

He laughed again and the world righted itself a little more.

"I actually had some moments of clarity there."

"Oh?"

The waiter came, set the cookies on the table between them and gave Sophie her coffee.

"Another coffee for me, please," Wyatt said before he lifted a cookie. "What were your profound revelations?"

"Really just one big revelation."

"And?"

"I realized I hadn't done anything wrong, so I didn't need to cower or be afraid."

He nodded. "Time away was a good thing for you after all."

She winced. "That and listening to your PR staff. I'm not sure I'd be so comfortable standing tall without their talking points and guidance about keeping a low profile without staying out of sight."

"They are good."

"You trained them well."

"No. I was talking about the cookies. Eat one so I can eat another."

She rolled her eyes but took a cookie.

"Oh, wow."

He pulled in a breath as he looked around. "I'd say we have to come here again some time, but I guess we only have another a week in Italy. I'll probably spend most of it with Bonetti."

Just like that her bubble burst.

Or maybe she had another moment of clarity. They had a few days together and she wanted them. She wanted time with him and Darcy, fun in the swimming pool, and romantic nights.

And she was going after it.

CHAPTER NINE

AFTER A TRIP to the basilica, where Sophie all but gave Wyatt a guided tour, they knew it was time to head home. Walking through town to the parking lot where he'd left the car, he gave her his phone so she could call Mrs. P. who agreed to tell Marco she didn't need a ride home.

He held the door for her and she climbed into the little red convertible sports car. When he sat behind the steering wheel, she smiled over at him, warming his heart.

"You're always taking me places or showing me new things."

He maneuvered the car through the streets until he got them to the road that would return them to the villa. She'd been happy all evening, which made him happy, and caused the cascade of wonderful memories he had every time he was around her.

"I have access to more things," he said.

"And you're not afraid to try new stuff."

He peered over. "You're not afraid either."

She took a breath. "That's the new plan."

They spent the balance of the drive discussing fear and life and how smart people go after what they want.

He was working to reinforce her decision to take charge of her life when they returned to Manhattan. But he got the impression the conversation meant something totally different to her.

He let her out at the front door, then drove the convertible into the garage. Silence greeted him when he walked into the house and up the short hall to the foyer.

About to start up the steps to his bedroom, he stopped dead when she called to him from the drawing room off to the left.

"I poured you a bourbon."

He turned from the stairs. "You did?"

"And a glass of wine for myself."

Their ritual.

When they were dating and they'd returned from an event, he'd check his phone before he turned it off, while she poured him a bourbon and herself a glass of wine. Then they'd sit in the living room and sip their drinks. To decompress she'd say.

But he always managed to seduce her, lure her back to the bedroom, and their glasses would sit forgotten on his coffee table.

He licked his suddenly dry lips.

She smiled and displayed the short glass with a splash of amber liquid on ice.

Too intrigued to walk away, he entered the living room and took the drink she offered him.

He sat on the sofa. She sat beside him.

"You liked the basilica?"

He let his gaze drift to hers. "I like everything about Lake Como." And he liked her. Always had.

He'd broken up with her to save her but tonight she didn't look like a woman who needed saving.

She took a sip of wine. "You really should buy a second home here."

"I'll have Trace run some numbers."

She laughed and turned to face him, her elbow on the back of the sofa. "For what? You have plenty of money."

"Yes." He glanced down at his bourbon. "But a smart person doesn't jump into things."

She smiled. "Why not?"

"Risk."

"You can afford to lose a few million dollars."

His skin began to tingle from her nearness. "Not all risk is about money."

"What do you think you'll lose by buying a house? If you change your mind, you can always sell it. Not everything is meant to be permanent."

He glanced over at her. "No. I guess not."

"And sometimes," she said, her gaze firmly holding his. "Things come into our lives for periods of time, or for reasons, or to help us through something. The trick is to enjoy them, then be able to let them go."

He studied her face, full lips, pert nose, serious eyes.

He was just about certain he knew what she was telling him and while part of him wanted to slide his fingers into the thick hair at the back of her head to hold her still so he could kiss her senseless, the other part held back.

She quietly said, "You're helping me a lot."

"It's what good people do."

She set her glass on the coffee table and faced him fully. "Exactly. You had the ability to help me, and you did. Now we're in this beautiful part of the world where we're having fun with your daughter and remembering all the good things we did together."

He said nothing, only watched her.

"You said it yourself this afternoon."

"I did."

She rose from the sofa. He sat back, watching as she unbuttoned the two closures at the top of her dress, then reached down to pull it over her head, revealing a pink bra and panties.

His breath stuttered.

She straddled him. Her wavy yellow hair drifted around her. "You said you wanted to get rid of the tension between us."

"We were doing okay in Bellagio tonight."

She laughed. "You've never been able to resist me, and I've barely been able to resist you...and we have a few days. No promises. No regrets. Some of the best things in life are temporary."

She leaned in and kissed him, and he let himself tumble over the edge. He speared the fingers of his right hand into her hair while his left hand undid the hooks of her bra, tossed it away and flattened against her naked back to press her to him.

That's when he realized he was fully clothed, and she was virtually naked. Every atom in his body had expanded with need and he sat there in a layer of clothes. She placed her hands on his cheeks to kiss him fully and he took advantage, unbuttoning his shirt and undoing his belt. Then he tipped her to lie on the sofa, giving himself space to remove his shirt and pants.

Finally happy, he leaned down and grazed his hands along the curve of her waist, up to her breasts and back down again. He'd never been so desperate or so hungry and when his fingers met the silk of her panties, they didn't pause. He yanked the little pink triangles down as he leaned in to run his lips over her torso.

Somehow, she flipped their positions, easing him down so she could reach him. They touched and tasted each other, both a little desperate with need and reverent with the sense of disbelief. He never thought he'd touch her again. Not even when he'd made the suggestion in the pool. But here they were.

When he finally joined them, he took a minute to savor. What he felt for her went beyond simple need. He liked her. His emotions went further than what he felt for his friends, beyond what he'd ever felt for another woman, but he wouldn't call it love because love was a tarnished word to him.

So, he worshipped her with himself. He took them to a place where want and need collided and then exploded in a shower of perfection.

Then they went to his room and did it again. They didn't talk. They lingered, their actions speaking much louder than words ever could.

Sophie woke the next morning to the sense of coming home. Not a feeling of déjà vu at being in Wyatt's bed content and happy, but a perception that she had come back to where she belonged. She knew this wasn't forever. But what was? Her mother's love had barely lasted through her toddler years. Her dad had moved on with his new family. Her house sitting job had been three years then done.

Plus, she and Wyatt always seemed to have a shelf life. This time it was two weeks and one of those weeks was already gone.

She could make more of this than it meant to him.

Or she could enjoy what they had. Take memories back to Manhattan with her. Then use them to help her get through the rough weeks when she got home and the even rougher year it would take to finish school while she struggled to find loans and grants and waited tables to make her rent.

That would be the smart move. And if there was one thing she was learning on this trip to Italy it was that she was smart. She didn't have to be timid. She didn't have to think herself less than because her mother had abandoned her. She was fine…just the way she was.

Realizing Wyatt was spooned around her, she smiled.

He nuzzled her neck. "Good morning."

She turned in his arms. "Good morning."

"I didn't hear the baby last night."

She winced. "I got up with her twice. Once there was a disaster in her diaper. Once she wanted to eat."

He laughed. "So maybe it was lucky I didn't hear her."

She nipped a kiss on his lips. "Or preplanned." She slid out of bed. "We have a choice. Quickly shower and hope she doesn't wake up. Or go wake her and start the day."

He rolled out of bed. Gloriously naked, he stepped into a pair of sweats. "I'll get her. You shower."

Surprised, she frowned. "Really?" He never missed a chance at shower sex.

"Of course, it *is* only six," he said casually. "If we hurried, we could probably shower and be out before she wakes."

"She was up at five. She's probably got another good hour of sleep in her."

He headed for the bathroom. "Let's not waste a minute."

She walked into the glass and shiny white tile shower. He followed her in and turned her around for a blistering kiss. The night before, he'd let her take the lead. This morning he was totally in command. Hot kisses morphed into a steamy trail of bites down her neck, as his hands roamed every inch of her.

When she tried to touch him, he held her hands behind her back, as if telling her he wanted his fun now. She let him have his way until they were both breathless with need then he pressed her against the shower wall and took her.

After a second session, she shared the shower spray with him, quickly washed her hair and got out, so she could tend to the baby.

She grabbed a fluffy towel to dry herself and the sounds of Darcy crying suddenly erupted from the baby monitor. "I'll get her."

She turned and reached for...nothing.

"I forgot! I don't have clothes!"

He stepped into the sweats again. "That's okay. You go to your room to dress. I'll get the baby."

Though it only took her ten minutes to comb out her hair and slip into a T-shirt and shorts, the nursery was empty by the time she arrived.

She raced downstairs to find happy Darcy in the highchair and Wyatt sitting at the head of the table, a T-shirt added to his sweatpants.

"That was fast."

She flipped her wet hair over her shoulder. "That's the good thing about long hair. I can let it air dry."

Mrs. P. walked in. "Good morning, Sophie. The usual?"

Wyatt intervened. "I think she should have pancakes this morning."

She gasped. "I haven't had pancakes in years."

Casually spooning some rice cereal into Darcy's open mouth, Wyatt said, "Three years, I'll bet."

She laughed, remembering how he could get her to eat pancakes every Sunday morning when she would have chosen fruit. "That might be a good thing."

"Not when you use a lot of energy." He fed Darcy another bite. "And sightseeing last night had us walking everywhere."

She smiled at Mrs. P. "Pancakes it is."

As the cook left, Wyatt said, "So what's on your agenda for today?"

"I was going to ask you the same thing."

"I'll probably see Bonetti. Listen to stories about his life. Trace said to try to get him talking about starting his business but any time I mention his business he ignores me."

She laughed. "Why don't you turn the tables and start talking about your life? Tell him stories about Darcy, your friends, Cade's island, Trace's vineyard."

His coffee cup stopped midway to his mouth. "That's not such a bad idea."

"You once told me that mimicking is a negotiating tool."

"It is."

"So use it. Talk about what he talks about."

He set his coffee cup on the saucer. "I don't normally talk about myself."

"Maybe that's what he's waiting for?"

"Trace thinks he's having trouble selling his company. His baby."

She shrugged. "Maybe. Or maybe he's been trying to draw you out so he can see who he's selling his company to."

He grimaced. "I should rephrase what I said before. I don't *like* talking about myself."

"Yeah, no kidding." She took a quick breath. "Keep the conversation on your friendships with your partners. After all, it's three of you buying the company. Talk about Cade. Talk about Trace. Talk about your friendship. Your bond."

Even as she said that the doorbell chimed. A minute later, Mrs. P. walked into the dining room with a short bald man.

Wyatt rose. "Mr. Bonetti."

Sophie's eyebrows shot up, but Bonetti grinned. "Good morning."

He motioned to Sophie who wasn't quite sure if she should rise and stay seated or bow. He looked like an aging statesman who deserved the respect.

"This is Sophie Sanders, Darcy's nanny." He pointed to the baby in the highchair. "And this is Darcy." He paused a second as Bonetti took the seat beside Sophie. "Would you like some coffee?"

"Yes. Thank you."

Wyatt nodded to Mrs. P., indicating he would get the coffee and she left the room.

"What brings you here?"

"I love this villa. I wanted to be sure you were comfortable."

Or he was checking up on them.

Wyatt poured the coffee and served it to Bonetti. "Sophie's been telling me I should buy it."

Bonetti laughed.

"I think his partners would really like it," Sophie interjected before Wyatt could say anything else. "Trace actually owns a vineyard in Tuscany. Cade's more of an all-American. He owns an island with a beach house."

Bonetti's thick, black eyebrows rose. "Oh?"

"Both are engaged. Trace's fiancée is general manager of his vineyard. Cade's fiancée owns a home nursing agency."

Bonetti nodded.

"They are great guys. Smart but normal. You know, they like boating and watching sports, as much as they like running big companies."

Wyatt stared at Sophie. Though Cade and Trace believed Bonetti was being nostalgic about selling the company he'd built, the old man seemed to be extremely interested in what Sophie was saying. As if she'd been correct, Bonetti wanted to know some personal details about the people seeking to buy his life's work.

He fed Darcy another spoonful of cereal, remembering again how smart Sophie was as she continued to tell Bonetti things about Trace and Cade, things she remembered from when she'd met them. Things he'd told her in passing.

The interesting thing about Sophie was that she was so accustomed to being observant and putting two and two together that she never saw how intelligent she was. Or, maybe more important, she didn't realize how rare it was that someone could use their intelligence so practically.

Bonetti stayed an hour, letting Wyatt take Darcy upstairs for her morning nap, while he continued to chit-chat with Sophie.

When he returned downstairs, Bonetti was gone and Sophie was grinning. "He said he'll see you at his house when you're ready to come over."

He returned to his seat at the breakfast table. "Thanks."

Sophie's grin grew. "He seemed more than interested in your partners."

"And you were doing a great job talking about them, so I let you run with the ball."

"It was fun."

"And you were aces at it." He wanted to tell her he now owed her, but he knew she'd brush that off. "I wish you'd let me help you." The words were out of his mouth before he realized he'd even formed them. But now that they were out, he stood by them.

"You are helping me."

"The only thing you'll seem to let me do is give you access to my PR department."

"Hey, bud, don't forget you're paying me a salary for being Darcy's nanny. And I expect a pretty penny. Enough for first month's rent and security deposit for a halfway decent apartment."

He hadn't forgotten. He just wasn't sure how much he could pay her before she'd have a hissy fit and refuse his generosity.

"If you'd let me, I could put in a good word for you with one of my business acquaintances to get you a job as an assistant so you could finish university."

"Oh, I plan to finish."

He remembered her saying that the trip had given her clarity. It looked like school had factored into that.

She took a sip of coffee, then said, "I worked all that out yesterday."

"While you were sightseeing?"

"Yes. With a clear head, I recognized I could get grants and loans like everybody else. I'll be filling out applications while Darcy naps today. I didn't come this far to quit."

His heart stumbled with relief. "I could actually pay you enough that it would cover your rent for a year."

She set her fork down and sighed. "Wyatt. I have to do this myself."

"Why?"

"Because you're not my reality."

His face scrunched. "Did you just say I'm not real?"

She snorted. "No. I'm saying that when we return to Manhattan, we will not be in the same world. You'll be working in Manhattan. I can't afford to live there, so God knows where I'll end up. But we'll probably never see each other again once we return to the States."

Though that thought had flirted with entering his brain, he'd never allowed it to fully form. Oh, he knew it was true, but he didn't want to think about it.

Or ponder how easy it seemed to be for her to accept it.

"Truth be told, this whole trip isn't my reality. I was lucky that you came up to my apartment and caught me when I was so gobsmacked I could barely think. I'd have been drowning in trouble right now if I'd stayed in New York. So though other people might consider this side trip delaying the inevitable, to me it was lucky you stepped in and offered me this job. A chance to get away to think and make some money."

At least she called it lucky that he'd offered her a job.

He stared at his empty coffee cup. "Darcy and I needed you too."

She grinned. "See? Lucky." Her smile dimmed a bit. "But when we get home, reality returns. I have to be prepared for that. Ready to stand on my own two feet."

There were so many ways he could help her, so many things he could do. It made his chest ache that she wouldn't let him do any of those, even as it made him extremely proud of her.

She'd come to terms with this and after a few days of looking for loans and grants and working with his PR team, she would be ready to go home.

He suddenly understood that was what her seduction the night before was all about.

She'd decided to enjoy what was left of their trip because when she got home, reality would hit. And hit hard.

As someone who liked her and understood her problems, he had to support her. He couldn't argue with her. He couldn't suggest alternatives to her plan.

He would go home to his penthouse that was like a palace, with a baby who loved him, two friends who supported him...

While she went home to trouble.

Only a selfish idiot would mess with what was undoubtedly a fragile peace she'd made with herself and her future.

CHAPTER TEN

AROUND NOON, WYATT left for Bonetti's. Sophie took Darcy for a stroll around the grounds, promising her a swim later that afternoon. The baby babbled and giggled and in general tired herself out. When Sophie took her upstairs to the nursery and fed her a bottle, the little girl immediately fell into a deep sleep.

Sophie leaned back in the rocking chair, staring at Darcy's beautiful face. Feelings she'd been avoiding with Wyatt's baby girl crept up on her. The warmth of love filled her chest, along with the desire for Darcy to have every good thing in life, and a protectiveness that shocked her.

Which made her wonder about her own mother. Darcy wasn't even her child, yet Sophie would face the forces of hell if anyone tried to hurt her. She couldn't imagine Darcy's mother simply deciding one day that she'd rather have a career than raise her child.

Yet, that's what she'd done.

That's what Sophie's mother had also done.

Maybe that was the connection she felt with Darcy now? Not maternal instinct but normal protectiveness. Sophie understood abandonment. She knew the deep hurt. The questions that bubbled up when she'd seen her friends shopping with their moms or dancing around their kitchens. She hadn't had that closeness and never would. She knew the emptiness of that loss and internally railed against Darcy someday facing that.

Of course, Wyatt might dance in the kitchen with his little girl. She also could see him taking Darcy shopping and sitting in a chair outside a waiting room holding her jacket.

Even without a mother, Darcy would have what Sophie never had. A place. While Sophie's dad struggled just to put food on the table, working long hours and sometimes two jobs, Wyatt called the shots in his life.

Something that felt a lot like self-pity tried to rise, but she reminded herself it was fate, luck of the draw who her parents were. She'd accepted that at fourteen. She'd used the knowledge to make herself stronger.

Plus, she loved her dad. Always had. Always would. He'd simply moved on, as a normal guy should. With a wife and two kids and a new mortgage there wasn't time or room for her in his life.

As Darcy slept on her arm, she allowed herself to realize just how strong a woman had to be to look around for the silver lining in her chaos—to choose to recognize that she had more than lots of people had and needed to take what she'd been given and make the best life possible.

She reveled in that strength, thanked God she had that strength and knew right then and there that no matter what happened, she would survive.

The baby snuggled against her, and her heart warmed as her chest filled with love. She might not get things the way other women got them, but she had time with two people she loved. Wyatt and Darcy.

She would only be kidding herself if she thought she didn't love them. This was her space of time to enjoy that. Not just Wyatt, but the baby too.

A whisp of common sense tried to remind her this was a slippery slope. She remembered how hard it had been to get over losing Wyatt—losing the baby would make it impossibly hard, but she shoved those thoughts away.

She was making memories. That was all.

She would need them for the difficult few years she had ahead of her.

Wyatt sat on a sofa in Signor Bonetti's huge office. Dark wood paneling covered the walls, a brown leather sofa and chair served as a conference area and a huge mahogany desk sat along the back window, behind a dark red oriental rug.

He'd been in a hundred offices like this. The workplaces of men on the verge or retiring, letting go of their life's work, accepting their accomplishments—big or small—as their legacy because they were done.

Some wanted to kick back and enjoy their upcoming free time. Some knew their best years were behind them. Others wanted their company to go on, strong and healthy. Not teetering because of mediocre leadership.

When Bonetti walked over to him from behind the desk and handed him the new five-year plan created by his employees, Wyatt knew that Sophie's chat that morning about Trace and Cade, and the friendship Wyatt shared with them, had resolved some of Bonetti's concerns about whether Three Musketeers Holdings could keep his company solvent.

But he realized two more things. First, Signor

Bonetti wanted his company to outlive him. Second, Bonetti had been stalling this past week while his employees finished the financial forecast that outlined what Bonetti wanted his company to accomplish in the next five years.

"This is ambitious."

Bonetti's eyes shined. "You cannot accomplish that?"

"Oh, my partners and I can pretty much do anything we set our minds to."

"Then, we are ready to discuss terms?"

"Yes and no." Wyatt glanced down at the small booklet in front of him. "First, we're going to have to talk money. There's no way we're giving your family twenty-five percent of the profits of a company we'll be running without them." He looked up at Bonetti. "If that's a deal breaker, I can go home now."

"I need to take care of my children."

"You're asking for billions of dollars for this business. Invest it wisely, and generations of Bonettis will live happily-ever-after."

Bonetti laughed. "Should be true. But you don't know my kids."

Wyatt rose. "And I don't intend to support them." He plucked his suit coat off the back of his chair and slid into it, then picked up his copy of the five-year plan. "I don't want to make promises or draw lines until I've read this. But let me give you a piece of advice. Teach your kids how to invest...or put the money in trust for them."

He said the last to give Bonetti some guidance that might ease his mind enough to accept the offer Wyatt was pretty sure he'd be making. But he didn't want to say anything definitive, not even to himself, until he read the five-year plan.

"I'll see you tomorrow."

Bonetti rose. "Okay. Tomorrow."

He returned to the villa and found Sophie and Darcy in the pool. He walked outside, loosening his tie. "If you don't mind, I'm going to spend the afternoon reading this." He displayed the five-year plan.

She swirled Darcy through the water, earning a giggle. "No. We don't mind. Go. Do whatever."

He returned the house and walked straight to the office. After hanging his jacket on the back of a chair and draping his tie over that, he took a seat behind the desk and began reading.

Though the plan was detailed, it only took about two hours to read it and realize that Bonetti wanted Three Musketeers Holdings to keep the company pretty much the way it was. Which was ridiculous. The point of buying a big company like Bonetti's was to improve on it.

He skimmed the whole plan again and when he let go of his own agenda and simply looked for Bonetti's, he realized the old man didn't merely want to assure his kids and their kids and their kids would forever be rich. He also wanted his current employees to have job security.

It was a great idea. Actually, it showed Bonetti was a kind man.

But business was business. He probably would keep most of Bonetti's employees. But he couldn't promise anyone forever.

No one could.

The thought gave him a funny feeling in his gut. He knew that was true. So why did it feel odd, out of place?

A sound had his head jerking up and he looked at the door to see Sophie holding Darcy. "She's going down for her second nap."

He nodded, but also allowed his gaze to take a quick tour of Sophie's long legs.

If she noticed, she didn't show it as she casually said, "Did you have lunch?"

"No. I basically bugged out of Bonetti's to get home to read the five-year plan he wants us to follow."

"Can a guy really tell you how he wants his company run after you buy it?"

"He can tell us anything. The real bottom line to an agreement is enforcement."

"Oh."

"Don't think I'd buy his company and then disregard an agreement to follow his five-year plan. There's integrity involved too."

She smiled.

For some reason, a wave of pride poured through him. She always seemed to see the best in him, or maybe bring out the best in him. Which was one of the reasons he enjoyed having her around. He'd worked for decades not to turn into his dad. She reminded him he hadn't.

"Anyway, I'm taking the baby to the nursery." As if on cue, Darcy rubbed her eyes sleepily. "Wanna kiss her good-night?"

He rose, walked over and kissed Darcy's forehead. "I'll see you later."

She snuggled into Sophie's chest.

Memories of their night before and morning in the shower rippled through him. He wanted more. Not just sex. But time. He wanted to laugh and talk and let his brain forget about the Bonetti family and their big dreams of being rich forever without doing anything.

"You and I should go out to dinner tonight."

She caught his gaze. "We could."

"Yeah. We could. When she gets up, I'll spend a few hours with her. Then we can leave her with Mrs. P. and head into town."

Just the thought made him feel ridiculous things. Happy. Content. Normal.

Happy and content he understood. Normal perplexed him. How could he feel normal when he had no idea what normal was?

He didn't have time or mental energy to debate it in his brain. He simply let it go.

"Do you want me to find a place, or do you want to?"

She smiled. "Surprise me."

She turned and headed to the nursery, and he chuckled as he returned to his seat behind the desk. The emotions rumbling through him and his behavior were just silly, then he realized there was something different about her too. Probably the result of having made her decisions about school. Or maybe she'd found some grants and loans and some of her tension had eased?

Deciding that was probably it, he chose a restaurant in Bellagio, if only so they didn't have to waste too much time driving. The night was beautiful, and he had the top down on the convertible, but he had plans for when they returned. Maybe a moonlight swim.

They strolled to the restaurant and were immediately seated.

She looked around in awe. "It's so quaint."

He followed her lead, taking in the linen table-cloths, stone walls and shelves of wineglasses beside the wooden wine rack. "All the reviews say the food is wonderful."

She grinned. "I can't believe I'm here."

He took a menu from a waiter with a murmured, "Thank you," as her words settled in on him. That was what he should be feeling. A sort of disbelief that a woman from his past was suddenly in his present. But none of those emotions ever struck him.

That was what the *normal* feeling had been about. He'd always been comfortable with her. Which was probably why it had been so easy for him to ask her to join them as Darcy's nanny.

They ordered wine and the waiter left them to look over the menu. He saw a few things that intrigued him, but he couldn't stop thinking about how comfortable he was with her. How his schedule and his life would go back to the madness he hated when they returned to Manhattan.

And she'd go back to trouble.

He bit his bottom lip, then glanced over his menu at her. "Has it ever crossed your mind that maybe you should continue as my nanny when we return to Manhattan?"

She blinked, so surprised her expression froze comically.

He gaped at her. "It *never* crossed your mind?"

"When I think of going back, I keep seeing myself homeless."

He laughed. The waiter returned with their wine, plus a basket of warm bread and a plate of olive oil. They ordered their dinners and the waiter left again.

"You think it's funny that I'm going to be homeless?"

"No. I think it's awful. And I will *never* let that happen. But I also can't believe that it never dawned on us that you could be Darcy's nanny while you're finishing your education. I think the easiest thing to do would be night school. You could study while Darcy was napping, and on nights that I couldn't get home in time for you to go to classes we could hire a sitter." He sniffed a laugh. "Nosey Cade has found two services that will provide fill-in nannies. Our schedules would run like clockwork."

She took a breath as she reached for her wineglass. He expected her to gasp with happiness. Instead, she frowned.

"You don't agree?"

She sighed. "Wyatt. I like you guys. But you aren't my life. You're like the fairytale where the poor wench meets a prince who rescues her and then the book ends. Everybody thinks it's a happy ending but in real life, the wench goes back to sweeping the hearth and scrounging for grain to bake bread because that's who she is."

"That doesn't have to be true. Not with a job offer on the table."

She shook her head. "No. These two weeks were a break. A much-needed break for me to get my head on straight. But it's not my reality."

He hated the punch-in-the-gut feeling he got from her words. Part of him wanted to argue. The other part had no idea what his argument was. She was an intelligent woman who needed to get an education and move on. She was right. He and Darcy weren't her reality.

So why the hell did that make him feel awful?

Because working for him as Darcy's nanny could make the next year easy for her. Plus, her working for him solved a problem for them both. Yet she discounted it without thinking it through.

"I understand what you're saying, but I still need a nanny and even if you don't want to be with us forever, working for me for a year might be the answer to how you get your degree."

She played with her wineglass. "Maybe."

"No maybe about it. I am offering you the job."

"And I don't think it's the right choice for me."

Her tone of voice said the conversation was over and the waiter picked that precise moment to deliver their food.

Wyatt whipped his linen napkin off the table, not sure why he was so angry when she was an adult who had the right to make her own choices, but he was.

Her love of her dinner softened his annoyance. The way she took his hand as they walked to the convertible melted it a bit more. The moonlight drive, with her leaning across the seat to snuggle into him completely obliterated it.

As they got out of the car and exited the garage, he said, "So, how about a swim?"

"Now? It's midnight…" She glanced at her watch. "No, wait. It's only eleven."

At the bottom of the steps in the foyer, he laughed and pulled her to him. "If it's time you're worried about, we can undress as we race to the pool."

Her smiled grew. "And skinny dip."

"It's the best way to do what I have planned for us in the water."

She laughed.

"There you are!"

The sound of his father's voice coming from the living room sent a lightning bolt of confusion and revulsion down his spine.

Stretching to see beyond the foyer, he moved away from Sophie. "Dad?"

"And me too." His mother entered the foyer, glass of brandy in hand. "You are in so much trouble!"

"If it's curfew you're worried about Sophie just told me it's only eleven," Wyatt quipped.

"Don't screw off with us, Wyatt!" His dad's angry voice sent another chill down his spine. "It takes a maid to tell us we have a grandchild?"

CHAPTER ELEVEN

WIDE-EYED, SOPHIE shifted around Wyatt. "I think I'll head up to my room."

An odd sensation shuffled through him as he watched her climb the stairs. He'd be racing away himself if these weren't his parents. But it somehow felt significant that she'd gone. That she hadn't stayed even long enough for him to introduce her to his parents.

"And who is that?" Wyatt's dad waved his hand indignantly at Sophie who had reached the top of the stairs. "Some floozie you dragged along on your fancy trip to Lake Como?"

"That's Darcy's nanny," Wyatt replied, so angry he could have spit fire. He eyed them suspiciously. His short, thin mom had brown hair cut in a blunt line. His dad was tall and thin with the same dark hair Wyatt had. Both were dressed as if they'd just come from the yacht club. "What are you doing here?"

"We heard you were here and wanted to surprise you," his mom said before taking a sip of brandy. "Guess we're the ones who got a surprise and not a good one."

Wyatt gaped at her. That was just like his parents. They never considered anyone but themselves. "Did you ever stop to think that if you'd let me know you were coming there wouldn't have been a surprise?"

His dad huffed out a sigh and headed to the living room. "I don't get it. I have absolutely no idea how we could have ended up with such an ungrateful son."

"I'm not ungrateful." The sting of being reprimanded hit first, but it was quickly followed by the knowledge that they didn't know him at all. They didn't see his successes. They didn't see his struggles. All they saw were their needs. He never spoke unkindly about them in public. He also gave his dad credit for pointing him in the direction of investing. He might not be the best son, but he was the kind of son they'd raised him to be. Quiet. Distanced. Available for their functions and always polite.

He was who they wanted him to be.

And the first time he didn't do exactly what they thought he should do, they were angry? No. He was not allowing that.

Wyatt followed his parents into the living room and walked directly to the bar where he poured himself a bourbon. The word *ungrateful* rattled through him. Still, he had a choice. Take a stand right now or say and do what he had to do to avoid arguments. After all, nothing he said or did would change them. Fighting would only make everyone uncomfortable. He chose the avoiding arguments route.

"You educated me and now I am self-sufficient."

"It would just be nice to see you now and again," his mom said, sitting on the sofa.

"You do see me at all your charity events."

His mom said, "Hmmm," as if she agreed.

His dad jumped right over that and went for the jugular, as he plopped down on the sofa beside his mother. "You kept a baby from us!"

He would have kept Darcy away from their toxicity forever if he could. He didn't want her paraded around Manhattan as their granddaughter and ignored at holidays. He didn't want her confused by an overabundance of attention one minute and absolutely no contact for weeks. He knew what it was like to be a child longing for affection and being ignored. He hadn't quite figured out how to protect his little girl, how to shield her, but he would. Right now, though, he stuck with facts, giving them the information his father wanted.

"I got her a few months ago from an old...girlfriend. We'd broken up over a year ago. I had no idea she'd gotten pregnant. But when she found out, I don't think she intended to tell me. I got the feeling she was enamored with the idea of being a mother. Then a job opportunity came up for her, and she suddenly didn't want to be a mom anymore. Her career came first. And I stepped up."

Horrified, his mom said, "You make her sound like a one-night stand! You got a baby from a one-night stand?"

"No. We dated a little longer."

"Fine. What kind of woman is she? Does she come from a good family? Good Lord, Wyatt? Do you even know anything about your child's background?"

His dad gaped at him. "Does she want money? Is she suing you? Is that what this is all about? She got pregnant to get at your money?"

"Dad, at this point I wouldn't care. I have custody and I also have lawyers. On top of that, I have a pretty strong case to keep custody, as Darcy's mom abandoned her."

"You've checked into it?"

He sat back in his chair. "A bit. But I've kept better tabs on Shelly. She's setting the world on fire and very happy in her job. After what she told me when she dropped Darcy in my lap, she's not coming back. If she does, I will deal with her."

His dad took a breath. "Have your lawyer draw up an agreement where she gives up her rights to the baby. Take it to her and make sure she signs it."

"No! I'm not having her give up her rights. At some point, Darcy might want a relationship—"

His mother groaned. "Are you insane? She sounds like trouble and the best way to head off trouble is nip it in the bud. Get that agreement signed now!"

"And never let Darcy know her mom?"

"She'll be better off for it."

"I disagree."

His father shook his head in disgust. "Just as I thought, you can't handle this."

"Actually, I can and I am. If you knew me better, you would realize no one pushes me around." Not even them. Not anymore.

Watching the amber liquid in her glass, his mother let out a disgusted breath. "I'm not sure how we'll introduce your child to society."

"You won't, Mom. I don't intend to raise her that way."

"Oh, Wyatt. Don't be ridiculous. She might be less than a year old, but she's *our* grandchild. Not only will the world want to see her, but there are some things we should be doing. Most parents get their children on waiting lists for the good schools before the baby's even born. If you haven't done that, I'd be happy to."

"I might home school her," Wyatt said. He'd always

known this would be the real fight of his life. Giving his daughter a happier, healthier environment than the one he'd lived in. He hadn't realized it would start so soon. "Plus, Manhattan isn't the only place that has good schools. Or the only place I'm considering living."

His mother's horrified expression returned. "You might *leave* New York?"

"Cade owns an island. It might be nice to build a house there."

She flopped back on the sofa.

His dad stared at him. "You've spent years *building* a career—"

"And I have enough money that if I chose not to work ever again, I wouldn't have to." Maybe this was why he and Bonetti couldn't seem to get down to business about transferring ownership of his company? Maybe he wasn't supposed to throw himself into another project now? Maybe he would need all his energy to shield his daughter from his parents' need to run her life, to turn her into the perfect little princess who wouldn't really have friends because everyone was competition?

Not ready to get into that argument, he rose from his seat. "It was a long day for me, and I have another long day tomorrow. If you don't mind, I'm going to bed."

He turned to leave but spun around again. "I'm assuming Mrs. P. got you settled in."

"She did."

"Goodnight, then."

After leaving Wyatt in the foyer with his parents, Sophie went to the nursery and checked on the baby then began walking across the room to the connecting door to her suite. It had taken heavy-duty self-discipline not to listen to the conversation taking place as she'd climbed the steps, but she hadn't. She wasn't part of this. After only a little over a week of working as Darcy's nanny, she had no right in a discussion with Wyatt's parents about their granddaughter.

She hesitated by the door to her bedroom. She'd spent the night before in Wyatt's room and they'd more than made plans to sleep together that evening. But with his parents' arrival those plans had gone out the window.

She opened the door to her room. It was better for her to be beside the nursery anyway. Not only was she closer to the baby but she didn't have clothes in Wyatt's room.

She tried to tell herself that the change of plans didn't matter, but the hollow feeling she'd had at her father's home the last year she'd lived there formed in her chest. At the time, she'd thought it was simply her eighteen-year-old self, longing to be out on her own. Now, she knew the urge to leave, to find her place, had been more about being an outsider looking in. Her father had a new wife, new kids, a whole new life and for the two years she'd lived with them, she'd been like a fifth wheel.

Just like she felt now.

She stopped those thoughts as she washed her face, brushed her teeth and slipped into her favorite silky pajamas because the empty feeling of having no one, belonging nowhere, filled her chest again. She stopped it by reminding herself that this was her time with Wyatt. Time to make memories. Time to relax and have some fun before she went home and faced God knew what. Having his parents arrive suddenly would certainly put a damper on that. But knowing Wyatt, he'd figure out a way for them to be together.

Focusing on that was much better than dwelling on the fact that she didn't really have a place in Wyatt's life, either.

Turning off the bedside lamp, she remembered Wyatt suggesting that she take the job as his nanny when they got home and for a few seconds she considered it, but she had to reject it. Their attraction was too powerful. They'd never have a simple working relationship. She would be a nanny having an affair with her charge's father. She'd be a cliché, but, worse, there were bigger things to consider. She liked him and Darcy so much that if she stayed a year, got accustomed to being in their lives that way, she'd probably never move on. There'd always be a reason to stay.

As his nanny.

Deep down inside she knew Wyatt didn't want her permanently. He liked being mobile. Being free. Plus, he was a guy who went after what he wanted. If he wanted her in his life forever, she'd know. He wouldn't have asked her to stay on as Darcy's nanny while she finished school.

Didn't matter. She would get her education, get a fabulous job and become someone. She wouldn't find her place. She would *make* her place.

She couldn't forget that.

Her bedroom door opened suddenly, and Wyatt walked in. "Can you believe them?"

Sophie only stared at him. He hadn't knocked. He entered as if he'd done it a million times before.

"Seriously, my mom's talking about schools already. Discussions about horseback riding lessons and competitions aren't far behind."

Realizing he needed a sounding board, someone to

talk this out with, she raised herself to her elbows. "And that's bad?"

"Oh, dear God," he said, yanking off his shirt, then moving on to his belt.

She blinked. That was a little more than sounding board material.

"They ran my life like two drill instructors. I didn't have friends. Everybody was a potential competitor. And I didn't even have my parents. I saw them once or twice a week when my dad would grill me about my grades and my mother would remind me she would be mortified if I embarrassed her. It wasn't merely a lonely way to grow up. It was confusing." Without hesitation or question, he crawled into bed with her. "And now they want Darcy."

She almost said, "You'll figure it out," but he hadn't reached for her to make love. Instead, he lay beside her, his arms behind his head, on the pillow. His behavior was so casual, they could have been an old married couple or longtime lovers.

"You are Darcy's dad. You don't have to let them run her life."

"I know. I'm just furious that I have to keep them in line." He groaned. "They're horrible people. No. I should take that back. They aren't horrible. They're just not real. They live for what other people think and they never, ever considered my needs. Actually, most of the time I felt they never considered me a person. I was more like a possession that came with responsibility. After I got old enough to realize that, I also saw I wasn't the problem. They were. And that was a relief." He paused for a second. "But it's a lonely way to live."

Their parental troubles might be different, but the

result was the same. Both she and Wyatt had had lonely childhoods. "Tell me about it."

He turned his head on the pillow to look at her. "I know. Your dad left you alone a lot too."

The fact that he remembered and understood filled her with happiness. But she wouldn't let herself make too much of it. She'd promised him this time to enjoy themselves while they were in Italy, but in moments like this she had to wonder how she could keep that promise without getting her heart broken. They always seemed so perfect together.

"My dad had no choice. He was working two jobs. Couldn't afford a sitter."

"Yeah."

The room grew quiet again. They were talking about loneliness—she'd been thinking about loneliness before he'd come into the room—but his opening up to her wrapped her in a warm, fuzzy feeling.

She squeezed her eyes shut, half letting herself bask in it and half reminding herself that this wasn't permanent.

But at least now she understood why he had so much trouble connecting to people. He'd never really been taught to make friends. He'd never experienced love or acceptance from his parents. He'd had to leave home to find reality.

He rolled over to kiss her goodnight and as he pulled away she smiled up at him.

He chuckled softly. "How can I feel better when my parents are still in the living room?"

She could have told him that their connection was as good for him as it was for her. But that was a Pandora's box best left closed.

"I don't know. Maybe out of sight, out of mind?"

He rolled his eyes. "I wish."

She walked her fingers up his chest. "I know a way we can take your mind off them."

He laughed, but he kissed her again. "We're supposed to be skinny dipping right now."

She shrugged. "I like it here." She smiled at him again. "We might want to consider checking to see if the door has a lock though. Your dad seems to enjoy barging in on people."

He snorted, but he locked the door before he returned to bed and made love like a guy who enjoyed her so much, he could never get enough of her.

But she'd already reasoned all of this out in her head. If he really couldn't get enough of her, he wouldn't have asked her to remain on as his nanny. He'd think of her very, very differently.

The next morning, Darcy woke them, and they simultaneously rolled out of bed and stumbled into the nursery.

Sophie found clothes for the baby while Wyatt changed her diaper. Then he brought Darcy into Sophie's room while she quickly dressed in something suitable for breakfast. Then they all went to his room.

He sat Darcy on the bed. "You know, you could take her to the dining room and get the breakfast ball rolling."

"Not on your life." She swung Darcy off his bed and to her hip. "I'm not risking saying the wrong thing to your parents."

In fact, she didn't intend to speak at all.

He laughed, wrestled a T-shirt over his head then

took Darcy from Sophie before they went to the dining room together.

His parents were already eating. His dad quickly rose and pulled out a chair for Sophie.

"Thank you."

Wyatt slid Darcy into the highchair. "Mom, Dad, I didn't introduce Sophie to you last night. She's Darcy's nanny."

Sophie smiled at the petite woman with a sleek brown bob, wearing white pants and a sleeveless red top, and the tall, slender man with dark hair, wearing blue jeans that looked to have been ironed if the crisp crease was anything to go by. "How do you do."

"Sophie, my mom and Dad are Connie and Bruce."

Both nodded in acknowledgement, as Wyatt took his seat at the head of the table.

Mrs. P. arrived and Wyatt asked her to make Darcy whatever fruit and cereal she thought appropriate. Then he asked for eggs and bacon before he nodded to Sophie.

"I'd like my usual fruit platter."

"With cinnamon toast," Mrs. P. said with a sidelong glance at Wyatt's parents.

Stifling a laugh, Sophie said, "Sure."

Wyatt busied himself pouring coffee for himself and Sophie, then refilling his parents' cups. She knew he'd done it to avoid real conversation, but she also sensed that dichotomy again. He was part of their lives. He hadn't rebelled and shouted that he never wanted to see them again and disowned them. But he also wasn't *part* of their lives. He was cool. Rigid. And very much in control.

Mrs. P. arrived with Darcy's food first and Wyatt fed her. When his food and Sophie's arrived, he gave the baby a toy to play with while they ate. His parents stayed around for light conversation about the weather and their flight to Italy, and though on the surface it seemed perfectly normal, Sophie felt the undercurrent of Wyatt's distance.

"I can't wait to sightsee today," his mom said buoyantly. "You'll come with us, won't you, Wyatt?"

"We've actually been into town a few times," Wyatt began, but his father interrupted him.

"Good! That means we'll have a tour guide."

Cool and emotionless, Wyatt said, "Sure."

Because it was already after nine o'clock, Sophie saw herself with the rest of the morning and a few hours in the afternoon to look for loans and grants. She took Darcy upstairs, packed a diaper bag and waved goodbye when the cool, composed family headed into town.

But three hours later she heard the sound of the SUV returning. She almost stayed in her room and pretended she didn't hear them but realized that they'd probably come home because Darcy hadn't napped in the stroller as she usually did, and she was fussy.

She raced downstairs and met them in the foyer, where she took Darcy's carrier from Wyatt. "Let me guess. She needs a nap. Right?"

"Among other things," Wyatt said, heading for the bar in the living room.

Happy to scurry away, Sophie took Darcy upstairs, fed her a bottle and changed her into pajamas for her nap.

Walking to her room and her laptop to go back to investigating her future, she heard Wyatt and his parents talking though she couldn't quite make out what they were saying. Curiosity overwhelmed her and she tiptoed to the top of the stairs and quietly sat.

Wyatt's dad was half arguing, half whining. "I'm not saying we didn't like Bellagio. I'm just not one to walk around and look at things. We should have taken out the boat."

"Yes," Wyatt's mom agreed with her husband. "The boat would have been better."

So they hadn't come home to put Darcy down for a nap but because his parents had been bored—

In beautiful Bellagio?

Wow. Who gets bored in one of the most beautiful towns in the world?

The conversation stopped, then his mom said, "I'm going upstairs to check on the baby."

Sophie scrambled to her feet. She ran to her room, but not wanting Wyatt's mom to wake Darcy, she changed her mind, walked past her bed and slipped into the nursery. She was rifling through the little laundry basket, sorting clothes that needed to be washed by laying them out in several piles on the changing table, when his mom stepped inside.

"Oh, Sophie, you're here."

Sophie made a shushing motion with a finger to her lips.

His mom lowered her voice. "Sorry."

"It's okay," Sophie whispered. "Once she's sleeping you can talk. She just needs a few minutes to fall into a deep sleep."

As Sophie said that, Connie walked to the crib. She watched Darcy for a few seconds, while Sophie continued to sort through Darcy's dirty clothes.

Then finally she said, "I never thought I'd be a grandmother."

Sophie laughed softly. "The lament of all parents."

She strolled to the crib, standing beside Wyatt's mom. When she saw Darcy was in a deep sleep, she didn't stop Connie when she continued the conversation.

"Wyatt's always been so busy with his work, that we were fairly certain he wouldn't find a wife." She smiled at Sophie. "Now he doesn't have to."

Sophie conceded that with a nod, though a weird feeling tiptoed through her. Wyatt's mom didn't know Sophie was sleeping with her son. She was only talking about having a grandchild. But the sense of being an outsider again tightened her chest, hinting that she'd made a mistake sleeping with Wyatt.

But just hinting.

Just enough that she recognized the feeling.

Still, the sensation was incorrect. She hadn't made a mistake. She'd known what she was getting into. She wouldn't see Wyatt again once they returned to Manhattan. She'd miss him. She'd miss Darcy. But when she went home, she had a life to straighten out. She'd need space to get her act together. The memories of this time in Italy would bolster her.

"Anyway, now that we have a grandchild, I intend to see that she's raised properly."

That was exactly what Wyatt wanted to avoid—and she understood why. They seemed to have had an "on call" relationship with Wyatt. As a child, he'd been left alone and felt abandoned. He also felt pressured to be the best if his comment about friends being competition was anything to go by.

"Wyatt doesn't know a damned thing about good

schools, dance lessons and getting a child on the right track for success."

That was so far off the mark that Sophie defended him without thinking. "He made a success of himself. I'm pretty sure he'll be a good dad."

Connie White turned from the crib, her eyes bright with anger. "Excuse me?"

Sophie gulped. She shouldn't have said anything, but defending Wyatt came so naturally she doubted she would have been able to hold back.

Besides, she'd only spoken the truth. She wouldn't apologize for that.

"I believe my husband and I had a hand in his success. We are the ones who raised him."

Oh, Lord. His mother was ridiculously clueless. But despite the urges she'd had to defend Wyatt, it wasn't Sophie's place to correct his mother.

Maybe an apology was in order after all?

"I'm sorry. That just slipped out."

Connie's eyes narrowed. "See that nothing like that slips out again." She straightened regally. "I don't care how long you've worked for Wyatt. Another slip gets you fired." She turned to the crib to look at her granddaughter, but quickly faced Sophie again. "Or if you really wanted to be a good nanny to this little girl, you'd get on board with making sure she has the suitable training."

For three seconds, Sophie was glad she wasn't Darcy's permanent nanny, then a hundred possibilities cascaded through her brain, things Connie could do if Wyatt hired a malleable caregiver for his daughter. Sophie could see Wyatt's mom turning Darcy's nanny into a spy. Or, worse, using her to take Darcy to schools or events that Wyatt hadn't approved. Now that Wyatt's mother was in Darcy's life, he'd have to be more careful than ever about whom he chose.

"I'm sure you have friends, connections," Connie said, holding Sophie's gaze. "Perhaps someone from your agency could help us get Darcy into the correct preschool."

"She's not even a year old yet."

"And if you're any kind of nanny at all, you know there are waiting lists to get into those academies." She studied Sophie. "Of course, you know that." She smiled stiffly. "You're sticking with Wyatt's side of things like a good nanny. But good nannies don't always listen to their boss. They think ahead." Her smile turned brittle. "Remember that." She headed to the nursery door. "And straighten up this room. It looks like a pigpen."

She nearly told Connie that she was sorting things to prepare to do laundry but bit her tongue. The less dealings she had with Wyatt's mom, the better. Plus, this was Wyatt's fight.

She stopped sorting as more pieces of Wyatt's puzzle fell together. He might have had trouble connecting with reality because he'd never seen it, but his parents were bullies. She'd watched Wyatt handle them by placating them half the time and standing up to them the other half. But she also recognized how difficult it must have been to break away, to create his own life—

And why he believed he had to keep them out of it. If he gave them an inch, they would take a mile.

But with a baby? Someone for Connie to spoil and show off? The comfortable life he'd built for himself was about to implode. There was no way Connie would stay out of her granddaughter's life, and once she squeezed in she would take over—

That had been his entire life. Not love. Not acceptance or encouragement. Demands until he erected walls and barriers.

It was no wonder he didn't believe in love, trust love. The people destined to be his first teachers hadn't ever shown him love. He'd spent his entire life battling for his sanity and freedom.

That's why he was so sure he'd never want to marry. Love had only ever hurt him, imprisoned him.

CHAPTER TWELVE

As HIS PARENTS took cocktails to the patio, Wyatt raced to the office to call Signor Bonetti. The older man almost sounded relieved when Wyatt explained that his parents had arrived unexpectedly, and he was showing them around.

"Go! Have fun! Let me know when they leave."

"No. I'll contact you as soon as I can. I don't have to hold their hands. Just entertain them a bit."

Disconnecting the call, he took a breath and leaned back in the leather office chair. He closed his eyes and released all the tension that had accumulated that morning while sightseeing. He could legitimately stay in the office for fifteen minutes, pretending the call had gone on longer, before he had to go outside and sit with his parents. He should enjoy them.

But he couldn't. He had to think this through. He knew what would happen now that they knew about Darcy. There'd be phone calls, a barrage of things he "had to" do and people he had to meet. His daughter wouldn't be a baby to them or even a person. She would be an item on a to do list. Someone they had to control to protect their image.

The way he saw it, they had now become the people

he had to control to protect his daughter. But controlling them was never easy. They were strong and committed to the life they'd created. If he really wanted to protect Darcy, he would have to get her away from them.

Suddenly, the house on Cade's island didn't seem like a pipe dream. It felt like an escape.

But wasn't it a shame he had to run away to protect his child?

A knock on the office door had him opening his eyes. Seeing Sophie, he smiled. "What's up?"

"Your mother is a piece of work."

He laughed. "No kidding. I was just realizing that if I want to protect Darcy, I'll probably have to build a house on Cade's island and home school her."

"You can't do that." She walked into the office and gingerly sat on the chair across from his desk. "She'll need friends, socialization."

He remembered being alone most of his childhood, until he was a teenager and able to make some of his own choices. It had been his first taste of the real world. University, though, was where he really grew enough to see that his parents' lives were cold and sometimes cruel.

Not what he wanted. Certainly not what he wanted for Darcy.

"You're right." He pulled in a breath. "There are actually a few families in the Montgomery."

"Readymade friends," Sophie said with a laugh. "But that's not to say you shouldn't build a *vacation* house on Cade's island." She frowned. "Unless, of course, there are enough rooms in Cade's retreat that even if he and Trace are already there, you and Darcy could still have a room. I imagine spending long weekends there with friends is really fun."

Damned if she wasn't right again.

"In twenty seconds, you've totally talked me out of building a house."

"I guess I have."

"I'm still going to have trouble with my parents if I stay in Manhattan."

"You can keep your distance."

He shook his head. "No. If you think that, you don't understand. My parents are like dogs with a bone. I broke away. But Darcy's fragile."

"Not fragile, just vulnerable. The best way to protect her is with the stability of a permanent home."

"I had a home in Manhattan my entire life, and all the markings of stability. It didn't help with parents who monitored my every move and scheduled my life into infinity, while barely having any contact with me aside from the few times they would order me downstairs and browbeat me on my schoolwork or scold me about embarrassing them." He took a breath. "No. A permanent home didn't help."

"Okay, if that's true, then the reverse should be true."

He eyed her as if she were crazy. "What?"

"If Darcy had people in her life who loved her, she would be fine wherever she lived."

"You would think that would be true."

"It will be if you set lines and limits for your parents."

"It's not going to be easy. They'll sneak in while I'm at work, probably bribe the nanny to report on my comings and goings."

Her face shifted. Her happy expression disappeared,

and she quickly looked down at her hands. After a few seconds, she looked back up at him again. "Your mom already approached me about some of that."

He gaped at her. "What?"

"She mentioned that if I wanted to be a good nanny, I should help her do the things she wants to do with the baby. Like, get her into the best school."

He closed his eyes and sighed. "She's only known she has a grandchild for twenty-four hours and already she's undermining me. This is going to make finding a new nanny doubly hard."

Sophie caught his gaze. "What if I stayed on as Darcy's nanny… At least until I finished school."

His breathing froze. "When I suggested that you said no."

"I changed my mind. Your mom is formidable. In this year, while you're establishing the ground rules for how your parents are allowed in Darcy's life, I'll stay. I'll help. You know she can't bribe me or threaten me. I'm not afraid of her."

Even though her suggestion shocked him, he could feel a smile forming, and relief pour through him. "Really?"

Before Sophie could answer, his phone rang. He picked it up and rolled his eyes heavenward. "It's my dad." He turned toward the big office window that showcased the pool and waved at his father.

"He called you?"

His phone rang again. "Either they want me outside to entertain them or they need their drinks refilled."

She rose. "I'll do it."

"No." He couldn't have been more emphatic. "If you're staying on as Darcy's nanny for the year while you're in school, I don't want them deciding you are the maid." He rose from his chair. "Stick to your duties."

He started out of the office but stopped by Sophie's chair, leaned down and kissed her. "Thank you."

That night, Sophie declined dinner with his parents. Wyatt said he was taking them to the little restaurant they'd found in Bellagio, and she suggested she stay home and care for the baby.

He didn't seem happy about her decision, but he was the one who had told her to make sure she kept her job duties clear. As much as that meant she couldn't slip over into maid duties, it also meant not hanging out as if she was part of the family.

He and his parents left without her, and she and Darcy had a good time, waltzing through the house until it was time to get her ready for bed.

The baby fell asleep immediately, and though Sophie had some applications to fill out, she stayed in the nursery a few minutes longer than necessary trying to get adjusted to the fact that she'd agreed to be Darcy's nanny for a year.

It was going to be hard.

So hard. Not only would she not split with Wyatt when she returned to Manhattan and regain her bearings, but also she'd have another year of falling in love with both him and Darcy.

She'd be a cliché.

She'd get her heart broken.

But when she looked into the crib, at sleeping Darcy, she knew exactly why she had done it. Wyatt might be excellent at thinking things through, but he also had the money and connections to make spur of the moment decisions that wouldn't be right for Darcy.

She couldn't live on an island with no friends and no influence except adults. She had to be around people her own age. She had to have experiences with other kids.

And like it or not, she needed contact with her grandparents.

Just very careful contact.

She tucked a cover over Darcy's tiny form and turned away from the crib. She would sacrifice a year.

Not just a year. Her heart.

She was going to have one hell of a broken heart when she graduated university and moved on.

But she *would* move on. That was a promise she was making to herself. When her schooling was done, no matter what the situation with Wyatt, she would move on.

Wyatt and his parents returned a little after ten o'clock. She saw the car drive up to the house and turned off her light immediately to discourage Wyatt from coming to her room.

Ten minutes later the door opened and though she kept her eyes closed, he slipped out of his clothes and crawled into bed with her.

She turned toward him.

"I hope I didn't wake you."

"No. I hadn't even really started to drift off."

"Worried about your decision to stay on as nanny?"

It could have impressed her that he was concerned about her, but she knew he was a considerate man, a man who saw all angles of everything. Though the question showed his innate kindness, she didn't take it as anything more than it was.

"No. You need me. Darcy needs me. I'll have somewhere to live while I finish school. It's win-win."

He chuckled. "I told you that yesterday."

She could have argued that there were lots of things he wasn't taking into consideration, like her broken heart, but that was her cross to bear. "How was your night?"

"My parents hated that we had to walk to the restaurant from the parking area, loved the restaurant and griped about the walk again."

She laughed.

He said nothing for a few seconds, then he shook his head. "They're snooty and condescending but, in a way, that makes their behavior very predictable."

"Which should give us the ability to stay one step ahead of them."

He said, "I have for the past twelve years," then snuggled against her. "Knowing Darcy's caregiver is on my side, I can protect her."

He said nothing for a few minutes. She let the silence linger in case he wanted to talk some more but soon she heard the deep, even sound of his breathing. The day had been difficult, and she knew he needed the rest.

She turned on her pillow with a satisfied smile, happy he was relieved she'd decided to take the job as his nanny for a year, and content that she could do this for both him and Darcy. She could make that sacrifice.

Then the weirdest thought hit her.

What if this was real love? Not just romantic love. But deep, abiding love.

Sacrificing for him and Darcy, letting him talk, letting him fall asleep naturally. All that was real love. He needed her as more than a nanny. He just plain needed her. But as long as things were running smoothly, she didn't think he would realize it.

The sound of the baby fussing came through the monitor speaker, and she rolled out of bed and headed for the nursery.

Wyatt was right behind her.

Seeing Darcy's diaper needed changing, she removed it and Wyatt handed her a dry one. Then she put the baby in the crib again and rubbed her tummy until she fell asleep and she and Wyatt tiptoed back to bed.

But as they both slid under the covers, she realized that they were forming a family. They talked about issues. They both cared for Wyatt's little girl. They both wanted what was best for her. And Wyatt didn't make her feel as if she was giving an opinion when they talked about Darcy. They made decisions together. Like equals. Like *parents*.

It felt like a family to her.

But no matter how much they talked, how much they drew conclusions and worked things out, they weren't forming anything permanent. Wyatt didn't want anything permanent, and she understood why. His clearest example of marriage and family wasn't a good one. Actually, he believed it was a bond to be fought against. He'd been fighting against it since he was eighteen. He'd fight it forever. And she refused to be the woman who thought she could change a man.

The next morning, Wyatt's parents finished their breakfast and announced that they were going to see the vineyards in Tuscany.

Sophie glanced up from her fruit and cinnamon toast.

"We've been there before, of course," Connie said

with a laugh. "But it doesn't hurt to have another visit or two on your social résumé."

Sophie struggled to keep her eyebrows from raising at that.

"We've actually called a real estate agent to show us around," Wyatt's dad picked up the conversation. "We're considering buying a place there. All our friends are."

"I don't think we should," Connie said. "Every once in a while, it looks good to be the person who doesn't follow the crowd, right, Wyatt?"

This time, Sophie blinked. How his mother could compare the choice not to buy a villa with Wyatt's life choices was beyond her.

"Anyway," Bruce said, tossing his linen napkin to his plate and rising from his chair. "It will be worth a day out and about."

"With an appropriate tour guide," Connie said, as she too rose. "Not someone who will take us to common tourist attractions—"

Sophie almost winced at that, but Wyatt remained emotionless.

"Someone who knows what he's doing."

Out of politeness, Wyatt stood as his mom did. "I thought you were looking for a place to buy?"

"Maybe yes. Maybe no," Bruce said. "With the amount of money we would be spending if we did buy, the agent knows a day of showing us around is worth the gamble."

Wyatt simply said, "Well, enjoy yourselves."

His parents left the dining room and Wyatt took his seat again, sending her a smile.

She shook her head in response as he dug into the rest of his breakfast.

He didn't have to say a word. Neither did she. They acknowledged that his parents were a bit absurd with a few looks.

The thought almost made her laugh. She loved their connection and knew it would help as they dealt with his parents over the next year.

Everything felt like it was falling into place.

Wyatt finished his coffee, then said, "I talked with Signor Bonetti before breakfast. He told me to come over any time this morning."

"Okay."

Groaning, he stood up. "God knows when I'll be back." He leaned in and kissed her.

"Then I'll see you when I see you."

Later that morning, when Darcy was napping, Sophie found an email from Wyatt's staff with an attachment that was her statement for the media.

It was short, simple and perfect. Just a line she could toss over her shoulder to keep reporters at bay.

If she ever actually saw one. Going home with Wyatt, living in his penthouse, not signing a lease for another apartment, put her off the grid. She got the sudden, unwanted feeling that it could look like she was hiding. But she couldn't exactly call the media and tell them she hadn't rented an apartment because she'd taken a job as a nanny.

A nanny.

The word rattled through her. No matter how close she and Wyatt had become, no matter that it felt like they were forming a family, they weren't. Her primary place in his life was as Darcy's nanny, an employee.

She'd made it official when she agreed to keep the job when they returned to Manhattan.

With her emotions jumbled, she didn't leave her room when she heard the sounds of Wyatt returning. Because he didn't come upstairs to check on Darcy or to change into swimwear, she figured he was still working.

She could go to the office and see what was going on, but her confused feelings had her walking to the door one second and turning away from it the next. A nanny wouldn't run downstairs to see what he was doing. A *girlfriend* would. But she wasn't really a girlfriend.

She was a nanny…with confidences?

She had no idea what she was. He'd talked to her about important things on this trip. When she was his girlfriend, he hadn't. They'd connected. They were caring for his daughter like parents…not people dating. Not a nanny and her boss.

Pacing her bedroom, she raked her fingers through her hair. She understood his feelings and fears about relationships. She also knew, absolutely knew, how easy it was for her to see more in their interactions than he intended—

That was why he'd broken up with her. She'd taken their romance as more than he intended. Right now, they had a sweet deal. He got a nanny. She got a place to live while she finished her degree. They also had each other.

It might not be forever, but the next year could either be happy or make her crazy with confusion.

She opted to be happy with her choices. After all, she was going to get her degree in this year too. If she kept her wits about her, this could be one of the happiest years of her life.

Still, part of her ached for more from their relationship. She'd never had a connection with anyone that was stronger. She'd already realized this was real love—

But what if it wasn't?

What if, like when they were dating three years ago, she was making more out of everything he said and did than what he meant?

She could not face that embarrassment again.

If there was more between them, he had to be the one to say it.

CHAPTER THIRTEEN

WYATT WALKED DIRECTLY into the office, closed the door and opened his laptop, immediately calling Trace and Cade.

Both said, "What's up?"

If Wyatt hadn't been in a mood, he might have laughed at how in sync they were. "I'm just back from what I think will be my last visit with Bonetti."

Trace winced. Cade laughed.

"It's not what either of you think. Last night Bonetti got a call from his daughter saying she and her family were going out on her yacht, sailing to Monaco, and they invited him along. So he gave me a little slip of paper." Wyatt waved it at the computer. "And he told me that's his price."

Trace sat up. "He gave you a number?"

"Yep." Wyatt read Bonetti's asking price to his friends.

Cade whistled.

Trace sat back in his seat. "He's had this number all along?"

"No. He said he based it on things we'd discussed. But he has conditions. He showed me a five-year plan a couple days ago. I told him we could not promise we would adhere to it. He wants his employees to keep their jobs. He also wants financial security for his family. If you think the number is high, that's why. He believes that number reflects the fact that we're not giving his family a percentage of the profits. So the purchase price needed to be higher."

Cade said, "Do we get a chance to counteroffer?"

"I'm guessing we can if we get it to him tonight. Tomorrow he's gone. If we're going to counteroffer, it has to be our best and final."

Trace said, "So what do you think?"

"I say we spend the afternoon running numbers."

They spent the rest of the day and part of the evening working up a counteroffer. Wyatt called Bonetti and after only a second's hesitation, he took the deal.

And just like that Wyatt was free.

He felt as if a burden had been lifted from his shoulders until he walked out of the office and heard the sounds of his parents in the living room.

Tired beyond belief, he headed to the living room anyway. "I just finished the deal with Signor Bonetti."

His dad said, "Fabulous. Let's have a drink to celebrate."

He ran his hand along the back of his neck. "Actually, Dad, I'm exhausted. I think I'm going to shower and go to bed."

Neither of his parents looked happy as he turned to walk out of the room, but he pivoted back again. "Did you find a vineyard or villa you liked?"

"Two." His dad winced. "But honestly I don't think we're made to live abroad."

"Okay. We'll see you in the morning."

He turned away again on a course for Sophie's room. He opened the door without knocking and found her leaning over her computer.

"What's up?"

"I got the statement from your PR department today."

"Oh, that's great." He walked over and slid his arms around her shoulders. "I bought a great big company today."

She turned in his arms. "You did?"

He grinned. "Yeah." He bent and kissed her. "What to join me in the shower?"

She hesitated. She tried to hide it, but he saw. Still, she said, "Sure."

She stood up and unbuttoned his shirt.

His eyebrows rose. "Are we getting a little ahead of ourselves here?"

"With a baby sleeping in the next room, it's always best to take advantage of the time."

He laughed, then realized there was no humor in her voice. For a second, he wondered if something was wrong with her. Especially when she reached up and kissed him, almost desperately. But desperation became a hot tango of lips and tongues as heat and need ignited his blood. Even thoughts of his parents in the living room didn't bother him. Everything was better now. He had his company. Sophie had agreed to be Darcy's nanny for a year.

He could not have asked for a better outcome to this trip.

He half kissed, half danced her into the bathroom connected to her bedroom. The place was smaller than the bath for the primary bedroom, but it was still comfortable and spa-like with a marble shower, gray floors and natural wood shelves for fluffy white towels and toiletries.

He yanked her T-shirt over her head, and she stepped out of her sweatpants. He grabbed a bottle of body wash as they entered the shower.

They stood under the spray, and he closed his eyes and pretended they were outside, in a gentle storm, just the two of them happy and content.

He ran kisses down her neck and didn't protest when she slid her hands over his chest and back. There was something so perfect about being with her that he couldn't capture the feeling, except to know that when she was wet and naked against him nothing else in the world mattered.

He pressed her to the shower wall and sank into her, relishing the feeling, so glad she'd be with him for the next year that for once in his life he didn't have a care in the world.

CHAPTER FOURTEEN

THE NEXT MORNING, they left his parents in Italy to fend for themselves, and headed for the private airstrip to return to Manhattan. Their two weeks weren't up, but with the deal done, he needed to go home to set things up.

Though he'd never felt better, happier, more in control, he could see something was bothering Sophie. She'd been quiet at breakfast, quiet while they packed Darcy's things, quiet when they'd said goodbye to his parents. Now, getting ready to take off, he could see something in her eyes.

Her silence unexpectedly reminded him of the cold wars his parents had, but he told himself that was idiotic. There was absolutely nothing Sophie could be trying to get her way about by using the silent treatment. They'd made their deal like consensual adults. She'd gotten what she needed and he was getting what he needed.

When she buried herself in her book, he decided he had to be imagining things. And comparing her silence to the silence of his mother? He probably made that connection because he'd just spent two days with his parents.

Still exhausted from his long, confusing ten days of dealing with Bonetti and his parents, he fell asleep on the flight and woke when Sophie told him the pilot was getting ready to land. He snapped Darcy in her car seat and Sophie buckled in herself, perfectly normal behavior for two people with a baby.

A limo awaited them when they landed at another private air strip, this one close to New York City. Carrying Darcy, Wyatt led Sophie to their ride. They climbed inside and Wyatt buckled Darcy into a car seat.

As the limo pulled away from the private jet, Wyatt leaned back. "Well, here we go. I now have a new business to organize, and you need to get enrolled in school, while we both figure out a way to deal with my parents and you handle the fallout from your mother's embezzling."

Beside him on the bench seat, she sat oddly prim and proper.

She was never prim and proper. She knew when to be polite and dignified, but she never had the tight look of someone playing a role—

Unless she was upset? Or scared? She'd mentioned at least twice that returning to Manhattan was returning to trouble.

"Are you nervous?"

She jumped when he spoke. "Huh?"

He laughed. "I asked if you were nervous because of everything going on with your mom. Although," he drew the word out as he realized something. "If you don't rent an apartment or do anything public, you'll literally be hidden in my house."

She took a breath. "I thought of that yesterday."

"So this is good for you?" he asked, pointing back

and forth between her and Darcy, wanting confirmation that she was okay.

She said nothing.

Her silence reminded him of his mom again. His dad always had to play twenty questions, trying to get her to talk.

But after a few more seconds, she took another long breath. "Yes. The arrangement is great."

Her answer should have relieved him, but confusion overwhelmed him. Never in their relationship had she behaved this way. He knew something was wrong, but she clearly didn't want to talk about it.

He settled back on his seat, rejecting a sliver of anger that tried to form. He understood that she didn't want to talk. He understood that she was nervous. He would let her alone to deal with her feelings.

The limo grew silent. The closer they got to the Montgomery, the more her expression tightened and the more worried he became.

"Sophie?"

She faced him. "What?"

"You know, you don't have to deal with whatever is bothering you alone. We can talk about anything."

Her head tilted. "Really? *Anything?*"

"Yes!"

She took a breath and blew it out slowly. "Okay, then I want to talk about us."

"Us?"

"What are we doing, Wyatt?"

Totally not comprehending, he looked at her. Right now, they were on their way to his house. She was going to be Darcy's nanny. He would help her with school. None of that should make her unhappy or confused or nervous.

"I'm not sure what you mean."

"When we're alone, we're lovers. When your parents were around, I was Darcy's nanny. For the past few days, I've felt like two people."

Once again, his parents' involvement had screwed things up. "That was to protect you."

"You're saying you'll be yourself when we're around Trace and Cade?"

He blinked. "Why would we be around Trace and Cade?"

"We're not going to go out? Ever?"

"Go out?"

"Are we dating again? Am I just your nanny? What are we doing?"

"I need you as my nanny. And you're the one who made it sound like you're unhappy with the *dating* aspect of our relationship."

"I feel like your dirty little secret."

Insult poured through him and he blinked. "What?"

"Think it through."

Her hesitation before making love the night before popped into his mind. He'd been correct that something was bothering her.

He tried seeing the situation through her eyes but didn't see what she obviously saw. They were friends. Or so he thought. They talked about everything. She was in on every decision they'd made.

"We never did or said anything that we didn't agree upon."

"That's true. But things changed while we were in Italy."

They'd talked. She'd agreed to stay on as Darcy's nanny for a year. Damn it! They *were* friends. "I thought things changed for the better."

"It was better."

"Until my parents came."

She winced. "That's part of it but not the whole deal. Wyatt, you're missing a big piece of the picture. You're missing why you want me to stay on as Darcy's nanny and why I hated thinking of you returning to Manhattan without someone to help you with your parents."

"I thought that was because we were friends."

"We're more than friends. With time to ourselves and caring for Darcy together, our feelings for each other grew."

His breath stalled as he finally understood what she was saying. "You think we fell in love."

"You don't?"

His heartbeat slowed down then revved up as fear collided with disbelief. "No. I don't think we fell in love." He'd just spent two days with parents who epitomized everything he hated and wrapped it up in a package they called love. "The past two days you were with my parents. Honestly…is *that* what you want out of life?"

"Absolutely not. From what little I saw, your parents don't know how to love. But you do."

His heart stuttered to a stop. He didn't believe in love because he'd never seen it. He'd always acknowledged that. Now, Sophie was telling him he loved her? Memories of feelings he'd been unable to identify jumped into his brain. Feelings while they made love, while she cuddled Darcy, while they did simple, happy things.

What if he did love her?

No. He couldn't. A person could not "do" something they'd never seen let alone been taught.

It was much easier to believe all those emotions he'd felt were passing things. Hormones. Endorphins. Dopamine. Good moods that would dissipate over time and leave two people floundering to either protect what never really existed, the way his parents had, or hurt each other and move on.

He wouldn't inflict that on either one of them.

He pulled in a breath. "Look. We had a good time in Italy. We absolutely connected and we made plans that benefitted both of us. Don't turn that into something it isn't."

His words stung like the crack of a whip. They made Sophie feel small and stupid, but she wasn't letting him miss the bigger picture. "So, you'd rather take me back to Manhattan, install me in your house as Darcy's nanny, sleep with me, and raise Darcy together but never commit."

"Commit?" He gaped at her. "Is that what this is all about? You want a ring?" He laughed. "After what? Ten days together?"

She'd thought his last comment had hurt? A knife in her chest would have done less damage. Still, meeting his parents, seeing his life up close and personal, she understood why he was so resistant. Though she hadn't wanted to try to change him, she finally realized forcing him to recognize his feelings for her wasn't changing him. It was pointing out the obvious. Getting him to see reason. Setting out facts in a way that he could see what had happened between them.

If she had to fight to do that, she would fight.

"If we really break down everything you've said today, you're avoiding making a commitment because you don't believe ten days is long enough to trust me forever."

"I don't trust *anyone* forever."

"You trust Trace and Cade."

"As business partners. They stand to lose as much as I do. We have to trust each other. But that doesn't mean we'll be together forever. Business partners move on. I'd like to think we'll be friends for our entire lives. But I simply don't believe in fairytales."

The thought that he thought he and the two guys he considered to be like brothers might drift apart astounded her into silence.

"Sophie, listen to me. My parents raised me in the worst, most empty way, and if there is such a thing as love, I never saw it. I can't believe in something that's insubstantial at best. And, at worst, is a way for people to hurt each other."

She stared at him, suddenly feeling like it was three years ago. His arguments hadn't changed. His beliefs hadn't changed. Even the way he behaved hadn't changed.

And she finally saw that he might have learned a thing or two from his parents after all. He could have created his beliefs to protect himself, but he did not seem to recognize that he was hurting her.

And if he did, protecting himself was more important to him.

The hurt was so deep, she wasn't sure she could move or speak. But she also saw he'd never led her on, always been up front with her. If there was blame to be placed it was on her.

He'd always told her the truth. She'd simply never understood it because to her it was so obvious they were good for each other.

And she'd loved him.

Familiar streets appeared around her. Even as her heart shattered into a million pieces, her brain righted itself. She'd fought for what she wanted, and she'd lost. She hated leaving Darcy, hated breaking a commitment, but there was a time in every person's life when they needed to face truth and act accordingly.

"Tell your driver to stop."

"We're two blocks away from the Montgomery."

"I know. I'm going to get a ride share and go to my dad's." When he only looked at her, she said, "Tell the driver to stop."

His face registered his recognition of what she was really saying. She wasn't going home with him.

"Come up to the condo. We can talk about this some more."

"No. I love you. I really, honestly love you." The liberation of saying that rode through her. For once she got to say what she felt without worry. He'd already broken them apart. Her telling him she loved him made no difference, except to free her.

"You don't feel that for me. If I work for you for an entire year, it will kill me. I'm sorry about Darcy. I'm sorry I said I would be her nanny and now I'm bailing. But you know what? Lots of people have hurt me too. I always accept it, but this time I can't. For once I'm going to do what's right for me."

"All your suitcases are in the trunk of the limo."

"I'll get them tomorrow while you're at work. Leave

them with Pete. Tell him I'll be by." When he only stared at her, she said, "Stop the car."

He did as she asked and she jumped out, reiterating that she'd get her things the next day. Then she closed the door on Wyatt White and his adorable daughter.

The sights, sounds and scents of Manhattan surrounded her. Tall buildings and people. Taxi horns. Hot dogs and bakeries.

None of this was hers anymore. She had to find an apartment she could afford, get a new job, and, hopefully, fit in her last year of university.

All with a broken heart.

Her fault this time.

Still, she was lost, alone, so empty she wasn't sure how she found the strength to stand.

The limo pulled into traffic again.

She'd made a mistake, a huge mistake in restarting their romance, because she now loved Wyatt. For real. In that earthy, honest, vulnerable way that causes a person to open their soul, sacrifice and share everything...

And he'd rejected her.

Getting over him this time was going to hurt much worse than the last heartbreak she'd gotten from him.

But she was stronger than she was three years ago. He might not believe in love, but she did. She knew love was out there and someday she'd find it.

It didn't stop the hurt of losing him, of losing something that could have been great. No one ever confided in her as he had, no one ever listened to her the way he had. They'd had a one-shot opportunity at perfection, and he hadn't wanted it.

Her soul ached at the thought, but she yanked the strap of her purse higher on her shoulder and started walking.

She'd call her ride share when she was sure she was done crying.

That night after putting Darcy to bed, Wyatt sat in his grand living room, with thoughts of Sophie getting out of the car haunting him.

Even though she'd been the one who promised to be Darcy's nanny for a year then bailed, he felt like he'd let her down.

He hadn't. He'd been up front with her from day one. Plus, three years ago he'd told her he didn't want a commitment. He didn't believe in love. He owed her nothing.

Except money for being Darcy's nanny in Italy and he had no idea where she was.

He could call her, but he got out his laptop and searched her dad's address and found it easily. He would take care of the money issue in the morning. Face to face. Fairly because he was fair.

Having a plan to fulfill his responsibilities to her should have eased his mind, but it didn't.

He tossed and turned in bed and woke grouchy.

When he walked into the suite for Three Musketeers Holdings, Cade frowned but Trace strolled into the office and groaned when he saw Darcy in the carrier on Wyatt's chest.

"You told us you had a nanny."

"I did." He winced. "She quit."

Cade said, "No big surprise there." But accustomed to having Darcy around, he got down to the business of going over potential articles of agreement for the purchase of Signor Bonetti's business.

Wyatt stopped him once so he could feed Darcy and put her down for a nap in the play yard he kept in his office.

When he went back to work, neither Cade nor Trace said anything about the pause. As if they'd never stopped, they picked up the next article for the batch they'd be giving to their lawyers.

Trace said something about the financing schedule and Wyatt zoned out. He knew there was plenty of money. He didn't care if they dipped into their personal fortunes to buy something new. But Trace always liked knowing everybody was on the same page. So Wyatt let him ramble even if it did make him smile.

When he realized he was smiling, happy to be with his two friends, he remembered telling Sophie that he believed their partnership wouldn't last forever and maybe even their friendship would break down eventually.

It was foolish to think otherwise. Trace now lived in Italy. He could decide to bow out of Three Musketeers at any time. So could Cade. He could choose to live the life of a reclusive island guy—

The thought tightened his chest. He didn't want to lose contact with either of his friends. He loved the women they'd chosen to marry...

And the thought that either one of them would marry and then divorce also made him feel funny.

He yanked his mind away from those things and focused on the articles they were drafting.

Darcy woke a few hours later and Trace suggested they call it a day. He'd brought Marcia to Manhattan to shop and, just like that, Wyatt could see Sophie showing Marcia around Manhattan, having fun with her.

He shoved those thoughts aside and followed his partners to the private elevator.

"You're welcome to have dinner with us tonight. I know Marcia would love to see you."

Wyatt glanced over at Trace with his glasses and ever-present smile. He pointed at Darcy. "Still no nanny, remember?"

"Yeah. How did you lose this one?"

Cade's question made Wyatt suck in a breath. He did not want to explain fully. He didn't feel comfortable embarrassing himself or Sophie that way.

"I thought we'd struck a deal for her to stay on once we returned from Italy. She had second thoughts and left."

"I know this has something to do with you," Cade badgered. "I mean, Trace and I see your goodness, but you can be gruff."

"I'm not gruff."

The elevator stopped in the basement parking garage.

"You are gruff," Trace said. "But we get it. You have a lot of responsibilities on your shoulders."

Glancing down to be sure Darcy was asleep, Wyatt said, "Thank you."

But for the first time he realized that he didn't do such a good job of hiding the pressure. He thought he was strong, above the normal feelings that usually plagued a leader, but they knew. They'd seen.

"Well, whatever your nanny's reasons for abandoning you, she must have been a gem because we've never seen you so calm."

Wyatt's breath stuttered. "She didn't abandon me." And she had pointed out that they were good for each other. At least twice. He'd heard. He'd agreed. But here in Manhattan with the two people he trusted the most in his life, those simple words carried more weight.

Or something.

Hours later, pacing the big main room of his penthouse, with the floor-to-ceiling view of the Upper East Side, he tried to get thoughts of Sophie, being happy with Sophie, out of his brain, but his nerve endings shivered with something he couldn't identify, and it made him crazy.

First of all, he'd hated that Trace thought Sophie had abandoned him. She wasn't like that. If anything, he'd pushed her. He could have placated her in that limo, but his need for protection drove him. Plus, he didn't want to get into something then hurt *her*. It was better to be the guy who didn't believe in love, than the guy who tried a real relationship and ended up hurting her even more with a bad marriage.

Second, he'd never worried about a former lover or girlfriend, but he couldn't stop thinking about Sophie. Not really worrying. She was a tough cookie. She'd taken him on a few times. After only ten days of being together, she would get over this quickly.

Wouldn't she? Of course, she would. But his heart expanded with pain as he envisioned her thinking their breakup was no big deal. That she'd move on and he'd never see her again. He'd never see her smile. Never hear her laugh. Never see her play with Darcy or have her play with him. No swimming. No pastries. No laughing at cinnamon toast.

Third, his parents kept tiptoeing into his brain. The idea that they deserved each other morphed into a realization that they'd made their choices. Whether it seemed lopsided to him or something like torture, it hadn't been his choice to make. It had been theirs.

He flopped onto the sofa but the whole idea of choices wouldn't let him go.

How people made choices and did things because that's what they wanted.

That edged over into the idea that he always thought of love in the negative. Always saw it as hormones, dopamine or wishful thinking. But if someone had something good—as he'd had with Sophie—it didn't matter if they called it hormones or love.

If they really wanted it to last, they could do things to assure it would last. They could make choices that took them and the relationship in the direction of stability and longevity.

This time when his chest tightened it was with the strangest feeling.

Hope.

The entire time he and Sophie were in Italy, he'd been happy. He knew that was because of Sophie. She'd always made him happy. But he wouldn't let himself tip over into acknowledging it or, worse, seeing what she'd seen, that they really had connected this time. That they'd done things for each other. That they enjoyed each other's company, shared their concerns, both wanted the best for the other.

He wouldn't because he'd been so sure he was right. That there was no such thing as love.

But what if he was wrong?

Even if love was dopamine, hormones and wishful thinking, a person had control over what they did and didn't do. A smart guy could make it last.

He frowned.

A smart guy *could* make it last. If he wanted loving her to last a lifetime, it would. He was a very determined man.

The thought made him laugh out loud.

He *was* a very determined guy. And he knew nothing in heaven or hell could stop him if he decided to make their love work—forever. No shelf life.

Under ordinary circumstances, he'd give himself a day or two to think this through. But his gut clenched and his chest tightened.

He'd let her leave the limo without so much as an argument. He'd let her think he didn't love her, didn't want her, was only upset that she was breaking her nanny commitment—

Realizing how much that would have hurt her, he fell back on the sofa.

He couldn't bear the way he'd hurt her.

Sophie took the pillow from her stepmom and fluffed it a bit before she set it on the pull-out sofa bed.

"If I forgot to tell you yesterday, thank you for letting me crash here."

Her stepmom sat on the arm of the oversize floral chair on which her dad sat in the basement family room of the house they'd recently remodeled.

"We tried to call you when we heard about your mom on the news, but the calls didn't go through."

"I was in Italy. I don't have an international phone plan."

Her dad laughed. "I'm still not sure I understand that whole thing with Wyatt."

"He needed a nanny while he was in Italy. I needed

to get out of town to think things through. It was perfect timing."

"Isn't he an old boyfriend though?"

"Yes," Sophie said, working not to wince. "But he was negotiating most of the time we were there." She didn't tell them about the romantic sightseeing trips or the boat ride with Darcy or swimming. "That's why he needed me. He also had his staff write me a really good 'no comment' statement for the media."

Her stepmom laughed. "Isn't 'no comment' enough?"

"Not quite. I guess I'll be testing it out when I go apartment hunting."

"I don't think you'll have a problem," her stepmother said. "The news died down quickly. Apparently, people embezzling isn't a big story anymore."

She fluffed the pillow again.

"We're just glad you're okay." Her dad rose and gave her a hug. "We were worried. But we also think it will be nice to have you around for a few weeks. We're sorry a bed in the basement family room is all we have."

"It's fine, Dad. It's great, actually."

He squeezed her again. "Good. Stay as long as you want."

Warmth suffused her. She never doubted her dad's love. Just always believed he was too busy for her. "Thanks, Dad."

An unexpected knock at the door had everyone looking toward the stairway. "Who could be here at this time of night?"

Her stepmom said, "I'll get it."

"I'll come with you," her dad said. "We'll let Sophie get ready for bed."

She smiled. "Thanks."

She heard the muffled sounds of her parents talking to someone, then there was silence. This would have been the perfect time for a shower, but she hadn't had guts enough to go to the Montgomery and get her luggage. She didn't want to run into Wyatt. She wasn't ready to run into anybody yet. It was strangely wonderful to catch up with her dad and stepmom and two half siblings.

Luckily, her stepmom had some sweats she could borrow.

"Sophie?"

At the sound of Wyatt's voice, she spun around on the sofa bed. Her heart skipped a beat then she realized he was carrying one of her suitcases. Of course, he couldn't let something go undone. She'd said she'd pick up her suitcases, and since she hadn't, he was bringing them to her.

"Thanks for bringing my things," she said, trying not to sound tired and sad. She loved how he thought of everything, but there was a hole in his chest where a heart should be, and she had to remember that.

"I just brought this one case."

Detail guy Wyatt had forgotten something? "Really? Where are the other things?"

"In my condo?"

She stared at him. "Are you asking me or telling me?"

"Okay. They're in my condo." Carrying her overnight case, he walked down the steps. "Because I think you and I need to talk."

Oh, no. She wasn't going through that again. She'd cried enough to be dehydrated. They did not need to talk.

"I think we said everything that needed to be said when I got out of the limo."

He shook his head. "No. Well, yes. Maybe. At the time."

She frowned at him. He was never indecisive. Certainly never at a loss for words. His babbling was so out of character, she had no idea what to say.

"I have a couple of things I need to tell you."

Great. His side of the story. Just when she'd gotten herself to understand him in such a way that she could deal with the pain of losing him, he was about to muddy the waters.

Then it struck her that he was alone. A single dad with a baby and no nanny couldn't just go gallivanting in the middle of the night. "Where's Darcy?"

"I left her with Pete."

Her eyes widened. "The doorman?"

"The father of three. His shift was over. He agreed to watch her for a few hours while we straighten this out."

"I'm not going to be Darcy's nanny. I love her and I know I made a commitment, but I have to think of myself."

"Agreed."

She frowned. "You agree with me?"

"Yes."

"Then what do you think we need to straighten out?"

"I thought long and hard about what you said in the limo. I understand how difficult it would be for you to be Darcy's nanny. I even understood the part about you sleeping with your boss. Even though that's not quite how you said it. I believe you called yourself a dirty little secret."

She winced. "Thank you—I think."

"You're welcome. But the big thing I understood was that I don't have to be my parents."

Her heart stopped. This was new. "Okay."

"You're not hearing what I'm telling you. I spent most of today with Trace and Cade and realized we'll never stop being friends."

She frowned. "That's good."

He laughed. "It is good because it made me see that we're all masters of our own destiny—once I realized that, I also knew I feel the same way about you."

"That we'll always be friends?"

"That we can be anything we want." He took a quick breath. "I love having you around. My world is simply happier with you in it. Sophie, you were right. *I love you* and if I set my mind to loving you forever, I will."

Her heart brightened with hope, but she also would never again misinterpret him. "You don't have to sound so surprised."

He laughed, but not like someone who was happy. Like someone who was relieved. "You're so wonderful. You're a partner. Someone I trust enough to confide in. Someone who can confide in me." He shook his head. "I can't explain it."

Her hopeful heart opened a bit. But just a bit. She heard what he was saying. She knew he meant it. But he'd hated the thought of commitment a little too staunchly to let it go so easily. And that was the thing keeping her from throwing herself into his arms.

"Don't you get it? I finally saw that I was holding myself back from something I really wanted and it was wrong. I saw you in my future and it was like the whole world opened up to me."

Tears formed in her eyes. She wished that meant he

wanted what she wanted, but she'd said her piece and he'd rejected it. He had to be perfectly clear.

"Come home with me. But not as a friend or nanny or even the woman I love. As the woman I am committed to." He reached into his jacket pocket and pulled out a ring box. "Will you marry me?"

Gobsmacked, she stared at the biggest diamond she'd ever seen.

"Wow. I'd take it."

Sophie glanced over Wyatt's shoulder to see her dad and stepmom standing on the stairs, watching everything.

"Not because of the gorgeous ring," her stepmom quickly amended. "But because I think your guy is serious."

Wyatt caught her hands. "I am serious. I've never felt for anyone what I feel for you. Never wanted to share my life. But thinking of having you with me forever makes me incredibly happy."

Sophie glanced down at the ring. Now that her dad and stepmom were settled into their new house, there was a place for her with them. She wasn't desperate, but she loved Wyatt. More than she'd ever thought she could love anyone.

And her real place was with Wyatt and Darcy.

Especially since deep-thinker Wyatt wouldn't say any of this lightly.

"I love you, too."

"And you'll marry me?"

"I'll marry you."

Even as she said the words, Wyatt caught her around the waist and twirled her around.

Her dad and stepmom laughed. Apparently awoken

by the commotion, her six-year-old half brother and five-year-old half sister appeared at the top of the steps.

Her brother said, "What's going on?"

Her dad laughed. "I think Sophie is getting married."

Her little sister gaped at her. "You're leaving?"

"Yeah." She grinned at them. "But I'll be back a lot for visits."

Both siblings ran down the steps and hugged her and she suddenly realized how lucky she was. She had a great dad, stepmom and half brother and sister. She'd been so afraid of disturbing their happiness, she hadn't even considered they might miss her too. If she hadn't desperately needed a place to stay, she might not have figured that out.

And she had Wyatt and Darcy.

She suddenly saw that the horrible thing her mother had done actually brought out the best in her life. She had Wyatt's love. She would be a mother to Darcy. Her dad and stepmom had found a place in her life, and all was right with her world.

EPILOGUE

THEY WAITED TWO years to get married. Cade and Reese tied the knot on his island. Marcia and Trace got married in Italy. Wyatt and Sophie said their vows at St. Patrick's Cathedral on Fifth Avenue.

She wore a gown created by a designer Wyatt's mother found. After months of hitting roadblocks with Wyatt about Darcy, his parents had had a real heart-to-heart talk with Wyatt, and his mother had decided that going with Wyatt's way of doing things was better than never seeing her granddaughter.

Sophie's stepmother had been with them every step of the wedding planning process. The three women had chosen cakes, bridesmaid dresses, centerpieces, table-cloths, lighting, silver, bouquets…and become unlikely friends. Even Wyatt's stuffy dad was coming around.

And no one had enrolled Darcy in preschool yet.

Now Sophie stood at the back of a very long aisle, her hand tucked in her dad's arm, ready to walk to Wyatt and become his wife.

When her stepmom was seated and the last brides-maid had taken the walk down the aisle, a hush fell over the church before the organ began to play Jeremiah Clarke's "Trumpet Voluntary."

She took the walk with her dad, who kissed her cheek and handed her over to Wyatt. The ceremony was solemn and elegant and when they walked out of the church Wyatt faced her.

"Well, we certainly can't break those vows."

She laughed and kissed him. "Yeah, they really made it feel extremely official."

He wrapped his hands around her waist. "Because it is. I wanted something like this because what I feel for you is special, important."

"It's not the nicest thing you've ever said to me, but I'll take it."

His face scrunched. "You keep track?"

"Not officially, but I remember things."

Bridesmaids, groomsmen and guests began spilling out the door to greet them. "What was the nicest thing I've ever said?"

She glanced at the growing crowd, stood on her tiptoes and whispered something he'd once said in bed.

He laughed heartily.

And their life together began officially. To have and to hold from this point forward.

With kids and goofy parents and enough money to enjoy it all, Sophie believed she'd found nirvana.

Especially since they'd bought the villa in Lake Como.

* * * * *

COMING SOON!

We really hope you enjoyed reading this book.
If you're looking for more romance, be sure to
head to the shops when new books are
available on

Thursday 12th May

To see which titles are coming soon, please visit

millsandboon.co.uk/nextmonth

MILLS & BOON®

Coming next month

TEMPTATION IN ISTANBUL
Hana Sheik

"I'm not tethering you to the house," he said with a frown. "You're free to go where you want. Take Zara with you. I'd like her to see Istanbul."

"And where will you be?" She ignored the alarm bell clanging in her head and the tightening mix of panic and ire pressing down onto her thumping heart. Leaping to a conclusion wouldn't do her any good.

"As I said, I'll be busy closing this partnership deal for my company. But by tomorrow afternoon, my schedule is free." His face relaxed, his frown softer and his eyes less troubled. The dark beginnings of a beard raked his jaw and climbed to his high-boned cheeks. He palmed the lower half of his face, his nostrils twitching with an audible sigh.

Suddenly the air around him shifted.

He smiled charmingly. "I was thinking a city tour might be a good way to celebrate the closing of this deal. If that's something you'd be interested in? I'm a pretty good tour guide."

His smile unleashed a fluttering in her stomach and a rush of heady warmth over her body.

"I think Zara would like that," she said.

"And you?"

She heard the rest of his question. Would you like it? After drinking down to the dregs in her cup, Maryan placed it on the tray and watched as Faisal mirrored her with his mug. She stood and grabbed the tray handles, her eye contact with him unsevered and stronger than before. He tensed his shoulders slightly as if anticipating her rejection. Even so, his smile remained sunny on his too-handsome face.

"I've always wanted to see the Hagia Sophia."

It took a few seconds, but his bright teeth flashed at her. "Then we'll add it to the tour." He stared at her afterward, his smile edging on playful and his eyes dropping to her mouth.

"Sounds good," she agreed.

"It's a date," he added.

She couldn't unglue her tongue from the roof of her mouth to give him a comeback. So she did the next best thing. Bobbed her head, lifted the tray with their empty mugs and walked away from him before she combusted from blushing too much.

Continue reading
TEMPTATION IN ISTANBUL
Hana Sheik

Available next month
www.millsandboon.co.uk

JOIN THE
MILLS & BOON
BOOKCLUB

* **FREE** delivery direct to your door

* **EXCLUSIVE** offers every month

* **EXCITING** rewards programme

50% OFF
YOUR FIRST
PARCEL

Join today at
millsandboon.co.uk/subscribe

JOIN US ON SOCIAL MEDIA!

Stay up to date with our latest releases, author news and gossip, special offers and discounts, and all the behind-the-scenes action from Mills & Boon...

 millsandboon

 millsandboonuk

 millsandboon

might just be true love...